P9-BZC-000

HE WAS 1996. SHE WAS 1958. TIMES HAVE CHANGED.

She knew he was going to kiss her again. His lips brushed over hers. The extreme tenderness of it caused her to inhale deeply and she felt his breath flow into her. He kissed her forehead, and when her eyelids drifted shut, he caressed each of them. As his mouth touched her nose, then her cheeks, she became frustrated with his gentle teasing and reached up to still his head. He responded to her wordless hint with a low groan.

It was her only warning.

In a heartbeat, he pulled her hard against him and his mouth descended on hers with raw hunger. The shock of his tongue forcing its way between her teeth cleared the sensual haze around Beverly's brain. She pushed against his shoulders and squirmed until he freed her mouth. "*Stop*," she moaned. "I . . . I can't do this."

He blinked at her in confusion, then released his grip, and took a step backward.

"I'm sorry if I led you on, but I'm not that kind of girl."

⬙ TOPAZ

OUT OF THIS WORLD ROMANCES BY MARILYN CAMPBELL

☐ **WORLDS APART** When a beautiful army nurse and a powerful soldier are thrown together on a military plane en route to the U.S. from the Orient, fate thrusts them into another world where they must find their way through time and space to work for freedom—under the protective cover of a fiery love that crosses all boundaries. (405226—$4.99)

☐ **STOLEN DREAMS** When a beautiful scientist and a handsome archeologist take off into a past lurking with danger, they find all their reasons for opposition giving way to attraction. (405005—$4.99)

☐ **STARDUST DREAMS** Cherry Cochran, a beautiful actress from earth who witnesses a murder is suddenly swept toward the remotest stars in the spaceship of her mysterious abductor, the handsome Gallant Voyager.... Interstellar intrigue, deadly danger, and a burning desire for love. (404130—$4.99)

*Prices slightly higher in Canada

Buy them at your local bookstore or use this convenient coupon for ordering.

PENGUIN USA
P.O. Box 999 — Dept. #17109
Bergenfield, New Jersey 07621

Please send me the books I have checked above.
I am enclosing $_____ (please add $2.00 to cover postage and handling). Send check or money order (no cash or C.O.D.'s) or charge by Mastercard or VISA (with a $15.00 minimum). Prices and numbers are subject to change without notice.

Card #_____ Exp. Date _____
Signature_____
Name_____
Address_____
City _____ State _____ Zip Code _____

For faster service when ordering by credit card call **1-800-253-6476**

Allow a minimum of 4-6 weeks for delivery. This offer is subject to change without notice.

JUST IN TIME

Marilyn Campbell

A TOPAZ BOOK

TOPAZ
Published by the Penguin Group
Penguin Books USA Inc., 375 Hudson Street,
New York, New York 10014, U.S.A.
Penguin Books Ltd, 27 Wrights Lane,
London W8 5TZ, England
Penguin Books Australia Ltd, Ringwood,
Victoria, Australia
Penguin Books Canada Ltd, 10 Alcorn Avenue,
Toronto, Ontario, Canada M4V 3B2
Penguin Books (N.Z.) Ltd, 182-190 Wairau Road,
Auckland 10, New Zealand

Penguin Books Ltd, Registered Offices:
Harmondsworth, Middlesex, England

First published by Topaz, an imprint of Dutton Signet,
a division of Penguin Books USA Inc.

First Printing, July, 1996
10 9 8 7 6 5 4 3 2 1

Copyright © Marilyn Campbell, 1996
All rights reserved
Topaz Man photo © Charles William Bush

 REGISTERED TRADEMARK—MARCA REGISTRADA

Printed in the United States of America

Without limiting the rights under copyright reserved above, no part of this
publication may be reproduced, stored in or introduced into a retrieval system, or transmitted, in any form, or by any means (electronic, mechanical,
photocopying, recording, or otherwise), without the prior written permis-
sion of both the copyright owner and the above publisher of this book.

BOOKS ARE AVAILABLE AT QUANTITY DISCOUNTS WHEN USED TO PROMOTE
PRODUCTS OR SERVICES. FOR INFORMATION PLEASE WRITE TO PREMIUM MAR-
KETING DIVISION, PENGUIN BOOKS USA INC., 375 HUDSON STREET, NEW YORK,
NY 10014.

If you purchased this book without a cover you should be aware that this
book is stolen property. It was reported as "unsold or destroyed" to the publisher and neither the author nor the publisher has received any payment for
this "stripped book."

To Josephine Campbell, a unique mother-in-law and the dear friend who introduced me to the spiritual world. Though you are now with the angels, *nous nous verrons encore.*

With thanks to Patricia Roenbeck and Barbara Ryan for sharing their knowledge of the Mohawks and Native American traditions with me.

And to Dr. Robert Campitelli, Laura De-Mato, and the staff of Western Communities Family Practice, where all too much of this book had to be written.

Chapter 1

"*Happy birthday dear Beverly, happy birthday to you!*"

Beverly Newcastle smiled over the glowing candles at her mom, dad, and kid brother. The fact that there were ten tiny flames on the round cake rather than thirty was her mother's way of being kind.

"Make a wish, sis," Allen reminded her.

She twisted her mouth from side to side as though she were seriously considering what to wish for. The truth was, she stopped believing in wishes seven years ago, when her husband's body was shipped back from Korea. Recalling the big story in the week's news, she said, "I wish the army hadn't shaved off all Elvis's hair."

"C'mon, Bev," Allen protested. "A real wish."

Her mother added, "Yes, dear, one for you."

Her father looked up at the clock on the kitchen wall. "Ed Sullivan comes on in five minutes."

"Okay, okay." As long as it was only pretend, Beverly decided to make her wish a doozy. "I wish for a tall, dark, and handsome stranger to sweep me away on an exciting adventure filled with danger and romance." As Allen groaned and her mother sighed, Beverly blew out every candle with one breath.

"I'll have my cake and coffee in the living room," her father said, flipping up the light switch on his way out of the room.

"A very small piece for me, Mom," Bev said. "The girls probably have another cake waiting for me at The Alley Cat."

"So? You're so skinny a breeze could knock you over. Maybe an extra helping of cake would help you fill out a little." She cut a three-inch-wide slab of chocolate fudge cake and placed it on her daughter's plate. "You would think for such an important birthday, you and your friends could do something different. You go bowling *every* Sunday night."

Beverly gave a little shrug. "Mercerville isn't exactly the social center of New Jersey."

"You could drive into Trenton, or better yet, head down to Fort Dix. There's certainly a lot of single men around there."

"I'm gonna go sit with Pop," Allen muttered, quickly picking up his plate and escaping the mother-daughter talk he saw coming.

Beverly wished she could disappear as easily as her brother. Even though he was only seventeen, he was the *son*, which granted him the privilege of avoiding their mother's well-intentioned nagging, while she, the *daughter*, got to help clean up the dinner dishes and listen to the same old advice. She wondered how long it would take to get to the subject of marriage.

"How are the plans coming for Peggy's wedding?" her mother asked brightly.

She answered the question as if that was what her mother was really thinking about. "The last I heard, she still couldn't decide whether to hold the reception in her parents' backyard or at the firemen's hall, plus she's changed her mind half a dozen times about the color of our dresses. But that's nothing new for Peggy. I'm sure we'll be talking about it some more tonight."

"Well, whatever she decides, I'm sure it will be better than her first wedding. What a disaster that was. They should have known any marriage that started off like that wouldn't last. Peggy should take some hints from yours. Now *that* was a wedding to be proud of. For something planned on such short notice . . ."

Beverly took a slow breath and carried her unfinished piece of cake to the sink. She didn't need to listen to her mother's words to know what she was saying. Everything about the day of her marriage to Billy Newcastle had been perfect, from the weather to the beautiful four-tiered cake with the smiling bride and groom on top. The miniature man's tuxedo had been painted over to look like combat fatigues—a joke from the best man since Billy was leaving for boot camp two days later.

Neither Beverly nor her mother could let go of the memory of that day, but there was one major difference. For her mother, it had been a moment of triumph to be relived over and over again. For Beverly, it was just one of a thousand memories that were permanently stuck in her heart like pins and needles. For her mother's sake, however, she smiled and nodded in all the appropriate places.

At least she no longer burst into tears at the mention of a wedding or babies. It had taken a while, but she could now listen to her mother or her friends talk about love and marriage and feel absolutely nothing. Well, almost nothing.

"I just don't understand it," her mother was saying. "You and Hope Sommerfield are both attractive women, even if you do insist on dressing in those awful blue jeans and hiding your pretty blond hair under scarves, yet there you are, living together in a little apartment like two old maids."

"That's because that's what we are," Beverly said with a forced laugh, then made a show of looking at the clock. "Holy cow! I had no idea how late it is. I told the girls I'd meet them five minutes ago." She hurriedly dried her hands on a dish towel and gave her mother a hug. "Thanks for dinner and the cake and the new sweater. I love it."

Her mother frowned. "At least take some cake with you."

"Thanks, but no thanks. Hope's on one of her diets again, and she'd kill me if I brought that home. Allen will probably finish it off tonight anyway." Having surpassed her time limit to be mothered, Beverly gave everyone a hug and kiss and took off with her birthday presents.

Claire Winetke stood in the doorway until her daughter drove away. She wished there was something she could do to put a spark of life back into her child, but nothing she said or did seemed to make a difference. Closing the door, she sighed and looked at her son. If she was ever going to have grandchildren, she supposed it would be up to him to give them to her.

Unfortunately, he seemed more interested in loafing with those bum friends of his, with their long, greasy hair and black leather jackets than dating

girls. She was fairly sure he had started smoking cig-
arettes like they did, too. What was this younger generation coming to, she wondered with a weary shake
of her head.

"You make a better door than a window," Paul
grumbled at his wife, startling her out of her reverie.

"Oh, sorry," she said and quickly sat down out of
his way. Ed Sullivan was saying good night, and Allen was heading to his room ... to do whatever it
was he did in there for hours on end. She wished she
could talk to her husband about the children, but
he had enough to worry about with all the layoffs at
the plant. That reminded her of the other subject
she wanted to discuss with him, but she waited for
the commercial to come on before speaking.

Careful to keep her voice in a chatty tone, she
asked, "Did you hear that Dottie got a job at
Woolworth's?"

Paul's mouth tightened into a thin line. "No. I
didn't realize things had gotten that tough for them.
Too bad."

"I don't think it's that bad. She said it was her way
of helping, what with their son going into college
next fall and everyone so worried about the layoffs,
and—"

Paul held up a finger to cut her off. "Now don't
you start worrying about that. If the worst happens
at the plant, I'll find something else, and Allen will
go to college if he and I both have to get second
jobs." He reached over and patted her knee. "Don't
worry, puss, the day will never come that my wife
has to go out and earn money. It's bad enough my
daughter is out there waiting tables like some poor
orphan with no man to take care of her."

Claire decided that the point she was trying to make was worth risking his displeasure. "But Beverly says she *likes* working, and Dottie is looking forward to getting out of the house."

"Of course they say that, puss. But we both know that's just a way to hide the shame they're feeling. Now how about cutting me another piece of that delicious cake you made before Allen finishes it off?"

Claire smiled at the compliment and carried his plate and coffee cup back to the kitchen. Dottie had told her the manager at the five-and-ten was looking for another salesgirl and preferred someone older, but she supposed it was foolish to have thought Paul might allow her to apply for the job. After all, he had gotten them through the Great Depression without any help from her. He always knew what was best for the family, and she knew better than to question his decisions.

Beverly parked her Chevy in one of the few empty spaces in front of The Alley Cat and turned on the interior light. Using the rear-view mirror, she checked her teeth for remnants of fudge icing, combed her fingers through her bangs, tightened her ponytail, touched up her lipstick, and pinched her cheeks.

The effort didn't help much. Her light blue eyes looked very gray tonight, as they always did when she was feeling sad, and her friends were sure to comment on it. She should have canceled. Dinner with her parents was always difficult enough, without it being her thirtieth birthday.

Thirty! She didn't feel that old, but she was born in 1928 and it was now 1958. A girl couldn't argue with the calendar.

Before getting out of the car, she took her new or-
lon cardigan sweater out of its gift box, put it over
her shoulders, and attached the pearl sweater guard
that Allen had given her. It didn't really go with her
rolled-up blue jeans, bobby sox, and Keds, but she
figured the sweater's soft shade of pink might make
her look happier than she felt.

Determined not to ruin everyone else's fun, she
pushed her mouth into a smile, grabbed her bowling
bag, and headed toward the glass doors, where she
could see Hope watching for her.

"It's about time!" Hope exclaimed and latched on
to Beverly's elbow to stop her from heading toward
the cocktail lounge immediately. "Dee-Dee's already
on her third beer. Had another fight with that creep
husband of hers. Wait until you see what he did to
her lip."

Beverly clucked her tongue. "Doesn't she realize
it'll only get him madder if she comes home drunk?"

"You know Dee-Dee," Hope said with a shrug.
"Half her fun is provoking that man. They'll fight,
then they'll make love, and she'll probably end up
pregnant with number five tonight. I just wish I
could be in her shoes for one day. I'd beat him so
bad, he'd never lay a hand on her again."

The image of Hope fighting with Dee-Dee's husband brought a real smile to Beverly's face. Frankie
Giammarco was a cowardly pip-squeak compared to
Hope, who stood close to six feet tall in her pumps,
and whose red hair and freckles were perfect for her
fiery personality.

As soon as they entered the lounge, she saw Dee-
Dee and Peggy at a table for four. Three gift-wrapped
boxes were stacked in front of an empty chair.

"Hey, Don, put one of those little umbrellas in Bev's beer," Hope loudly told the bartender as they passed. "It's her birthday."

Several of the regular patrons instantly shouted, "Happy birthday," much to Beverly's embarrassment. As she shoved her bowling bag under her chair, she noticed the absence of any others. "What did you guys do with your stuff?" All three women glanced at each other and giggled.

"We're not bowling tonight," Hope said.

"We have a surprise for you," Dee-Dee added.

"What kind of surprise?" she asked warily.

"None of your business. Just open your gifts."

Beverly tried not to stare at the cut on Dee-Dee's lip. In high school, the two of them had often been mistaken as sisters because of their long blond hair and short, boyish figures. But four pregnancies and a taste for beer had left Dee-Dee with an overly plump body, and she now kept her hair short and curly since that was how Frankie liked it.

Hope's gift to her roommate was Elvis Presley's *Golden Hits* album, which was hardly a surprise since she had practically had a fit when Beverly had mentioned she was thinking of buying it herself. Dee-Dee gave her a purple wallet with a picture of the late, great James Dean inside, and Peggy's box contained a photo album.

"The pictures from my wedding can be the first ones you'll put in it," she said, which opened the way for her to report on the progress she and her fiancé Calvin were making with their plans.

Beverly was certain that Peggy wasn't so much in love with Calvin as she was in love with the idea of getting another chance at a big wedding. Though it was very unusual to celebrate a second marriage in such grand style, no one ever criticized Peggy. She was too sweet, too sensitive, and too empty-headed. Her first husband was almost a carbon copy of her, which was why they were doomed to failure from the start.

Calvin, on the other hand, was fifteen years older, owned a hardware store, and had no problem making decisions. From the sounds of Peggy's update, he had apparently decided it was time to step in and help her make some choices.

"I have some news, too," Hope said after Peggy covered every possible detail.

Beverly looked at her curiously. What could have happened since they had talked this morning?

"Stanley is taking me to Atlantic City next weekend!"

Dee-Dee arched an eyebrow at Hope. "Won't his wife and kids wonder why he took his secretary on vacation with them?"

Hope's pink complexion flushed a bit more. "They won't know I'm there. It's a weekend sales conference, not a vacation, so it's perfectly reasonable for him to go without them and for me to attend. Of course, we'll have separate rooms in the hotel."

Dee-Dee smirked. "Oh yeah. I'm sure that'll fool everybody."

Hope lifted her chin defensively. "I know you don't believe Stanley will ever leave his wife for me, but at least he doesn't use me as a punching bag!"

"No, he just uses you as a spare toilet for his—"

"Whoa!" Beverly interjected before things got out of hand. "It's my birthday, and I refuse to let anybody fight within my hearing. Besides, I've waited long enough. What's the surprise?"

"You have to have another beer first," Hope told her, then motioned to the bartender for another round.

Beverly's suspicions rose. "Swear to me this has nothing to do with fixing me up with anyone, or I'll—"

"Swear," Hope said, raising her right hand. "There are no men involved in this surprise. It's just something you need to be real open-minded about."

That didn't go far to reassure Beverly, but as long as it wasn't one of Hope's attempts to push some man on her, she figured she could go along. While Dee-Dee and Hope apologized to each other and moved on to gossiping about another one of their acquaintance, Beverly felt herself slipping into that place where she just sat and watched what was going on around her without really being involved.

The four of them had been friends since junior high school and Dee-Dee was the only one who had come close to living her life the way she had expected. She had wanted to marry a man who could support her and a houseful of children. It was too bad she hadn't been more specific about the man.

On the contrary, Hope had been very specific about what her man would be like. He just never showed up in her life, nor did any others find her to be their type . . . until she went to work for Stanley Tucker.

While Hope's coloring matched her disposition, her name was perfect for her romantic nature. She had been secretly seeing Stanley for three years, during which time he fed her every line in the book about why he couldn't leave his wife until some future time. Yet she never gave up hope that he would be free to marry her one day. As strong as she was, both physically and mentally, Hope was a bowl of strawberry Jello around that man.

Peggy never knew what she wanted, so she was never disappointed by anything that happened to her.

For a brief moment in time, Beverly had been given exactly what she had wanted out of life, and then it was snatched away.

"Time to go," Hope announced, giving Beverly's ponytail a tug. "We'll take my car."

"To where?" Beverly asked as she retrieved her bowling bag and Peggy gathered up the presents for her.

"You'll find out when we get there," Dee-Dee said.

"Maybe I should take my own car," Beverly offered, thinking of providing herself with a means of escape in case whatever they had planned was really awful.

"Not a chance, Chicken Little," Hope said, giving her a nudge toward the exit. "Knowing you, we'll head in one direction and you'll go back to the apartment and go to bed."

"But *dahling*," Beverly countered in a bad Tallulah Bankhead imitation. "You don't know who I have waiting for me in that bed."

Hope rolled her eyes, and a few minutes later Beverly's things were stowed in the car's trunk.

Beverly's curiosity wasn't at all satisfied when Hope drove them into a development of tract homes, most of which were still under construction. "Don't tell me. You bought me a new house. Really guys, it's too much."

"Here it is," Hope announced, pulling into one of the few graveled driveways that led to a finished house.

Though drapes were drawn in the windows, a hint of light shone through to give evidence that someone was in residence.

Hope, Peggy, and Dee-Dee climbed out of the car, but Beverly stayed put. "I'm not moving one inch until somebody tells me who's inside that house."

"I guess it's safe to tell you now," Hope replied. "Inside that house is Madame Lavonda. She's a fortune-teller!"

Beverly groaned. "Is this a joke?"

"Don't be such a party-pooper," Hope said and pulled her out of the car. "Some kid handed me one of her fliers when I was leaving work the other day, and I thought it sounded like fun. Don't you want to know what the future holds?"

"I already know," Beverly answered. "Ten years from now, the four of us will meet at The Alley Cat to celebrate my fortieth birthday. The only difference will be that we'll all have a lot more gray hair."

"You know what I love most about you?" Hope asked. "You always see the world through rose-colored glasses. Come on, Bev. You've got nothing to lose."

Hope was right about that, she thought. She had nothing at all to lose.

The front door opened before they reached it, and Beverly had to stifle a laugh. The woman standing before them looked like a Gypsy for a carnival side-show, from the purple turban on her head, enormous gold circle earrings, and multiple necklaces, down past her yellow peasant blouse and long, gathered red-and-blue patterned skirt. She jangled the dozen bracelets on her arms and smiled, showing badly yellowed teeth and a space where one was missing.

Beverly leaned toward Hope and whispered. "This is some kooky friend of yours, isn't it? You can tell me. I won't ruin anyone's fun."

Hope shook her head. "I swear, I never met her before."

"Come een, ladies," Madame Lavonda said in a heavy French accent. "I have been waiting for you."

"You mean you *knew* we were coming?" Peggy asked in amazement.

"Of course. I know all there eez to know. You will be zee first." She waved Peggy toward a door leading into another room.

"Oh, but it's Bev's birthday."

"I know that also, but she must wait until I am ready for her." Again she showed Peggy where she wanted her to go, and with a shaky smile, Peggy obeyed.

The others sat down in the living room, which was dressed in the same gaudy fashion as Madame Lavonda. It was both comical and weird at the same time, but it gave them something to talk about while they waited.

Peggy came out of the back room less than five minutes later. Her smile let them know she had been given good news. "She said I'm going to live happily ever after with Calvin, and we're going to have twins—two beautiful little girls who will be just like their mommy."

Poor Calvin, Beverly thought, then scolded herself

for being mean. Leaning toward Hope, she mumbled, "Some fortune-teller! I could have guessed that much."

"She wants to see Hope next," Peggy declared as she sat down next to Dee-Dee.

Hope returned about ten minutes later with a thoughtful expression. "She told me I'm going to live happily ever after, too, but not with Stanley. She said he's never going to leave his wife."

"Oooh. Isn't that a big news flash," Dee-Dee said with a smirk.

Hope made a face at her. "You're next, smarty-pants."

As Dee-Dee left the room, Beverly asked, "Did you tell her about Stanley?"

"No. She told me about him. Not by name actually, but she described him perfectly."

"Yes," added Peggy. "It was the same with Calvin."

"Well, it doesn't mean anything," Beverly said patiently. "I read a story one time about how these people do their tricks. They pick up on little things you say or how you're dressed, and then they keep their predictions real vague so that you can interpret them any way you want."

Hope scratched her head. "I don't know. She told me a few things that were pretty specific, like how I'm going to meet a dark-haired giant in a place where there are sick people, and he's going to help me see how I'm wasting my time with Stanley. She said I'm going to marry this guy and move to California. Can you believe that?"

What was important was that Hope appeared to believe it, and Beverly figured anything that weaned

Hope away from Stanley was a good thing. "Sure. Why not? Maybe you'll go to Hollywood and be Lucille Ball's stand-in."

Dee-Dee didn't come back for nearly a half hour, and when she did, they could all tell she had been crying.

"Did she tell you something bad?" Peggy asked with wide eyes.

"Whatever she told you, don't believe it," Beverly said, trying to reassure her, even though she knew there was a strong possibility of something bad happening in Dee-Dee's future. "She just makes this stuff up and sometimes it hits home by accident."

"I . . . I don't think she was making it up." As if in a daze, Dee-Dee walked to the front door and opened it. "If you don't mind, I'd kind of like to be alone for a while. I'll be in the car."

"You said this was supposed to be fun," Beverly said to Hope.

"I said I *thought* it would be fun. So far it's two happily-ever-after romances to one tear-jerker. Go on. It's your turn."

"Swell," Beverly said as she stood up. "Mine will probably be the comedy."

Madame Lavonda's workroom was exactly as Beverly expected. Burning candles were the only light. Fringed shawls covered every piece of furniture, and a crystal ball sat in the middle of the table in front of the Gypsy woman.

"Look, madame, my friends insisted I come in here, but it really isn't necessary for you to waste any time on me. I don't believe in any of this."

"I see," she said with a nod, but her piercing gaze seemed to challenge Beverly's statement. "Perhaps, just for zee sake of your friends, you should sit down for a few minutes and pretend that you are not so much a skeptic."

Beverly shrugged and sat across from her. "Could I ask you a personal question?" Lavonda cocked her head. "Do you actually live like this, or is this all just part of the show because that's what people expect to see?"

Lavonda's mouth curved into a crooked smile. "People usually see what zey expect to see. Show me your right hand."

Beverly chuckled lightly, but placed her hand on the table. Lavonda turned it palm up then traced several of the lines there with her index finger.

"Your entire life eez een zee palm of your hand—from birth to death."

Beverly tried to tone down her sarcasm, but it was tough. "Are you telling me you can tell when I'm going to die?"

"I could, but eet eez not good for a person to know too much about their future—only enough to guide them toward good decisions." She touched a spot on Beverly's palm. "You had a surgery when you were a little girl, *oui*?"

She thought a moment, then smiled. "I had my tonsils and adenoids removed. But so did most of the kids I know."

Frowning, Madame Lavonda tipped Beverly's hand this way and that and stretched out the skin on her palm. "Thees eez *très* strange. Eet eez as eef you have no future. You had a good childhood and a love een your life—You were married, *oui*?"

Beverly flinched, but Lavonda held on to her hand. "Yes, I was married."

"But not for very long. When he passed over, you wanted to also, but eet was not your time. And now you go on like ... how you say, a zombie, zee living dead. You have no husband, no children, no dreams."

"Look, it's obvious that Hope put you up to this, but I don't want to play along anymore." Again she attempted to retrieve her hand but Lavonda squeezed tighter.

"Deed you not wish for an adventure and passion with a handsome stranger?"

That stopped Beverly from tugging. "You could have guessed that."

Lavonda nodded. "*Oui*, but eet eez your wish, and I can give eet to you." Satisfied that Beverly was not going to run away, she released her hand and rose from the table with a jangle of bracelets.

Beverly watched the Gypsy open a cabinet on the other side of the room, take something out, then sit back down.

With a dramatic gesture, Lavonda placed a small purple-and-gold perfume bottle in Beverly's hand. "Een thees bottle eez a powerful potion that can change your life forever. Eef you drink eet, you will have an adventure unlike anything you can imagine, and you will meet a man who will reawaken your heart."

Beverly arched an eyebrow in disbelief. Hope was always pulling one trick or another to get her to meet men, but this was crazier than any of her previous schemes. It was going to take some thinking to pay her back for this one. She tried to twist the stopper out of the ornate bottle to get a sniff, but it wouldn't budge.

"Eet will only open for someone who believes een eets powers and eez prepared for zee changes eet will bring."

Beverly set the bottle back down on the table. "Then you may as well keep it, because I will never believe in fortune-tellers or magic potions. Besides, I'm perfectly satisfied with my life the way it is."

Lavonda placed both her hands on the crystal ball and closed her eyes for a second. Abruptly they popped open again and she stared deeply into the ball. "Tomorrow, a waitress who works at zee diner with you will ask you for advice. She eez expecting a baby and eez *très* upset. You must be gentle, yet wise when you speak at her."

Beverly narrowed her eyes. There were three full-time waitresses at Pete's Place besides herself—two were married and wouldn't be upset if they became pregnant, as long as it was by their husbands, and the other was a widow without any men friends, as far as she knew. That left Nina, the high school senior, but she only worked on weekends, never Mondays. Perhaps Hope found out a secret about one of them and told it to this woman.

"You think your friends tell me zeez things," Lavonda said, stroking the crystal ball as if it were a lover's face. "So, I will tell you some things they could not know. Een seven days, there will be a fire een zee house of someone you are acquainted with. No one will be hurt, but possessions will be lost. And since you are such zee skeptic, I will give you something *plus grande*. Soon, you will read een zee newspaper about a revolt een Algeria. Because of that, General Charles de Gaulle will become active een

France's government and eventually be named President."

Beverly shook her head and sighed. "You're really very good at this. For a second there, I almost believed you." She picked up the pretty bottle and examined it more closely. "What's really in here? A shot of vodka or what?"

"Eet eez nothing you would be familiar with, but I assure you that eet will not harm you in any way." Beverly started to set the bottle down again, but Lavonda forced her fingers closed around it. "Take eet with you. Even eef you never do believe there eez magic inside, eet eez very pretty, *non*? But eef you think about your life, you will know I have told zee truth, and you will know that eet eez time to make eet better."

Beverly shrugged and put the bottle in her purse. Rising, she smiled and thanked Madame Lavonda for entertaining her and her friends.

"Happy birthday, Beverly," the Gypsy said with another piercing look, then murmured, "*Nous nous verrons encore.*"

Chapter 2

"I'm sorry to cry on your shoulder, Bev, but you're the only person I could think of to talk to. I couldn't possibly tell my mom, and I'm afraid my friends would spread it around school."

"It's okay, Nina. I'm glad you felt you could come to me." When the girl had called the diner and asked her to meet her in the park after she got off work, she automatically guessed the reason. At first, she kept expecting Nina to say, "April Fool's," and admit that the whole thing had been a crazy joke of Hope's. But Beverly quickly realized that Nina was truly upset . . . and three months pregnant. She didn't know how Madame Lavonda had gotten her information, but she had been correct.

Be gentle yet wise, the Gypsy had advised. How could she do that when she had no experience with pregnancy herself? "Does the father know?"

Nina shook her head. "I'm afraid to tell him. It's all my fault. Andy and I have been going together for two years, and for the longest time, I kept saying no, and he respected that, but then I got tired of saying no. I mean, I know I shouldn't have given in, but I just love him so much, and I was afraid, if I didn't,

somebody else would. It isn't like we weren't careful
. . . most of the time." She hung her head sheepishly.

It was on the tip of Beverly's tongue to tell her that
if Andy really loved her, he would have waited, like
Billy had, but that wouldn't be very *gentle*. She figured the *wise* thing to do would be to guide Nina
into making a decision herself. "What choices do you
have?"

Nina turned her head away and said quietly, "I've
heard of a place where, um, the pregnancy could be
ended."

"Have you also heard how dangerous that is?"

Nina faced her again and grimaced. "I don't think
I could do that anyway."

"Next choice then."

"I could go away to one of those homes for unwed
mothers then give the baby up for adoption." She
paused for a moment. "But I don't think I could
stand that either." Another hesitation. "I suppose I
could tell Andy and see how he feels about being a
father. Maybe he'd be willing to marry me when
school lets out in June. I could probably hide my
stomach for another two and a half months. Maybe
the other kids would believe I was just gaining
weight."

Beverly knew that was probably the only logical
solution, but thinking of Dee-Dee and Frankie compelled her to give one bit of advice, even if it was
somewhat radical. "I know it would be really difficult to raise a baby without a husband, but it can be
even more horrible to live with a man who isn't
ready to grow up and take on the responsibilities of
being a father. Even if Andy is willing, be very sure
that you love each other one hundred percent and

that he's going to help you get through this, not just be another child for you to take care of."

The look on Nina's face told her that she would consider that unusual advice, but it wasn't likely that she would turn down a marriage proposal if one came out of Andy's mouth.

When Beverly returned to her apartment, she was somewhat relieved to discover that Hope wasn't home. Had Hope been there, Beverly might have been tempted to tell her about Lavonda's prediction coming true just to see if Hope would confess to having put the Gypsy woman up to it.

What she was afraid of was that Hope might be able to convince her that Lavonda was legitimate. If her forecast about the pregnant waitress had really appeared in the crystal ball, what else might be true?

As she took off her waitress uniform, her gaze latched on to the little purple bottle. Though she didn't believe it contained any magic potion, Lavonda was right about the bottle itself. It looked very pretty sitting in the center of her dresser. Just for fun, she tried to remove the stopper again. It didn't give, but Beverly distinctly felt the bottle growing warm in her hand, and for just a second she thought she saw a spark of light coming from inside.

Ridiculous! It was just a pretty perfume bottle; probably didn't have anything inside at all. In fact, it was probably like those sugar pills they give to hypochondriacs to make them believe they're taking medicine, so that they'll think they're getting better. Yes, that made sense. By Lavonda suggesting that the bottle held the power to change her life if she believed it strongly enough, she could make it happen.

Beverly returned the bottle to its spot on the dresser and headed for the shower.

It wasn't as if her life really needed changing. Sure, there were times she was a little bored, times when she thought of how her life would have been if Billy hadn't been killed . . .

They would have had children by now. Two, maybe three. They would have had their own home, with a yard. And a dog. Billy always wanted a German shepherd.

And the gift shop—the one they had planned on opening together—the reason he had majored in business in college. He would go to the store every day to manage it and keep the accounts. She would do the buying and decorate the windows—a different display for each month, depending on the holiday.

Billy always complimented her on her taste. He had thought she had a good sense of what would sell and how to put shapes and colors together to make something appealing to the eye. She had always admired his organizational and planning abilities.

They would have made a great team.

Beverly felt the sadness about to overwhelm her again and physically shook it off. So, her life hadn't turned out the way she had expected. Was it really that bad?

She called up the answer that she usually gave to others who worried about her. She was content. Waiting tables at Pete's Place wasn't what she had planned, but it filled most of her hours, and she liked visiting with all the different people who ate there. Hope was a good roommate, and she enjoyed their Sunday nights at The Alley Cat with Dee-Dee and Peggy and all their other acquaintances.

Her life wasn't an exciting adventure, but then whose was?

As she lathered her chest, she cautiously checked the underside of her left nipple. A few months ago she had felt something like a little BB gun pellet there. Since she didn't exactly make a habit of feeling her own breasts, however, she assumed it had always been there; she just hadn't noticed it before. Now she wasn't so sure. It seemed to have gotten a little larger. Or was it just that she was more aware of it? If her family doctor was a woman, she might ask about it, but she couldn't imagine bringing it up with a man.

"Beverly!" Hope's shout was accompanied by three hard knocks on the bathroom door. "Hurry up! I've got to tell you what happened!"

"Okay, okay. Hold your horses. I'll be right out." Beverly rinsed off, wrapped her hair in a towel, and donned her cotton duster. When she opened the door, Hope was pacing the bedroom like a caged animal. "All right. What happened?"

"You are not going to believe this, but I swear it's true. It happened. Exactly the way Madame Lavonda said it would."

Beverly lifted her eyebrows in surprise. "You talked to Nina?"

"Nina? The kid at the diner? What does she have to do with my dream man?"

Beverly waved her hand. "Never mind. Go on with your story."

Hope plopped onto the bed with a bounce. "Stanley had to be rushed to the hospital this afternoon."

"Since you're smiling, I gather it wasn't serious."

"Nah. He thought he was having a heart attack, but it turned out to be indigestion. The doctor sent him home with some Maalox and a bland diet chart."

"So your weekend in Atlantic City is still on."

"Well, actually, it is as far as Stanley's concerned, but I'm not so sure I want to go now."

That was the best news Bev had heard in a while, but she didn't want to jump to any conclusions. "Oh?"

Nervous energy had Hope bounding up from the bed again. "I met him, Bev. The man the Gypsy told me about. He was the internist who ran the tests on Stanley. He's a doctor, Bev. A *doctor!* And there he was, a giant of a man with dark hair, in a place where sick people are. I swear, he's six foot five if he's an inch. When he stood beside me, I felt . . . I felt *little!* Can you imagine?"

Knowing how self-conscious Hope was about her size and being anxious to see her attracted to anyone besides Stanley, Beverly gave her a big smile. "Wow. He sounds terrific."

Hope's excitement was bubbling out of control. "It gets better. He came out to the waiting area to tell us about Stanley—Oh, didn't I tell you his wife was there, too? She was very sweet; not at all the way he'd described her. Anyway, Jacob—that's his name, Dr. Jacob Mauser—took one look at me and forgot what he was going to say about Stanley."

Beverly couldn't help but catch some of Hope's giddiness. "Did he ask you out?"

"No, but he will. He asked for the number at work so he could call and check on Stanley tomorrow."

Beverly sent up a little prayer that the doctor was truly as interested in Hope as she thought.

"I've got to tell you, I really didn't believe what that Gypsy told me, but how can I not believe now?" She sat back down on the bed with a bit more grace. "Why were you asking about Nina?"

Beverly hesitated to add another feather to Madame Lavonda's fortune-telling turban, but then she thought it might help Hope believe Stanley should be forgotten. "Nina's in trouble."

Hope's face fell. "Oh, dear. What's she—" Comprehension hit abruptly. "She was the one Lavonda told you about! Oh my." She rapidly rubbed her forearms. "I have goose bumps all over. This is really scary. We'd better tell Dee-Dee. Or maybe not. Do you think you can prevent a bad fortune from happening if you know about it ahead of time?"

Beverly grimaced. "First of all, we don't even know what Dee-Dee was told. Second, I'm still not convinced these two things weren't just enormous coincidences. But if I did believe, I'd have to say that a prediction is like a warning. You always have free will, so you should be able to intentionally do something differently than you normally would, and by changing directions, you could stop a prediction from coming true."

"That makes sense. Yeah. I like that. We'll warn Dee-Dee, and maybe she can prevent whatever it was the Gypsy told her. But what about you? Didn't she give you any personal predictions?"

Beverly glanced at the purple bottle. "Not really. She told me about the pregnant waitress, and the fire, and that crazy stuff about Algeria—"

"The fire! Shouldn't we warn somebody about that?"

"Oh, sure. Let's call the fire department and tell

them a Gypsy said there will be a fire in some house next weekend. I'm sure they'll put all the volunteers on full alert for that."

"You are such a skeptic! And I think you're lying about her not giving you a personal prediction. Come on. Tell me what else she said."

"It wasn't anything you haven't told me a thousand times yourself: I lead a very dull life."

Hope snorted her agreement. "Still, it was nice of her to give you a birthday present."

For a moment, Bev was confused, then she noticed Hope's gaze on the bottle. "Oh, that wasn't really a birthday present. I just said that because her explanation was so ridiculous." She leaned closer and pretended to be imparting top-secret information. "You see, the bottle has a magic potion inside, and when I drink it, I'll meet a handsome stranger and have a wild adventure. My whole life will change."

"So what are you waiting for? Drink up!" Hope said, laughing.

"Can't. The stopper will only come off if I truly believe," Bev replied with heavy sarcasm. "Nice catch, huh?"

Hope got up and tried to remove the top herself, but it wouldn't budge.

"See? It's just a scam. The Gypsy expects me to return to ask for help in getting to the potion. Then she'll ask me for money."

"But why you? Any one of the rest of us would be easier to con than you. Sorry. I think you're wrong about her. And I also think you should take a chance on anything that might put a spark in your life."

Bev took the bottle from her and tried to remove the stopper, without success. "It's probably all one piece and . . ." Suddenly the bottle grew very warm and a golden glow began radiating from within. Bev set it on the dresser as quickly as possible, and the eerie light vanished.

"How did you make it do that?" Hope said with wide eyes.

"Do what?"

"Light up like that."

Bev made a face at her. "It was just the way the lamplight hit it."

"Bullshit." Hope picked the bottle up and turned it one way and another, then held it directly under the lamp. The golden glow failed to appear. "Okay, fine," Hope said, returning the bottle to the dresser. "Believe what you want. I'm happy with Madame Lavonda's prediction for me, and I'm going to call Dee-Dee and warn her."

Though Bev held to her belief that Nina's pregnancy and Hope's new gentleman friend were just enormous coincidences, she didn't think there was any harm in passing the stories on to Dee-Dee.

One week after her birthday, Bev's staunch skepticism was shaken to its core. Early Sunday evening, her mother called with bad news. There had been a fire that afternoon in the Granger house, barely a block away from their own property. The family had gone out and must have left something cooking on the gas stove. The kitchen was destroyed, but the firemen saved the rest of the house, except for smoke and water damage. At least no one was hurt.

Beverly's hand trembled as she hung up the phone. Another one of the Gypsy's predictions had happened exactly as she had said it would.

"You look like you've seen a ghost," Hope said in a worried tone. "What happened?"

Bev had to force her voice to work. "The Grangers' house . . . a fire . . ." Hesitantly she related what details her mother had known.

"Just like Lavonda said," Hope whispered. "Oh, those poor people! Is anybody taking up a collection to help replace what they lost?"

"Mom will let me know what we can do."

"You have to tell Dee-Dee. She wouldn't listen to me when I tried to talk to her. She won't even tell me what Madame Lavonda predicted for her that was so upsetting. Maybe when you see her at The Alley Cat tonight, she'll have a few beers and you can convince her to—Are you listening to me?"

Bev slowly shifted her gaze from the purple bottle to Hope. "Yes, that's a good idea."

"Are you going to try it again?" Hope nodded at the bottle. "I mean, now that you can't help but believe?"

Bev didn't have an answer. She had been so sure it was all malarkey.

"Well, if you decide to take the chance, don't do it till I get back. It shouldn't be too late. I mean, it *is* only our first date." A glance at the clock spurred her to action. "Good God! Jacob will be here in an hour, and I haven't even started on my hair."

Bev smiled as Hope rushed into the bathroom, yanking rollers out of her hair along the way. Dr. Jacob Mauser had taken five days to progress from calling to check on Stanley's condition to asking Hope out for a date, but Hope had never had a doubt that he would get around to it eventually. Bev couldn't help but wonder if Hope would have been as confident if the Gypsy hadn't put the idea in her head to begin with.

Five minutes before he was due, Hope's doctor knocked at the door. He truly was a giant of a man, but the bouquet of delicate pink rosebuds and baby's breath in his large fist and the shy smile on his pleasant face kept him from being the slightest bit intimidating.

"Hi. I'm Jacob. You must be Beverly."

Bev liked the fact that he didn't introduce himself as Dr. Mauser and was wearing a suit and tie, and when he shook her hand, it was warm and solid, and best of all, his third finger didn't have a wedding ring on it. His eyes and her intuition said he was a good man. They didn't have a chance to exchange more than a few words, however, before Hope joined them, looking prettier and happier than she had looked since they were teens.

The instant the couple's eyes met, they forgot Bev was in the room. Beverly herself felt a little embarrassed at witnessing the strong force that passed between them, and she discreetly backed out of the living room.

Not until she heard the front door close did she allow herself to think about that force. A wave of sadness washed over her as she remembered how it had felt to have a man look at her like that and how it had felt to look back. Love at first sight. Happily ever after. *Till death do us part.*

A tear ran down her cheek and onto her blouse, followed by another, before she put a stop to it. If she was so damned content with her life like she kept telling everyone she was, why was she crying? She tried to tell herself they were tears of joy for Hope, but that was a bald-faced lie. The truth was, she was crying because she knew exactly what Hope was feeling, and it hurt terribly to think she would never experience that kind of happiness again.

The Gypsy's words echoed in her mind. *You will meet a man who will reawaken your heart.* Perhaps, if she tried to remove the stopper now . . .

Before her fingers touched the bottle, the telephone rang and the distressed voice on the other end commanded her full attention.

"Beverly? This is Mrs. Vivianno, Dee-Dee's mother. She asked me to call and, um, oh dear, just a moment."

Bev heard the woman pleading with Dee-Dee's children to behave. Apparently, Frankie had once again found something better to do than stay with his children for the few hours that his wife got out of the house.

"I'm sorry. The children are rather upset this evening. Oh, yes. I'm calling to let you know that Dee-Dee won't be able to meet you tonight."

Something was making Mrs. Vivianno nervous and Bev didn't think it was only the children. "What's going on Mrs. V? Tell me the truth."

"Oh, dear. Frankie practically ordered me not to, but I think Dee-Dee would want me to tell you."

"Please do. Maybe I can help." She heard the woman sigh and try to hush the baby, who was beginning to cry near the mouthpiece of the telephone.

"She's in the hospital with a broken jaw. The doctor decided to keep her overnight for observation. She said she fell, but I'm sure *he* did it to her. In all our years of marriage, her father never broke one of my bones. Sure, he may have pushed me around a little, but—"

"What hospital is she in, Mrs. V? I want to see her." As soon as Beverly could end the conversation, she called Peggy to tell her bowling was canceled, without explaining why. Peggy really wouldn't want to know.

In record time, she reached the hospital and found the room number Mrs. V had given her. To her relief, Frankie was nowhere around. Bev lightly touched Dee-Dee's hand, and she opened her eyes. There was no mistaking the look of fear in them before she recognized her friend. Rather than feeling sympathy, anger fueled Bev's speech.

"What happened this time, Dee-Dee? Did you forget to wash his lucky poker shirt in time for a game tonight? Or were you five minutes late getting dinner on the table?" The wire contraption on her swollen face prevented Dee-Dee from being able to answer, but Bev doubted that she would have anyway. Or worse, she would have blamed herself for Frankie's rage as she had dozens of times before. "How much is enough, Dee-Dee? When are you going to call it quits? That business of staying with him because of the kids doesn't make sense anymore. What are those kids going to do if he beats you to death? Who will protect *them* from him if you're gone?" Dee-Dee's gaze darted beyond Bev's shoulder and that fearful look returned.

"Still don't know when to mind your own goddamned business, do you, Winetke?"

Bev whirled around to see the cocky sneer on Frankie Giammarco's face and wished she was a man for just five minutes.

"Visiting hours are over," he stated flatly as he walked to the opposite side of Dee-Dee's bed and took her hand in his. "I'd like to say goodbye to my wife now . . . in *private*."

Bev read the look in Dee-Dee's eyes that begged her not to cause more trouble, and she nodded. She wanted to know if this was what Lavonda had predicted for her, but she couldn't think of a way to ask that wouldn't rouse Frankie's suspicious nature. It would just have to wait until she could speak to her alone. She leaned down and gave her friend a kiss on the forehead. "I'll check on you tomorrow. If you're still here, Hope will—"

"She'll be back home tomorrow morning," Frankie interrupted. "And she won't need no visitors upsetting her."

Bev squeezed Dee-Dee's hand and left without saying any of the things she wanted to say to her or Frankie. She knew it wasn't right for her to interfere in the couple's private business, but the way Frankie treated Dee-Dee wasn't right either. There had to be something she could do to help. But what?

Knowing she wouldn't be able to sleep until Hope got home and shared every detail of her date, Bev put her new Elvis album on the phonograph and settled in bed with the Frank Yerby novel one of her customers had given her as a birthday gift. It was supposed to be quite risqué, but she couldn't keep her mind on the story or its characters. She couldn't blame her distraction on Elvis's wailing complaint about his "hound dog" either. Her gaze kept drifting off the printed page and on to the purple bottle on the dresser.

She was nearly certain now that the Gypsy had

warned Dee-Dee about what was going to happen to her. Why hadn't Dee-Dee done anything to prevent it? Was it because, like her, she didn't really believe in the fortune-teller's ability to predict the future, or did she simply believe there was nothing she could do about it?

If Madame Lavonda was correct about all those other things though, then might it also be possible for Bev to change her entire life, just by drinking a potion? Beverly recalled what the Gypsy had said her future held if she chose not to change it: *You have no future . . . a zombie . . . zee living dead.*

At least her life was better than Dee-Dee's. Or was it? No matter how badly Frankie treated her, she adored her children, and had often said she would marry him again just to have those kids. When Beverly saw Dee-Dee with them, she always felt a little envious. And when Nina was confiding in her about her pregnancy, there had been a moment or two when Bev wished it could have been her instead. And when she had seen Hope and Jacob together earlier, hadn't she been just a little jealous of them as well?

She tried to force her attention back to the book, but a phrase about someone having a dream for their future made her remember another comment of the Gypsy's. *You have no husband, no children, no dreams.*

She could have gone ahead with the idea of owning a store, except that had really been Billy's dream, not hers. Her interest in it had always been centered around decorating the store, particularly the windows. She supposed if she moved to Trenton, or better yet, New York, she might be able to do that for one of the big department stores, but whenever she thought of moving away from her family and friends, living alone, and starting over, she would come to the conclusion that she was perfectly content waitressing at the diner.

Side one of the album came to an end, and she closed the book and slipped out of bed. She flipped the record over and waited for "Don't Be Cruel" to begin before turning back, but her feet stopped in front of the dresser. Purposely ignoring the little bottle, she studied the image she faced in the mirror.

People were always asking why a girl as pretty as she was didn't have a husband, but her appearance wasn't important to her. In fact, she paid very little attention to it. She only put on makeup so that she wasn't featureless. Her gray-blue eyes were too pale, and her eyebrows and lashes were nearly invisible. And as far as her long blond hair was concerned, she only let it grow because a pony tail was more practical for work and easier to deal with the rest of the time.

No one ever complimented her figure, however. She ran her hands down the oversized man's dress shirt she liked to sleep in, but there were no obvious feminine swells anywhere. In a blouse and jeans, she could be mistaken for a young boy. But that didn't matter to her either, since she wasn't trying to win a beauty pageant or attract a husband.

Her gaze drifted to the bottle despite her intention to ignore it. To her bewilderment, a flicker of light seemed to be coming from inside, and she wasn't even touching it this time. She moved from side to side to determine if it was a reflection, but the glow stayed where it was. With a mixture of fascination and wariness, she touched the purple glass with one fingertip. As she expected, it was much warmer than it should be.

For several seconds, she just stood there, frowning at the Gypsy's tricky little bottle. "Oh, what the hell," she mumbled, picked it up, and gave the stopper a tug. It came out so easily she almost dropped both pieces. The shock of what that might mean caused her to immediately replace the stopper and set the bottle back on the dresser again.

She received a second shock when Hope appeared in the doorway a heartbeat later.

Looking as happy as a woman possibly could, Hope gushed, "No wonder you couldn't hear me come in. You're in here dancing with Elvis!" She stepped closer and raised Bev's chin with a finger. "Wow, that must be some album. He's even got you blushing."

Bev took a deep breath and gathered her wits. "How was your date?"

"Fabulous! I have no idea what I ate, or what we talked about, but it was the most wonderful evening of my life. And when he brought me home—it was so sweet—he wanted to be respectful, but he couldn't resist at least one kiss good night, and my God, what a kiss! We are going to be so-o-o happy."

Beverly angled her head at her. "Doesn't knowing what's going to happen take some of the fun out of it?"

Hope laughed. "I don't see what's so *fun* about worrying whether a guy likes you or not, or whether he'll call again, or if the relationship is going somewhere. I wasted enough years with Stanley, wishing and hoping for something that was never going to happen. I'm too old to enjoy playing that game anymore."

Bev listened to what details Hope did remember about the evening, then she told her about Dee-Dee.

"I agree that there must be something we can do to help," Hope said. "But *she* has to want to change her life first."

"Well, maybe this time will do it. After all, he never put her in the hospital before. And maybe when we tell her about Madame Lavonda's other predictions coming true . . ."

"Whoa! What's that I just heard? Could it be that my skeptical roomie has had a change of attitude?"

Bev made a face at her, then decided to be honest. "Right before you walked in, I tried to open the bottle again. The stopper came right out."

Hope didn't know whether to be excited or disappointed. "You were supposed to wait for me!"

"Oh, I didn't drink it. I got scared and closed it up again, but I think I want to try it now that you're here. This way, if it turns out to be poison, and I pass out or something, you can call for an ambulance."

"Cool!"

Bev reached for the bottle, then hesitated. "Maybe—"

"Just do it!" Hope ordered.

Bev nodded and picked up the bottle. Immediately, it warmed and glowed, and when she lifted the stopper, it came out effortlessly.

Hope peeked inside and took a sniff. "Champagne?"

Bev did the same and had to wipe her nose where some of the escaping bubbles had tickled it. "Could be, but it's not even enough to get silly on let alone give me the nerve to change my whole life."

"So what? You've got nothing to lose."

Hearing those words again was the final spur. To the accompaniment of her very favorite Elvis hit, Beverly brought the bottle to her lips, closed her eyes, and swallowed the contents in one gulp.

She had never had a drink go straight to her head with a mere sip, but before the liquid even reached her stomach, she felt dizzy. Suddenly she was spinning amidst colors and shapes as if caught inside a toy kaleidoscope tube. It was incredibly beautiful, but she was too panic-stricken to appreciate it. She had heard of drugs that do strange things like that to your brain.

Somewhere outside of the kaleidoscope she could hear the words to "Jailhouse Rock" and she latched on to the sound to try to clear the drug out of her brain. Gradually, she could feel the floor beneath her feet, the colors and shapes faded away, and she felt perfectly normal again.

Except for her eyes; they wouldn't open. And her ears; the music was so loud she could feel it vibrating through her. With great determination, she was able to raise her eyelids, but what she saw made her squeeze them shut again. Several times she opened and closed her eyes until she was convinced the scene around her wasn't going to change back to her bedroom.

She seemed to be in a nightclub or lounge, but she had no idea how she got there. More astonishing, however, was the sight of Elvis Presley—*in person*—performing the song she had been listening to in her room just seconds before.

But it couldn't be Elvis. He was in boot camp, and his head had been shaved. The man on stage had all his hair and was gyrating more suggestively than the censors would ever allow. And he was wearing something no celebrity rock 'n' roller would be caught dead in. It was all white from neck to ankles and was decorated with rhinestones and fringe.

Bev glanced around her and noticed other oddities. The customers were almost all women, and some were screaming very unladylike phrases at Elvis, such as "Shake some of that this way!" and "Let's see some buns!" There was something about their clothes and hair that didn't look right. Then she spotted the waiters—at least she guessed that's what they were since they were carrying trays loaded with drinks— but these men were bare-chested, muscular, and extraordinarily handsome, and a few of them had very, very long hair . . . and wore *earrings!*

A collective squeal from the audience drew her attention back to the stage in time to see Elvis strip his rhinestoned outfit completely off his body.

Chapter 3

Elvis Presley was stark naked in front of a roomful of screaming women!

Well, practically stark anyway. The white, rhinestoned triangle of material below his navel couldn't even pass for underwear.

"Have you lost your way, sweetheart?"

Startled, Bev jerked toward the male voice and had to reach out to balance herself. It was one of the long-haired waiters and her hand was pressed against his tanned, hairless chest. Good grief! His breasts were larger than hers. The rock-hard muscle flexed beneath her fingers.

"Do you need help finding your seat?" he asked in a tone that suggested he meant something else.

She quickly withdrew her hand, then looked up to see a sexy grin, and looked further up to meet his eyes. The look he gave her made her cheeks flame. How dare he! Then she noted the way he scanned her from head to toe and realized exactly why he dared. She was still dressed in her nightshirt with nothing but panties underneath. Her calves and feet were bare. "I . . . I have to go," she stuttered.

He pointed behind her. "Restrooms are that way."

She shook her head. "No. I mean, I have to get out of here."

His grin broadened with some private joke, and he pointed toward a red-lettered sign.

Before she made it to the exit, she banged her right baby toe twice on chair legs, tripped over someone's purse strap, and bumped into another Adonis. She had this idea that if she could just get out that door the weird dream would end, and she'd be safely back with Hope.

She pushed her way through the door, fully expecting to find herself in her bedroom once more. Instead, she was outside, in a parking lot, and she could still hear the music and cheering women inside the lounge. How had she gotten here? Where was *here*?

A shiver overtook her as the chilly night air crept under her shirt, and she thought she smelled cigarette smoke. She couldn't remember ever having a dream anything like this. It wasn't just vivid; it was solid . . . as solid as that waiter's chest had been. Thus, she returned to the theory that the Gypsy's potion was some sort of strange drug that was giving her hallucinations. She decided to run a little test.

"Two times two is four. Four times four is sixteen. One hundred fourteen plus twenty-nine is . . . one hundred forty-three. Columbus discovered America in 1492. My name is Beverly Newcastle, born Winetke. I live in Mercerville, New Jersey."

If she was drugged, her mind seemed perfectly clear, and that didn't seem to be right either. Didn't drugs make your brain fuzzy? She felt the panic rising and ordered herself to calm down. Whatever was happening to her, getting hysterical wasn't going to help.

"Okay, Hope, I don't know how this stuff works, but I'm going to assume I haven't really gone anywhere, and you're still standing in front of me. Just stay cool. I seem to be fine, just having a very strange hallucination. To be on the safe side, though, don't let me leave the apartment until I'm back to normal. If this doesn't wear off soon, maybe you'll have to take me to the emergency room for an antidote."

Only then did she realize she was still holding the purple bottle in her hand, and tucked it in her shirt pocket to make sure it got to the hospital with her body. For some reason, however, she felt confident that the drug would wear off before that became necessary.

The lighting in the parking lot was minimal, but sufficient for her to make out another peculiar vision. The cars were all different from any models she had ever seen before. A long, low vehicle in the front row caught her eye, and she decided as long as she couldn't stop the hallucination she would try to relax and take a closer look at some of the odd things she was imagining. Slightly favoring her injured foot and being careful to avoid pebbles and glass, she began a leisurely inspection of the unusual cars.

From his assigned post beside the exit door, Josh Colby remained perched on his Harley as he watched the intoxicated woman doing her damnedest to walk a straight line. He wondered if she even realized she was barefoot. Probably left her shoes with the imaginary friend she was talking to.

From what he could hear, it sounded like she had

taken something a lot stronger than alcohol tonight. He only hoped she had simply come outside for some fresh air and that she had at least one nonimaginary friend inside who would be driving her home. Otherwise, it looked like he might actually have to earn his money tonight.

Amanda James, the owner of The Bullpen, had recruited him in a bar one night when he was between construction jobs and low on cash. She had wanted him for her stable of dancers and waiters, but conceded to hire him on as a doorman/bouncer, with his primary duty being to make sure no one got behind the wheel of a car who was too drunk to walk a straight line to it.

The money was decent, the job was easy, and he had nothing better to do with his evenings. Even after he got hired on at another high-rise construction site, he continued to work for Amanda on weekends whenever he was in town.

Of course, there were a few concessions he had to make for such a flexible part-time job. His black-and-red Harley-Davidson Heritage Softail came to work with him; the women loved it. He wore a black leather jacket, pants, and boots. Beneath the jacket was a fitted black muscle shirt.

Amanda said the outfit made him look both sexy and tough. She also insisted he accentuate his Mohawk heritage by keeping his straight black hair long and loose and wearing a beaded headband or choker. Tonight it was a turquoise-and-coral choker. The silver hoop in his left ear had been her idea, too. But he wouldn't have done any of it if it hadn't suited him to begin with.

Their personal relationship suited him as well.

They were two mature adults, who got together every so often when it was mutually convenient—no ties, no promises, no emotion, just some laughs and physical gratification. Neither of them wanted anything more.

The blonde had made her way down the front row of cars without trying to get into any of them, so Josh stayed put while she staggered back toward him. It was his policy to talk to the patrons only when absolutely necessary. There were plenty of guys inside who were available for "socializing."

He and his bike were far from invisible, but he could tell by the woman's expression that she hadn't noticed him until she was about to go back inside.

"Oh," she said. "How nice. I was just thinking that I should try talking to someone, and here you appeared. Are you able to answer questions for me? I mean, I know this is my hallucination, but I don't seem to be controlling it in any way."

Josh stood away from his bike in case he had to catch her or defend himself.

"You see, I've been giving this a lot of thought, and I figured the potion might have been like the plant Indians eat to have visions that help a person see into the future, only I don't know how to interpret what I'm seeing."

For someone stoned out of their gourd, she was speaking very clearly. "What are you on, lady?"

She looked down at her feet and back to him. "Asphalt, I guess. Is that important?" She stopped and checked him out from hair to boots. With the light behind him, his face was in shadow, but from what she could see he seemed to have striking features, and the rest of him was outlined in black leather. The fancy motorcycle gave her a clue. "Wait a minute. If Elvis is in there taking his clothes off, you must be ... let's see ... James Dean! Right? And since he's dead, that *must* mean something. Something to do with Billy maybe."

Josh suddenly realized that she didn't appear to be either drunk or drugged; mentally handicapped was more likely. "Did you come here with someone?" he asked in a gentler voice than he normally used. "Can I help you find them?"

She shook her head. "No, I seem to be alone, but can you tell me where I am?"

He didn't really have the patience for this sort of thing, but he also didn't know what to do with her, other than play along until someone came to claim her. "You're at The Bullpen."

She looked thoughtful. "I never heard of a lounge called that around Mercerville, or Trenton for that matter. I guess I need to make my questions more specific. What *city* am I in?"

"New Rochelle." When she didn't seem to recognize the city name, he added, "New York." The pathetic bewilderment in her eyes made him think of a lost child, but he wasn't in charge of the lost and found department. "Why don't you let me call you a cab. Do you know where you live?"

She clucked her tongue at him. "I'm confused, not stupid. Let's try something else. I was in my bedroom in Mercerville at eleven-thirty. What time is it now?"

He pulled back his jacket sleeve to check his watch. "A few minutes to midnight."

"Sunday?"

He shook his head. "Not for a few more minutes."

He wondered how much longer he should wait to call the police to take her back to whatever institution she had escaped from.

She sighed and shook her head with frustration. It was Sunday night a half hour ago, now it's Saturday. Could she have had amnesia for a week, and traveled to New York in the meantime? "I don't understand any of this." Rubbing her arms against the cold, she paced a few feet one way, then the other, staring at the cars. Abruptly, she stopped and came back to him. "What is the exact date?"

"April 6, 1996. Now listen, lady—" Josh's words hung in the air as the woman vanished before his eyes. He reached out into the space where she had been standing one second ago, but there was absolutely nothing there . . . and not a soul around to confirm that he hadn't been talking to himself.

"Thank God!" Beverly exclaimed when her second kaleidoscope ride ended, and she found herself facing Hope in her bedroom. She gave her roommate an exuberant hug, then stepped back again to assure herself it was really Hope. "*That* was the scariest, weirdest thing that has ever happened to me. It was so real. Could you hear me talking, or was I just imagining it? Was I moving around in here, or did I just stand here the whole time? Why are you staring at me like that?"

Hope's eyes were huge and her voice came out in a higher pitch than usual. "You were here, then you weren't, then you were. Then you were gone again, and now you're back."

Beverly touched Hope's forehead to check for fever. "*I'm* the one who drank the potion. What's wrong with *you*?"

Hope swallowed hard and blinked a few times. "You admit that you drank the potion?"

"Of course." She pulled the bottle out of her pocket and turned it upside down. "See? Empty. From what I could tell, it made me have a very realistic hallucination, but if it was supposed to give me a hint about my future, I couldn't make any sense of it. What did you mean, I was here and then gone?"

Hope rubbed her temples as she attempted to sort out what happened. "This is going to sound crazy, but I swear I only had one cocktail before dinner and I'm perfectly sober. I watched you drink the potion. A second later, you just disappeared—nothing was left, not even a puff of smoke like in the movies. I blinked, and you were back, only your eyes had changed. They were completely gray, no blue at all. And when I asked you about the potion, you shrugged and told me you 'threw that stupid bottle in the trash' while I was out with Jacob.

"I kept thinking you were pulling my leg for some reason, but you got really bugged at me so I dropped it. We were talking about what we could do for Dee-Dee when you vanished for another second or two. Now you're here with the empty bottle and bright blue eyes. And you want to know what's wrong with *me*?"

Bev scratched her head. Hope's explanation made as little sense as her own hallucination. She glanced at the clock. It was five after twelve. "Tell me this, is it now Monday, April 7, 1958?" Hope checked the time, then nodded. Slowly, so as not to miss a single detail that might be important, Bev related what had happened to her during the last half hour.

Even before she was completely finished, Hope came to a conclusion. "*The Time Machine,* by H.G. Wells. Remember, we read it in high school."

Beverly arched an eyebrow. "You think the potion was like a time machine, and I really *was* in New Rochelle, New York thirty-eight years in the future?"

"Wait right here. I can think of one way to check." Hope hurried to her room and came back with an almanac. "This book has a perpetual calendar in it. It'll say what day of the week April 6th will be on in 1996. If it isn't Saturday, then you weren't really there." She found the page and narrowed her eyes as she figured out how to read it. "There," she said, pointing her finger at one line. "Saturday it is."

"Hmmph. That hardly proves that I traveled through time."

"It's as good as your Indian plant vision theory."

"But neither one explains how you were talking to me about Dee-Dee while I thought I was talking to James Dean."

Hope wrinkled up her nose. "But the you I was talking to swore you didn't take the potion, and the eyes were different, kind of flat, like when you're sick with a cold or something." She gave an exaggerated shudder. "It's too spooky for me. I think you should go back and see Madame Lavonda and ask her what it was all about."

"Ah-ha! You see? Didn't I tell you there was some sort of con game where I would need to go back to see her again, and then she'll ask me for money. No thank you. I had enough of an adventure one time around."

* * *

"You're right; I know you're right," Dee-Dee told her three friends a week later at The Alley Cat. "But I can't change the fact that I have four young children. I can't expect my mother to take care of them all day so that I can go to work. And even if she was willing and able, what kind of job could I get?"

"You were one of the best in our typing and shorthand classes," Bev reminded her. "You could practice up."

Dee-Dee bowed her head. "It still comes down to money. I don't even own a dress to go on an interview, let alone go to work in an office every day. I'd need a car and a place big enough for me and the kids . . . Face it, a secretary doesn't make enough money to support five people."

Peggy had been quietly following the discussion up until then. "She's right. What she needs is another husband, preferably an older gentleman, like Calvin." Dee-Dee's groan prompted her to say, "All you'd have to do is pretty yourself up a little, like you used to, and I'll bet lots of men would come sniffing around."

"Peggy's got something there," Hope agreed. "Hey, if I could accidentally meet someone as wonderful as Jacob in an emergency room, why couldn't you?"

Dee-Dee made a face. "I was just in the hospital, and I didn't meet anyone worth remembering. Now did we come here to bowl or make me more miserable than I already am?"

As they got back to their game, Beverly's mind stayed on the problem of how to help Dee-Dee. She had finally admitted that Lavonda had foretold of an event far worse than a simple broken jaw. A child's life, she couldn't say whose, would be in mortal danger because of one of Frankie's drunken rages.

All week Bev had fought off thoughts about Madame Lavonda and her bottle of potion, but she couldn't deny that the woman's predictions had been accurate. Although the potion had not changed her life in any way, she had begun to think about making some changes. She had had a pretty wild adventure, even if she couldn't understand what had happened. And she had sort of met a whole bunch of handsome strangers, though none of them had reawakened her heart. She figured a few details might have gotten mixed up in the translation.

The fact was it seemed rather foolish now to ignore the Gypsy's words completely, in which case, Dee-Dee could be facing a tragedy in the near future.

"How about another trip to Madame Lavonda?" Hope suggested, almost as if she had been hearing Bev's thoughts. "I'll pay the fee. It can be a, uh, an early birthday present from Bev and me."

Dee-Dee looked interested for a moment, then shook her head. "The only night I can get out is Sunday, and I think Frankie's been checking on whether I'm here or not."

"Then go during the day, while he's at work. Bev's off on Tuesday. She can drive you."

Beverly narrowed her brows meaningfully, but it was too late. Dee-Dee was already considering the outing.

"But the kids—"

"Surely your mom would watch them for another hour or so," Hope said confidently.

"Bev?"

Dee-Dee's expression was too hopeful for Bev to refuse. "I'll pick you up at noon."

Bev had a few words to say to Hope that night about getting her into things without consulting her. Nevertheless, Tuesday afternoon she and Dee-Dee were knocking at Madame Lavonda's door.

"So, you have finally returned," the Gypsy said to Beverly.

"We're here for Dee-Dee," she quickly replied.

Lavonda nodded and waved them inside. "I do not know that you will like what zee crystal ball has to say, but we shall see. Perhaps eet has some advice you can use. Come."

Dee-Dee followed the Gypsy into her back room with an air of resignation. A short while later they returned to the living room together. Bev could tell that it hadn't been good news, but at least Dee-Dee wasn't crying.

"And now you," Lavonda told Beverly.

"Oh, no. That's all right. What do we owe you?"

"Hmmph. I do not want your money. I want a moment of your time. Come."

"Really, I have to get Dee-Dee back home."

"It's okay, Bev," Dee-Dee said. "I have a while yet."

"I can explain your journey," Lavonda offered. "Are you not curious about what happened to you last Sunday night?"

Bev didn't bother to ask how she knew when she drank the potion, she just followed the Gypsy into her room and sat down at the covered table. Before joining her, Lavonda went to the cabinet she had gone to during Bev's first visit and took out another bottle. As she set it on the table, Bev noted that this one was blue and silver, even prettier than the first. "Another magic potion?" she asked with a half smile.

"A stronger one," Lavonda replied and sat down. "Give me your palm." Again, she examined the lines carefully as she spoke. "You took a small chance, but not enough to change your life. You are still zee skeptic, *oui*?"

"Not as much as before. Most of the things you predicted happened. But I don't want any more of your potions. The last one didn't do anything but scare and confuse me."

Lavonda grinned, revealing the space where a tooth was missing. Beverly could have sworn it was on the other side of her mouth the last time.

"That eez because you deed not believe what you were seeing and hearing. Eet was, how you say, a preview of coming attractions. But I will explain now. Zee potion took you on a journey to a time and place where you are much needed."

"But was I really in New Rochelle in 1996, or was I just hallucinating?"

"Eet was completely real. You were there."

Hope had been right after all. The potion was like a time-travel machine. It was totally ridiculous . . . and made perfect sense . . . sort of. "What about the me that Hope talked to in my bedroom while I was away? Explain that."

It took Lavonda a moment to understand the question, then she grinned again. "When you departed from thees time and place, a shadow of your essence was left behind to continue on as zee person you would be had you chosen *not* to take zee potion. Een other words, they were both you, but on two different paths—one who took zee risk, one who deed not. I know what you are thinking now, but do not be afraid. The two will never be een zee same place at zee same time. Eet eez impossible. Eet eez also impossible to stay on two different paths for *très* long. Eventually one must choose one's destiny."

"Okay, let's say I understand the theory, and maybe I can even believe I took a trip through time. But what was the purpose of it?"

Lavonda looked at her curiously. "Deed you not meet a man? Someone who interested you?"

Beverly made a face. "I don't think *interested* is the right word. I saw Elvis taking his clothes off, and a lot of other half-dressed men. They were all pretty interesting. I talked to one of them. Then there was another guy, who probably thought I was drunk or crazy. But no, I didn't actually *meet* anyone."

Lavonda rubbed her crystal ball and stared intently into it for several seconds. "Now I see more than I deed before. A beautiful, happy future awaits you, but you must earn ect. There eez something *très* important you must do, a life you must save, before you can be rewarded."

"A life I must save? Whose? How? Is it Dee-Dee or one of her kids?"

"You will help your friend one day, but she eez not zee one zee crystal speaks of. Zee key to your happiness can only be found een zee time and place that zee potion sends you. To perform thees service and change your life, you must take another journey. That eez all I can tell you. Zee rest eez too cloudy." She fell back in her chair as though exhausted. With a tired wave of her hand, she dismissed Beverly. "Take zee potion, and thees time, pay better attention.

There eez someone who needs your help desperately, and there eez very leetle time left."

Beverly rose and put the blue bottle in her purse. She wasn't sure she was going to try it, but taking it away was easier than arguing about it. As she opened the door to leave she heard Madame Lavonda say, *"Nous nous verrons encore."*

Lavonda waited until Beverly and her friend left, then walked over to the calendar on the wall. Lifting the top page, she began counting backward from April 30th: *fifteen days*. She could only pray that it was enough time, and that she had chosen well with Beverly, for she would not be given another chance to right the wrong that had been done.

If only the rules were not so rigid—No, she knew that was not possible. She could enlist a mortal's aid one time, if the cause was deemed truly worthy, but she could not come right out and tell the chosen one what they must do. All she could do was create situations and give vague hints. The mortal had to *want* to help and had to do so on her own, out of the goodness of her heart.

Lavonda had no doubt that Beverly had a good heart, and that eventually she would figure out what she needed to do, but she didn't have the luxury of *eventually*. The rules were quite clear about the timing also—Lavonda was given extraordinary powers for only thirty days from first contact with the mortal of her choice. If Beverly did not succeed within that time, Lavonda's wish would be permanently denied.

On the way home, Dee-Dee told Beverly what Lavonda had predicted. "Frankie will keep drinking

more and getting meaner. Big surprise, huh?" She
touched the brace on her jaw. "This wasn't the last
time I'll be in the hospital because of him."

Bev frowned. Rather than voice her agreement, she
asked, "But what about the child? Did she tell you
more about that?"

"A little. She thought the injured figure she saw lying on the floor was a boy, but it could have been a
girl with very short hair and dressed in boy's clothes.
Either way, she described the child as being fourteen
or fifteen. If that's true, it's not something that's going to happen immediately. Tina's the oldest, and not
only did she just turn twelve, she's all girl."

But kids change, Beverly thought. Tina could suddenly decide to cut her hair and be a tomboy.
"Lavonda told me I'd be able to help you one day.
Believe me, Dee-Dee, if there's a way, you know I
will. In the meantime, will you at least start brushing
up on your secretarial skills?"

Dee-Dee shrugged. "Sure. But I don't see what
good it'll do."

Beverly didn't know either, but it might at least get
her friend thinking about independence. Meanwhile,
she was glad that Dee-Dee was so caught up in her
own problems that she didn't think to ask what else
the Gypsy had said.

Life had been so simple two weeks ago. All she
had had to do was wake up in the morning, go to the
diner, eat, sleep, and gossip about people she had
known forever. Two weeks ago, she had been certain
Madame Lavonda was a fake, and it was easy to dismiss anything she said.

Suddenly, because of that same Gypsy's words, she
felt responsible for someone else's life . . . or lives if

she counted Dee-Dee's and her child's along with the desperate someone Lavonda spoke of. After everything that had come true, she could hardly ignore the warning. Changing her own life and falling in love again might be nice, but she didn't feel strongly compelled to do anything about it. But this new information . . .

Lavonda implied that she was the only one who could help. And the only way she could do it was by going on another trip through time. It looked as though she would have to risk her own life to save someone else's, someone she didn't even know.

By the time she dropped Dee-Dee at her house and entered her apartment, she had her answer. She had never turned her back on anyone who needed help in her life. She couldn't start now.

She took the bottle out of her purse and started to remove the silver stopper when she thought of some things she should do first. In case Hope came home from work before she returned, she scribbled a note telling her she took the potion again. Not knowing what her "shadow" might do if she saw the note from herself, she pinned it to Hope's bed pillow.

The first journey had been a blind experiment for which she had not been prepared in any way. This time, she was wearing a watch, was fully dressed in blue jeans, a short-sleeved sweater, socks, and shoes, had a purse with identification and some cash in it, and was carrying a jacket in case it was cold wherever she ended up. This time, she knew what to expect, so she didn't need to be afraid or waste most of her visit trying to figure out what was going on. This time, as Lavonda had instructed, she would pay better attention.

Certain that she was as prepared as she could be, she swallowed the potion and tried to enjoy the kaleidoscope ride. She was almost doing that when she felt something firm beneath her feet again.

"What the hell?" a man's voice uttered in shock.

Beverly opened her eyes and saw *him*—her James Dean from the strange lounge in New Rochelle—staring at her with his mouth open. Then she noticed her surroundings ... most of which was air.

She was standing at the end of a narrow metal beam of a building under construction, and she was closer to the clouds than the ground.

"Don't look down!"

His harsh command jolted her and the jacket slipped off her arm. Without thinking, she reached for the blue material and instantly lost her balance.

Chapter 4

As the woman's body pitched forward, she instinctively tried to grasp the nearest solid mass, which happened to be Josh. His thighs clamped around the beam he was straddling, and his arms closed around her waist a heartbeat before she took a nosedive. If he had been standing, she would have taken him with her on a fast and very final trip to the first floor.

For several seconds, neither moved as she hung there, half across his lap and half suspended in midair. Far, far below, her jacket continued its leisurely float to the ground, where a few workmen were trying to figure out what was going on up there.

"Could you help me up please?" she asked in a squeaky voice.

"Only if you swear to me that you're not planning to jump," Josh replied angrily. "Or at least that you'll do it somewhere that I'm not."

"I wasn't trying to commit suicide. I'm not stupid. I just lost my balance."

There was something familiar about her voice or her attitude, but he couldn't place it. "What the hell did you think you were doing coming out here like that?"

"Help me up, and I'll tell you," she said, as if *she* were losing patience with *him*.

He carefully pulled her upright and held her steady while she straddled the beam facing him. Fortunately, she didn't weigh any more than a couple of two-by-fours. "Are you dizzy?" he asked with more annoyance than concern. "Do you think you could shimmy your way back to the platform?"

She seemed to test herself for a moment. "I think I can do that."

"Good. Now, keep your hands and butt on the beam and your eyes on me. We'll do this nice and slow, just scoot a few inches at a time." Josh made the first move backward to demonstrate. As she took her turn forward, he glanced down. A fair-sized audience had gathered to watch their slow trip back to safety. He was tempted to leave the foolish woman on her own and simply stand up and walk away. He was going to see to it that somebody caught hell for letting her get up here and almost killing him.

"You don't recognize me, do you?" she asked after her second scoot.

He stopped and squinted at her. "We've met?"

She laughed. "Not exactly. We spoke for a minute or two last Sunday, I mean, Saturday night . . . outside of the, um, what did you call it?"

"The Bullpen?" He looked at her features, the blond hair, her small body. Like her voice, there was something familiar about the package, but all the women he saw at the club tended to blend—He stilled as awareness set in. "You! I thought I imagined you. How did you disappear like that?"

She made a face. "The same way I appeared a minute ago."

"Like hell. Whoever let you come up here—"

"Nobody *let* me come up. If you'll think for a second, the platform is *behind* you. I'm in *front* of you, and there's nothing behind me but air. I *popped* in, the same way I *popped* out on you last week."

She was nuts. She had to be. Unless he was. Last week, no one saw her but him, so he figured he must have dozed off and dreamed of her without realizing it. But he was wide awake today and from what he could tell, plenty of other people down below saw her, too.

"You're not crazy," she insisted, as though she had read his mind. "But I think you're in danger of some kind. And I'm supposed to save you somehow, but I—"

"Save me!" Josh exclaimed incredulously. "You almost killed me with that stunt."

Her spine straightened defensively. "I didn't do it on purpose."

He rolled his eyes and scooted back another foot.

"Listen to me! There's this Gypsy named Lavonda. She gave me a potion and said it would take me to a time and place where someone needed me desperately. Since it brought me to you both times, you must be that someone. I can't help it if you happened to be doing a high-wire act when I drank it."

"Stop," Josh ordered, holding up his hand. "I don't want to hear anything else you have to say." He stood up, walked the last two feet of the beam to the platform, and pointed to the control box. "See this red button? It will take you down to the ground. Use it, and don't come near me again."

Beverly watched him turn his back on her and stalk off onto another beam, then another, and another, with a graceful leap wherever there was a gap, until he reached the opposite side of the building framework. From there, he jumped down onto another platform that took him up to the next level. If he hadn't been so rude, she would have been extremely impressed with his agility.

As she completed her awkward progression to the platform alone, she thought she might have been impressed with more than just his agility . . . if he had been a little more gentlemanly. It struck her that she could have been mistaken about why the potion took her to him twice. Rather than his being the "desperate" someone whose life she had to save, maybe he was supposed to be the "interesting" someone instead.

He certainly was handsome with his deep tan, dark eyes, and prominent cheekbones. And he was at least her age, probably a little older, midthirties at the most. His straight black hair was a lot longer than appropriate for a man to wear, but she knew from her last trip that quite a few men in this time period grew their hair long. At least his was neatly brushed back today and tied at the base of his neck. The cloth band he was wearing around his head was probably to keep the sweat out of his eyes—she couldn't help but notice the damp sheen on his muscular arms and chest—but the headband also made him look very much like an Indian, which she also found intriguing.

She had heard of Indians who specialized in working dangerously high construction jobs like bridges and skyscrapers because they had no fear of heights. His striking features made her think he could be one of those men.

He was strong, too. He had caught her and reposi-
tioned her as if she were weightless.

Overall, he was quite nice to look at. He just
wasn't very nice. In fact, he hadn't even introduced
himself. Besides, not only had he shown absolutely
no interest in her as a woman either time, he wanted
to get as far away from her as possible.

No, she decided, he couldn't possibly be the man
who was supposed to reawaken her heart. That
meant he *had* to be the one she was supposed to save.

When she reached the ground, several men surrounded her, asking if she was all right, and one
questioned how she had gotten up there without
anyone seeing her. Knowing she couldn't tell the
truth, she put on her prettiest smile and imitated her
friend Peggy. "I'm fine, thank you, gentlemen. I
guess I was daydreaming and got on one of those
funny elevator things." She giggled lightly and
shrugged. "Anyway, that sweet man up there helped
me. Could you tell me his name?"

Several of the men looked at each other doubtfully.
"Sweet man?" one asked another, who replied, "I
thought Colby was the only guy up there." They all
laughed at that.

"Colby?" Bev asked, maintaining her dumb blonde
act.

"Yeah," the first man answered. "Josh Colby, our
token Native American. But I never heard nobody
call him sweet."

"But I am," said the second man, openly eyeing
the slight swells beneath her sweater. "And it's almost quittin' time. What's say you an' I go have a
cold one at Hank's, and you can tell me all about
your daydreams."

"Hank's?" she asked as if she would actually consider taking him up on such a rude invitation. "Is that where you all go after work?" She purposely let her gaze drift over the entire group.

"Yeah," the first man repeated with more of a smile. "It's a bar down the block."

"Well then, I have a few errands to run, but maybe I'll see you all there a little later."

As she fetched her jacket, she felt male eyes following her and had the sudden urge to look up. There, forty or fifty stories above, she saw a figure move out of sight and was certain it was Josh Colby. He had been watching her, too. She smiled. At least now she knew his name.

She was afraid if he saw her hanging around he might never come down, so she walked toward the corner where a group of people were preparing to cross the street and tried to blend in. She had thought Trenton was a big city. This place made that seem like a small town.

Every inch of the wide streets was packed with cars, especially taxi cabs. So many of them were sounding their horns she assumed it must be a way the people signaled each other here. Between the horns, radios blasting, the buzzing and banging sounds from the construction site, and the street vendors competing with each other for attention, she wondered how anyone could hold a conversation outdoors.

The WALK sign came on and the little crowd around her stepped off the curb in a rush. As the light changed to a flashing DON'T WALK almost immediately, she understood why they were moving so swiftly. However, they kept going at that speed even after they reached the other sidewalk. Why were they all in such a hurry?

She found a spot where she was able to hide behind a man selling hot dogs from a cart with a big umbrella. From there, she would be able to see the workers when they filed off the construction site and headed toward Hank's, but they wouldn't see her. She wasn't exactly sure how she was going to convince Mr. Colby to listen to her, but she had the idea that those other men might help if she approached him once they were all inside the bar.

As she waited, she tried to orient herself. Mr. Colby had acknowledged seeing her a week ago, so that answered the date question. Since she had first seen him in New Rochelle, and now he was working on a very high building on a very busy city street where most of the other buildings were higher than she had ever seen before, she figured she had to be in New York City.

Looking around, she found confirmation of her location everywhere—on a manhole cover, a trash container, a building wall covered with poster advertisements for Broadway shows. She recalled that she had recently been thinking of what it would be like to live and work there. Had it been a premonition? She no longer believed anything was impossible.

Nearly an hour passed before the men she had seen before started walking down the street, and for another fifteen minutes there was no sign of Mr. Colby. What if he had decided not to go to the bar tonight? What if she popped back home before she had a chance to speak to him again? Would that mean she had failed in her mission to save him? All those questions proved unnecessary, however, when he finally made an appearance with another, older man.

They were intently discussing something and didn't even glance in her direction, but she waited until they were inside Hank's before moving away from the hot dog cart, just in case the sight of her sent him running in the opposite direction.

She made herself wait another two minutes, long enough for him to order a beer, then headed toward the bar. He saw her the instant she walked through the door, and his scowl let her know she had her work cut out for her.

"Oh, Josh, *honey*, please don't be like this," she said walking to him with a look of total adoration. "We have to talk."

"I told you to stay away from me," he said in a low but deadly serious tone, then turned his attention back to his beer.

"That's not what you said two months ago," she whined. "You wanted me near you then, when I kept trying to hold you off." He was determined to ignore her, but she had the attention of most of the men around him, so she went a little further. "You told me you loved me and wanted to marry me. Damn you, Josh Colby. This is your baby I'm carrying!"

That did it. He stood up so fast, his bar stool toppled over. His friends looked as though they were paralyzed, or maybe they were afraid to move lest the rage on his face might turn on them. As his fingers closed around her upper arm and steered her toward a booth in the corner, she knew she had gone too far. For all she knew, he was another Frankie Giammarco. On the other hand, she did have his undivided attention.

Behind her, she heard murmurs and a crude laugh. It didn't look like she could count on any of his coworkers to help her after all.

"Sit," he barked, releasing her arm.

She slid into the booth and began before he sat down. "Mr. Colby, if you had only listened to me before—"

"Now I'm *Mr.* Colby? What happened to *Josh honey*? I don't *want* to listen to you, lady. I want you to leave me alone. And if you don't, I will get a restraining order against you."

Beverly didn't know what that meant, but it sounded serious. Nevertheless, she had to convince him she wasn't a lunatic. "I don't blame you for being upset, but if you'll just hear me out, *completely*, I think you'll understand." His scowl didn't soften in the least. "*Please*. If you still want me to leave you alone when I'm finished, I promise I will."

"Fine," he said, leaning back against the booth wall and crossing his arms. "I'll give you five minutes to talk, then you'll get up, tell all those guys you were kidding, and never come near me again."

"Deal." She smiled and held out her hand to shake on it, but he glared at it like it was a rattlesnake. Remembering how skeptical she had been helped her to remain patient with him. She realized that her mistake out on the beam was in opening her explanations with the ending, but she had been too upset by her nearly fatal accident to think clearly. Thus, she now started at the beginning, with her birthday visit to Madame Lavonda, and went forward as sensibly as possible from there.

Occasionally, it was necessary to the story to explain a bit about the people involved, like Dee-Dee and Frankie, but Josh's attention stayed on her despite the detour. The five minutes he had allowed her passed, as did twenty more. She considered it very promising that he was still listening, but she didn't want to take any chances. When she came to the point where she popped in at the construction site, she pulled her wallet out of her purse and extracted her driver's license. "Look at my birth date—March 30, 1928. Do I look like I'm ... um, sixty-eight? And look at the address—Mercerville, New Jersey, just like I told you."

He glanced at it without touching it. "There's no picture on it. How do I know it's not somebody else's old license, or one you had made up?"

"Why in the world would I do that?"

He shrugged. "You tell me."

She was on the verge of screaming, but she knew that would do her more harm than good. Frustrated, but not willing to give up yet, she pulled out an insurance card, her social security card, and the birthday note Dee-Dee had written and stuck inside the wallet. "I swear, I am Beverly Newcastle." Thinking of what else she had that was dated, she removed all the cash she had in her purse and showed him that not one bill or coin was dated after 1958. "I don't know how else to prove what I'm saying. My popping in and out should be enough to convince anyone that something strange is going on."

He thought for a moment. "Okay. Pop back to 1958, while everyone's watching, and bring me the newspaper for today, April 15th. Then I'll believe the rest."

She closed her eyes and concentrated on returning

to her bedroom, but nothing happened. "It doesn't seem to work that way."

"Of course not," he said snidely.

She huffed with annoyance. "This is only the second time I've traveled through time! I don't know how it works, I just know I've been sent here to save someone's life, and that seems to be you."

"Who played center field for the Yankees in the 1958 season?"

She wrinkled her nose at him. "How would I know? I'm not a baseball fan." She paused to think. "But I do read the newspaper, and I know that the Milwaukee Braves beat New York in the last World Series. How's that?"

He looked like a cat who had cornered a mouse. "Don't you mean the *Atlanta* Braves?"

"No, I'm sure the Braves are Milwaukee's team."

He turned toward the bar. "Hey, Hank! Was there ever a team called the Milwaukee Braves?"

The man tending bar didn't hesitate to reply. "You bet. They won the World Series over the Yankees in 1957, four to three. The Braves didn't move to Atlanta until 1966."

"Thanks," Josh said and shifted slowly back to Beverly with a perplexed frown.

"Why would you ask me a question about baseball, if you don't even know the answer?"

He shook his head. "I have no idea. They do it in the movies when they want to catch a spy. I couldn't think of anything else."

"Oh, for heaven's sake. I'm not a spy. I'm just a woman who's been given a very strange job to do." His expression now held more bewilderment than skepticism. "Just think how I feel! I was perfectly content with my boring, meaningless life, and all of a sudden I'm popping in and out of the most peculiar places, traveling through time, and trying to convince a hard-headed man that he's in danger, when he doesn't want to know about it. Try to put yourself in my shoes for a minute!"

Josh was having too hard a time in his own shoes to try on hers. He wanted to dismiss her as a royal nut case and get back to his beer. He wanted to come up with a perfectly logical explanation for everything she had said and send her slinking out the door.

Maybe there was a hidden camera somewhere, filming his reaction to a crazy joke, all to be shown at a later date on a national television show. But since he wasn't playing along or doing anything remotely humorous, wouldn't they have given up on him by now?

Or perhaps she was the front person in an unusual con game where he was the mark. But what could he be conned out of? He lived from paycheck to paycheck and his Harley was his only possession of value.

Besides, no matter what explanation came to mind, it still didn't cover how she had materialized in front of him today like one of the *Star Trek* crew. He might have guessed that she was a hologram and her appearance was performed with lasers or mirrors or something like that. But he had had his arms around her, and she was definitely a real, living, breathing woman.

He studied her eyes, looking for a hint of deception. A man could get lost in the innocence he saw there. Her light blond hair was neatly arranged in a ponytail with straight bangs across her forehead, making her look more like twenty than the thirty she claimed. When he had first seen her at The Bullpen, it was dark, and her hair was loose and kind of wild, blowing around her shoulders and hiding part of her face. That's why he had thought she was a lonely man's dream that night, and why he didn't recognize her today.

"Mr. Colby? Can't you even *try* to believe the story I've told you?"

"Just for the sake of moving this conversation along, let's say I believe your fairy tale. Now what?"

His turnabout was so unexpected it took her a moment to shift mental gears. "Well, I don't really know, except that I must do something to save your life, then I can go back and my life will be improved."

He lifted one eyebrow. "That's it? Won't I *owe* you something for such an incredible, selfless favor? Maybe there's a certain dancer at The Bullpen you'd like me to fix you up with."

She sighed with exasperation. "And I thought *I* was a skeptic. Okay. You win. I'll go away." She slid out of the booth and avoided meeting the men's eyes as she passed the bar and headed toward the door. Before it closed behind her, she remembered the rest of her promise to Mr. Colby. "Just kidding, guys," she called out with a forced smile and a wave goodbye.

What was she supposed to do now? Skulk around behind him, looking for an opportunity to perform her lifesaving task? Considering the fact that she had never been to New York in her life and skulking was hardly one of her skills anyway, it looked like the best thing would be to find a comfortable place to wait until the potion wore off, and she popped back home.

Beverly stood in front of Hank's with the full expectation of being whisked back through time at any second. As far as she could tell, she had done her best and there was nothing left to be accomplished by staying any longer. Also, the first trip had only lasted a half hour. Although Lavonda had said this potion was stronger, it had already been close to two hours.

When several of the men exited Hank's sometime later, she was still standing there, but her feeling was now closer to anxiety than expectation.

Someone put a hand on her back. "Are you going to be okay, honey? You look lost."

She turned and saw a stocky man with a shaved head, several earrings in each earlobe, and a gold ring piercing the side of his nose. But he had a pleasant smile. "I'm uh . . . yes, I'm lost. Could you direct me to a motel that would be nice but not too expensive?"

He shook his head with a look of sincere regret. "I don't think there is such a thing in Manhattan. About the cheapest *nice* rooms you're going to find cost around a hundred and a quarter, and they're usually all reserved way in advance."

"One hundred twenty-five *dollars*? Oh, no, you misunderstood. I only need a place to stay for one night."

"That *is* for one night," he said, giving her a strange look.

She tried to laugh off her mistake. "Maybe you could think of somewhere not quite so *nice*. I only have forty dollars on me."

"What about plastic?"

"Plastic?" His expression told her that he wasn't sure if she was pulling his leg, or if she was truly that much of a rube.

"You know," he said slowly, as though he were speaking to someone who didn't know English. "Mastercard, Visa, Discover. *Plastic.*"

"Uh, no. I don't have any plastic."

"Well, then you'd have a hell of a time renting a room in a hotel around here. It's usually required even with cash."

"Oh." She assumed the plastic he spoke of was a form of identification. Although she normally used her driver's license to identify herself, it would be impossible to convince a desk clerk that it was hers considering the birth date. "What about a YWCA? Is there one around here?"

He shrugged. "I couldn't tell you, but hey, I'm headed to Queens. I know that area better. I could help you find a place to stay there, if you want to come with me."

She knew she couldn't simply stand there, especially in front of a bar after sundown. Normally, she would never go anywhere with a strange man, particularly one as strange-looking as this one, but surely she would be vanishing any moment, and at least he was being more helpful than Mr. Colby. "That would be very kind of you, Mr. . . . ?"

That made him laugh aloud. "No mister. Just call me Stud-Man. Everybody does . . . 'cause I'm a riveter. Get it?"

She didn't, but she smiled, and kept smiling, despite her unease when he put his arm around her shoulders and pulled her close to his side as he led her away from Hank's.

"Beverly! Where the hell do you think you're going?"

She whirled at the already familiar sound of Mr. Colby's annoyed voice. Stud-Man stopped and turned around only because she dug in her heels.

"I told you to wait for me," he said, marching toward them with an expression that made Stud-Man drop his arm from Bev's shoulders and take a step back.

She stood her ground, however. "I thought you said—"

"Since when do you listen to me? You got me mad! After how long we've been together, you know I don't mean what I say when I get like that. Now quit fooling around." He grasped her arm and drew her away from Stud-Man. "It's getting late, and I want to get home."

She wasn't sure what was going on, but she knew, of the two men Mr. Colby's touch felt safer. As he hurried her away, she glanced back at Stud-Man. "Thank you anyway."

"That's two," Josh murmured through clenched teeth.

Chapter 5

"Two, what? And what was that all about? I thought you didn't believe my *fairy tale*. And stop dragging me around!" She pulled away from him until he let go of her arm. "Thank you. I'm beginning to understand how poor Raggedy Ann feels."

"Raggedy Ann? Who's—Never mind. I don't care. Are you coming with me or not?"

"Where?"

"Back to the construction site."

He resumed his long-legged, rapid stride, and she hustled to catch up. "Two what?" she asked again.

"Two times that I've saved your behind. Did you really believe we call him Stud-Man because he's a riveter? Yes, I was listening to your conversation, and I decided you were either zapped here from a small town in the fifties, like you said, or you're an alien. And personally, I prefer the time-traveler angle. At least that makes you human. How is it you're still here?"

"I don't know. It must have something to do with my mission." They reached the locked fence gate at the site and she was struck by a frightening thought. "You're not going to make me go back up where I popped in, are you? I'm sure that wouldn't do any good."

He smirked at her. "My bike's here." The guard on duty greeted him by name and let them in. "I may not be totally convinced, but just in case you're for real, I figure you're better off going home with me than Stud-Man."

Beverly smiled up at him. "Thank you. I'm sure I'll be popping out any minute now, but I really do appreciate your help in the meantime."

"Have you ever ridden a cycle before?" She shook her head, and he grimaced. "Okay, the main thing to remember is to become one with the bike." He could tell that didn't explain it for her and tried again. "Most people's instinct is to lean the opposite way the bike does in a turn, and you can't do that. The best thing would be for you to attach yourself to my back and move with me."

He helped her don his spare helmet, then ran down a list of other instructions for safe riding. "Put on your jacket," he advised as he pulled his own out of a compartment. After they mounted the bike, he glanced back at her uncertainly. "Are you going to be okay?"

She chuckled. "After the trip I took earlier today, this will be a walk in the park."

With a ferocious roar of the Harley's powerful engine, they were on their way. Traffic had finally thinned somewhat, but even in tight spots the motorcycle was able to find a passageway. It was impossible to ask any questions over the noise of the engine, but her eyes were taking in as much as possible. She was hoping to see streets named Broadway, Wall Street, or Fifth Avenue—especially Fifth Avenue. She wanted to get a look at the famous store windows of Macy's and Gimbel's. What she saw instead were streets numbered E 67, 68, 69, and up.

Nevertheless, as they sped along, her mind and body seemed to be filling with an unfamiliar sensation. There was something about the city itself that spoke to her, crawled right inside and excited her. She would have called it electric, but she had never actually been electrocuted to know how that would feel. This had to be close, though.

When they crossed the bridge to the Bronx and left Manhattan behind, she expected the feeling to fade away, but it didn't. If anything, it seemed to be expanding. Despite the cool wind, she felt overly warm, and she had to concentrate to take a deep breath.

"Sit still!" Josh shouted back at her.

She hadn't even realized she was fidgeting. His reprimand stopped her mental wanderings and made her abruptly aware of why she was so warm. The heat was coming from him. She hadn't given a thought to the impropriety of their positions. Even with his leather jacket between them, it was terribly intimate. Her chest was pressed to his back, her thighs clenched to his hips, and her arms were wrapped around his waist so tightly she could feel the hard muscles of his abdomen as well as if he was—

She cut off that thought before it settled into her head. It certainly would not do to be distracted by his physical attributes. Not only was she merely visiting, she could never allow herself to become attracted to a man who might not live much longer. Of course, she was going to do whatever she could to save him, but since she was playing it all by ear, she couldn't be sure that she would succeed. Then, too, he still didn't seem very nice.

Perhaps it wasn't him or the positions of their bodies that was causing wicked thoughts to form against her will. Perhaps it was just the motorcycle. She had heard talk about *some* women who enjoyed riding the powerful bikes because of the sexy way the engine made them feel. Yes, she liked that explanation a little better.

She had no idea how long they had been riding, but it was nearly dark when they reached New Rochelle. He came to a stop in the rear of an apartment building.

"You can let go now," he said a few seconds after turning off the bike's engine.

He sounded annoyed again, but she couldn't help it if her muscles wouldn't relax.

"Just move slowly," he said a bit more patiently. "The vibrating will stop in a minute."

She took his advice and was able to peel herself off him and the bike. They were in front of a row of doors with metal grates and big padlocks. There were no windows on this level. "You live . . . in one of these?"

He was obviously about to make some smart-aleck comment as he dismounted, but he restrained himself. "No, but the Softail does. They're *storage* rooms. I can't get her upstairs to my apartment, and she's safer here than on the street."

"*She?*"

He shrugged and went to unlock the grate. Once his back was turned, she shook each leg and arm and wiggled her fingers to get them back to normal. By the time his "girl" was safely locked up, the sensation that she was still on the bike was almost gone.

He cocked his head to indicate which way they were headed, but she stopped him with a light touch on his arm. "I just wanted to say thank you again for bringing me with you." She looked up into his dark eyes, hoping he could see sincerity in her own. For the first time, he didn't glare back through narrow slits or pick some spot behind her head to look at while she spoke. She had noticed his handsome features before, but when he directed that gaze right at her, he went from handsome to devastating. She had to remind herself to take a breath.

His expression softened as his gaze moved slowly over her face. She stood very still as he raised one hand and tucked a stray lock of hair behind her ear. "I couldn't very well leave you on your own."

"Yes, you could have," she countered quietly. "But you didn't. You know what I think, Mr. Colby? I think you're not nearly as mean as you want people to think you are."

The warm expression in his eyes cooled instantly. "Stop calling me Mr. Colby. It sounds ridiculous." He turned on his boot heel and walked into the alleyway on the side of the building.

Beverly remembered how Stud-Man had laughed when she called him mister. Had things changed so much in thirty-eight years? She caught up to Josh and asked, "Don't people use that title anymore?"

"What?"

"Mister. You said it sounded ridiculous."

They reached the front door of the old brick building and Josh quickly unlocked it. "Under the circumstances, it is. We still use *mister*, but maybe not as much as they did in the fifties. I don't think we're as formal as people used to be."

"All right then. Under the circumstances, I'll call you Josh, if you'll call me Beverly, or Bev for short." His only response was a shrug.

In the foyer, there was a yellow light bulb in the ceiling, but it wasn't bright enough for Bev to see much. Josh led her up a narrow flight of stairs with a wooden railing too splintered to grasp. By the time he stopped to unlock his apartment door on the second floor, her eyes had adjusted to the dim light, but there still wasn't much worth seeing. The hall carpet was threadbare, and the paint on the walls and his door was cracked and peeled off in some spots to reveal a lighter color.

He pushed the door open, then remembered his manners at the last second and let her enter first. One quick glance covered the whole apartment, which was really more of a motel room. A bathroom was immediately to the left. To her right, another door was open enough for her to see that it was a small closet, and beyond that was a compact kitchenette. The rest of the room was taken up by a bed, a nightstand, and a dresser with two broken handles.

Everything was beige or brown or white; not a hint of color anywhere. There were no pictures or photos on the walls, nor any knickknacks to personalize the room. On the positive side, it was neat. She searched for a polite comment. "It looks . . . very comfortable."

"It's all I need," he said tersely, closed the door, and went over to the dresser. He pressed a button on a small rectangular object on which a red light was flashing. It made a high-pitched sound, followed by a woman's voice.

"Hi, sweetie. Amanda here. Rick called in sick for tonight. Any chance you can cover for him? I need to know by eight. Even if you don't get this message until late, call me at the club anyway. I've got another need you could take care of at any hour. It's been quite a while. *Ciao*, baby."

For some reason, Bev had just assumed there wouldn't be a wife waiting for him at home, but whoever that voice belonged to obviously had an intimate relationship of some kind with him. "What is that?" she asked, pointing to the box.

Josh looked at her curiously as he pushed another button, the box made a whirring sound, then a green light came on. It took him a moment to understand what she was asking about. "Oh, that's right. You wouldn't have had answering machines then." He raised the lid and pointed inside. "One tape has a recorded message from me that plays if I don't pick up the phone. The other records the caller's message if they want to leave one. Then I can play it back when I get home."

Beverly didn't understand how something so small could do all that, but she nodded approvingly. "Cool. I can see how that would come in handy. Um, that message sounded personal. If you'd like, I could go take a walk—"

"Not in this neighborhood. The call can wait. You hungry?" he asked as he crossed the room and opened the little refrigerator. "I have chicken fried rice, spaghetti, or"—he opened a white container—"something brown."

Bev laughed at the face he made. "Spaghetti would be fine. What can I do to help?"

"Nothing. The restaurant down the street made it. I just have to nuke it for a minute."

"Nuke it?"

He sighed as if he were frustrated by her ignorance, but his mouth turned up on one side, letting her know that he was amused in spite of himself. "I guess, besides saving your butt, I'm going to have to introduce you to modern technology."

Beverly was fascinated by the microwave oven, but even more so by the discussion it prompted over dinner.

In the years between 1958 and 1996, women's lives had apparently undergone a drastic change. According to Josh, there had been a sort of rebellion—"women's liberation," he had called it. Appliances like the microwave oven helped reduce the time spent on household chores. There was one that washed dishes, and another that dried clothes that never needed to be ironed. Families were smaller, and there were places called day-care centers where children of any age could be left while the mother went to work. Men were encouraged to accept more responsibilities at home, and jobs that were formerly only held by men were being filled by women now. There were women doctors, lawyers, business executives, senators, even a supreme court justice. It was absolutely amazing!

As incredible as all the changes and inventions were, however, time travel was still beyond the capabilities of science, yet she had somehow done it by drinking a Gypsy's potion. She knew Josh didn't fully believe that story, but at least he was going along with her for lack of a more practical explanation. It might have been easier to convince him if she had told him she had used a time machine. Unfortunately, she hadn't thought of that in advance.

While she rinsed their dishes in the sink, he told her about cars with air conditioning inside, and planes that could fly from New York to Europe in a few hours. She wasn't sure whether to believe him about a man walking on the moon in 1969, but he swore he had watched the event on television when he was ten years old, and that she would find proof in a library . . . if she hung around long enough to visit one.

His mentioning his age made her realize that he hadn't even been born in the year she had come from. "I just thought of something interesting. Assuming I succeed in whatever it is I'm supposed to do to save your life, and I get to go back home, I could come to see you in 1996. Of course, I'll be really old by then, but it would still be interesting to visit with you after the me that's here now goes back."

"Weirdly enough, I understood that," he said, arching an eyebrow at her. "I'll look forward to seeing you again . . . I guess. Although that's not always the way it works in time-travel movies. I'm not sure either one of us will remember this meeting."

She cocked her head at him. "You mean, I might not remember any of the things you told me about the future?"

"Who knows? Even if you did remember, there's not much you could do with anything I've told you."

She gave that some thought. "Unless you told me who won a certain world series, or a boxing match, or a horse race. I could bet on the outcome and make a lot of money. Or I could invest in the stock market if you told me the names of really successful companies today." Her brows raised with a flash of comprehension. "Oh my. That would be completely dishonest, but I'm not sure I wouldn't be tempted. Okay, just in case I do remember meeting you—because I did the first time—promise you won't tell me anything real specific."

He agreed, and immediately wondered if he could be as honest if their positions were reversed. Not many people could. But then, there was something about her that made him think she wasn't like any of the people he knew ... and not simply because she might have come from another time period. It was something else.

Innocence. The word came to him without having to think about it. How could a thirty-year-old woman as beautiful as she seem so innocent? Before his curiosity pushed him into asking her personal questions, which would give her the right to ask the same of him, he got back to the discussion about inventions, beginning with the digital alarm clock on the nightstand, then moved on to beepers, cellular phones, and finally computers.

He couldn't remember the last time he had done so much talking, and he never remembered enjoying it at all. Talking was one of those things you had to do a minimum of to get by. But every time she gasped in amazement or her eyes lit up over something he told her, it made him grin—another thing he didn't do very often, at least not when he was sober.

It was the genuine amazement that finally convinced him of her honesty. He kept looking for her to make a slip, a look, a movement, a word, anything that would confirm that she was lying about where and when she had come from. He didn't believe in fairy tales, but he couldn't seem to stop himself from believing her.

He also knew it was only her ignorance that was making him feel so smart, and the rapt attention that was making him feel so special was only because there was no one better for her to turn to.

On this particular evening in time, he was her entire world, but he didn't feel smothered by that as he normally would. Nor did he have to keep her at arm's length as he did with most women. He didn't have to worry about her misunderstanding his intentions or expecting something from him that he couldn't give. He could be as relaxed as if he were completely alone, because this evening didn't mean anything in the long run. Any minute now, she would vanish, just like she did before . . . leaving nothing behind but a memory that seemed more like a dream than reality.

"Listen," he said as it passed eleven o'clock. "I need to take a shower and get some sleep before it's time to go back to work. Do you think you'll stick around for a few more minutes, or should I say goodbye now?"

Bev smiled. "Last time I popped back right around midnight. Maybe the witching hour has something to do with my traveling. So, if you hurry I should still be here when you get out of the shower."

"Do you want to watch the news? I don't know what else is on, but you can check for yourself."

She hesitated only because the television was on a trunk at the foot of the bed, and the best way to view it clearly would be by sitting on that bed. She had gotten past the fact that she had spent an entire evening in a strange man's bedroom by pretending not to notice the largest piece of furniture in it, but there seemed to be no help for it now.

He noticed the blush that colored her cheeks, the way her gaze skittered away from the bed, and recalled how naive she had been about Stud-Man's invitation to help her find a place to stay. She truly was an innocent, something he knew absolutely nothing about. It was one thing to tell her about women's liberation, another to update her regarding male-female relations. Instead of commenting on the bed, he showed her how to use the remote control and decided to leave it up to her if she wanted to sit or remain standing.

"Oh!" she squealed when the picture instantly appeared. "That was so fast! And it's in *color*! Just like at the movies. I heard that it was coming to television eventually, but that it would be very expensive."

He felt himself grinning again. "Well, I'm sure it was at first, but just about everybody has a color T.V. now. I remember my mother telling me I was born the same year *Bonanza* came on in color. Apparently, it was a very big deal."

Without giving it another thought, Bev sat down on the bed, her eyes focused on the colored picture that was more than twice the size of the television screen on her father's set. She could hardly wait to tell Hope that she would be able to see Adam Cartwright in technicolor by next year!

She didn't notice Josh walking away, but when she heard the shower turn on, she took off her shoes and made herself more comfortable on the big bed. With the pillows propped behind her and the remote in her hand, she discovered why the television was situated where it was. It was quite comfy.

For a few seconds, she switched channels just to watch the picture change, then she left it on the news program where the people's faces seemed the friendliest. To her dismay, their expressions contrasted with the news they were telling. Within a five-minute period, they related information about a mother murdering her children, a bomb exploding in a school, and a state governor being accused of sexual harrassment by his secretary.

She was searching for a less depressing program on another channel when Josh's phone rang. Josh called something out from the bathroom that sounded like, "Answer that," so she picked it up and said hello.

"Who is this?"

Bev was fairly certain it was the same voice that had left a message on his answering machine and didn't want to say anything that would get Josh in trouble with his lady friend. "This is Beverly. Josh's . . . cousin. Who's this?"

"Josh never mentioned having any *cousins*," the woman said suspiciously.

"Oh, that's probably because we'd never met until this afternoon. Our families weren't very close." Hoping to give a reasonable explanation why he hadn't returned her call, Bev added, "It took us all evening to catch up on each other's lives. We, uh, we just got in a few minutes ago."

"Let me talk to him," she demanded.

"I'm sorry. He's in the shower, but I'll be glad to give him a message."

The woman's voice had icicles dripping off the edge. "Yes, you give him a message, sweetie. You tell him he's on Amanda's shit list."

Bev flinched as the woman hung up with a bang. She had obviously mishandled the situation and hoped Josh wouldn't be too angry with her.

A minute later, Josh exited the bathroom wearing what looked like a pair of swimming trunks . . . and nothing else. She supposed it wouldn't bother her if they were at the beach, but under the circumstances . . . She felt herself blush again and tried not to gape at his incredibly formed body as he rubbed a towel over his long black hair.

"Was there a message?" he asked from beneath the towel.

She swallowed hard and concentrated on answering his question. "Yes. It was Amanda. I'm afraid she seemed rather upset. I tried to explain—"

"You *what*?" He stopped drying his hair and stepped closer. "Didn't you hear me say not to answer it?"

Bev's mouth opened and closed. "I thought you said 'Answer it,' " she replied sheepishly, then relayed the exact conversation to him. Instead of being furious with her, however, he burst out laughing.

"That's priceless," he said, still chuckling. "I was going to call her back when I got out of the shower, but it looks like you saved me the trouble."

Beverly wrinkled her nose at him. "I don't get it. Don't you have a, uh, *relationship* with Amanda?"

He chewed on the inside of his cheek. "Now that's an interesting question. I suppose it's a matter of interpretation. She's the owner of The Bullpen, and I am one of her employees. We're also friends . . . sort of."

"Considering how jealous she sounded just now, I can guess what 'sort of' friends you must be," Bev teased then thought better of it. "I'm sorry. It's none of my business, and I really am sorry if I messed something up for you."

"Not a problem," he insisted, sitting on the bed and picking up the remote. "She was probably just putting you on. There's no way she could be jealous with the stable of boys she keeps."

Bev was pretty sure she understood that comment and decided to let it drop, but Amanda's call did make her think of something else. "Would you have gone to work for Amanda tonight if you hadn't brought me home?"

Josh flipped through the channels until he found the station he wanted. "I don't know," he said indifferently. "Maybe."

Her eyes widened, and she sat down beside him. "I had been thinking that I had to save your life by *doing* something, like pushing you out of the way of a speeding car. But maybe all I had to do was be here. Think about it. What if, I *wasn't* here and you decided to go to The Bullpen, and on the way there, or back, you were in a fatal accident? If you look at it that way, I might have already fulfilled my mission by preventing you from going out tonight."

"It makes sense, except for one thing. I'm not convinced that I'm the person you're supposed to save. I'm nobody important. If I was killed tonight, no one would care. It wouldn't make a damn bit of difference. So why, out of a whole world full of important people, would you have been given the ability to travel through time to save my life?"

She understood his argument, but all she could think of was how sad it was that he was so alone. She had the strongest urge to put her arms around him and hug him until he believed that somebody did care whether he lived or died. But that wouldn't be very proper. "Maybe it isn't you directly. It could be that a child of yours—one that isn't conceived yet—is supposed to accomplish something important in the future. If you died now, that child would never be born.

"Then again, maybe you weren't the one who would have died in the accident. Maybe you were just riding along and someone driving a big truck didn't notice you on the motorcycle until the last second. They swerved and crashed into a limousine carrying a senator. Because he dies in the accident, he never does whatever important thing he was supposed to do, and then—"

"Okay, okay, I get it," Josh said, raising his hand to stop her runaway imagination. "But if you've already done the good deed you were sent here to do, why haven't you popped back out yet?"

She glanced at his digital alarm clock and shrugged. "It's not midnight yet."

"Right." He shifted toward her and placed his crooked index finger under her chin.

She sat very still as he tipped her head slightly back and stared deeply into her eyes, as though he were searching for a secret there. "What is it?" she whispered, not understanding, but not wanting him to look away either.

Rather than answer, he dipped his head and gave her a soft kiss on the mouth. The contact was brief. He barely touched her. It could hardly be called a kiss. Yet he practically stole the breath from her body. It had to be her imagination, or the fact that she hadn't been kissed by a man for many years.

When his mouth returned to hers a heartbeat later, she knew it wasn't her imagination or lack of experience. The touch of his lips on hers filled her with the same electrical sensation she had had riding on the bike behind him through the most exciting city in the country. Before she could decide whether to return his kiss or put a stop to it, he raised his head and blinked at her. He looked as surprised as she felt.

"I . . . I wanted to say goodbye . . . and thank you . . . for possibly saving my life."

"You're welcome."

"That was a lie."

"I know." Her heart was pounding much too hard, and he was sitting much too close. Her head felt all fuzzy, like she was going to faint.

"The truth is, in about fifteen minutes you'll probably disappear again, this time for good, and I wanted to know if you tasted as innocent as you look."

His words caused an unfamiliar trill of pleasure to run through her. She knew it would be extremely forward of her to encourage him, but she couldn't seem to resist. "Did you find out what you wanted to know?"

"No," he said, frowning. "It was the weirdest thing. All of a sudden I felt like I was taking advantage of you. I mean, you are pretty much at my mercy here, and I'd like to think I'm a little better than Stud-Man."

"What if . . ." She shyly lowered her eyes. "What if . . . I kissed you instead?"

Chapter 6

Josh's stomach did a fast flip. What was wrong with him? He couldn't remember getting this nervous over kissing a girl since he hit puberty. It was just something you had to do to move on to the main event. She was obviously willing. What was he waiting for?

Beverly came to her senses while Josh hesitated. "I'm sorry," she said, quickly putting space between them. "I don't know what I was thinking. Of course, you're right. The circumstances are hardly—"

He pressed a finger to her lips. "Sh-sh-sh. Let's just forget it."

He rose from his bed, so she did as well. She assumed they were going back to sitting at the little table where they had talked and eaten, and kissing was the furthest thing from either of their minds. Instead, she watched him turn down the bedcovers, rearrange all the pillows in the center of the headboard, then return to the scene of the crime.

Josh leaned back and patted the spot next to him. "You've still got five minutes to liftoff. You may as well be comfortable while you're waiting. Besides, this guy is usually pretty funny."

She was still a tiny bit embarrassed about forgetting herself, but not enough to forego his offer of comfort. She really was terribly tired. She smiled, then tried to get situated beside him without actually touching any part of him. Then she remembered her shoes on the floor and started to fetch them when he put an end to her fidgeting by placing his arm behind her head and tucking her closer. The full-body contact caused her to tense up.

"Would you rather I didn't?" he asked without looking at her.

She knew what her answer should be, but also knowing that she would probably never see him again, and might never again feel the way he was making her feel right now, she answered honestly. "I think, I'd rather you did."

With that admission, they both pretended to relax and turn their attention to the comedian on T.V.

A moment later, Josh pulled the covers up to their waists to keep her from seeing how little control he had over his body's response to her.

Thank God she was only passing through. Otherwise, he was certain her contradiction of sexy innocence would be the death of him. She was the kind of woman a man falls in love with and wants to hold on to for the rest of his life.

She was also the kind of woman who would never have anything to do with a man like him under normal circumstances. The second she learned the truth about him, she would take off, just like Elise had.

He had known the second he saw Elise that she wasn't for him. But she had looked back, and he stopped thinking with his head. She was the first and last woman customer at The Bullpen that he had gotten personal with, except for Beverly.

He and Elise were the definitive example of oppo-
sites attracting. He had been drawn to her because
she positively reeked of class. She had been drawn to
him because of his lack of it. He had seen her as
someone he would have been proud to bring home
to meet his parents, if he had any. She had taken him
home to meet hers, as a gesture of defiance, a threat
that if she didn't get her way, she just might marry a
worthless bum like him. The fact that he was half
Mohawk had appealed to her only because she knew
it would horrify her mother to imagine one of her
grandchildren being born with anything less than lily
white skin.

Not that Elise was the only woman who had ever
dumped on him, she was just the one who brought
the hard lesson home with a kick to the groin. After
her, he stuck to women who were just looking for a
night's distraction; women who didn't care what he
was, or where he had come from, or who his father
was; women like Amanda James.

He just wished he could stop time, right now. She
wouldn't go back, nor would either of them go forward. And the rest of the world could go to hell.

Amanda James drummed her crimson-painted
sculptured nails against her desktop as she watched
the minute hand on her clock creep closer to the
twelve. Fortunately, business was fairly slow tonight
and she could close up on time. It was also fortunate
because Josh's services as a doorman hadn't been
necessary after all.

The other service she had requested of him ...
now *that* was another matter. Amanda couldn't remember the last time a man had ignored her invita-

tion. Recalling the female voice that answered his phone irritated her so much she rose from her chair and began pacing the office.

"Cousins, my ass," she muttered to her full-length reflection in the wall mirror. "If she's Josh's cousin, I'm his sister." She took a step closer to her image. "Mirror, mirror on the wall, are any of my parts starting to fall?" There wasn't an inch on her that hadn't been tucked, sucked, or lifted already, but at the first sign of aging, she would have more work done. She had turned forty last year, but no one ever guessed that when they looked at her face or her body. Everyone thought she was under thirty, and she certainly wasn't going to correct them.

She smoothed her burgundy-glazed, chin-length hair. It had just been styled in the latest movie-star fashion and she had wanted Josh to see how flattering it was. She had worn the body-hugging black minidress for him tonight, too. The last time he saw her in it, he got so hot he hadn't even waited for her to take it off.

She smiled at the memory. That was the best thing about Josh. He liked it hard and fast, and he was man enough to get her ready for him with no more than a look.

Had she waited too long between invitations this time? She thought she had him completely figured out. The best way to keep him interested was not to pursue too diligently. She had been certain that he would balk at anything that smelled like a real relationship. And when it came to Josh Colby, she had decided sometime ago that whatever she had to do to keep him around was worth the sacrifice.

She might have forgiven him if he had called when

he got out of the shower . . . if that was truly where he was. She might have believed that he had unexpected company that he couldn't get rid of . . . if his excuse had sounded even the slightest bit regretful. But nearly two hours had passed since her second message, and he hadn't bothered to call back. She wasn't sure how she would punish him for such rudeness—he was the one man in her life that she had no hold over—but she would think of something before he arrived for work Friday night.

In the meantime, she had been anticipating some quality time with him and now she was left with an annoying problem. She opened her office door and motioned to her floor manager. As always, he stopped what he was doing and came to her.

"How long has that waiter been with us? You know, Ben something."

He followed her gaze to see who she was referring to. "The one by table 14? About a month. His name's Ken."

"Ken, Ben, who the hell cares. We're going to change it anyway. Send him in to see me after he's off duty."

Fifteen minutes later, the beautiful young man stood in front of her desk, smiling too much. Amanda couldn't help but enjoy the fact that he still had that fresh, eager-beaver attitude. "When I first interviewed you, you said you were willing to work as a waiter since it was the only opening I had, but that you wanted the chance to dance on stage. Is that still true?" It didn't seem possible, but his smile got even wider.

"Yes, ma'am," he said politely.

"Do I detect a southern accent, Kenny?"

"Texas, ma'am."

"Hmmm. We could use that, if we called you The Lone Ranger, and you wore a black mask, cowboy hat, and boots. That would fit in with the fifties nostalgia theme. Do you know how to use a lasso? Don't worry, you can fake it. What do you think?"

"Wow. I'd truly appreciate the opportunity, ma'am."

"I think I could find a place for you . . . if you can move."

"Hey, no problem there."

She swiveled her chair around and pressed the play button on her recorder. As the music began, she turned back to him. "Show your stuff, cowboy. You're on."

Ken quickly found the beat, proving he could move, but could he follow directions?

"Good. Can you do that and strip at the same time?" His hands roamed seductively up his shaven chest to his muscular neck and undid the clasp on his bow tie. His shoes and pants came off in a fairly sexy way as well. When he hooked his thumbs in his briefs and hesitated, she gave him a nod, and he bared the rest of what nature had endowed him with. He turned his back to her and flexed his buttocks, just to show her he knew what the ladies in the audience wanted to see.

Amanda got up and came around the desk, and he stopped showing off. "Do you know what this is for?" she asked, holding up a small rubber band. He looked at it warily without admitting his ignorance. "The boys don't strip completely down anymore, but they still need to have a sizeable swelling in their G-string, or the ladies might laugh when they're not supposed to. Of course, they could use a substitute, but I prefer my boys to do it au naturel. Well, almost."

She noticed that he had swollen somewhat without any help. "Not bad, but I need more than that to show you how they do it. Let's see if I can help." She stroked him softly, and he responded, but not enough. "Maybe you need a different kind of incentive." With little more than a tug and a wiggle, her dress slipped to the floor, and she gave him a close-up view of her incredibly perfect, nude body. Satisfied with the effect she had on him, she gave his erection a smile of approval and a squeeze. Then before he could protest, she placed the tight rubber band at the base of his penis, keeping the blood right where she wanted it.

"Damn! That hurts . . . ma'am."

"Only at first. You'll get used to it. They all do." She circled around him, running her hands over his hard body. "I think you'll do just fine, cowboy. I just have one problem." She stopped in front of him, pouted, and waited. When he looked sufficiently worried, she ran her hands up her own body, lifting her breasts and toying with the nipples. "Interviewing you has got me all . . . tensed up inside. Do you think you could help"—she moved close enough to rub her breasts and stomach against him—"relax me?"

The newly promoted dancer grinned down at her. "It would be my pleasure, ma'am."

When he had performed the best he could, she let him go. He was good enough to take the edge off, she thought with a sigh.

But he wasn't Josh.

* * *

Beverly smiled as she felt Billy snuggle her body a little closer to his. She knew it was only a dream, and that he would be gone when she awoke, but as she always did when she dreamed of him, she resisted leaving that misty world. And, as always, she lost the struggle.

Her mind rose slowly from the mist, but the realistic dream held on.

"Oh, shit! I forgot to set the alarm!"

Beverly surfaced with a jolt as Josh lurched from the bed and staggered to the bathroom, muttering more obscenities along the way.

"Do me a favor," he said from the doorway in a brusque tone that made his request sound more like an order. "Pour me a cup of coffee. Light, no sugar. Wait. First call the site and tell them I'm on my way."

"What's the number?" she asked before he shut the door.

"Just push the first memory button. It's programmed in."

Setting aside the confusion she felt over waking up in Josh's bed, she hurried to help him. His instruction for the phone call made no sense to her, but she figured it out after a few seconds. He had shown her the coffee machine with its automatic timer last night, but she was still amazed to see the pot of fresh-brewed coffee on the counter. She quickly fixed him a cup and handed it to him as he rushed out of the bathroom.

Minutes later, he was dressed, and his empty cup was in the sink. He was about to fly out the door when he turned back to her, looking as though he just realized she was there.

"Go on," she said. "I'm a very trustworthy person. Everything will be right where you left it when you get back."

"What about you?"

She had no idea how to answer that, so she just shrugged and shooed him out.

Caught up in his need to race to work, Beverly didn't think about what she had done until several minutes after he was gone, and then it was too late. The fact that she hadn't popped back home yet suggested that her mission had not been completed, as she had assumed last night. A jumble of thoughts crammed her brain all at once.

What if *today* was the day she was supposed to save Josh? She should have accompanied him to work! Of course, she could always try to catch up with him, *if* she knew the way, and *if* she had transportation, and *if* she had a key to lock up his apartment when she left.

She poured herself a cup of coffee to clear away the cobwebs. Her first clear thoughts, however, had nothing to do with her mission. She had slept with a strange man last night. The fact that sleep was all they had done, didn't make it all right.

A fragment of her dream came back to her and she knew they *had* done a bit more than sleep, even though neither of them were conscious at the time.

And don't forget about kissing him last night, her conscience reminded her.

Damn! Her brain was jumbled again. If she had known she was still going to be here today, she would have slept on the floor, and she never would have asked if she could kiss him. She felt herself flush with the memory. Good Lord. What had come over her to behave that way? He must think she was one of those "easy" women. Why, he wasn't even her type—

She giggled, knowing how Hope would respond to that. How could she know what her type was when she hadn't been out on a date with anyone but Billy in over a decade.

With a shake of her head, she got back to the more practical matter of her mission. Since she hadn't gone back last night, how much longer might she stay? It had never occurred to her to pack a change of clothes.

On top of everything else, she felt like kicking herself for missing an opportunity to see all the wondrous things she had heard about in New York City.

Suddenly the door opened and Josh was back. He looked angry or frustrated, or both.

"I forgot to tell you to keep the door locked," he said, frowning at her without moving from the doorway.

"I was just about to do that. But I'm glad you came back. You have to take me to work with you."

His eyebrows rose a notch. "I have to what?"

She quickly slipped on her shoes and grabbed her purse and jacket as she explained her reasoning.

His frown changed to a look of disbelief. "No way are you going to follow me around on the job." He took a deep breath and finally came the rest of the way into the apartment. "Look, I don't know whether you're really a time traveler on some mission, but whatever you are, I do believe you're stranded. By the time I got on my bike, it hit me that

I couldn't leave you alone up here. I can't explain it. It was just a weird feeling I got, like . . ."

When he couldn't seem to find the right words, she finished the sentence for him. "Like we're supposed to be together for some reason?"

His mouth turned down again. "Yeah. I guess that was it."

She cocked her head at him. "Which is pretty much what I've been trying to tell you." He gave her a look that warned her not to rub it in. "Aren't Indians supposed to be able to see the future?"

Instantly, his features hardened. "I'm only half Mohawk. Anyway, that spiritual crap is all bullshit. It comes from drinking too much cactus juice."

She backed away from what was clearly a sensitive subject. "Okay, so what do you think we should do now?"

Josh scratched his head and looked around the tiny room. When his gaze lit on the unmade bed, he cleared his throat. "I guess hanging out here all day wouldn't be such a good idea, huh?"

"No, it's not," she said firmly. "But if you're going to take the day off work, I have a better idea." Given the alternatives, it wasn't hard to convince him to take her to see the sights of New York City. "And if you wouldn't mind, maybe we could stop at a store. I could really use a change of clothes. I've been in these since yesterday morning."

He realized that she would probably like to take a shower also, but was too modest to even suggest it. Talk about innocent! She gave the word new meaning. "I have an idea. Wait here. I'll be right back."

When he returned, he had a small pile of clothing

in his hand. "These belong to a woman upstairs. I
told her my sister just arrived in town, and the airlines lost all her luggage. She's a little taller than you
are, but I figured you could manage. If you want to,
uh, freshen up, there's a clean towel in the bathroom
you can use. I've got to call the site and give them
some excuse for not coming in after all." As soon as
he saw the way her eyelids lowered self-consciously,
he knew he had guessed right about her modesty
hang-up.

As he tried to decide what story to tell his boss, his
gaze kept wandering to the closed bathroom door.
He felt his temperature and manhood rising at the
images that flickered in his mind. She was hardly the
first woman to take a shower in his apartment, but
she was the first one who was so shy about it. For
some ridiculous reason, that made it sexier for him
than actually being in there with her, as he had been
with most of those other women.

With considerable effort, he shut out the sound of
running water and picked up the phone. He had
never called in sick before, so his claim of being bit-
ten by a violent flu bug was believed without question. He then turned on the television to drown out
the sound that was making his skin itch. Unfortunately, when it stopped he had to deal with the realization that she was rubbing *his* towel all over her
naked body.

He opened the one window in the apartment, letting in the cool morning air and the sounds of a city
waking up.

Beverly stared wide-eyed at her reflection. It was
incredible! The woman's brassiere was padded in

such a way that it actually made it look like she had
cleavage. And the cut of the panties was so low, they
made her waist look so much smaller than her hips.
She decided she would have to buy some underwear
like this to take back and show Hope. Maybe she
should buy a set for her trousseau for when she mar-
ries the doctor. She laughed at how she no longer
questioned any of Lavonda's predictions.

As her fingers examined the cups of the bra in
amazement, she gave some thought to the hard
lump she felt beneath her skin. She no longer believed it was her imagination. It had gotten larger
than it had been when she had first noticed it. As
much as she hated the idea of asking her doctor
about it, she supposed she should. Perhaps after she
got back, she would make an appointment. With
that decision made, she returned her thoughts to
what she would be doing today and hurried to finish dressing.

The top Josh had borrowed confused her for a moment. It was like a short-sleeved, scooped-necked
jersey, yet it had a strange hem with snaps in the center of the front and the back. As soon as she figured
out what they were for, she could see how snug the
top was . . . and how much of her new cleavage was
exposed. She undid the snaps and pulled the jeans
on over the tails. Much better. After her behavior last
night, she wanted to be very careful not to do anything forward again. The pants fit well enough once
she rolled the legs up a few times.

As soon as she stepped out of the bathroom, she
shivered from the drop in temperature.

"Oh, sorry," Josh said and quickly shut the window. He noticed her wet hair and the brush in her

hand. "There's a blow dryer under the sink if you—"
He supposed he would have to demonstrate that for
her also. "Allow me to show you another advantage
to this time period." He took her hairbrush and
directed her back into the bathroom. "I happen to be
a little familiar with long hair."

She smiled, relieved to hear that the annoyance
was gone from his voice again. She was also anxious
to see what advantage he was referring to.

He spritzed something into her hair then used his
fingers to spread it into the roots and work it
through the ends. "This keeps the hair from tangling
and frizzing up."

She didn't care what it was for; she just liked the
way he was massaging her scalp. He was telling her
something about how often he considered cutting his
hair to save himself time and trouble, but her mind
was distracted by the gentle way he ran the brush
through her hair, carefully separating any knots with
his fingers. She watched the movements of his hands,
and how the muscles in his arms flexed with each
stroke; so strong, yet graceful.

She was disappointed when he set down the brush
and picked up the blow dryer, until she felt the warm
air touch her scalp and his fingers threaded their way
into her hair.

One section at a time, his fingers eased in at the
base, then very, very slowly slipped through to the
end accompanied by a wave of heat. She watched
the hypnotic action in the mirror until he turned her
toward him, presumably to do her other side. But the
moment she met his gaze she was enveloped by a
different kind of heat wave.

She watched his Adam's apple move as he swallowed hard, and she licked her lips, partly because they were suddenly parched and partly because she knew he was going to kiss her again. It seemed to take an eternity for him to set down the dryer and bring his free hand up to touch her cheek, but in that time she saw something in his eyes that could only be described as reverence. She wanted to ask why he was looking at her as though she were the Madonna, but the question fled as his lips brushed over hers.

The extreme tenderness of it caused her to inhale deeply and she felt his breath flow into her. He kissed her forehead, and when her eyelids drifted shut, he caressed each of those. As his mouth touched her nose, then her cheeks, she became frustrated with his gentle teasing and reached up to still his head. He responded to her wordless hint with a low groan.

It was her only warning.

In a heartbeat, he pulled her hard against him and his mouth descended on hers with raw hunger. The shock of his tongue forcing its way between her teeth cleared the sensual haze around Beverly's brain. She pushed against his shoulders and squirmed until he freed her mouth. "Stop," she moaned. "I . . . I can't do this."

He blinked at her in confusion, then released his grip and took a step backward.

"I'm sorry if I led you on, but I'm not that kind of girl."

His eyes narrowed as her words sank in. "No. I'm the one who's sorry. I should have known you wouldn't want somebody like me." He turned and walked out of the apartment before she could stop him.

"Josh!" she called, rushing to the door. She was prepared to run after him if necessary, but she found him leaning against the wall right outside with his arms and ankles crossed.

With a huff of frustration, she said, "When I was a teenager, I remember a boy who used that line to get a girl to feel sorry for him so she would go all the way. But I got the distinct feeling that you really believed what you said just then. Am I right?"

He pushed himself away from the wall and shoved his thumbs into the pockets of his jeans. "If you still want to go sightseeing, get your purse, and we'll go."

"Fine. Right after we have a little talk." She crooked her finger at him to beckon him back inside. He didn't like the gesture or the order, but he obeyed.

The instant the door was closed, she demanded, "Explain why you said what you did."

"You know what I can't stand about women? They all think they have a right to know everything that's in a man's head, even when it's none of their damn business."

"I am not angry with you, Josh. Please don't be angry with me. All right. I'll go first. I am . . . an experienced woman." She stared at the floor and forced herself to say what had to be said, no matter how embarrassing it was. "I know that men cannot, um, help the way they, um, act, once a woman . . ." She waved her hand, searching for the right phrase. "When a woman flaunts herself at him. I can't explain why I keep forgetting myself around you, but I assure you that you're completely wrong about what you said. In fact"—she turned her back on him and mumbled the rest of her confession—"the problem seems to be that I *am* attracted to you."

Chapter 7

She felt his hand on her shoulder and stepped out of his reach. Facing him again, she saw that he was no longer angry, but she wanted to make sure that he didn't misunderstand. "Don't you see? I *can't* be attracted to you. There is no hope for a relationship between us. And although I know the younger generation doesn't think that matters, it still does to me."

Between her old-fashioned belief about males having no control and that last sentence, Josh couldn't hold back a grin. "The *younger* generation? Oh, yeah. That would be the kids that set the stage for the sixties. Free love and acid rock. Have you ever heard the expression, 'You ain't seen nothin' yet'?"

"I am trying to be serious, but if you can't—"

"I'm sorry. You'll understand better why I laughed in about ten years . . . your time. Things, *morals*, have changed a lot since the fifties. I'll try to remember that for the rest of the time you're around. But if I forget again, just kick me."

She smiled softly. "And if I forget that I'm a lady again, I'll kick myself." Holding out her hand, she asked, "Friends?" He enveloped her small fingers in his, and she pretended that the contact didn't make her stomach flutter.

"Friends. So, what would you like to see first?"

Beverly brightened instantly. "The Empire State Building. No, the Statue of Liberty. Oh, wait, I really want to see all the stories on Fifth Avenue. Could we take a subway?"

Laughing at her exuberance, Josh handed her purse to her and ushered her out of the apartment as she continued.

"And Central Park. And Broadway. I don't suppose we could see a play. Ooh, I almost forgot about Chinatown and Greenwich Village. Do beatniks still live there?"

Josh shook his head in amazement. He didn't know how she did it, but she had him feeling terrific again. He wondered if this was what happiness felt like. Never having been "happy" before, he couldn't be sure, but he decided to appreciate it while it lasted . . . whatever it was. One thing he was sure of, the feeling was the strongest when Beverly's eyes lit up with excitement. Funny how no other women had ever affected him that way. At any rate, it seemed worth a little extra effort to keep her smiling as much as possible.

To eliminate the problem of finding parking for his Harley, they took the train into Manhattan and relied on the subway and bus systems to go from there. Because Josh had lived around the city all his life, he had never viewed it as a tourist, and because Beverly found everything to be so awesome, he enjoyed his role as guide immensely.

As entranced as Beverly was by the city, she never forgot about her mission. She kept a constant lookout for speeding cars when they crossed a street and for objects plummeting from high-rise buildings when they were on the sidewalks. While waiting for the subway, she held tightly to his arm to prevent his accidentally falling off the platform. Despite her size compared to his, she felt physically and mentally prepared to save him, whatever the threat turned out to be, but nothing even slightly scary ever occurred.

Nor had they begun to scratch the surface of her list of "must-sees." The wait to get to the top of the Empire State Building plus the Statue of Liberty/Ellis Island tour took up most of the time. Josh promised to take one more day off to see how much more ground they could cover if they set their minds to it and got started earlier.

Since the only clothing Beverly had acquired that day was a souvenir T-shirt Josh had bought her, he took her to the local mall when they got back to New Rochelle. There, she discovered how little could be purchased with her forty dollars. After several minutes of useless arguing, she allowed Josh to buy her a pair of jeans, another T-shirt, and some socks, while she spent her money on underwear and some tailored pajamas . . . while he waited elsewhere, of course.

Having used up most of his own cash during the day, Josh took the opportunity to teach her about "plastic." He owned one bank credit card for emergency purposes only, but he figured this qualified. Though she still didn't feel comfortable with his paying for everything, whether it was by cash or credit, she really didn't have any other choice.

The huge indoor mall was a discovery in itself, with the most interesting place being a store devoted to collectibles. Comic books, baseball cards, autographed photos of celebrities, toys, and gadgets bore price tags that made no sense to Beverly.

"Good heavens," she exclaimed, pointing to an object in a locked case. "That's the Elvis album Hope gave me for my birthday two weeks ago. Who in their right mind would pay three hundred dollars for it?"

Josh hushed her and whispered, "That attitude's not going to gain you any friends in here. Have you seen enough? I'm starving."

"Oh, sure. But I think we emptied your refrigerator last night."

"That's okay. I figured we could eat at the restaurant here in the mall."

She frowned. "My debt to you just keeps adding up, doesn't it?"

"It will all balance out when you save my life," he said with a wink.

On the way to the restaurant, most of the stores were already closed for the night, but Bev still enjoyed looking at the displays in the windows.

"That's what I want to do," she blurted out in midthought.

Josh glanced around curiously, but no one was doing anything particularly interesting.

"I'd like to be a window dresser. I think I'd be very good at it." She stopped in front of a toy store. "See how they just stacked all those games in a pile and surrounded it with a mixture of sports equipment and dolls? It would be much more eye-catching if it was less cluttered and more balanced. A theme grouping rather than a hodgepodge would help also."

"You sound like you know what you're talking about. So, why don't you do that?"

"I really don't know. It was something I had planned with my husband, and when he died, I guess I just lost interest."

Josh fought the temptation to tread into *personal* territory until they were seated in the restaurant and had ordered, but the urge was too strong. "You don't seem old enough to be a widow," he said, for the lack of a more sensitive opener to the subject.

Bev sighed. "I didn't think so either. But the North Koreans didn't agree."

"Koreans? Oh, the war. Believe it or not the United States got into a messier one than that in Vietnam in the sixties." He had successfully gotten himself out of personal waters, however he couldn't seem to let the original subject drop without knowing more. "What year was your husband . . . in Korea?"

"In 1951. He went to boot camp after our honeymoon, then I saw him once more before he shipped out."

He felt an unfamiliar tugging in his chest, and he knew it wasn't indigestion. "Geez. That must have been awful for you."

She shrugged. "Life goes on . . . whether we want it to or not."

Again he tried to hold back the next question, but it slipped out anyway. "Did you remarry afterward?"

She shook her head. "I guess I lost interest in that when he died, too."

He didn't need to hear more. That one sentence had filled in all the blanks for him. When she had said she was "experienced," it had been a gross exaggeration. He knew without being told that she had remained a virgin until her wedding night, or at least her husband was the only man she had had sex with. Then after a few nights of marital bliss, she had remained celibate for the next seven years.

No wonder she seemed so innocent! She was. While he, on the other hand, was about as far from innocent as a man could be. She didn't even belong in the same decade with him let alone the same bed.

What the hell were they doing together?

It was time for the television news when they got home, but what was going on in the world took a back seat to what was going to happen within the apartment.

"I'll sleep on the floor" was Bev's first statement after they walked in.

Josh rubbed his chin. The chivalrous thing to do was insist that she take the bed, but if he spent the night on the floor, he wouldn't be able to walk tomorrow. "I've got a better idea," he said and pulled the mattress onto the floor at the foot of the box springs. "This way, neither one of us has to be a martyr. Your choice."

Relieved that he didn't even make an attempt to convince her to share the bed, she smiled and opted for the mattress. A short while later, comfortably, yet discreetly clothed in her mannish pajamas, she settled into her makeshift bed, and Josh turned out the light.

"I had a wonderful time today," she said into the darkness. "Thank you."

"I'm glad. I enjoyed it, too."

"She really was wrong, you know."

"She, who?"

"The girl who broke your heart. The one who made you think you weren't good enough for her." She heard him sigh as if she couldn't be more wrong, but she instinctively knew she had guessed right. "*She* was the one who wasn't good enough for you. You're a very good man, Josh Colby, and you deserve a very good woman. You probably just haven't met her yet."

"You're crazy. Go to sleep, or I won't take you to see Fifth Avenue tomorrow."

She smiled, knowing he wasn't nearly as annoyed with her comments as he sounded. Satisfied that he had gotten over her refusal to get intimate, she rolled over onto her stomach and closed her eyes. Talking to him about Billy had helped emphasize the fact that she must be extra careful not to fall in love with Josh. Losing one love in a lifetime was more than enough.

Josh stared at the spot of light on the ceiling caused by a crack in the window blind. He was glad she didn't push him to confide in her. After he had asked so many personal questions of her, he feared that she would feel he owed her the same courtesy. He was also afraid that he might end up telling her everything. Then she would be disgusted with him or feel sorry for him, and he couldn't stomach either one.

Sure, Elise and a few other females over the years had let him know he was some sort of lower life form—something to be looked at, examined, and maybe even played with, but not something to bring home to the family. However, they were only part of what gave him such a high opinion of himself. Whether it was because of his half-breed origins, his father, his troubles with the law, or his jobs, there had been more than enough people in his life who had been anxious to let him know exactly where he belonged.

He might have laughed at Beverly's suggestion that he just hadn't met the right woman yet, if it hadn't been the least funny thing he had ever heard. As usual, life seemed to have set him up for another fall on his face. It was beginning to look like the right woman had been dropped directly into his lap, only he couldn't keep her. At any moment she would pop back to where she came from and he would be exactly where he was before she appeared. Alone.

Part of him wanted to spend every minute of the time they had left as they had today—together, having fun, laughing, talking about nothing important. He didn't even want to go to sleep for fear he might be wasting the few hours they had left.

The other part of him wanted to make her disappear right now, before he got used to that happy feeling she gave him and began thinking he needed it . . . or her . . . to survive.

It seemed as though his alarm went off only minutes after he had finally fallen asleep. He should have been exhausted, considering how much of the night he had spent arguing with himself and trying to get comfortable on the too-firm box springs. Instead he arose, anxious to get started on another day as her tour guide.

He knew in that instant that he was in serious trouble.

As Josh had predicted, by starting earlier they managed to cover more ground, including every block of Fifth Avenue and the theater district. The only discovery that was somewhat disappointing to Beverly was that Gimbel's had gone out of business years ago. Having heard of the competition between Gimbel's and Macy's for the best window displays, comparing the two had been high on her list that day.

Despite how much she saw, however, there was still one large piece of property, namely Central Park, that she had yet to explore.

"You'll have to see it to understand why we can't fit it in today," Josh told her late in the afternoon. "But I have a surprise for dinner that I think you'll enjoy. It's a place called Planet Hollywood."

She had given up protesting since all it did was delay the inevitable concession on her part. She liked the restaurant a lot, though she was unfamiliar with many of the movie stars whose things were displayed throughout. Again, she was made aware of how valuable certain items from her time were now.

She decided, if she could go back and forth once more, she would have to bring Josh a special gift. She already knew he wasn't much of a baseball fan and she didn't notice any records or comic books in his apartment. What could she bring him that would have enough value to repay him for all the money he had spent on her?

As they were leaving, they passed a wall of autographed photos. "Do you have a favorite movie star?"

His gaze scanned the portraits. "I don't know. I always kind of liked James Dean." They both laughed, remembering what she had said about him being James Dean when she had first seen him.

She now knew what she would bring him.

It was late by the time they got home again, and Josh had made it clear that he had to go to work early the next morning, so they went right to bed. Beverly guessed that he had planned it that way, and was glad he had. She wasn't prone to lying to herself, and the truth was she didn't trust herself to be alone with him.

There was something about him that made her want to forget that she had always been a "good girl." During the day, while they were out in public, it was easier to fight that urge, though even then, there had been *incidents*. Touching each other for the slightest reason had become accepted on both their parts. In fact, she had to admit she had started to look for a reason when one didn't turn up after a few minutes.

Why was this happening? She didn't remember it being like this with Billy. From the day they met in eighth grade through their marriage, they had always been comfortable together. They had gone out on half a dozen dates before their first kiss, and it was probably a year after that before tongues got involved. Waiting until their wedding night to have sex was by mutual agreement, even though that date was postponed until Billy graduated from college.

She had loved Billy with all her heart, yet she knew his kisses never turned her knees to jello, the way Josh's did. She had never wanted to do more than what was proper based on where they were in their relationship. With Billy, she had never forgotten that she was a lady. With Josh, she had to remind herself of that every hour.

Thank God he wasn't the kind of man to take advantage of a woman just because she was available, alone with him in his bedroom, and had admitted that she was attracted to him.

She heard Josh punch his pillow for the third time since he had shut off the light and knew he was having as hard a time falling asleep as she was.

"I'm sorry, Josh."

"For what?"

"For still being here, for . . . intruding on your privacy."

"Don't worry about it. It's only temporary, right?"

"Well, I thought so. But it's been three days, and although I've had a wonderful time, nothing remotely dangerous has happened to you, or around you. Maybe it's like I said the first night, and my being here prevented you from doing something that would have been disastrous. What if the danger is passed, but my return trip has somehow been delayed? What if I can't go back at all?"

Josh's heart picked up its pace. Was it possible? Could she be here to stay? Did he want that or not? Since he wasn't sure of the answer, he resorted to sarcasm. "Well then, I'd say you'd better start looking for a job so you can get your own apartment. I don't intend to navigate over that mattress every morning for the rest of my life."

He was right, she thought. She had imposed on him too long already. She refused to believe she wouldn't go back to her own time eventually. That possibility didn't bear thinking about yet. Until she returned, however, she needed to find a way to support herself.

He had been very firm about her not going to work with him tomorrow. As an alternative, he agreed to take her with him to and from Manhattan and meet her for lunch. While he worked, he suggested she visit Central Park and the museum.

"Josh?"

"What now?"

He was using his annoyed voice again, probably to make her think she was keeping him awake, but she knew better. "I don't think I'll go in with you tomorrow, if you don't mind. I'd like to go to the mall again, if there's a bus I could take from here."

"What about Central Park?"

"It's not going anywhere. And apparently, neither am I at the moment."

The next morning, he forced some cash on her, gave her his spare apartment keys, and showed her where to catch the bus.

"You're sure you'll be okay?" he asked, frowning with worry.

She smiled, pleased that he wasn't pretending to be indifferent. "I'm a grown woman. I know how to ask for directions if I get lost."

He took a deep breath and walked away, but came back an instant later. Without warning, he dipped his head and quickly kissed her. "Be careful."

She touched her lips as she watched him walk away. She wished he wouldn't do things like that. Now she would be thinking about his mouth all day instead of what she had to do.

The first problem she encountered was her lack of clothing appropriate for a job interview. She only hoped Josh had been honest when he said women wear jeans everywhere today, even to work.

There were two sit-down restaurants in the mall. The first wasn't looking for help. The second asked her to fill out an application. Twisting the truth as little as possible, she managed to complete the form, stating that she had just moved from Mercerville,

New Jersey, and giving Josh's address and phone number for current residence. She gave Pete's Place as her last employer, figuring they wouldn't bother to make a long distance call to verify it. The only important facts she lied about were dates.

Since the assistant manager at the second restaurant didn't sound very encouraging, she decided to stop in every store and inquire about clerk positions. Several took her name and number, and a few had her fill out applications, but no one asked her to start immediately.

She had the least expensive lunch she could buy in the food court, then made her way around the different booths to see if any of them were hiring. She met a lot of friendly people, but no one needed help. From there, she proceeded to cover the last wing of the mall.

When she got to the toy store she had seen with Josh the other night, the elderly manager was very sympathetic, but told her business was too slow to hire any additional employees. As she walked out, the cluttered display window caught her eye again, and she went back inside.

"Excuse me," she said to the white-haired man. "I couldn't help but notice your window. I think you might attract more customers if you used that space a little differently."

Mr. Fisk's mouth turned down. "My wife, God rest her soul, she had an eye for that sort of thing. I try, but, you see for yourself how it turns out."

Beverly could empathize with the sense of loss. "My husband and I had plans to open a store. He knew management and I was going to take care of the decorating. He passed away also." They were both quiet for a moment, then she smiled to change the mood. "Would you like some suggestions?"

"If the advice if free, I'll listen."

She gave him a summary of what she thought was wrong, then asked him about which toys were most popular. He gave her a brief tour of the store, during which she had dozens more suggestions regarding the design and layout of his merchandise.

After another promise that she was not expecting payment for her services, he agreed to let her try her hand at his window and the entranceway displays.

She was having such a good time that she was stunned when Mr. Fisk told her he would be closing in a half hour. She had been working nonstop for five hours.

"I had no idea it was so late! Do you know when the last bus comes by?"

"A bus? You don't want to take a bus at this time of night." He went to the register and took out a twenty-dollar bill. "Take a cab, little one. There are always a few waiting by the main entrance. It's safer."

"But I agreed to do this for free," she protested, though she didn't relish the idea of walking from the bus stop to Josh's apartment in the dark.

"Consider it a loan. You come back tomorrow and finish what you started, and we'll be even."

She took the money and shook his head. "Deal. I'll see you tomorrow morning when you open your doors."

Her mind was still rearranging Mr. Fisk's store as she got into the cab. She couldn't wait to tell Josh about her day.

The realization of her thoughtlessness hit her like a

rock. Good heavens! She should have called Josh hours ago to let him know where she was. What must he think happened to her? "Please hurry," she urged the cab driver. "I forgot something very important."

Five minutes later, she was racing up the rickety stairs to Josh's apartment. "I'm so sorry," she gushed as she unlocked the door. The apartment was dark, except for the beam of light coming through the blind. A sharp intake of breath drew her attention to the bed. "Josh?" She moved to the bathroom and switched on the light.

"Shut that off!"

She did so immediately. "You're very angry with me, aren't you?" He gave no answer. "If I come over there to explain, will you promise not to hit me?"

"I've never hit a woman in my life."

His voice sounded very nasal, like he had a bad cold. He even sniffed at the end of his statement. "I didn't think so, but a lot of men do when they get angry enough." She made her way over to him, avoiding the mattress on the floor, and sat down on the edge of the bed. "I deserve any insult you want to throw at me. I should have called hours ago, I know that. But I got caught up in a project and had no idea what time it was. Josh, please, just yell at me and get it over with."

He inhaled deeply, then remained quiet.

"I don't know what else to say," she said in a hushed voice. "Except that I am truly sorry if I made you worry."

"I thought you had gone back."

Only then did she realize that he wasn't just worried that she had gotten lost or hurt; he thought she had vanished again. And it had really upset him. She had been so caught up in trying not to fall in love with him, she hadn't considered whether he might be falling in love with her.

The walls around her heart collapsed and her eyes got teary. What could she say to make him feel better? That she would never leave him was a promise she couldn't make. Not knowing what else to do, she moved closer and laid her head on his chest. She felt him take another deep breath, then as he let it out he wrapped his arms around her and held her tightly to him.

There were no words that would make either of them feel better, but holding one another kept it from hurting quite so badly.

When the alarm went off in the morning, she was still in his snug embrace, and she wondered if he had slept at all. She certainly hadn't.

He only said one thing before leaving. "Do you want to come with me?"

"Thank you, no. I'm going to the mall again. I'll be here when you get home, and I'll tell you all about it then. Okay?" she added hopefully.

He nodded and left.

She assured herself that he would understand when she explained everything later. In the meantime, she had a job to finish. Of course, it wasn't a *paying* job, unless one counted the cab fare, but she had a good feeling about it anyway.

Mr. Fisk was standing in front of his store talking to another man when she arrived. "Aah, here's my girl wonder now. Beverly Newcastle, meet Ed Garwood, the leasing manager here at the mall. He was complimenting me on my new window display."

"Fisk told me how you twisted his arm to let you play with his toys. I like what I see. If you've got some cards, I'll be glad to pass them along to some of the other tenants."

"Oh, I'm afraid I don't—"

"She doesn't have time right now," Mr. Fisk interrupted. "She's got a lot of work to do this morning. I'll send her to see you when she's done."

After Mr. Garwood left, Mr. Fisk told her why he had cut her off. "You have talent, Beverly. Just like my wife did. There's no need to waste your time working as a salesperson for a few dollars an hour, when you could have your own business. There's a machine down by the food court that can make up cards for you instantly. They won't be anything special, but you can upgrade later. For now, make twenty or so to give to Garwood. And one for me to tape in my window there for everyone to see. Put your name, phone number, and a fancy-schmancy title in it. And something like 'Let me dress your store for success.' So why are you just standing there staring at me like I'm a crazy old man?"

"I don't think that at all, Mr. Fisk. In fact, I think you're pretty incredible. This would be wonderful if I could actually make money at it. I've only got one problem. I have no idea what I would charge if someone asked me."

"Good question. You get to work for me, and I'll get to work for you . . . on the phone. Some of the stores here used an outside company to help set them up. By the time you're done, I'll know what your competition charges and what their names are. And if the changes you've made bring me more customers, I'll be a paying client for you next month . . . with a discount of course."

Bev laughed. "For you, half price."

By the time she left Fisk's store that afternoon, she was in business for herself. Knowing that it was only a temporary situation didn't matter. What was important was that she might have found a way to support herself while she was here.

It got more exciting when she received a call, minutes after entering the apartment, from one of the mall store managers who wanted her to give them an estimate the next morning. A call from Mr. Fisk followed that one. He had just spoken to a friend who owned a gourmet food store in a strip center in White Plains, and he might be interested in her services as well. She began to wonder if the kindly old gentleman was really a guardian angel in disguise.

Josh barely made it in the door before she started telling him all her news. To her disappointment, he didn't seem the least bit impressed or pleased for her. "Are you still angry with me?"

He had brought home a pizza and had started on a slice while she spoke. "I'm not angry. I'm just tired, and I forgot what day it is. I've got to go to The Bullpen tonight. I can't cancel out at the last minute or I really will be on Amanda's shit list. Have some pizza. I didn't know what you liked so I got half pizza and half with everything."

"Plain is good for me," she said, taking a piece and sitting down across from him. He may have said he wasn't angry, but he wasn't "just tired" either. She wished he would tell her what he was thinking, but by now she knew talking about himself was one thing he avoided whenever possible. Their first morning together he had made it very clear what he thought about women who stick their noses in where they don't belong.

Since he hadn't shown any interest in the events of her day and made no attempt to open any other discussion, she remained quiet as well.

As soon as he was done with his half of the pizza, he got ready to leave. The only other words he uttered were on his way out the door, and they made her more uncomfortable than she was already.

"Don't wait up. I don't know when I'll get back."

Chapter 8

By the time Josh rumbled into The Bullpen parking lot, he had it all figured out. Beverly's forgetting to call last night was the best thing she could have done. It showed him just how stupid he had gotten.

The fact that she came back meant nothing. Tonight, or tomorrow, or the next night, she would go away and *not* come back. Her leaving was inevitable; only the time was unknown. After last night, he knew he had to get her out of his system now, while it only hurt a little. There could be no more laugh-filled days, or nights of holding her close. That kind of stuff would only make it worse when she finally left for good.

If he planned it right, he could avoid her completely most of the time. From what she said this evening, she might even be self-supporting in a short while . . . if she stuck around much longer.

What he needed tonight was a strong reminder of who Josh Colby was and where he belonged. And he knew just the person to jog his memory.

He parked the Harley beside the front door and strode directly to Amanda's office. The door was closed, but he walked in anyway.

Amanda was "inspecting" a masked man's cowboy getup and was about to snap at whoever had dared to intrude, when she saw that it was Josh. "Why is it that you're the only one of my employees who can't seem to remember that if my door is closed, you are to knock before entering?" Her voice was stern, but her eyes raked over him with lewd intent. As she expected, he didn't bother to apologize. "Josh, do you know Ben? We just promoted him from waiter to dancer."

"The name's Ken, ma'am," the Lone Ranger said, trying to keep his smile in place despite the tension in the room.

"You're excused, Ken," Josh said, and the younger man grabbed his cowboy hat and rope and took off.

"You are such a bastard," Amanda hissed and took a deep breath that made her torpedo tits jut out even more than they already did.

Josh reached out with his right hand, stuck his fingers in the low bodice of her dress and pulled her toward him. "I heard I'm on your shit list." His left hand cupped her bottom and squeezed while his right palm moved over her rapidly contracting nipple. "I suppose you're expecting some kind of apology or at least an explanation."

She tried to be coy, but she knew he could feel the way her heart was racing. She licked her lips. "That would be nice."

"Yeah, it would." He dipped his head to bite her earlobe and murmured the rest into her ear. "But we both know *nice* isn't what gets you hot."

She raised her one knee to his hip and pressed herself against the tight leather clinging to his thigh. "Do it now, Josh. You've made me wait too long already." Her hand sought out the snap on his waistband, but before she got it open, his fingers encircled her wrist and raised her hand to his mouth. Staring into her eyes, he licked her palm, then released her.

"As much as I'd like to oblige, *ma'am*, I'm on duty at the front door of this establishment starting"—he glanced at the clock—"now."

"Bastard," she whispered at his back as he walked out of her office, but as she turned toward the mirror, she was smiling. Whoever the "cousin" was, she must not have been very satisfying.

Though it was strictly against policy, Josh got a bottle of beer from the bar and downed half of it before he got outside. What the hell was wrong with him?

Amanda looked sexy as ever tonight. She would have been ecstatic to have him take her right there on her desk, no preliminaries, no sweet talk or gentle kisses, no resistance. He could have been in and out in sixty seconds flat and she would have thanked him for stopping by. He had done it before and felt pretty damned good afterward.

So what happened? When he looked at her tonight, instead of doing what came naturally, he was thinking that her lipstick and nails were much too red, and her hair was a clownish shade of purple, and her body was ... well, there was just too much of everything. Rather than being turned on, he couldn't wait to get out of her office, away from the smell of heavy perfume and cat-in-heat. He couldn't have *done* her if his life had depended on it.

His mind got off Amanda as the patrons began arriving for the early show. He greeted the women entering by twos and in small groups—young, middle-aged, an occasional senior citizen; tall, short, thin, overweight, light, and dark. Not one of them made him want to take a second look.

Maybe he was just tired, like he had told Beverly. God knew he hadn't had more than a few hours' sleep since she popped into his life five days ago. The moment he thought her name, he felt a stirring in his stomach that threatened to move to lower regions if he didn't stop it immediately. Obviously, he wasn't *that* tired.

He wasn't one of those *modern* men who thought it was necessary to "get in touch with their feelings." He always figured he was much more comfortable not knowing he had a feminine side. But if he *was* one of those men, he would probably tell himself that Beverly turned him on because she represented all the good, innocent things he had always wished for, but never had. He couldn't have her, so he wanted her more.

There. That was it. No big deal. And now that he had it straight in his head, he could forget about Beverly and plan on enjoying Amanda later. Once the show was under way, he got another beer, knowing full well that one of Amanda's boys might decide to tattle on the big bad wolf at the door. In fact, he hoped one of them did. Sex with Amanda was always best when he refused to let her be the boss.

The fourth beer got her attention.

"What do you think you're doing?" she demanded with her fists planted on her hips. "You know I can't control those boys in there if they know I let you break the rules. The no drinking rule applies to everyone, no exceptions."

Josh hadn't realized how drunk he was getting until he tried to focus on her face and saw nothing but a colorful blur. "I was thirsty."

"You can have all the soda you want. What's wrong?"

He shook his head and snorted. "Just like a woman. A man has a couple beers, somethin' must be wrong. You know wha's wrong? Women. Tha's wha's wrong." He drew her close and palmed her bottom. "But not you, baby. You aren't like that, are you? You don't care if I have dirt under my fingernails, do you? Just so my dick gets hard on cue." He held her head still for a hard, wet kiss, then abruptly released her. "Don't worry, I've had my quota for tonight. I gotta drive home."

She slipped her hand beneath his jacket and kneaded the hard muscles of his chest. "You don't have to drive home after work. We'll pull out the sofa bed in my office and we can play till the sun comes up. Just like last time."

He rubbed his eyes. He was definitely tired, and the alcohol had his head spinning. "I don't know. I should go home. She'll—" He cut himself off when he felt Amanda's nails dig into his chest.

"She'll, what?" Amanda said tightly.

"What?" He was sober enough to realize his slip.

"You said *she'll*. Is your *cousin* still staying with you?"

"My cousin? Oh, yeah. Her."

"Now, Josh, you and I have been friends for quite a while. You can tell me the truth. She's not your cousin is she?"

Josh laughed. "To tell you the truth, Mandy, I don't

know what the hell she is. Hell, I don't even know *when* she is. All I do know is she's drivin' me nuts."

Amanda stroked his cheek. "That's okay, sweetie. After tonight, you won't care. I'll make sure of that." She turned to go back inside, but added a warning. "But no more beer until you get off, okay?"

Josh saluted her. "You got it, boss lady." As soon as the door closed behind her, he reached down behind the bike where he had stashed two more bottles. "Right after I finish these." He was going to keep drinking until Amanda looked good again ... or at least until he stopped seeing Beverly when he closed his eyes.

Amanda marched straight to her office and picked up the phone. She didn't care if Josh screwed a different woman every night, as long as it didn't take anything away from his performance with her. Oh, he was trying to act normal, but her sexual antennae were picking up a serious abnormality, and she was going to get to the bottom of it.

Whoever *she* was, she wasn't a cousin or any other relative. The important question was, was her answering the phone in Josh's apartment the other night a coincidence, or had he changed his attitude about live-in relationships? Josh's home phone rang four times before it was answered.

"Hello?"

It was the same voice. "Hi," Amanda said with forced friendliness. "This is Amanda James, at The Bullpen."

"Oh my God. Don't tell me he never got there. He left here hours ago!"

"No, no, don't get upset. He's here, safe and

sound. He's just been partying a little too much to-night, and he asked me to give you a call. I'm sorry, I forgot what he said your name is." She sensed the girl's uncertainty in her delayed response.

"Beverly."

"Oh, yes, Cousin Beverly. Well, anyway, he won't be home till sometime tomorrow. Actually, I wouldn't count on seeing him for the rest of the weekend. Don't worry, I'll take good care of him. I know just what he needs when he gets like this."

"Oh. Good. Thank you for calling."

Amanda knew she had her worried, but she wasn't satisfied with causing a little concern. She was aiming for big trouble. "No problem. I think it's so nice that Josh has family visiting. I was beginning to think we'd have to hire someone to sit on the groom's side of the church."

"Ch-church?"

"Well, the plans haven't been finalized, but when they are I'm sure he'll want you to be involved. If you're going to be living here now, maybe you could be one of the bridesmaids."

"Um, I, uh, I'm only visiting. I'll be leaving soon."

"Oh, that's too bad. Well, we should at least have lunch before you go. How's tomorrow?"

"Tomorrow? Oh, I'm sorry, I have to work."

"Work?" Amanda knew she had her now. "I thought you said you were just visiting."

"I am. It's . . . it's just temporary until . . . until I go back home."

"Well, sweetie, you let me know if it looks like you're going to stay awhile. If so, I definitely think we should meet."

Amanda was smiling again as she hung up the

phone. That was certainly easy enough. She must be a very stupid little twit. Amanda could almost visualize the girl packing her things with tears running down her youthful cheeks. Perhaps she was so upset by the news that Josh had a fiancée that she would be gone before he returned. She didn't worry about the lie backfiring. If anything, Josh would probably reward her once he came to his senses again.

Now to figure out how to keep Josh here long enough to back up her story ...

Beverly told herself there had to be a reasonable explanation for what she had just heard.

She distinctly remembered Josh referring to Amanda as his boss and "sort of" friend. He hadn't even bothered to return her call that first night, even though Beverly had offered to step out of the apartment to give him some privacy. He had laughed when she had told him Amanda sounded jealous.

Could it have been an act? Could he be a deceitful man like Hope's Stanley? Josh was certainly secretive about his personal life, but she had never guessed one of his secrets might involve a fiancée and wedding plans.

She had always considered herself a good judge of character and found it hard to believe that she could have been so wrong about Josh. But if he wasn't lying, that meant Amanda was, and she couldn't imagine why that woman would make up something so easy to prove false.

And what was that about his "partying" too much? He was supposed to be working, not playing. She had made it sound as though he was drunk, which was also confusing. The only time she had seen Josh have a drink was at Hank's, and she was fairly sure that was just one beer. Could he be an occasional heavy drinker like Frankie, and had kept it hidden from her this week, while he was trying to seduce her?

None of it made any sense, but she knew men were not always as honest and open with women as Billy had been with her. On the other hand, she trusted all the women she knew. The only conclusion she could reach was that if Josh didn't return all weekend, then Amanda was probably telling the truth, which meant one thing to Beverly. Mission or not, she couldn't wait any longer to find another place to live until she popped back to her own time.

She put her mind to that problem rather than dwell on how she felt about Josh spending the night in his fiancée's bed. She had absolutely no business having any feelings about that one way or the other.

Josh managed to remain upright, with the support of his bike, but it was fortunate that no one required his assistance. When the last customers drove away, he was determined to be right behind them, but Amanda came out in time to put a stop to that foolish idea.

"You're the one who's supposed to *stop* drunks from getting on the road."

"But I gotta go."

"I know, sweetie, but come have a cup of coffee first."

He stood up and the world spun around him. "Coffee. Good idea."

Amanda told her manager that she would take care of locking up, and had one of the boys bring

Josh's bike inside. Josh pulled himself together enough to walk into her office on his own.

"Sugar, no cream, right?" she asked as she poured him the promised cup of coffee. He grunted and dropped onto the sofa. His eyes were closed a second later, and she took advantage of his inattention to grind up two of her sleeping pills and melt them in the hot liquid. She knew from personal experience that, on top of a few beers, the pills would knock him out for about twelve hours without causing him any real harm. Then she added an ice cube to cool it off. "Now don't go to sleep. You want to get home to Beverly, remember?"

He opened one eye a fraction. "You know Beverly?"

She handed him the mug. "Drink up." He obeyed, emptying it in a few swallows. "Now this one." She handed him a glass of water and stood over him until he finished that as well. "Now let's get you a little more comfortable." When she tried to remove his jacket, he resisted, but she convinced him he would sober up faster if he was cool. That made enough sense for him to let her help him take off his boots and leather pants as well.

While he made a trip to her private bathroom, she opened the sofa bed, slipped off her dress, and posed seductively amidst the satin sheets.

The look on his face when he came out and saw her took a chunk out of her confidence, but she had to play it out. "You'll feel better if you just lay down for an hour, sweetie." She patted the pillow beside her. "Come on now. You can hardly stand up. If you try to drive home, you'll end up wrecking that beautiful bike of yours."

He took a step toward that soft pillow, then stopped. "I should call . . ."

She quickly rose and went to him. "I already called for you." Guiding him to the bed, she talked to him like a little boy. "I told Beverly you weren't feeling well, and we had a nice, long chat."

Amanda could see that he was confused by that, but he was unable to form a coherent question. Minutes later he was unconscious, and she removed the rest of his clothing. Things may not have gone the way she had hoped, but he didn't need to know that. When he awoke, she would convince him it was the best time they had ever had, then seduce him into doing it all over again. If she could keep him away from the little twit in his apartment long enough, he would surely forget she ever existed.

Beverly did her best to hide the dark circles under her eyes, but her supply of makeup was limited to what was in her purse. Though Josh had not come home, she still wasn't completely convinced that she had been all wrong about him. Before she left for her appointment at the mall, she wrote him a note to let him know where she would be, just in case he returned before she did. Knowing it was his habit to check his answering machine as soon as he walked in, she placed the note on top of the unit.

As she paid her bus fare, she couldn't help but think of how low her cash supply was. Between what Mr. Fisk had given her for cab fare and the money Josh had given her two mornings ago, she was down to seven dollars, and she had eaten the last of the pizza last night.

She had already decided that no matter what the

truth was about Josh she could not continue to share a room with him and depend on him for food. What she needed was a miracle, nothing major, mind you, just enough to tide her over.

Her prayer was partially answered when her morning appointment turned into an immediate job with payment to be made in cash upon completion, which she estimated would take two full days. It was a store devoted to kitchen- and cooking-related items, and she enjoyed the work even more than she had at the toy store.

When she took a break to get something to eat, she stopped by to see Mr. Fisk, and much to her pleasure, he insisted on treating her to lunch.

"Make sure you call my friend in White Plains," he reminded her after she told him about her successful morning.

"Yes, I planned to do that before I went back to work. Mr. Fisk, you have been so much help to me, I wish there was some way I could repay you."

He laughed. "You don't think working for free for two days was enough? You worry too much, little one. You're a good girl, believe me, I have a sixth sense about these things." He narrowed his eyes and studied her for a moment. "But my guess is you're having a little trouble right now. There's probably a man involved, hmmm?" He didn't wait for a verbal admission, her expression told him enough. "I give pretty good advice for an old man."

It was Beverly's turn to laugh. "You give *great* advice. But I'm afraid my situation is too complicated for advice. Unless you know of a place where I could get room and board for about a dollar a day."

"As talented as you are, it won't be long before you can afford a lot more than a dollar a day."

"Unfortunately, even you can't make that happen by tonight."

His expression grew worried. "That bad, eh? Sure you don't want to talk about it?"

She smiled. "If I change my mind, I'll come see you first."

When they left the food court, he suggested she use the phone in his store to call his friend. "Every quarter saved helps," he said with a wink.

She made an appointment to see the woman on Monday, assuming she would have the money from the kitchen store job by then and could afford the trip to White Plains.

Before she could leave to return to work, Mr. Fisk stopped her again. "I have an idea, but I want to make sure you understand I'm too old to have any ulterior motives, and I'm too frugal to give things away just to be nice. I believe in honest, fair trading, and I have a trade I'd like to offer you."

Beverly looked at him curiously. She had already decided that anything Mr. Fisk had to say was worth listening to.

"Since my dear wife passed on, the store is not the only thing that's suffered."

She patted his shoulder. "I know how you feel. After all these years, I still miss my husband."

"Yes," he said with a nod. "I miss her. But I also miss her cooking, and cleaning, and doing laundry. I know, call me a male chauvinist pig, but she spoiled me. I don't want another wife. I need a housekeeper. But affording one is another matter altogether. Unless you're one of those women who think all those chores are beneath them, I think we could make a good bargain here."

She wasn't certain she was following him and told him so.

"I have a spare bedroom and feeding such a skinny thing as you would hardly bankrupt me. If you'd like to help me with the chores, you could stay at my house, as long as we got along, or until your new business takes off. What do you think?"

She was so surprised by the offer she didn't know what to think. It sounded almost too perfect to be true. Before making any move, however, she owed it to Josh to speak to him first. "Could I let you know tomorrow?"

"Of course, little one. Oh, I almost forgot one more thing you should know about. I have two grandchildren who come to visit sometimes. They're beautiful little girls, but they can be a handful."

"I love children," Bev assured him and had to hold back the urge to accept his offer on the spot. Again it crossed her mind that Mr. Fisk seemed to have been appointed as her guardian angel.

Amanda spent a nerve-wracking afternoon fretting over whether Josh would ever wake up and worrying about how she would keep him there when he did. He was so still, she kept checking to make sure he was breathing. It had never occurred to her that the pills that she took on a regular basis would put him into a coma. After all, he was a lot bigger than she was.

By five o'clock, she started to panic. It was time to open for business again. "Josh," she said close to his ear, "you have to wake up." When all that got her was a groan, she became more aggressive. Shaking his shoulders, she spoke a bit louder, and he growled at her.

A knock at her office door nearly gave her a heart attack. "I'll be out in a few minutes," she called, then gave Josh's hair a hard yank.

"Ouch!" he exclaimed and swatted the air in front of him.

"Josh! You have to get up! You've been asleep all day."

He forced one eye open and found the source of the nagging voice.

"Does your head hurt?" Amanda asked with some concern. "Do you want ice? Aspirin? Coffee? I hate to rush you, but I have to get to work, and I need you at the front door. We're shorthanded tonight, and there's no one to cover for you."

Josh rubbed his eyes. There was a dull ache in his head and his mouth was desert-dry, but it was bearable. The real problem was that he felt like he was still asleep. "Time?" he croaked.

"It's after five," Amanda said, pulling him upright. "Come on. I'll help you into the shower, but I can't get in with you, as much as I'd like to." He let her guide him into her bathroom and leaned against the wall while she turned on the water.

"I must say, you were a very naughty boy last night, Josh Colby." She ran a wet, red claw over one of his nipples, then tweaked it. "I should make you shower in ice water. But no one, not even you, has ever satisfied me that well before, so I won't punish you for breaking my rules about drinking this time. Just don't do it again. Now hurry up. I need you out front in half an hour." She closed the door behind her, and Josh stepped under the lukewarm water.

Slowly, the drowsiness left his mind and his memory returned. Rather, *some* of his memory returned. He remembered having a few too many beers and being overly tired. He sort of remembered lying down on Amanda's sofa bed. But he had no recollection of taking his clothes off or doing anything that would put him in her sexual hall of fame. He only remembered *not* being able to service her.

That thought led to another. *Beverly.* He had told her not to wait up for him, but he knew she might have anyway. Damn! She probably figured he had had that fatal accident she was supposed to save him from and was wallowing in guilt. Remembering how upset he had been when she hadn't checked in with him made him feel awful. He wanted her out of his life, yet he didn't want to worry her.

There was a fresh pot of coffee, a sandwich, and a bottle of aspirins waiting for him on Amanda's desk, and his clothes were neatly laid out on the closed-up sofa bed. As soon as he was dressed, he called his apartment.

When the machine picked up, he wondered if she was out or just ignoring the phone. "Beverly? If you're there, pick up. Okay, I guess you're not. It's about five-thirty and I wanted to let you know I'm still alive and well. No accidents. I just couldn't get home today. I . . . well, I'll explain later. I mean, tomorrow. I'm working again and Saturday's usually a late night. I just wanted to—" The machine cut him off before he could say he was sorry if she was worried about him. He would have to take care of that tomorrow as well.

By the time he headed out front he felt fairly good . . . physically. He supposed he really needed the sleep, but fourteen hours seemed unbelievable. It was just one of the things his mind wasn't satisfied with. Not remembering sex with Amanda was another.

The third was the most bothersome of all though. He had arrived there yesterday with every intention of using Amanda to get Beverly out of his head. Apparently, he had done what he had intended. So, why, instead of feeling cured, did he feel like he had done something really bad?

Beverly had hoped to get back to the apartment in time to have dinner with Josh, but as soon as she walked in, she knew her rushing had been futile. The note she had written that morning was exactly where she had left it, as was everything else in the room.

Josh hadn't come home.

She noticed the flashing red light on the machine and pushed the play button. Josh's voice sounded strange, and she didn't think it was the fault of the recording. It was the voice of a man with a guilty conscience.

Amanda had told the truth.

All day she had stopped herself from thinking about what that woman had told her. Every time the word *fiancée* crept into her mind, she ordered it away. She had no claim on Josh. She shouldn't even care if he lied to her, or why. He was just a person whose life she was supposed to save. She knew there was no possibility of the two of them having a future together, so it was completely unreasonable to be upset. It wasn't as though they had a relationship and he had cheated on her. If anything, *she* had almost been the other woman.

So why was there such a terrible pain in her chest and tears gathering in the corners of her eyes?

She couldn't allow herself to get emotional. A logical plan of action was needed, and it needed to begin immediately. She found the number for Mr. Fisk's store in her purse and called.

As soon as he answered, she wasted no more time giving him her decision. "If the offer is still open to move in with you, I'd like to take you up on it."

"Wonderful!" he exclaimed. "When can you move?"

"Would tonight be too soon?"

He laughed. "Not at all. Give me your address and I'll pick up you and your things on my way home after I close."

She gave him directions, thanked him profusely, then went about making her departure preparations. She threw her few belongings into a shopping bag and left the borrowed outfit on the bed for Josh to return to his neighbor. Next, though it was no easy task, she got the mattress back onto the box springs and remade the bed.

The even harder part, however, was writing a farewell note to Josh. Three times she started and three times she tore up the paper. Finally she managed to get all the necessary information written without sounding overly emotional.

When the buzzer sounded, letting her know that Mr. Fisk was downstairs, she took one last look around, locked the door, and slipped the key under the loose carpeting in the hallway. Telling herself she was doing the best thing for everyone, she walked away, prepared to begin a new chapter in her strange adventure.

Chapter 9

Dear Josh—

No, I have not popped back to 1958. I have just moved to a place where I will not be in the way. I'm sorry I intruded on your privacy as long as I did.

Thank you very much for taking me in when I had nowhere to stay, for feeding, clothing, and entertaining me. I am especially grateful for the time you spent showing me New York City. I will treasure the experience always. I hope that my presence in your life was not too disruptive. I don't suppose we'll ever know if I really saved you from something, but I want to believe that I did.

If I don't pop back, I should be able to repay you all the money you spent on me in the near future. I do need to ask one last favor, however. I gave your phone number to several prospective clients. If I get any calls, I'd appreciate it if you would pass the message on to Mr. Fisk at the mall toy store.

I wish you had told me the truth about being engaged to Amanda right from the start. She seemed very nice when we spoke last night. I wish you both good luck and I hope that my staying here hasn't caused any serious problems.

Thanks again,
Beverly

P.S. Your key is under the carpet outside your door.

Josh read the note twice before all of it sank in, and even then, he was dumbfounded by most of it. Engaged to Amanda? Obviously the two women had a conversation that he was unaware of, but what could Amanda have said that would have led Beverly to believe they were engaged?

How could she have found a place to stay? She had no money, no friends or relatives, barely knew her way around. Stud-Man's face flashed in his mind. No, that couldn't be. He had warned her about him.

But what if another, more subtle man came along and offered his help? She might have accepted just to give him back his privacy.

Isn't this exactly what he wanted—her out of his life?

Absolutely. He just hadn't expected it to be by her choice. Her note suggested that she felt she had to move out, that she was in his way. He knew he was partially to blame for that, except for the bit about Amanda. He thought he had been fairly honest with Beverly about that relationship.

However, if he was engaged and had kept it a secret from Beverly, that would be reason enough for someone like her to feel obliged to clear out immediately, especially after the kisses they had shared.

But it wasn't true.

It didn't matter, he told himself. She was gone, and that was best for both of them. What he needed now was another fourteen-hour nap. In spite of the multitude of questions in his head, he was asleep minutes after he lay down.

Unfortunately, when he awoke late Sunday afternoon, all the questions were still whirling around in his brain without answers. As much as he wanted to let it go, he couldn't. He picked up the phone and dialed The Bullpen, knowing Amanda did her bookkeeping on Sundays.

"Well, hi sweetie," she said brightly. "Changed your mind about that encore?"

Josh could hardly promise an encore when he had no recollection of the original performance. "I want to apologize for the other night. I don't know what got into me."

"I told you I forgave you."

"Did you also tell me you had a talk with Beverly?" She paused long enough for him to know she had. "It's okay. It's all over anyway."

"Yes, we spoke. What do you mean, it's over?"

"She's gone. I was just trying to figure out how she came to the conclusion that you and I were engaged."

"Don't you remember? You told me how she was driving you nuts and you wanted her out of your life. I just gave her a nudge in the right direction."

The fuzzy picture was rapidly clearing up. "So you lied to her?"

Amanda laughed. "It worked, didn't it? I told you I'd take care of your problem and I did. You can come over and thank me tonight if you've got your energy back."

Josh tried to keep the anger out of his voice long enough to clear up one more question. "And that was also a little fib about how good I was Friday night, wasn't it?"

She laughed again. "All in a good cause, sweetie. It was obvious that your ego needed a big boost, and I knew you'd make it up to me later."

"You're a real bitch, you know that?"

"Everyone knows that, sweetie, but no one appreciates it quite as much as a real bastard. That's why you and I are so good together."

Once upon a time, not long ago, he would have agreed with those words, and probably would have made a trip over to The Bullpen to confirm them. But today, they gave him a sick feeling in his stomach. "Go to hell, Amanda." He heard her confident laugh as he hung up the phone. She believed everything was status quo.

He knew everything had changed.

For the umpteenth time, Beverly assured Mr. Fisk that she was fine. His guest bedroom was as comfortable as her own room back in Mercerville. He had given her money to buy groceries and loaned her his car to drive to the store. She had cooked a good dinner and enjoyed sharing it with him. She had finished the job at the kitchen store and gotten paid for it. She had even bought herself a pretty new blouse to celebrate.

Other than being able to pop home, she could not have asked for a more ideal situation.

She wondered if the girls were bowling tonight. Would anyone besides Hope notice that the Beverly they were with was only a shadow of herself? She knew her family wouldn't know the difference. They barely noticed when the real her was around. And what about everyone at Pete's Place? Would her shadow be as friendly as she always was?

She realized those were silly questions since Lavonda had explained that the shadow was exactly the same except for taking the time-travel risk. She also remembered that Lavonda had said that her two selves could not continue on separate paths for very long. Then why was she still here?

"Don't feel you have to stay up and keep me company if you're tired," Mr. Fisk said. "I'm a bit of a night owl."

"I'm a little tired. It's been a busy weekend." She thanked him again for taking her in and went to her new room. If only she could tell him the truth about herself, he would probably be able to give her the perfect advice. But there was also the chance that he would think she was a lunatic and throw her out of his house.

Once she got into bed, she found she couldn't sleep, so she leafed through the brochures she had picked up at the collectibles store at the mall that afternoon. Of all the amazing things she had seen on her visit, the most unbelievable was the value of certain items from her time.

Ten-cent Superman comic books now demanded prices ranging from a thousand to over a hundred thousand dollars. An autographed picture of James Dean was available for the mere payment of five hundred. That one made her laugh. In her keepsake box at home, she had several signed pictures of Dean along with the letter that came in his fan club package. If she took very good care of that package and the Elvis album, she would have a nice inheritance to pass on to her children.

Children? The likelihood of her having children was getting smaller and smaller with each birthday, and she usually tried not to think about it.

Oh, Josh. Why couldn't you have existed in my time?
She tried to make that thought go away, too, but it

hung on until she gave it some consideration. If he had been in her time, things might have worked out between them. There was certainly plenty of mutual attraction. They had had a lot of fun together once he quit thinking she was crazy. She could have helped him get over whoever made him feel bad about himself. He could have helped her get over losing Billy. Of course, in her time period, he wouldn't be engaged.

She tried to imagine what Amanda must be like, but a woman who owned a nightclub with male strippers and half-naked waiters was so far out of her experience, she couldn't form a picture. Something Josh had said about Amanda that first night came back to her—something about her keeping a stable of boys. She had thought she understood what kind of a woman she was from that comment. Why would Josh say such a thing about the woman he was going to marry? Was his opinion of himself so low that was the type of wife he thought he deserved?

She sternly reminded herself that it was none of her business. Josh was free to go on with his life any way he chose and one day, hopefully soon, she would return to hers.

The only question left was the most important one. Why was she still here?

The next day she paid a visit to Mr. Fisk's friend in White Plains and introduced herself to the other tenants in that shopping center. She didn't close any deals, but there was considerable interest.

When Mr. Fisk got home, he was tickled to discover a cooked meal waiting for him. While he ate, she filled him in on her day, and he gave her a few suggestions about how to turn a customer's maybe into a yes.

Over dessert, he said, "You know, little one, only one thing would improve this meal—if you would tell me what terrible thing is making you look so sad."

Since that was what she wanted to do very much, she took the risk of letting him in on her secret. "It all started on my thirtieth birthday . . ."

Mr. Fisk listened attentively for over an hour without interrupting as she related her strange story. When she was up to date, his first comment was hardly what she would have expected.

"Mrs. Fisk and I celebrated our tenth anniversary in 1958. Our son would have been, let's see, four years old. It was a good year for business, too, I think."

"Mr. Fisk, do you understand what I've told you?"

"That you've traveled through time? Of course. I understood everything you said."

"And you believe me? Just like that?"

He shrugged. "Why not? You have no reason to lie to me. You must realize, for me, this is the future. I read H. G. Wells when I was a boy. People were supposed to be able to travel through time and live on the moon by now. Besides, everything about you says you're an old-fashioned girl, not like the girls today, with the tattoos and earrings in their noses, to say nothing of other unmentionable places."

She smiled at the face he made. "So, now that you know, what do you think?"

"I think you left out some important information about that young man, Josh—like how you feel about him."

Her cheeks grew warm, and she lowered her head. "It doesn't matter how I feel."

"Did he reawaken your heart?"

Her head bobbed up. "What?"

"Didn't the Gypsy say you would meet a man who would reawaken your heart?"

"Yes, but—"

"No buts. You assumed he was the one you were supposed to save, but nothing dangerous ever happened. I think you got your wires crossed. I think he was the special man you were supposed to meet, and I'm the man whose life you were supposed to save."

"You? But you're the one who has helped me. Just like Josh."

He waggled a finger at her. "That's where you're wrong. I was very lonely and depressed before you came along. Who's to say I wouldn't have gotten worse and worse until I finally just laid down and died? I was very close to selling the store, you know. You showed up one day, and suddenly I have things to think about again, someone to worry about, and now I even have someone to come home and have dinner with. Believe me, little one, you saved me."

He made it sound like she was the guardian angel instead of vice-versa. "I'm glad I helped. And I'll admit that Josh did reawaken my heart, but it would have been better if we hadn't met at all."

He frowned at her. "I don't believe that. Instead, I think that there might be some alternate possibilities that you haven't considered. Such as, what if you were supposed to save him from marrying this Amanda creature by showing him what a good old-fashioned girl is like? Or, what if he was supposed to remind you that you are still a desirable woman, so that you'd be prepared when the right man comes along in your own time?

"But here's the one that gets my vote. What if *he's* the right man for you, but in order for you to be together, you had to be transported into a different time period? Maybe this time is where you're supposed to stay now."

Bev blinked at him. "I can't believe I'm not going back. I didn't make arrangements to leave for good. I didn't say goodbye to anyone."

"You wouldn't be the first person who left a place without saying goodbye."

"I suppose you're right. I just hadn't let myself consider the possibility that I'm here to stay."

He arched an eyebrow at her. "And yet, you went looking for a job, started a business, found suitable living arrangements. Funny, that sounds like someone who was preparing to stick around awhile."

"I'm a very practical person." She sighed. "I guess you're right again. If I was going to pop back, it should have happened already. But that doesn't change anything as far as Josh is concerned."

"Maybe not. Then again, maybe you gave up too easily."

"Gave up? He's engaged to marry another woman. I'm not a home wrecker."

Mr. Fisk chuckled. "Seems to me that you were the one in his home, not her. That must mean something. Did he treat you with respect?"

"Oh, yes. He was more of a gentleman than any man I've ever met, and the circumstances were . . . let's say, he could have taken advantage of me easily if he'd had a mind to."

"But he didn't, which says a lot about him. And

yet, you say he purposely kept his engagement a secret from you. Doesn't that seem like contradictory behavior to you?"

"Yes, it does," Bev admitted. "But I've never pretended to understand how a man's mind works."

Mr. Fisk winked at her. "And none of us men understand women either, but that's never stopped any of us from trying to overcome our differences. So, what are you going to do about all of this?"

Beverly rose and began clearing the table. "I'm going to keep doing what I've been doing. Expect to pop back at any time, but find ways to get along while I'm still here. I think tomorrow would be a good day for me to see Central Park. It can be my day off since I worked all weekend."

"And your young man?"

"He's not *my* young man. Anyway, if he wants to talk to me, I told him he could reach me through the store, but I'm not expecting to hear from him. I'm sure he's extremely relieved to have me out of his hair. Which, by the way, is much too long."

By Tuesday afternoon, there wasn't a man on the construction site willing to go near Josh. His boss told him he was acting like a bear who had been awakened in the middle of hibernation. The secretary was afraid to be alone with him in the construction trailer. He had done more work in two days than he normally did in a week, yet it still wasn't enough to burn off his lousy mood.

Although the last thing he felt like doing was socializing, he stopped in at Hank's for a beer in the hopes that it would help him unwind before the long drive home. The only empty bar stool was next to Stud-Man, so he took it and ordered a draft.

"Word is you're havin' some trouble with the little woman," Stud-Man murmured so that no one else could hear.

Josh shot a narrow-eyed glare at him, but said nothing.

"Don't get me wrong," Stud-Man said, continuing to keep the conversation private. "I'm not tryin' to stick my nose in your business or give you any advice like some of the old guys like to do. I just want to know what the status is. I mean, if you're through with her, you know, I'd like to have a turn at bat. I mean, she ain't got no tits, but you know what they say about good things coming in little packages, especially nice, tight little—"

Josh's fist connected with Stud-Man's chin and knocked him off the stool. The riveter was so stunned he just sat there on the floor rubbing his jaw as Josh threw some bills on the bar and stepped over him.

Josh was halfway home before he noticed the ache in his hand. Stud-Man's face had the resilience of a brick wall. How the hell did he know about Beverly anyway? Had he seen her? Had he been with her? He nearly ran into the back of a truck before he got control of his rage.

Why did everyone assume that his bad mood had been caused by a woman? Couldn't he simply be disgusted with life in general? He sure didn't have anything to be particularly *happy* about.

The really rotten thing about Beverly was that he now knew what *happy* felt like. Before she interfered in his life, he didn't know and didn't care. Before her, he had thought Amanda was the perfect woman: half independent business person, half cat in heat. Now he couldn't stomach the idea of even working for her, let alone touching her.

His whole life had been turned upside down, and it was all Beverly's fault. And what had she done about it? Walked out on him, that's what. She hadn't even had the consideration to vanish in front of him the way she had before.

So what if she thought he was engaged to Amanda and had kept it a secret? She should have known—

He interrupted his own thought with a bit of logic. Beverly wouldn't know how someone like Amanda operated. Beverly wouldn't lie to save her life. Beverly was the type who would sleep in a box on the street rather than be the cause of a problem between him and his so-called fiancée.

An image of Beverly sleeping amidst the street people made his chest hurt. Surely she hadn't done something so drastic, just to give him his privacy.

Though he knew he was better off with her out of his life, he suddenly needed to assure himself that she was okay. Stud-Man's comments had made him realize how vulnerable she was without him. He didn't need to actually see her or talk to her, he just needed to know that she was safe. Rather than drive directly to his apartment, he took the road that headed toward the mall.

After rereading Beverly's note so many times, the name of the toy store manager was as familiar as his own.

"Mr. Fisk?" he asked the man at the cash register.

"Yes. Can I help you?"

Josh felt better already. "I hope so. A friend of mine gave me your name—"

"Beverly?" the white-haired man interrupted with a twinkle in his eye.

"Yes, she said—"

"Are you Josh?"

Josh hadn't expected to be identified. "Yes, I just wanted—"

"She's fine. Doing very well, in fact, considering her advanced age."

"Advanced? Are we talking about Beverly Newcastle, about so high, blond hair—"

"Big, innocent blue eyes, born in Mercerville, New Jersey, in 1928?"

Josh was shocked. "She told you?"

"She told me a lot of things."

"And you believe her? About the Gypsy's potion and traveling through time?"

A customer walked up at that moment, and Mr. Fisk took care of him before responding. Josh had the information he had come for. Beverly was fine, doing very well, in fact. He could leave and go to sleep tonight without worrying about her. But his feet refused to move from the spot in front of Mr. Fisk's counter.

"Now, what did you ask me?" Mr. Fisk asked Josh after the customer left. "Oh yes, if I believe Beverly's story. It really doesn't matter, Josh. What's important is that _she_ believes it, and that she's an honest woman with a good heart. That's enough for me. I'd think that would be enough for most men."

Josh knew that remark was directed at him and felt the need to defend himself. "Look, I don't know what she told you, but I didn't throw her out in the street."

"She told me she left on her own, after she learned of your engagement to Amanda. It was the proper thing to do."

"I'm *not* engaged to Amanda! I'm not engaged to anyone. I never have been." He tried to rub the tension out of the back of his neck. "I'm sorry I bothered you." He turned to walk away, but Mr. Fisk stopped him.

"Wait. Don't you want to know where she is?"

"No. I'm better off not knowing."

"Better off? How can two young people moping around like lovesick puppy dogs be better off?"

Josh met the older man's eyes. "She's moping around?"

Mr. Fisk shook his head and sighed. "The both of you are so afraid to tell each other how you feel, afraid that time is against you. Let me tell you something, son. Time is against all of us. I would give up the next ten years of my life the way it is now, if I could have just one more day with my beautiful wife. Not knowing what the future holds is what makes life an adventure. Grab every moment of happiness you can, son, because if you don't, I can assure you, one day you'll regret it."

Josh felt the man's words reach into his chest and squeeze his heart. "Where is she?"

"She's staying at my house. And before you get your testosterone in an uproar, it's a business arrangement only. Room and board in exchange for cooking and housekeeping. If I was forty years younger, you'd have some competition, but as it is, I'd rather have a hot meal and clean socks." He wrote down his address and gave Josh general directions. As Josh was leaving, he added, "I won't be home until at least ten-thirty."

Josh gave him an informal salute. "Thanks. Maybe I'll see you later."

He sat on his bike in the driveway for several minutes after he found the house. If he wanted to, he could still leave knowing she was fine and in a safe place, knowing that she cared enough to be "moping around" over him. But Mr. Fisk's words kept echoing in his head, until he finally gave in and walked up to the front door.

After working so hard to build up his courage, he didn't know what to do when there was no answer to his knock. She could be in the shower, or taking a walk. Should he wait? For how long? What if she was out for the evening? What if she had met another man and was out on a date? Considering his frame of mind, he was afraid he would punch that guy in the face, too.

He finally decided he should go down the street to the fast food restaurant he saw, have something to eat, and come back. If she wasn't home by then . . . well, then he wasn't meant to see her again.

He got to the corner just as a bus was letting off passengers, and was about to go around the obstructive vehicle when he saw her.

Chapter 10

Beverly heard the sound of a motorcycle engine being revved up and instantly tensed. Like the mating call of a wild beast, it demanded she notice it and the man who controlled its power. He pulled up beside her and waited for her to make the decision to climb on board for the ride of her life, or walk away and not look back.

Reminding herself that this whole strange journey was about taking risks, she mounted the beast.

When Josh turned the bike around and went straight to Mr. Fisk's house, she knew for certain that her "guardian angel" had been behind Josh's finding her.

She allowed Josh to get away without explaining until they were inside, but that was it. "Is there a button somewhere that I need to push to get you started talking?"

He narrowed his eyes and stuck his thumbs in his pockets.

"You told me you hate it when women stick their noses in your business, but you came to me this time, so that gives me the right to ask questions. Why are you here?"

He took a deep breath and ran his hands through

his hair before answering. "I wanted you to know that Amanda lied to you. There's never been a commitment of any kind between us. She just wanted . . . to cause trouble."

Beverly nodded, instinctively knowing that he was telling the truth. "You could have told me that over the phone."

"Yeah, but I also wanted to make sure you were safe."

"I'll bet you knew that two minutes after you met Mr. Fisk."

Josh threw up his hands in frustration. "Why don't you just tell me what you want me to say and then I'll say it?"

"Now that would make it a lot easier, wouldn't it? No. What I want is to hear something come out of your mouth that goes deeper than the surface. Oh, you talk enough when you're telling me about events and technology or showing me the sights, but you've never once told me anything personal about yourself. I let you get away with that while I was imposing on your hospitality and while we both thought that I was going to disappear at any second, but neither of those excuses apply now. So, either you give me a good answer as to why you're standing here, or you can just go back to your apartment, all alone, until you come up with one!"

Josh's mouth slowly curved into a grin. "You talk awful tough for such a little thing."

She didn't return his smile. "And no joking your way out of it either. Why are you here?"

His expression straightened again as he struggled to find the right words. "I'm not even sure if I know why I'm here. Being with you all the time, but not . . .

being *with* you, well, it was making me crazy. I was positive I wanted you out of my life, then when you were gone, I got even crazier. Does that make any sense?"

"Yes," she said softly. "It's been confusing to me, too."

He brushed his thumb over her mouth then placed his hand on her neck to bring her closer. "Nobody's ever made me feel the way you do."

She tilted her head back and gazed into his eyes. "And what way is that?"

"Good," he whispered with a smile. "Happy."

"Surely you've felt happy before."

With a negative movement of his head, he rubbed his nose over hers. "No. Never. It scared the hell out of me."

She eased her arms up and around his neck. "And now?"

His hands slid down her back and drew their bodies together. "And now, I want to feel happy, as long as you'll let me, even if it's only for an hour."

Their lips met in a tender kiss and held as he lifted and carried her to the sofa. Settling her on his lap, he stopped kissing her long enough to make a confession. "I've never been with anyone as innocent as you. I don't know what's right and what's wrong. You're going to have to give me some guidelines so I don't mess it up again."

She blushed at the memory. "You just moved a little too fast for me that time. If you want to kiss me like that now, I won't object. In fact, I think I'd like it very much."

He held her close and stroked her back. "I wasn't just talking about the kiss. I was remembering what you said about men not having any control, and I want you to know that you're wrong about that. You have all the control here." She shifted on his lap, making him groan with discomfort, and making her blush a bit more.

"Despite the evidence to the contrary, I don't want to push you into doing anything you're not ready for. I've been in this condition since our first night together and I've done a fair job of controlling myself so far. And as much as I want to . . . be *with* you, in every way, I can wait."

She buried her face in his neck. "What if I don't want to wait?" She felt his lower body respond to that possibility. "I think there's something you should know. Billy was the only man I ever . . . was *with*, and we waited until our wedding night, because we thought it was the right thing to do. After I lost him, I cried for months over all the years we wasted, waiting until it was proper. If I didn't want to be *with* you, Josh, believe me, I wouldn't be sitting on your lap right now."

He chuckled. "Then I guess that means I don't have to ask you to marry me after all."

She raised her head and pressed her mouth to his, thinking that was answer enough.

Rather than deepen the kiss, however, he drew back from her. "I would if you wanted me to."

"It's not necessary, truly." She leaned toward him, but he spoke again.

"What would you have said if I asked?"

"I beg your pardon?" she asked cautiously, not wanting to jump to any conclusions.

He couldn't meet her eyes, and his reworded question was mumbled. "If I had asked you to marry me, what would your answer have been?"

Her heart began pounding like a bongo drum. She knew exactly what he was doing. He was proposing without risking rejection. No matter what her answer was, he could always tell himself he hadn't really proposed. It was only a hypothetical question.

She pursed her lips and rubbed her jaw to show him that she was giving his question serious consideration. He expected her to say no, and from a practical standpoint, she should give him that answer. After all, she could disappear at any moment; she knew nothing about his background or his future plans; she didn't even know if he liked children. Saying yes would be the biggest risk she had ever taken.

"Ask me now, Josh. If you want to hear my answer, you have to ask the question and mean it. No ifs."

A muscle in his cheek twitched and he resituated her on his lap so that she was turned more toward him. "Will you—" His throat closed up and he cleared it nervously. "Will you marry me?"

Beverly let out the breath she had been holding. "Yes. It's completely crazy, but I don't care. I want to be Mrs. Josh Colby, just as soon as possible."

Their mouths came together in earnest now, without caution or fear of rejection. And when she felt his lips part, she did the same and welcomed his tongue with hers. It had been so long since a man had made love to her that she felt like a virgin all over again, except that there would be no pain or discomfort or inexperienced fumbling. Somehow, she knew with Josh there would be only pleasure.

Josh rose, lifting her with him, and she pointed out her bedroom.

"Are you sure?" he asked as he lowered her onto the bed.

"Do you love me?" she asked in return, gazing up at him adoringly.

"More than life itself."

"Then I'm sure."

He quickly yanked off his boots and started to peel down his jeans, but stopped when he noticed how pink she had gotten. "I'm sorry," he said, pulling the pants back up, but leaving them unzipped. "I did it again, didn't I? I swear, I'll learn how to go slower—"

"Or I'll get faster," she ended with a smile to relax them both.

He stretched out alongside her. "Just so we meet somewhere in the middle." He kissed her nose. "I love you, Beverly. I don't know what I ever did to deserve you, but it must have been pretty terrific to get you to travel so far to come to me."

She kicked off her shoes and turned on her side toward him so that they were meeting in the middle as he suggested. She ran her fingers over his shoulder, down his back, and onto his hip, feeling the hard muscles beneath his clothes and wishing he had taken them off the way he had started to. "I'm afraid I haven't had much practice at this. Feel free to offer directions."

He imitated her action exactly. "I will if you will."

She made a face at him. "Don't try to convince me that you're inexperienced, because I won't believe it."

He nipped her earlobe. "Experience has taught me that different women like different things. For instance, I already know you want me to go slow." He planted a trail of gentle kisses down her throat as he continued. "I just want to make sure I'm doing everything else you like, and I won't know that unless you tell me." He undid several buttons of her blouse and brushed his mouth over the skin exposed above her bra.

Her heart was beating wildly, and he hadn't even touched a private part of her body. She couldn't imagine how she was going to survive the rest. "I like what you're doing," she said breathlessly. "I think I'm going to like anything you want to do."

He raised his head to caress her mouth. "What a cooperative wife you're going to make."

Beverly tried to stay aware of what she was feeling, but there were too many places on her body all coming alive at once. His tongue played with hers while his hand bared her breast and his fingers were doing something to her nipple that caused streaks of pleasure to shoot downward to that place between her legs where his thigh was pressing and moving so expertly.

She moaned with a need unlike anything she had ever experienced before, and found some relief by rocking back and forth against his leg. She tried to slide her hand between their bodies to arouse him as well, but he moved lower, out of her reach.

And when his mouth closed over the nipple he had already teased to a hard peak, she forgot what she had wanted to do for him. She was on fire and agitated beyond coherent thought. She couldn't decide if she wanted him to continue or stop the torment.

As though he sensed her bewilderment, he made

the choice for her by unsnapping her jeans and slipping his hand beneath her panties. His fingers eased
inside her body as his palm massaged the sensitized
flesh, and suddenly the uncomfortable feeling increased a hundred times.

"Josh, ple—" Waves of delicious, bubbly pleasure
washed over her, stealing her thoughts and her
breath, making her want to laugh and cry at the
same time. When she finally opened her eyes, she
saw Josh smiling down at her.

"I gather that we can put that on the list of things
Beverly likes," he teased.

She shyly lowered her eyes.

"Uh-uh," he sounded, touching her chin to make
her look up at him again. "I think your blushes are
very pretty, but I don't want you to ever be embarrassed about anything that happens between us.
Okay?"

"Okay," she whispered with a soft smile.

"So, answer me. Did you like that?"

She giggled. "I definitely liked that. But now it's
time to find out what Josh likes." Her fingers barely
scraped the top of his briefs when he stopped her
progress again.

"We can't."

She glanced down at the muscle doing it best to escape from its cotton prison. "I think we can," she
said and curved her hand over his erection.

Josh inhaled sharply and placed his hand over hers
to keep it still. "I don't have any condoms with me."

She clucked her tongue at him. "We're going to be
married soon, and I want children. Don't you?"

He moved her hand to a less sensitive area. "Yes,
but I keep worrying about Mr. Fisk coming home

early. The truth is, I don't want to make love to you then have to get dressed and leave."

He moved over her, aligning their hips so that she would have no doubt as to how much he needed her. "I want to feel your body lying next to mine all night, and I want you to be with me when I wake up in the morning. Sort of like the first night, only without all these clothes."

She swallowed hard and managed to say, "Okay," despite how badly she wanted to feel him inside her.

Once decided, they straightened their clothing, wrote a short note to Mr. Fisk, and were off in ten minutes.

The trip from Mr. Fisk's to Josh's apartment was actually rather short, but for the couple already vibrating from desire, the ride on the Harley seemed to take hours. Either way one looked at it, however, it was long enough and the wind was cool enough for an ounce of reason to creep into Beverly's love-dazed mind.

As soon as they were inside Josh's apartment, he was more than ready to pick up where they had left off, but Beverly asked him to wait a little longer.

"I haven't changed my mind about anything," she assured him as they sat down on his bed. "I love you, and I want to sleep with you tonight and every night from now on, but I want something from you first."

He looked relieved. "Name it, love, and if it's in my power . . . No, whatever it is, I'll get it for you. Do you want a ring? We can buy one tomorrow."

She leaned forward and kissed him softly. "That's very sweet. Thank you. But it's not something you need to buy for me. It's something you already have." She tapped his forehead with her index finger. "In here. I want you to tell me about Josh Colby. I don't even know when your birthday is, or whether you have any family. I've told you almost every tiny detail of my life, and all I know about you is that you're the kindest, sweetest, most wonderful man in the world. That's enough, really, but I'd like to know how you got that way. Where did you come from?"

Josh rose from the bed and paced the apartment like an animal that suddenly discovered he had been caged. "Nothing about my life before I met you is important. You popped in and changed everything. Can't we just leave it at that?"

"Of course we can, if you insist. But I'd consider it a wedding present if you could trust me enough to tell me whatever you're so ashamed of. Consider this, if you tell me your life history and it makes no difference to me, then you'd never have to worry about me discovering your dark secrets later, and I might be more understanding when you get into one of your gloomy moods. On the other hand, if whatever you're hiding makes me change my mind about loving you, wouldn't you be better off without somebody so unforgiving?"

He had shoved his thumbs in his pockets again, and she knew what that meant. "Please, Josh, I want to be with all of you, not just the parts on the outside." As she waited for a reaction, she had a moment of light-headedness. She guessed that it was due to not having eaten since late morning, but she could wait awhile longer under the circumstances.

A few seconds later his fists unclenched and the thumbs came out of hiding. "At least sit back down with me. If you can't tell me about your life, then tell me what you've been doing since Friday."

He sat down on the edge of the bed with his back to her and removed his boots. She had no clue about what he was thinking until he spoke.

"I was born January 28, 1959, in Brooklyn. I was baptized Catholic, but haven't seen the inside of a church for over thirty years. My parents were both of Mohawk descent mixed mostly with French and a little English. My father was a high-steel worker, like his father was. One night after work, he got drunk, beat his boss to death with a pipe, then went home and got my mother pregnant. He was caught and sentenced to life in prison before I was born."

Beverly touched his back. "What your father did is not a reflection on you."

He turned toward her, defiance in his eyes. "No? What would you say if I told you I lost my temper and punched Stud-Man after work today?"

"Why did you lose your temper?"

He looked away. "He said something I didn't like."

"Something about being an Indian or something about me?"

His gaze darted back to her and he frowned. "About you, but that's still no excuse for using my fists."

"Let me ask you this. If he had said it to me, would I have slapped his face?"

He almost smiled. "Maybe."

"Then that settles that."

He shook his head. "You don't understand. I didn't even think about it. I just reacted. The thing is, it wasn't the first time. I once did six months in jail because of punching first and thinking later."

"What got you mad that time?"

"It didn't matter. I spent most of my life looking for a fight, and more often than not, somebody gave me one."

She took his hand and held it though he tried to pull away. "You once told me you never hit a woman. Did you ever pick a fight with someone smaller than you?"

He gave a dry laugh. "If I had, I may have come out on top more often."

"So, you're not a bully, just very angry."

"If you're thinking about psychoanalyzing me, don't bother. They forced me to listen to the shrinks in jail and it didn't do any good. I don't believe in any of that stuff."

"You didn't believe someone could travel through time either, but here I am." She squeezed his hand. "I'm no expert, and I would never try to analyze you, but I spend a lot of time listening to people who have all kinds of different problems. It seems to me that it helps them just to talk it out. Will you try?"

He shrugged. "What else do you want me to tell you?"

"Did you ever get to know your father?"

"Not really. When I was a little kid, my mother forced me to go with her on visiting days. I hated that trip more than anything. I don't remember exchanging more than two words with my old man—hello and goodbye—and that was only because my mother insisted. However, I remember very well what the other kids on the block said about him. They thought it was very funny to call him a murdering Injun and make jokes about how he was in the pen for scalping a white man. I got into my first fight before I even went to kindergarten."

"Children can be very cruel, especially when their parents give them ammunition to hurt with. It must have been hard on your mother."

"No sh—Excuse me. No kidding. She started cleaning houses and taking in ironing while she was pregnant with me, and after I was born, she'd take me with her until I was school age. Then I helped matters a lot by coming home every other day with a black eye or a note from the teacher reporting how disruptive I was. She got pneumonia when I was ten, but couldn't afford to take care of herself. She literally worked herself to death."

Beverly stroked his cheek. "Who took care of you then?"

"A cousin of my father's took me in for a while, but I messed that up. The state tried putting me in a few foster homes after that, but nobody could stand me for long. The juvenile detention center was my home until I was old enough to get a job."

The light-headedness came and went again. "Whatever happened to your father?"

Josh took a slow breath. "I got a letter eight years ago from the warden's office informing me of my father's death. Apparently, he just laid down on his cot one night and didn't wake up the next morning. The night after I got that letter was when I got arrested for assault and wrecking a bar. Six months later, I swore I'd never use my fists for anything but self-defense again."

"Did you keep that vow?" Beverly asked, though she was certain she knew the answer.

"I thought you said you were a good listener. I told you I punched Stud-Man tonight."

"And I don't think that should be counted against you. You're in love. That gives you special dispensation. The pope said so. Was there any other time in the past eight years?"

"No, that was the first." He shook his head in disbelief. "Is there anything I could tell you that you wouldn't have a positive answer for?"

"Well, I don't know. I'm still waiting for you to get to the deep, dark secrets that will make me run for safety. So far, all I've heard is a story about a boy who grew up to be a very good man, despite all obstacles. And even though it isn't finished yet, I'm predicting a happily-ever-after ending."

"You really love me, don't you? I mean, it's not my long hair, or leather, or my Harley, it's *me*."

She smiled. "I love those things, too, but only because they're part of you."

"Is there anything else you'd like to know about me?"

"Not at the moment."

He drew her into his arms. "Then I'd like to know more about you."

She arched a brow at him. "What else could you possibly need to know?"

He slowly unbuttoned her blouse. "Oh, there's lots of things I need to know. For instance, do you mind if I leave the lights on when I make love to you?"

His words made the dizzy feeling return in a rush.

"And is there any place on your body that's never been kissed?"

She inhaled deeply, and the dizziness got worse.

"I'm sorry, Josh. I hate to have to say this, but I . . . I'm suddenly not feeling very well."

He sat up immediately and pressed his hand to her forehead. "You're a little warm. What can I get you? A glass of cold water?" He jumped up from the bed. "I'll see if I have some aspirins."

Her eyes were playing tricks on her. Josh seemed to be going in slow motion. Then suddenly she saw colors at the edge of her vision and realized what was happening. She heard Josh's anguished cry a heartbeat before she was sucked into the kaleidoscopic tunnel and away from him.

Chapter 11

"N̲o-o-o!" Beverly cried, but her protest was of no use. A few seconds after she entered the tunnel, she was solidly in her bedroom in Mercerville.

Hope and Jacob appeared in the doorway a moment later. "What's the matter?" Hope gushed, then widened her eyes with awareness. "Jacob, will you excuse us for a moment, please?" She waited until he moved away, then quietly closed the door. Closing in on Beverly, she stared into her eyes. "It is you in there, isn't it? I mean the *real* you?"

Beverly nodded and took a slow breath to clear her mind.

Hope gave her a bear hug that squeezed the breath back out of her again. "My God, Bev. You've been gone a whole week. What happened? Are you all right?"

"Yes. And no. So much has happened. I kept expecting to pop back here, and I thought that was what I wanted. But then I changed my mind, and I wanted to stay there. I've got to go see Lavonda." She hurriedly scanned the room. "Do you know if I have car keys here? I left my purse behind. Never mind. Loan me yours."

"Whoa! I don't think you're in any condition to drive anywhere. For one thing, you should finish getting dressed."

Beverly looked down and noted her open blouse and bare feet. She went to her closet and slipped on a pair of loafers as she buttoned her blouse.

"For another," Hope continued, "I'm not letting you go anywhere again until I hear everything. Let me send Jacob home. I'll tell him you had a very upsetting conversation with your mother or something and I need to console you. Then if you want to go see Lavonda, I'll drive you ... after you explain."

Jacob was disappointed, but understanding. As he kissed Hope good night, he secured her promise to call him before she went to sleep, whatever the hour. The moment she closed the door behind him, she was back in Beverly's bedroom demanding details.

Bev's tale came out in a jumbled, nonsensical sequence until Hope insisted she start with last Tuesday and take it one hour at a time. It might not have taken that long to tell if Hope hadn't stopped her after every sentence with a question. Since she wanted to hear each tiny detail, particularly about Josh Colby, it was quite late by the time Beverly was finished.

"I just can't believe it!" Hope exclaimed, pacing the room. "After all these years, you finally fall in love and want to start living again, and it's in another time zone. There has to be a way we can make everything work out. You're right. We need to go see Lavonda. It just wouldn't be fair if I got to live happily ever after with Jacob, and you just got another broken heart."

"I agree," Beverly said, determined to get back to

Josh somehow. "Let's go. On the way there, you can tell me what's been going on here."

"The first thing that happened is the other you insisted that someone broke in during the night and stole her purse and some clothes. She was furious over having to replace her driver's license and her brand-new Keds."

"That answers one question I had. It's why she didn't have the potion bottle that first time. I had it with me. And since I took my purse, she was left without a license. I wasn't holding on to it when I popped back, so it's still there. That's good."

"Why is that good?" Hope asked as they got into the car.

"That means I can definitely take something with me from this time period, give it to Josh, and it won't come back when I do. I had a special present in mind for him." She briefly told Hope about the collectibles store, but when Hope asked another question, Bev put her off. "Tell me about Jacob first."

Hope's face instantly took on a glow. "What can I say? He's wonderful. He works a lot of hours, but we're together every spare minute he has. I don't know how long it's going to take him to ask me to marry him, but I know he will."

"How's Stanley?"

"Hmmph. Pouting. But I'm too good a secretary for him to fire me just because I won't sleep with him anymore. Wait until you hear this. Guess where Jacob wants to move to and start his own practice?"

Bev smiled. "Gee, Hope, I can't imagine. Let's see, could it possibly be . . . *California*?"

Hope laughed. "You should have seen me when he said that. It was all I could do not to tell him about

Lavonda, but I'm not sure how he'd take that. Maybe I'll tell him later, like on our twentieth wedding anniversary. Oh, and that reminds me of another thing. There was something on the news the other day about Algeria and DeGaulle. I wasn't really listening, but I'm sure it was whatever Lavonda had told you was going to happen."

Bev nodded. She didn't need to follow it up to know that it was. "Have you seen Dee-Dee and Peggy?"

"All's quiet on the Giammarco homefront at the moment. But Dee-Dee is really depressed. She needs to get away from him before Lavonda's predictions for her and her kids come true. I tried to cheer her up Sunday night when we all went bowling, but she and I ended up butting heads again. You know you're the one she always listens to. But the other you didn't cheer her up this time.

"Your *shadow* says and does all the things you would, but something's missing. It's like how her eyes are always a dull gray. The personality's pretty much the same color. I don't think anyone's noticed but me though.

"Peggy is . . . Peggy. Nothing new there. Let's see, what else? Oh yeah. You—I mean the other you— told me that Nina's boyfriend asked her to marry her right after they graduated. But Nina also told you, *her*, that your kid brother has been hanging out with a pretty tough crowd. Sounded like he's heading for trouble."

Beverly furrowed her brow. "What did I do about that?"

"Even less than you did for Dee-Dee. You said you'd try to talk to him, but as far as I know, you never picked up the phone. Like I said, there's just something about your shadow that's missing. I don't know what. It's as if you've always got your thoughts turned inside."

They were both relieved to see a light on inside Madame Lavonda's house despite the late hour. The Gypsy had the door open before they could knock.

"Eet eez so good to see you both," she said cheerfully. "Come een. Quickly." She looked at Hope and cocked her head. "You have met your doctor, *non*?"

Hope laughed. "I have met my doctor, *oui*! And he is *très magnifique. Merci beaucoup.* And there you have the summary of all the words I remember from high school French."

"You do not need to know zee French. But Spanish would help where you are going."

Hope glanced at Beverly and shrugged. "I guess I'll be signing up for night school next term."

"Eez good that you try. Now Beverly, come, we have so leetle time left."

Beverly followed Lavonda into her special room and sat down. "Do I need to tell you what happened?"

"A few questions only. I see by your eyes that your heart has come awake again. Does he love you?"

"I think—" Beverly smiled and began again. "Yes, he does. He asked me to marry him."

"And deed you accept?"

"Yes, but then I popped back here again. I can go back to him, can't I?"

Lavonda nodded. "Eet eez possible, *oui*. But you have not yet performed zee lifesaving task."

Beverly was stunned. "I didn't? But nothing dangerous ever happened. I thought maybe my being there was all I had to do." Lavonda shook her head sadly. "Why can't you just tell me what I'm supposed to do? I'll do anything, whatever it takes so that I can go back and marry Josh. I didn't think I'd ever fall in love again. I can't go back to how I was living before. Please, tell me what I have to do."

Lavonda sighed. "I would eef I could. But eet eez not so simple. What you must do, you must discover on your own, or zee magic will not take hold."

Beverly reached across the table and grasped Lavonda's gnarled hand. "A clue then. Surely you could give me a little hint to point me in the right direction."

The Gypsy appeared to be listening to something over her head, then with a nod she brought the crystal ball closer to her. With narrowed eyes, she peered into the cloudy sphere as her hands moved around it. "Deed he not tell you of heez family?"

"A little. It was extremely difficult to get him to talk about anything personal."

"Yes, I see that now. That eez why eet took so long for you to come back. But still, he deed not tell you enough. He deed not tell you zee one thing that you needed to know. And now we are almost out of time. *Mon dieu.* Such a difficulty. But wait. There eez yet hope. You may go to him again and ask him to tell you more about heez family. But be warned. You must leave immediately, and thees trip to the past cannot last more than two days. After that, all will be lost."

"I understand. At least I think I do."

Lavonda got up and retrieved another bottle of potion. This one was dark red and the stopper was a crystal heart. She handed it to Beverly and said, "God be with you, *ma petite. Bonne chance.*"

Beverly wrapped her fingers around the bottle. "Doesn't *ma petite* mean something like 'little one'?"

"*Oui.* Why do you ask?"

Beverly shook her head. "Just a coincidence I guess. But I met a very kind man in the future, Mr. Fisk, who was incredibly helpful. He called me, 'little one.' "

Lavonda shrugged. "Eet eez a term of affection. Do you know zee meaning of *bonne chance*?"

"Good luck, right?"

She nodded. "Now run along, and remember, only two days. *Nous nous verrons encore.*"

Beverly stopped again. "You said that the other two times I was here. What does it mean?"

"We will see each other again."

Beverly gave that a moment of thought. "So, I will be returning?"

"You must."

"But I don't want to. I want to stay in the future with Josh."

"As I said before, eet eez possible for you to stay where he eez, *eventually*, eef you complete zee task een time. I can say no more than that."

Beverly took a step and turned around once more. "One more question. You said I have two days. Is there any way I can control the moment of my return trip?"

Lavonda studied her for several seconds before answering. "I can only tell you that within a short time of your discovering what you must, you will be brought back. And when zee two days are ended, you will come back whether you have made that discovery or not."

Beverly filled Hope in on the way back to their apartment. "There's something in my bedroom I have to get before I go. Otherwise I would have drunk the potion as soon as she gave it to me."

"But she said you'll definitely be coming back, right?"

"Right. And I'll talk to both Dee-Dee and Allen then. But Hope, you understand that if there's any way I can go and stay with Josh, I will."

Hope smiled. "Of course I understand. I'm in love, too, remember. Just try to arrange it so we have some time together before you go."

"*If* I go. I really have no idea what it is I'm supposed to accomplish to make everything turn out right, and when I asked for a hint, all she'd say is that there was something that Josh had to tell me about his family. It makes no sense. I think he told me everything he knows about his parents, and it wasn't much."

"Maybe it's not about his parents. Maybe it's some other family member."

Bev remembered his mentioning a cousin of his father's, but he was only a young boy when he stayed with that family. "I don't know. I'll just have to make him wrack his brain until he comes up with something that sounds important. Damn! How am I supposed to know what's important and what's not?"

"You'll know when you hear it," Hope said confidently. "Lavonda hasn't steered us wrong yet."

As soon as they got home, Bev headed straight to her closet and pulled down a large box from the top shelf. Hurriedly, she sorted through prom souvenirs, pressed flowers, letters, and newspaper clippings. For the first time in seven years, she looked at the keepsakes from her years with Billy, and she could smile instead of cry.

When she caught sight of a photo he had sent her from boot camp, she picked it up and held it to her heart. "Goodbye, Billy," she whispered. "I'll always love you."

Finally she found what she was looking for. The packet she had received for joining James Dean's fan club. Hope had sent her name in as a joke, and Beverly remembered coming close to throwing it away. Now she was very glad she hadn't.

"Okay, I guess I'm as ready as I can get," Bev said to Hope after putting everything neatly away. She had the packet in one hand and the potion in the other. "Wish me luck."

"Hold it," Hope said, raising both hands. "Take those shoes off before you go. She'll have a fit if she loses another pair."

Laughing, Beverly placed the shoes back on the closet floor, exactly where she had found them. She gave Hope a kiss on the cheek, took a deep breath, and swallowed the bubbly liquid.

This trip seemed twice as fast as the first two, but Beverly had no objection to that.

The room was illuminated only by the light from the television, but it was enough for her to see Josh lying in the middle of his bed with his eyes closed. He didn't know she was there. She was about to go to him when he suddenly sat up.

"Damn it!" he cried and hurled a pillow across the room.

Beverly caught it in her face and threw it back at him. "I was hoping for a little warmer welcome."

"Oh my God," Josh said, lurching up from the bed. "Oh my God."

Beverly dropped the packet and the bottle, ran into his arms, and he lifted her and whirled her around. When he stopped, he kissed her for a very long time before speaking again. "I wasn't sure if I was doing it right."

Thinking he was referring to the kiss, she said, "I don't think you could do that wrong."

"Not that," he said, returning her teasing smile. "I was praying. Since I hadn't done that in a while, I wasn't sure anybody could hear me. But they must have, because you're back." His expression grew serious and he held her a few inches away from him. "You *are* back aren't you?"

"Yes, but only for a short while, then depending on something, I might be able to come back for good."

He couldn't decide whether to smile or frown. "I don't get it."

"I'm not sure I do either, but I'll tell you exactly what the Gypsy told me. Before I do though, I have a present for you." As she fetched the packet off the floor and placed the potion bottle in her purse with the other two, she said, "It's not so much a present as a repayment for all the money you spent on me."

Josh looked offended. "I wasn't expecting repayment. Besides, you've done more for me—"

"Oh, hush, and just look inside." She handed him the packet. His mouth dropped open when he saw what it was. "This ... this is incredible," he said, going through the James Dean memorabilia. "This stuff must be worth a small fortune. Are you sure you want to part with this?"

"It has no value to me, not even sentimental, but you could probably take it to that collectibles store and—"

"No way will I sell it," he vowed, holding the packet to his chest as though she might take it back, then he grinned and lifted a brow. "Unless we use it for a honeymoon trip."

Her stomach fluttered, and she stepped close to kiss him for that sweet thought. When he would have deepened the caress, however, she eased back. "Don't distract me until after I tell you what Lavonda said." Taking his hand, she led him back to the bed and sat down. As concisely as possible, she summarized what she had learned.

When she was finished, he shook his head. "I didn't hold anything back before, I swear. And as far as I know, there aren't any other close family members. The relatives I stayed with after my mother died weren't even first cousins. After I got kicked out of there, I never talked to them again."

Beverly massaged her temples. "Let me think. There has to be something. Lavonda specifically said I have to discover something, that you had to tell me more about your family. She made it sound like it was something you would know, or at least should know."

"I'm sorry, love. I told you how it was from the time I was born. I never spoke to my father, and if my mother ever told me anything important, I don't remember. Besides, I really don't see how some piece of information about people who are long dead is supposed to save my life or anybody else's."

"I don't either. But it's the only hint she'd give me, and since I want to be able to stay with you more than anything in the world, I have to figure it out."

"I don't know what good it would do," Josh said after a moment of frustrated silence. "But I could try to track down Tom and Alice, that's the cousins . . . if they still live in Buffalo, and don't have an unlisted number, and—"

"Just try! It's the only lead we've got."

Probably because it was after midnight, the information operator didn't mind giving Josh the phone numbers of every Thomas Chevalier in the Buffalo area. Fortunately there were only four of them and no Tom's or T's to contend with. After waking two Toms that were not related to him, Josh located his distant cousin.

He apologized and explained who he was. "I would never have called this late, but it really is terribly important. I'm not at liberty to explain more than that and can't even tell you exactly what I'm trying to find out."

By that time, Alice had awakened, and Tom had to relay everything to her. Between the two of them they told Josh what little they remembered about his parents, but it was even less than he knew already.

Alice took possession of the phone as Josh was about to hang up. "I just thought of something," she said, sounding much more awake than her husband. "After your mother died, her things were brought here with you. I gave away the clothes and such after you left, but I held on to her photo album in case you wanted it after you'd outgrown your wild streak. I put it up in the attic and forgot all about it until now. Would you like me to send it to you?"

"Hold on." Josh told Beverly about the album and asked her opinion.

"We don't have time for her to mail it. Can we go get it?"

"We have overnight mail now, but there's always a slim chance it could get lost. How do you feel about taking a trip to Buffalo tomorrow?"

"I don't think we have a choice."

"Alice? If it's not too much trouble, we'd like to come pick it up. I'm not sure if we'll fly or drive, but either way, we could be there by tomorrow evening."

She swore she would love to see him again and offered to pick him up at the airport if they flew in. She also gave him directions to their house in case they decided to drive.

The decision was made for them when Josh called the airlines. They could get out of New York, but not into Buffalo until the day after tomorrow, unless they wanted to try standby. It would have to be a road trip.

"Do you think you could stand eight hours on the bike or should we rent a car?" he asked.

"Which would be faster?"

"Figuring the time it would take to rent a car, I'd say the bike, but the car would be quieter and—"

"The bike. We might not be able to hold a conversation, but"—she put her arms around his waist and hugged him tight—"I get to wrap myself around you the whole time." She giggled as she felt his lower body instantly respond to that idea.

Josh kissed her nose. "You know, if we're going to take the bike anyway, we could leave now and get there in the morning. Traffic would be lighter."

"How much sleep did you get last night?" she asked with a challenging look.

"Oh, at least . . . fifteen minutes or so. I had something on my mind that wouldn't go away."

"Then we'll leave in the morning."

He kissed her ear and murmured, "What makes you think I'm going to get any sleep if we stay here for the night?"

His breath tickled her neck, and she squirmed in his arms. "Why, Mr. Colby, what are you suggesting?"

His low chuckle gave her another kind of tickle. "I'm suggesting we get back to finding out what Beverly likes."

"Hmmm. I suppose that would be all right, as long as we get to find out about Josh as well this time."

His hands covered her bottom and lifted her, bringing her legs around his hips. "I can give you a guarantee on that."

As his lips met hers, a spear of pleasure jolted through her, beginning where their lower bodies pressed together and ending in her fingertips. He invaded her mouth, starved for the taste of her, and she offered him all that she had.

He took a step, and she felt the wall against her back. Moving in an imitation of what was to come, he pushed himself hard against her, and she finally understood the urgency he had felt before. She didn't want to go slowly anymore. She wanted everything, and she wanted it immediately.

Her fingers tangled in his hair, and she forced his tongue back into his own mouth so that she was now the aggressor. The sound that came from his chest let her know he understood exactly how she felt. Neither wanted to wait a moment longer, but their clothes made their wish for instant fulfillment impossible.

Josh carried her to the bed and fell with her on top of him. "Tell me you want me to slow down, love, and I will."

"No," she said, shaking her head and raising herself into a sitting position. "I want you to go faster." She grasped the hem of his T-shirt and pushed it upward. And as her fingers explored the broad expanse of muscled chest she had uncovered, he opened her blouse and unhooked the garment that prevented him from doing the same to her.

The sensual contact was not nearly enough for either of them. The blouse and shirt had to come off completely, as did jeans and underwear. Their very lives suddenly seemed dependent on their being able to see and feel every inch of each other's body.

When Josh slipped his fingers between her legs, she nearly rose off the bed.

"No, Josh, please, not like that."

He stilled his hand, but kept it pressed to her heated flesh. "I thought you liked this." He moved one finger to demonstrate what *this* he was referring to. She arched her back in response.

"I do, but now I want . . ."

Josh waited for her to finish, but when she couldn't seem to, he helped her along. Kissing her tenderly, he stroked her with his finger again. "Do you want to please me?" She nodded. "Well, it would please me to have you so hot for me that when I do get inside you, you won't care that I'm not going to be able to make this first time last. I've wanted to be like this with you for too long. So, I need to make sure you're very *very* ready for me. Are you there yet, love?"

Her only response was a soft whisper.

"If you're too shy to tell me with words, what else can I do but find out for myself?" He eased two fingers inside her tight, but very damp opening and scissored them back and forth.

"*Please*," she moaned.

"Hmmm. I'm still not sure you're ready for me." He lowered his head to kiss her breast.

"Damn you, Josh Colby!" In a totally unexpected move she shoved him onto his back and straddled his hips. "You talk too much!" Without further discussion, she centered herself above him and slid down his engorged shaft, absorbing him, inch by inch, until there was no part of him that she did not possess.

His expression let her know he was extremely pleased with her act of aggression, but a heartbeat later she found herself on her back again with him above her.

He had been right to prepare her so well, for he was very large and she was nearly virginal in her tightness, and there was no patience on either of their parts.

With powerful thrusts, he drove her to the beautiful, erotic place he had shown her before. But he didn't join her. Instead, he paused for her to come back to the starting line so that they could take another trip together. Despite his earlier warning, he made it last until she cried out in frustration once more, and only then did he let go and ride the wind home with her.

Although he had teased her about how much sleep

they would get, they both drifted off almost immediately. Just before dawn, Josh awoke her with the gentle stroking of his fingers up and down her back.

They made love again, only this time, as they rested in each other's arms, Josh did something totally unexpected. His fingers moved to her left breast and touched the lump.

"Have you always had this?" he asked, gently moving it beneath his fingertips.

Beverly knew it was silly to be embarrassed after how well acquainted they had become with each other's bodies, but it felt as though he was pointing out a flaw. "I, um, well, I'm really not sure. I only noticed it a little while ago."

"Have you had a doctor look at it?"

"Heavens no. I'm sure it's nothing, and as you are well aware, I've been a little busy with other things."

He outlined the edge of it, then rose on one elbow to look down at her face. He looked terribly worried. "Has it always been this big?"

"Josh, it's nothing. Why are you so concerned about a little lump?"

He sat upright and made her do the same. "I guess women didn't talk much about this kind of thing in the fifties, but just like technology, the medical field has advanced quite a bit also. I'm not a doctor, and I sure wouldn't claim to know all that much about female problems. But I'd have to be deaf and blind not to have heard medical warnings to women about . . ."

He didn't dare say the C word aloud. ". . . about lumps in the breast. It might be nothing, like you said, but when a woman finds anything that hasn't always been there, she should have it checked out, especially if it's hard or grown or changed in shape.

From what I understand, if it's diagnosed early enough, it can be taken care of before it becomes . . . something serious."

Beverly could see that to Josh, it had already become something serious. "Okay. I'll have it checked out as soon as I have a chance." The worried look didn't completely leave his eyes. "I promise," she added, sealing it with a kiss.

They could have easily spent the entire morning learning more about each other, particularly about their personal preferences in bed, but Beverly's mission could not wait any longer.

Chapter 12

The sun was just beginning to rise when they mounted the Harley to begin the long trek across the state of New York. Knowing Beverly wasn't accustomed to riding, Josh made a lot more stops than he normally would. Thus, they didn't reach Tom and Alice's until seven that evening.

"Heavens to Betsy!" Alice exclaimed the moment she opened the door. "Lookie here, Tom. Don't he look just like our Charlie, only a little thinner, and with longer hair, and no earring of course. Come in. Come in." She took Josh by the arm and pulled him through the door.

Josh grabbed Beverly's hand to bring her along. "This is my fiancée, Beverly Newcastle. Bev—Alice and Tom."

Beverly shook Tom's hand and returned Alice's warm hug. She guessed they were both in their seventies, healthy, and content with their lives. She liked them on sight.

Alice directed everyone to go straight to the kitchen, where the table was already set for four. "I made roast beef and au gratin potatoes. As I remember, you liked that when you were here."

Josh smiled. "If *I* remember correctly, when I was

here, I wasn't polite enough to have complimented your cooking no matter how much I liked it."

"*Humph!* That's for sure," Tom said, then grinned so that everyone would know he held no grudge.

Alice clucked her tongue and gave him a look of rebuke. "Now, Tom, that was a long time ago, water under the bridge and all that. Anyway, we both know he had good reason to be angry with the world."

Josh shot a glance at Bev, and she winked back.

"And now, here you are," Alice continued in her cheerful tone. "A full-grown man about to be married. While we eat, you can tell us everything you've been up to for the last twenty-five years."

Beverly had to stifle a laugh, knowing how hard she had had to work to get Josh to talk about himself, but the tables were turned when Alice addressed her. "Then you can eat while Beverly tells us all about herself."

With a bit of joint creative effort, they managed to satisfy Alice's curiosity, then got her talking about her own family. It was after nine when the purpose for Josh and Beverly's visit finally made it into the conversation.

"I'm sorry I don't have more to tell you," Alice said sadly. "Your father and I had only met once or twice—you know, a funeral, a wedding, that sort of thing. But we never kept in touch. I never even met your mother. It was quite a surprise when we were told we were the closest living relatives. Of course, that didn't stop us from taking you in."

Josh placed a hand over hers. "I realize it's too late for it to mean much, but I am extremely grateful that you did."

"Nonsense, son. It's never too late to say thank you. And you're very welcome. Now, what are your plans? You're welcome to stay here tonight. We have a spare room."

Josh and Bev exchanged a glance, and he said, "Thank you, but we need to put a few hours of road behind us tonight so that it's not such a long trip tomorrow."

Alice was clearly disappointed, but she understood. "Well then, I guess I'd better get that album for you so you can be on your way."

As she went off to get it, Beverly started to clear the table, but Tom shooed her away with a smile. "After I retired, Alice put her foot down about sharing chores. Now she cooks and I clean."

"Good for you. I'm going to suggest my mother do the same thing."

Tom looked from side to side in a conspiratorial manner. "Just so you don't tell your father where the idea came from."

It took a while longer to say goodbye and actually leave the house.

"What nice people," Bev told Josh after they were alone outside. "We'll have to come back when we can stay longer."

Josh stroked her cheek. "You sound pretty certain that you'll be around to do that."

Beverly gazed up at him lovingly and sighed. "I have to believe that. Otherwise, I'd—well, I don't even want to think about it, okay? Anyway, I have a very good feeling about this album." She placed her hand on it. "I can almost feel it dying to give up some tidbit of information that will make everything make sense."

"I hope you're right," he said, then stored the album in the side compartment. "We passed a lot of motels coming in. I figure we can ride an hour, check in somewhere for the night and go through the album there."

"Sounds good to me," she agreed, donning the helmet he handed her.

As planned, about an hour later they were inside a comfortable motel room. Josh was ready to begin looking for the mysterious clue without further delay, but Beverly stopped him.

"No," she said, taking the album from him and setting it on the dresser. "Not yet. Lavonda said once I discover whatever it is that I need to know to save someone's life, I'll pop back to 1958. Even though she said it was possible for me to come back again to stay with you, if I successfully complete my task, she didn't guarantee it. Just in case something goes wrong . . ."

She lowered her eyes shyly, then raised them to him again and continued with the confidence of a woman who knows she's loved. "I don't want to leave you one hour before I have to. I want to spend another night with you, making love with you. Waiting until morning to look through that album won't make any difference."

Josh drew her into his arms and quickly assured her with his kiss that he was in complete accord with that line of thinking.

Their loving began gently, but quickened with the unspoken awareness that this night could be their last together, if the album held no clue. Beverly could be returned to her own time without having discovered the secret that would allow them to stay together forever.

Her hands memorized each of his features. His mouth clung to hers as though that alone could hold her there. With equal desperation they joined together, then forcefully reined in their passion to make the wondrous union last as long as possible.

Their need for release would not be put off, however, and a powerful climax robbed them of their ability to think for a long time afterward.

Uncertainty returned with the quieting of their hearts, and sleep refused to assist them in putting off the inevitable moment. Josh rose and brought the album back to bed.

As he opened the faded cover, he said, "I just wish we had some idea what we were looking for."

Beverly placed her hand over his. "Maybe it's better that we don't. This way we won't overlook anything."

The first photos were wedding pictures of Josh's parents Mason and Lucille.

"Good heavens, Josh, you look exactly like your father." He frowned at her, and she scolded him. "Now stop that. Look at their faces. That's not the face of a mean, angry man. That's a man in love. And your mother is positively glowing."

"I don't remember her looking like that. I only remember thinking she was old. Old and tired."

Page after page bore testimony to the fact that the couple remained very much in love with each other for two years past their wedding day. Photos taken on vacations, holidays, and at parties showed smiling faces. On the backs, Lucille had written dates and notes about the circumstances or other people in the scene.

"These don't prove anything," Josh argued when she repeated how happy they seemed. "Nobody keeps pictures that show the bad stuff."

"True, but people who aren't happy with each other usually don't take many pictures at all. These were taken by people who cherished their times together."

Even if she hadn't known the history, Bev could have guessed that a major change had occurred three-quarters of the way through the album. From one page to the next, there were no more photos of either Mason or Lucille, only their son.

The first five years of the boy's development were neatly chronicled. There was the sleeping newborn Josh, the laughing infant, the curious toddler, and the pouting little boy getting his first barbershop haircut. The photojournal became less detailed at age five, thinning down to a portrait on Santa's knee and a birthday shot. The last two photos that had been secured in the album were Josh's first- and second-grade class pictures.

"There's nothing important here," Josh stated in a tone that melded anger and frustration.

"What about the pictures with other people in them?" Bev asked, rather than give in to her own disappointment.

His reply was heavy with sarcasm. "Like we have time to start looking up every name on the back of a bunch of forty-year-old photos. I don't know who any of those people are. I can't remember anyone visiting my mother or us going anywhere."

Beverly started to close the album when a photo

fell out from the back. She flipped over the remaining empty pages and found a small collection of loose pictures, negatives, and papers that had been tucked into a built-in file pocket.

Here were Josh's class pictures for the three years prior to his mother's death, his and his parents' birth certificates, the Colbys' marriage certificate, and his father's high school diploma. There were also two yellowed newspaper clippings. The first was dated August 8, 1956 and contained a one-sentence announcement of the marriage. The other was dated July 20, 1958 and was long enough to warrant its own headline: LOCAL MAN SENTENCED TO LIFE IMPRISONMENT FOR BRUTAL SLAYING OF BOSS.

Beverly tried to hand the article to Josh, but he didn't want to look at it. "Do you mind if I read it?" Josh leaned back against the headboard and closed his eyes. Beverly didn't want to seem morbid, but she didn't want to take the chance of ignoring anything in the album.

The first two paragraphs covered the brief trial and how the defendant, Mason Colby, shouted his innocence even as they hauled him away. As Beverly went on to read a summary of the incident that led up to the case, she couldn't help but think that the evidence seemed to point toward Mason's guilt.

Suddenly, she gasped and shook Josh's arm. "Listen to this! 'Mason Colby admitted to having argued with his boss the afternoon before the murder and could not deny that it was his truck in which police found the pipe with the victim's blood on it. Nor could he disclaim the neighbor's account that he had had a loud argument with his wife after work and had left their apartment in a rage, not to return until well after the murder was committed.

" 'The only alibi Colby offered was that he took a long drive to cool down and ended up in a diner called Pete's Place, in Mercerville, New Jersey, where he used the men's room and returned home. Although that drive could account for the hours in question, and there is such a diner, no one at Pete's Place could recall seeing Colby.' "

Josh's sour expression didn't change.

"Don't you see?" Bev said, giving his arm, and his attitude, a shake. "*Pete's Place* is where I work. That's too strange to be a coincidence. It's got to be the clue I was supposed to discover."

"I'm not sure I follow."

It seemed so obvious to her she had assumed he had come to the same conclusion, but she had to keep in mind that he had believed in his father's guilt his entire life. "Your father claimed to have driven to Mercerville, but no one at Pete's Place could confirm it. If it was a busy night, and all he did was walk in and out, it's certainly possible that he wasn't noticed."

She frowned and skimmed the article again. "Does it say what day of the week that was? If it was a Friday—Oh my God! Josh, look at the date. The murder was committed on *Friday, April 25, 1958.* I usually work Friday evenings because of the big dinner crowd Pete gets on his special Friday Fish Fry. What's today?"

"Thursday," Josh replied, then, as awareness seeped in, he added, "April 25th."

"Oh my God. The same date in 1958 is one day ahead, so that means it's already Friday there. The murder happens tonight!" She vigorously rubbed her forearms. "Geez. I'm covered with goose bumps."

Josh pinched the bridge of his nose. "Let me see if I understand what you're saying. On the night of the murder my father was accused of, he went to the diner where you were waiting tables, but because it was busy, and he didn't sit down and eat, or do anything memorable, nobody paid attention to him."

Beverly nodded excitedly. "Including me. But with what I know now, I could look for him to come in and make sure I could identify him to the police later."

Josh's eyes were wide with wonder. "You could be his alibi."

They both sat in silence for a moment as they absorbed the immensity of the discovery they had just made. Because no one had recognized Mason Colby that night, he was unjustly sent to prison and died there. His wife met an early death due to overwork and poverty. His son grew up angry and bitter and alone. Had Beverly remembered seeing that poor man, she would have saved not one, but three lives.

But it could still be fixed, Beverly realized abruptly. All she had to do was go back to that day and make things right. And with that thought, she felt a familiar wave of dizziness.

"Josh, would you please bring me my purse?" He did, and she tucked it securely under her arm. "Now kiss me. *Quickly!*" He was most happy to oblige her that as well. "It's coming. I mean, I'm going. Soon. But I'll be back, somehow. I promise. It may take me some time though. I don't know how things will happen. I mean, if your father gets arrested anyway, and I need to testify in court or something, I'd have to stay there until it was over. So, don't give up on me. And please go visit Mr. Fisk and explain everything to him. I don't want him to worry either."

Another wave made the room appear to sway. "I'll be back as soon as I prove your father was innocent, *is* innocent. I love you so much."

She pressed her lips to his, but the kiss did not prevent her from being pulled into the kaleidoscope.

It took Josh a moment to realize he was kissing air. She was gone, just as she had warned. Only this time, she had promised to come back for good.

There was one possible problem with that promise, but he had purposely kept it to himself. After all, what did he really know about time travel? He had seen no good reason to upset her with what was worrying him. That would have accomplished nothing, since there were no alternatives.

She couldn't stay longer than another twelve hours anyway. And if she went back and didn't complete her so-called mission, she said she couldn't come to the future again. Either way, she was definitely lost to him. At least, if she did what she was supposed to—change history—it sounded like they had a chance to be together again.

He tried to relax and get a little sleep before he had to drive back home, but the worry wouldn't leave his mind. What if, like in the time-travel movies, when you change something in the past, more than just one event changes in the future?

What if she succeeds in changing his father's fate, what will that mean? Will he still have died eight years ago? Or will he have survived instead? And what of his mother? With a husband to help her, might she not have recovered from the pneumonia that stole her life?

But one question superseded all the rest. Would his and Beverly's memories stay intact, or would they forget that they had met and fallen in love?

Since praying had brought her back before, it was the only thing he could think of trying now. So he prayed that no matter what happened, she would come back to him, and they would somehow recognize each other . . . and remember.

Chapter 13

Only when she arrived in her bedroom did it occur to Beverly that she had taken a risk in kissing him at the moment of departure. Since *things* she was touching traveled with her, what if people did also? But he hadn't come back with her. Unfortunately. She would simply have to do without his company for a while. At least she had the consolation that they would be spending the rest of their lives together, sometime in the future.

She was anxious to talk to Hope, but a glance at the clock reminded her it was only 2 A.M. Conversation could wait until Hope got up for work.

That thought led her to check her calendar for her own work schedule . . . assuming her shadow would maintain the same habit of recording it that she always did.

Perfect. She was working the evening shift tonight, as expected. She would be on duty when Mason Colby walked into Pete's.

To make sure she didn't fall asleep and miss Hope, she wrote her a note saying she was back and to wake her up, then taped it to the coffeepot on the stove top. As she crawled into bed, she made a mental list of things she had to do while she was here:

She had to pay Lavonda a visit; she had to have serious conversations with her brother Allen and Dee-Dee; she had to say her goodbyes, with a believable explanation, to her parents and all her friends and coworkers—hopefully Lavonda could help her figure out how to manage that; she had to put together a collection of items that she could take with her into the future—nothing so valuable as to call unusual attention to herself, just enough to build a starter nest egg for her and Josh and their children. Comic books seemed to be the best idea, since they were easy to buy and wouldn't amount to much in weight or space.

Oh yes, and she must make an appointment for a checkup with her doctor, just to make sure she would be going to Josh as a healthy bride-to-be and potential mother.

Shortly after nine, Beverly got up, surprised that Hope hadn't awakened her. After checking Hope's empty bedroom, she went out to the kitchen and saw that her note had been replaced by another:

B—Welcome back! Overslept. Tried to wake you, but you were out like a light. No time to chat anyway. Will catch up when you get off tonight.

Love, H

Bev was actually glad Hope hadn't been able to interrupt her sleep. She hadn't realized how tired she was. Recalling her list of things to be done, she put food and a shower in the top two spots and decided she could arrange the rest after that.

It had become a habit to check the hard lump in her breast each time she took a shower, and she did so now. There was no longer a question of its growth. What had originally felt like a tiny B-B pellet was now the size of a marble. Feeling it again helped her decide the third item on her list. After she was clean and fed, she called her doctor and was able to get an appointment at noon.

There wasn't enough time to do any visiting before the appointment, so she filled the opening with a stop at the corner drugstore.

From the collectible store's catalog, she had learned that issues with low numbers were especially valuable in certain series, like *Superman*, *Green Lantern*, and *Captain America*, but since she hadn't thought of bringing the catalog with her, she decided she had better buy everything and deal with the values in the future. For less than five dollars, she was able to purchase one of every comic book on the shelves.

"Just try to relax, Beverly," Dr. Kanter said as his fingers examined the inner walls of her vagina. "This will only take a few seconds."

Beverly forced herself to keep her knees parted during the embarrassing invasion. The only other time she had had to undergo this intimate examination was before she married Billy. It wasn't much less humiliating now.

"Everything's exactly where it should be," the doctor said as he peeled off his gloves. "You can sit up now. Have you been feeling all right?"

"Oh, yes. I've been well. It's just—" She couldn't tell him that the reason for the visit was to have a premarital exam. If she told him she was planning to get married, he might decide to call her parents to congratulate them. Josh's concern about the lump in her breast came back to her, and as embarrassing as it was, she knew she had to mention it.

"It's not a problem really, at least I don't think so, but I noticed a . . . a lump, in my, um, left breast, and it seems to have gotten larger."

"Well then, let's take a look at it." He waited for her to reveal the breast and point to the spot. He turned his head away as he gingerly touched the lump. A moment later he backed away, and she covered herself again.

"I wouldn't worry about it," he said. "It's quite common for women to develop lumps of harder tissue in their breasts as they get older, especially when they haven't had the opportunity to get pregnant and nurse. You might think of it as your hormones rebelling. I would venture to say that the only reason you've noticed it is because of your size. That's another thing pregnancy can change you know.

"You're still a beautiful woman, Beverly. And although, we don't normally recommend pregnancy after the age of thirty, and certainly not to an unmarried woman, there are a few grace years there, if you take good care of yourself. You should give some serious consideration to finding a husband and starting a family as soon as possible. I guarantee you won't have time to be worrying about a little lump or two if you do what you were put here on Earth to do."

Since his advice was precisely what she intended to do, she didn't get annoyed as she did when her mother said things like that. Instead, she felt extremely relieved as she left his office.

From there, she drove to Lavonda's, but met with disappointment. There was no answer to her knock and all the blinds were drawn, so she couldn't see inside. She supposed a Gypsy had to go grocery shopping just like normal people, though she couldn't envision that. It was nearly time for her to get ready for work and prepare for the big moment, so she had no choice but to put off the visit with Lavonda.

As impossible as it seemed, sometime in the next few hours, she would be given an opportunity to change history, and hopefully, her life. The annoying voice of her pessimistic shadow whispered in her head, *If you're on the right track about Mason Colby being the person whose life you were supposed to save. You could be all wrong about everything.*

She just had to be patient a little longer to find out whether she or her shadow would come out on top.

When she got back to her apartment, she called her mother.

"What's wrong?" Claire Winetke asked immediately.

Bev laughed. "Nothing's wrong. I just wanted to make sure you wouldn't mind if I came for dinner tomorrow night."

"Sweetheart, you know I'd be happy to have you join us every night. Unfortunately, your father already promised the Grangers that we'd play cards with them tomorrow night. Would Sunday be okay instead?"

"Of course. That would be fine."

"Will it be just you, or are you bringing someone with you?"

Beverly knew what her mother was getting at. "Sorry, Mom, but I'll be alone as usual. I need you to do me one favor though. Please make sure Allen is there and doesn't make plans to go out. Tell him it's very important that I talk to him."

"I knew it. Something *is* wrong." Her voice filled with anxiety. "He's in trouble isn't he? He hangs around with those bums at the corner all the time now, and he never talks to me or your father anymore. Of course your father says it's just part of his becoming a man, but I don't know."

"Calm down, Mom. I don't know if he's in trouble or not. I just want to talk to him, so try to convince him to stay home for me, okay?"

Claire sighed. "Okay. What would you like for dinner? I have a nice pot roast in the freezer that I could thaw out."

"That would be perfect," Beverly said, knowing her mother lived for an excuse to make her pot roast. "I'm off at three Sunday. I'll come by right after that."

"Here you go," Beverly said, placing the tray on the edge of the table and passing her customers their drink orders. "One coffee, a vanilla Coke, and an egg creme. Your salads will be out in a few minutes."

For the thousandth time, she glanced toward the front entrance then at the clock on the wall. It would have helped if the old newspaper article in the album had mentioned the specific time that Mason Colby had come into Pete's Place. Since she didn't have that bit of information and knew that his passing through was extremely fast, she was afraid to take her attention away from the path between the front door and the men's room. Unfortunately, the diner was as busy as she had expected, and that prevented her from being as watchful as she wanted to be, which added to her nervousness.

She tried to look at it logically, but her facts were too limited. Mason said he had gone home after work, had an argument with his wife, and took an approximately two-hour drive. Did he get off at four or five? Without knowing where he was working, she couldn't guess how long the trip to Brooklyn took. Did he eat dinner or argue with Lucille the minute after he walked in the door? The only thing she could be certain of was that Pete's closed at eleven.

It was now a little after eight, and she couldn't be sure she hadn't already missed him. Her stomach was in knots, and she was taking care of her orders out of sheer habit. Three days without seeing Josh was bad enough. Knowing their future together depended on her noticing a stranger's fleeting appearance had her on the verge of a breakdown. At least she had seen pictures of Mason and knew what the man looked like—a dreamboat, just like his son.

Josh's image never left her mind. No matter what she had been doing, or who she had been talking to for the last three days, he was always there.

She saw him as he had appeared that first night, all in black leather, with his long, dark hair moving gently in the night breeze; the silver earring, the beaded choker, his dark eyes watching her with wariness. How handsome and strong he had looked when she popped in on him at the construction site, where he was shirtless and wearing a headband with his hair tied back. He had thought she was crazy.

The way she saw him most often though was how he had looked the night he asked her to marry him. There was so much love in his eyes it made her want to cry every time she thought of it.

The scenes playing in her mind were so vivid that she couldn't imagine not being able to return to him.

It seemed terribly unfair that her entire life now depended on one moment in time.

And suddenly, that moment was upon her. Seeing Mason Colby in the flesh brought two thoughts to mind. How could she have missed seeing someone that looked like him? It had to be that she was either in the kitchen, or her back was turned. The second thought was that he looked like he had the burdens of the whole world on his shoulders.

He was in the men's room before she could get to him but she was prepared for him by the time he came out. She stood poised outside the door, holding a large bowl of Brunswick stew in her hands, as though trying to remember who had ordered it. Mason was so immersed in his own gloomy thoughts that he never saw her step into his path. He only felt the hot brown soup hit his chest and run down the front of him.

"Oh my heavens," Beverly squealed, forcing her voice into a higher pitch than usual. "I am so sorry. I can't believe I did that. Don't move!"

Shocked and more than a bit uncomfortable, he looked down at the mess that had been his shirt and pants. Bits of meat and vegetables clung to him as though he were a living piece of abstract art.

Beverly grabbed several napkins and made an attempt to clean him up without getting overly intimate and without letting him get a good look at her face. "Buddy!" she called loudly to the busboy, maintaining her falsetto voice while making sure she drew the attention of every person in the diner. "Bring the mop, and see if there's an extra cook's uniform in the kitchen."

Mason began to regain his senses. "Really, miss. It's okay."

"It certainly is not okay," she said, continuing to fuss over him, yet keeping her head bowed. "If we don't rinse this out in cold water immediately, it's going to stain, and your wife is going to be furious. It will only take me a few minutes, but in the meantime, I insist you let me buy you dinner."

He glanced around, noticing all the attention they were receiving, and his discomfort increased. "Thanks, but I've already eaten, and I really need to get home."

Buddy arrived with the bucket and mop in one hand and white shirt and pants in the other, and Bev said, "There, you see how fast we are around here?" She pushed Mason around toward the men's room. "Now you go back in there and change into these. The drive home will be a lot more comfortable in clean clothes. Buddy, you go on in with him and bring his soiled clothes to me. I'll clean this up." To Mason's back, she asked, "What's your name, sir?"

Mason looked like a man who had been pinned to the front end of a speeding locomotive and couldn't figure out how to get off. "Colby. Mason Colby."

Holding an open menu up in front of her face, she asked, "Since you already had dinner, Mr. Colby, how about dessert? Do you prefer apple or peach pie? A la mode, or plain? Coffee, Sanka, or tea?"

Completely bewildered, he muttered, "Apple, à la mode, coffee."

While he was changing and she cleaned up the floor, Bev asked Nina to cover her tables and made sure she and the other waitresses had seen her act of monumental clumsiness. Not willing to take any chances, however, she held her ground between the restrooms and the front door.

Buddy came out and handed Beverly the dirty clothes. When Mason exited a few seconds later, Beverly took his arm and led him to a booth in Nina's section, occupied by two elderly gentlemen who never missed a Friday dinner at Pete's Place.

"Ray, Oscar, this is Mason Colby. I'm sure you saw what I just did to this poor man. Well, I was hoping you'd visit with him for a spell while I try to get the stew out of his clothes. I'm going to get him some pie and coffee, can I get you some, too? It's on me." As she expected, both men were delighted to have someone new to talk to, as well as the free pie. Mason, on the other hand, still appeared to be under the influence of the runaway locomotive.

Once she had served the desserts, she quickly hand-washed Mason's things, dried them as well as she could with towels, and rolled them up in heavy freezer paper. While she got back to work in her own station, she had Buddy return the damp shirt and trousers to their owner.

She had no doubt she had achieved her goal of making sure Mason Colby's presence was noted by a number of reliable witnesses. Unfortunately, she also realized that her attempts to avert her face and disguise her voice had been futile.

Before Mason left to return home, he had learned her name from Ray and Oscar and made a point of thanking her for being so nice, especially for introducing him to the two gentlemen. Apparently, they had gotten him talking about his problems and had given him some interesting advice.

There was nothing she could do about it now. If he

was still alive in 1996 when she got there, and still held some memory of her, she would worry about explaining it then.

Between the busy evening and the nerve-wracking experience she had been through, Beverly was exhausted by the time she got off, but she took a drive by Lavonda's in hopes of talking to her about what had happened. The house was completely dark, and though she knew it was impolite to keep intruding at such late hours, she knocked on the door anyway.

To her dismay, there was no answer, even when she knocked harder. Was Lavonda that sound of a sleeper, or was she still not home? Beverly chose to accept the first explanation, rather than consider the possibility that the Gypsy had abandoned her.

Hope wasn't home when she arrived, so she assumed that she had gone out with Jacob. As much as Beverly wanted to see her, she didn't have the energy to stay up and wait until who knows when. She decided to write another note and put it on Hope's bed pillow:

H—Have MUCH to tell you, but I'm dead tired and have to work the day shift tomorrow. Could we have dinner together? I may not be here much longer.—B

Beverly wished she could take tomorrow off, but she didn't know precisely when the police would come by to get statements about Mason Colby, and she wanted to be there when they did.

Even the belief that she had successfully completed the mysterious "lifesaving task" was not enough to keep her awake once her head touched her pillow.

When she awoke the next morning, she noticed

Hope's bed had not been slept in. Apparently, her relationship with Jacob had moved on to sleeping together. Because of her feelings for Josh, however, she could now be much more understanding about that sort of thing.

At Pete's that day, so many people had commented on how pretty she looked and how happy they were to see her good mood returned that she felt somewhat guilty for leaving them with her shadow for so long. It made her wonder how her shadow could appear to be so different to so many people, when Lavonda had assured her that the other one was exactly like her except that she hadn't taken the risk of trying the potion.

The answer came to her with a little thought. She had known her life had been at a standstill, but compared to how she felt now, she had barely been alive. Without taking the risk, she was destined to become what Lavonda had called her: a zombie, the living dead. Perhaps the decision not to take the potion would have accelerated her downhill slide.

But she had taken the risk, and her life had changed so much that she was no longer content in this time and place. She was anxious to move on.

Her shift came to an end, yet no police officers had shown up to ask about Mason Colby. She hoped it was just a matter of the wheels of justice moving slowly rather than something worse. The old pessimism tried to take over her thoughts, but she banished them with a shake of her head. Everything was going to work out just fine. It had to.

But pessimism reared its ugly head again when she went by Lavonda's house a third time without any luck.

It helped a little to find Hope home when she got there. After a warm hug of welcome, Hope held Beverly by her shoulders and glared at her. "Do you have any idea how crazy this is making me?"

Beverly laughed. "*You!* How would you like to be the one popping back and forth all the time, having your life turned into an adventure story, looking for mysterious clues—"

"And having a ball," Hope finished with a grin. "You are, aren't you?"

Bev thought about that before automatically agreeing. "If meeting Josh wasn't part of it, I'm not sure I'd be smiling about all the rest. It's really been terribly frustrating. But he is part of it, and I'm almost positive we solved the mystery."

"Great! I want a report of every minute you've been gone, but would you mind talking while I make some dinner? I'm starving."

Hope was always "starving." Being in love hadn't lessened her appetite one bit. Bev had always figured that it had to take a lot more food to keep Hope's body functioning than it did for hers, so she never questioned her constant hunger or the fact that she never gained weight. But one of the programs she had seen on Josh's television was about people who had eating disorders. A discussion of a problem called bulemia had made her think about Hope. Recalling the symptoms, she knew she would have to wait until after she was finished eating to know for sure.

While they prepared dinner, Bev told Hope about Tom and Alice and the photo album, and what she had done last night to set things right.

"What did Lavonda say?" Hope asked.

"I haven't seen her yet. I've been by her house three different times, but she hasn't been home."

Hope was as surprised by that as Beverly had been. "I was planning to go by and see Dee-Dee tonight; El Creepo will be out playing poker. If you want, we could go by Lavonda's again on the way home."

"Sounds good. I wanted to spend some time with Dee-Dee anyway. I've decided to tell her what's been going on. It's the only way I can think of convincing her not to ignore Lavonda's warnings."

Beverly watched Hope consume her usual large portions of food, then take her usual after-dinner trip to the bathroom. Only this time, she didn't clear the dishes while her roommate was absent. Instead, she went to the closed bathroom door and listened. As soon as she recognized the gagging sound, she banged on the door.

"Stop it, Hope. I know what you're doing, and it's very dangerous." She jiggled the handle and pounded on the wood again. "I mean it. You come out of there right now!"

Hope opened the door a few seconds later, but she wasn't happy about the interruption. "What the hell's wrong with you?"

Beverly glared up at her with her fists propped on her hips. "If you have to go to the bathroom, you go, but I'm staying in here with you."

Hope looked at her as though she had lost her mind. "I think all that popping back and forth has taken a few of your marbles away."

"It's your marbles that are lost. How long have you been vomiting after you eat?"

"Wha—How—" Hope knew she had been caught,

but she couldn't see the problem. "I only do it when I eat so much that I'm uncomfortable. Why are you acting like I've committed some kind of crime?"

"Because you have, Hope. Sit down so I can quit straining my neck. I have to explain something to you." She waited for her to lower the toilet seat and sit on it, then she told her about what she had learned about bulimia from the television program.

"You're making it sound like an addiction or alcoholism," Hope protested. "It's not something I *have* to do to get by."

"Then stop doing it. Right now. This minute. Prove to me and yourself that it's not a bad habit. I'm not making this up, Hope. I swear. In the future, young women die from what you're doing to yourself. You used to fit the picture of the kind of woman who does this sort of thing. Someone who doesn't think they're thin enough or pretty enough, someone who turns to food every time they feel lonely or depressed. And Stanley helped make you that way. But Jacob doesn't make you feel that way. He thinks you're the most beautiful woman in the world, and so do I."

Tears instantly filled Hope's eyes. "Really? You think I'm beautiful?"

Beverly handed her a tissue. "I know you are. And I want you to have a long, healthy life so you'll still be around in 1996. I intend to look you up when I go back."

That brought a smile back to Hope's face. "I hadn't thought of that. That would be so cool." A thought made her grimace. "Of course, you'll still look like you do now and I'll be an antique."

Bev tucked a strand of red hair behind Hope's ear.

"But I'm betting you'll still be a firecracker. I love you like a sister. I don't want anything bad to happen to you if you can help it. Promise me, Hope. Promise you'll stop hurting yourself."

Hope wiped her eyes and made another face. "Geez. I'll probably have to learn how to diet."

"You might even have to get some exercise," Bev added with a smile.

"Ee-yuck! Don't be disgusting. I'm trying not to throw up, remember?"

Beverly gave her a hug. "Let's go see Dee-Dee."

Walking into Dee-Dee's house was always like entering a foreign country where chaos was the norm. Although not a speck of dust could ever be found on the tabletop, the enormous amount of clutter made the house seem unkempt. Toys, pacifiers, clothes, newspapers, barettes, and so on were scattered haphazardly throughout. The crowded circumstances didn't help. Two adults and four young children lived in that two-bedroom, one-bath house.

Dee-Dee claimed that the children were fairly quiet and well behaved when their father was home, but the minute he left, all hell broke loose. Beverly didn't blame any of them. Anytime she was forced to spend more than a minute or two with Frankie, she wanted to scream also.

Thus, they arrived while the older children were running around making as much noise as possible, and Dee-Dee was trying to bathe the baby and get him ready for bed. In an attempt to restore enough calm that they could have a conversation, Hope and Beverly corralled the three wild things and convinced them to play a quiet game while Dee-Dee was with the baby.

Nearly two hours passed before all the children were settled in their beds, yet even then Dee-Dee couldn't sit down and visit. The kitchen had to be cleaned up from dinner and order had to be restored to the living room before Frankie got home. He was a real stickler about coming home to a clean house.

Especially after he had been out drinking half the night.

Beverly wanted to be married and have children, but if she thought for one second that this was the way it was supposed to be, she would be happy to die an old maid. There had to be something she could do to help Dee-Dee, but what? Here in the midst of Dee-Dee's chaotic world, she couldn't seem to see a way out. Remembering Lavonda's prediction, however, made her determined to find the exit no matter how hopeless it looked.

"Have you tried practicing your shorthand?" Bev asked while the three of them picked up the clutter.

Dee-Dee snorted. "Look around. This is normal. It isn't that I don't want to plan for a better future; I just haven't got enough hours in a day."

"Didn't you say the kids are better behaved when Frankie's here?" Hope asked.

"Of course. They're scared to death of him. But I can't let him see me doing something like practicing shorthand. He doesn't even like to see me read a magazine if he's in the same room. God forbid he might need another beer and my brain is occupied elsewhere."

Beverly knew she wasn't exaggerating. "I realize it's easy for us to give you advice when we're not the ones who have to follow it, but I have something to tell you that I hope will give you a push to try a little harder to find a way out."

Considering the prior evidence, it didn't take much to convince Dee-Dee of Beverly's time-travel story. Not only did Hope back it up with her eyewitness account, but Dee-Dee herself had noticed the difference between Beverly and her shadow.

Dee-Dee's response wasn't changed by the new information, however. "It isn't that I don't believe some awful thing is going to happen. I just can't see a way to prevent it. No matter how I look at it, it comes down to money. Frankie's paycheck isn't great, but we have a roof over our heads and food on the table.

"It would be lovely if some wealthy man came along and swept me and the children off to his villa in France, but I had to give up on fairy tales a long time ago. And as to breaking away on my own ... well, there's no reason to go through all that again. Thinking about it just depresses the hell out of me. You know what's really sad? Between Frankie and the kids and this house, I don't even have time to curl up in a ball and be depressed."

Beverly had no argument to offer. She was feeling depressed from simply being in that house for a few hours. As they were leaving, however, she still felt compelled to try to cheer Dee-Dee up. "When I talk to Lavonda, I'm going to ask her more about you. Maybe she'll be willing to give me a little extra reward for my accomplishment, like letting you win the Irish Sweepstakes, or something." They hugged, and Bev promised to call if she learned anything helpful from Lavonda.

On the way home, they stopped at Lavonda's

house, but it was completely dark inside, and again, there was no answer to Beverly's knock.

"Maybe there's still something more you're supposed to do before you can see her again," Hope said.

"More?" Bev asked, but what she was really thinking about was what she would do if Lavonda was no longer here.

"Yeah. You said she told you that for the magic to work, you had to solve this thing on your own, without a lot of guidance from her. Right?"

"Right."

"Then it would make sense that you have to go ahead with whatever else had to be done without her help or any more reassurance before you can be rewarded for your good deed."

Beverly brightened. "A test of my goodness, to see if I'm truly worthy? Yes. That sounds possible. And I like that a whole lot better than thinking she's abandoned me, and I'll never be able to get back to Josh."

She recalled something else. "Each time she gave me a bottle she said a French phrase that she translated to 'We will see each other again.' I have to trust that. But what else—" She snapped her fingers. "Of course. I haven't really succeeded until the police are satisfied that Mason Colby is innocent. I'll bet Lavonda will be back as soon as they complete their questioning at Pete's."

"I agree. Now, I don't know about you, but after spending an evening in the Giammarco house, I could really use a hot fudge sundae." When Beverly frowned at her, she added, "I swear, I'll digest every fattening calorie and start my new diet in the morning." Her vow was confirmed by crossing her heart and holding up two fingers. "Scout's honor."

"We were never Scouts," Beverly countered.

Hope wrinkled her nose. "Okay, I swear, if I break that promise, I'll turn Jacob down when he asks me to marry him."

Beverly smiled. "Hot fudge it is." Now if she could only solve Dee-Dee's problem as easily.

Between all of Beverly's news and the visit with Dee-Dee, Hope hadn't had a chance to talk about Jacob yet. But she made up for it over the next several hours. Beverly was more than happy to listen to every detail of how utterly perfect the man was. After all, she planned to leave soon, and this might be the last time she and her best friend would be together like this.

They stayed up talking part of the night and had breakfast together before Beverly went to work. Hope reminded her that she and Jacob were having dinner with her family that night and made her swear not to disappear until she got to see her one more time.

It was easy to agree to that since she had yet to speak to Lavonda. Without the Gypsy's help, she wasn't going anywhere. She wished she could be as optimistic as Hope, to be absolutely certain that it was just a matter of waiting for the police to clear Mason's name.

Unfortunately, she knew from personal experience that no matter how much you wanted something, that didn't mean you were going to get it.

Chapter 14

The police arrived at the diner shortly after Bev got there Sunday morning, and a dozen people testified to the fact that Mason Colby had been there Friday night. To her dismay, her name came up every time. So much for staying in the background. She supposed that she could have found another, more indirect way to draw attention to Mason, but it was too late now.

Before she left, she asked Pete for Monday and Tuesday off. She hoped that by the time she vanished and her shadow replaced her, the excitement would have vanished as well. As it turned out, the spilled stew incident was already old news by Sunday afternoon.

From the moment she entered her parents' home, she made an effort to be more attentive to them, to embrace them longer than she normally would, and to be extraordinarily patient with all the little things that usually made her want to go running from the house as soon as possible.

She complimented her mother's pot roast dinner until the woman was blushing with pride. She asked her father about how things were going at the plant, then actually listened to his answer. These were such small things, yet it clearly pleased them enormously. It hadn't occurred to her that she had been so neglectful in the past. Her decision to leave this time had been made, but she determined to pay her parents at least one more visit before she did.

As to her brother, she had to admit that she simply hadn't really looked at him in some time, and it surprised her to see what a sullen young man he had become. The great difference in their ages had kept them from ever behaving as a typical brother and sister. She had always felt more like an aunt. When he was little, she babied him, then played with him as an adult would, but as he matured, he had no use for her.

When Allen finished eating and got up from the table, she excused herself and followed him. "I want to talk to you for a minute, Al."

He continued walking toward his room. "About what?"

She followed him, but stopped in his doorway. "May I come in?" He gave her an indifferent shrug and dropped onto his bed. She moved his desk chair close to him and sat down. "I realize you and I have never been best buddies"—he rolled his eyes—"but we've always gotten along. You also have to admit that I have never butted my nose into your business."

He loudly cracked his knuckles. "Is this show going to get any better? If not, I'd like to change the station."

She narrowed her eyes at him. "Listen, buster, I used to change your diapers, so don't go getting smart-alecky with me. I've heard some rumors, and if they're true, I want to offer my help."

"You mean *advice*?" he asked sarcastically.

"If necessary. I was thinking more along the lines of listening to you."

He made a face. "What do you want to know?"

"Have you started hanging out with a tough crowd?"

His expression let her know she wasn't the first to voice her concern about the company he was keeping, and it agitated him. "They're just guys."

"From what I heard, these *guys* like to get drunk, travel to other neighborhoods and pick fights with other *guys*. And sometimes, just for an extra kick, the way they get to those other neighborhoods is in a stolen car." The way his gaze darted to her then away told her she had hit a bull's-eye. "Aw geez, Al. You're too smart to get yourself into that kind of mess."

"Oh, yeah?" he responded belligerently. "Well maybe I want to go to jail. At least then I—" He got up from the bed and walked over to stare out his window.

Beverly had to organize her thoughts before approaching him. What could possibly be so bad in his life that he would rather go to jail than face it? She tried to remember how she had felt at seventeen, but all she could recall was being in love with Billy and making plans for the future. She had never had a rebellious bone in her body.

"Al? Please talk to me. You know you can trust me not to repeat anything you say. And if I try to give you advice you don't want to hear, you can tell me to shut up, and I will." She watched his shoulders slump and his head bow. He was weakening. "Please. Sit back down and tell me why jail looks more appealing than this house." As soon as she said those words, she began to guess at the answer.

As a teenager, she was anxious to get out of this house, away from her parents, to be a grown-up, but she had always had something to look forward to. All she had had to do was be patient until the time was right. Allen had never been a very patient child, and it didn't sound like he had anything to look forward to. She heard him sigh and decided to test her assumption.

"You want your freedom, don't you?" He turned toward her, but didn't give her a verbal confirmation. "You graduate from high school in two and a half months. That's not such a long time."

"Graduate?" Defiance made his eyes glow with emotion as he came back to where she was sitting. "What good will that do? I'll still be here, in this house. The only difference is I'll be working at the plant full-time all summer. Maybe that wouldn't be so bad if I could use the money to get a car and my own place, but I have to put it all away for college. And then I'm looking at more years of school and homework that I don't care about, and working every spare hour I have at a job I hate. For what? Can you answer that, sis? For what? I'll tell you for what. 'Cause Pop couldn't go to college. Haven't you heard him? 'I want my son to have all the advantages I didn't.' He doesn't care what I want!" He slumped back down on the bed.

"What is it that *you* want?"

He made a face. "What's it matter?"

"It matters. If all you want is the freedom to hang out with hoodlums and waste your life, then I can't argue with Pop's thinking. But if you have something else in mind, I'd like to hear it."

"You'll think it's dumb."

"I dare you to tell me," she challenged, hoping that route might work.

He hesitated for another few seconds, then reached under the bed and pulled out a sketch pad. It took him another few seconds to decide to hand it over to her.

She raised the cover and stared in shock. It was a perfectly scaled-down drawing of an automobile. Not just any car mind you, but a car of the future. In fact, she was certain it looked exactly like the first sports car that had caught her eye at The Bullpen when she originally traveled to 1996. "Dear God, Al. I can hardly believe it. This is beautiful. I had no idea you could draw at all, let alone something like this. Where did you come up with the design idea?"

His fair cheeks pinkened. "I made it up," he said with a mixture of embarrassment and pride. As she looked at the following pages, he continued. "I see all these cars in my head and I just, well, it's like I can't stand to just leave them there. I have to put them on paper."

"You have to do something with this, Al. You have a tremendous amount of talent."

He shrugged and pinkened a bit more. Praise and encouragement were obviously not things he was getting a lot of in this house. "When I showed Pop one of my drawings, he told me to stop wasting my time. Artists don't get rich, he said. He wants me to major in business so I can be management instead of a laborer like him." He met Bev's eyes with a look of desperation. "I can't do it, Bev. I can't be what he wants me to be."

"So you figure if you get into enough trouble ... what? Are you hoping he'll throw you out in the street? What would you do then? I can promise you, you'd be so busy struggling to survive, you wouldn't have time to do any drawing." She grasped Al's hand. "It doesn't have to be like that. I know it's hard, but you need to be patient to get what you want.

"You can make a good living at this. Americans love cars. And I'm absolutely certain that what you've drawn are exactly what they're going to look like in the future. But you need to be more than an artist. You have to go to college and take engineering, so that you understand everything about automobiles in order to design them. You could end up working for Ford or Studebaker.

"If you're worried about bucking Pop, let him think you're majoring in business the first year. I don't think what you study is as important to him as the fact that you're studying to better yourself. Remember, you're *the son*. That gives you a lot more power than I ever had. But use that power in a smart way and you'll both end up happy."

One corner of his mouth curved upward. "Since when did you get to be so smart?"

Smiling, she ruffled his hair. "Wisdom comes with age, my child. Besides, I had a very special birthday this year."

She left her parents' house feeling confident that she had accomplished even more than she had hoped to. Of course, she had to admit that she might not have been able to offer Allen so much encouragement if she hadn't already seen the future for herself. Besides that, according to Hope, her shadow had made no attempt whatsoever to talk with him.

So far, her risky adventure had given her the ability to help two people who had nothing to do with Mason Colby. Hope's and Allen's futures might just be a little brighter now than they would have been had she not taken a chance.

Only one item was left on her list—the visit with Lavonda. She had fulfilled her part of the bargain. Now she wanted her reward.

Her faith faltered when she pulled into Lavonda's driveway and the house looked the same as it had for the last several days. All the blinds were drawn, and there was no hint of a light coming from inside. She sat behind the wheel of her car, staring at the front door, wondering what she would do if, as before, she knocked and no one answered. What if Lavonda was gone for good? How could she possibly find her?

How could she live without Josh, now that he had reawakened her heart? And Mr. Fisk. She wanted so very much to see that dear man again.

She was nearly paralyzed with the fear of discovering that Lavonda was gone, yet she couldn't drive away without confirming it. She looked down at the door handle, and taking a deep breath, made herself open the door and step out. When she looked up again, her worries vanished.

The front door of the house was open and Lavonda was standing there smiling at her.

"*Bonjour, ma petite*. Eet eez a beautiful day, *oui*?"

Beverly ran to the Gypsy and hugged her, in spite of the fact that they had never shared such an affectionate greeting before. "I can't tell you how happy I am to see you!"

Lavonda nodded. "I am sorry I could not be here for you before. Eet was not possible until zee task was a fait accompli. And though I am here now, eet can only be for a short time, and we have many things to discuss. Come een."

As Beverly made herself at home in Lavonda's workroom, she noticed something different about the way the Gypsy was looking at her, or perhaps it was just a different look in her eyes. Yes, that was it. She had always seemed rather sad, and today she seemed . . . *happy*.

It made her think of the time in Mr. Fisk's house when Josh told her he had never felt happy until he had been with her. Lavonda's eyes now reminded her of his. In fact, so much so that she wondered how she hadn't noticed it before.

"You have done well," Lavonda said, settling into her chair across from Beverly.

Beverly didn't realize how much she had needed to hear that until the words were out. "Then it *was* Mason Colby whose life I was supposed to save."

"*Oui.* Mason, his wife, and his son. By opening your eyes and your heart, you changed their lives."

"Do they ever find out who the real killer was?"

"When eet eez clear that someone tried to frame him for zee murder, zee police will investigate more better than they deed originally. Now the true murderer will be caught and punished."

"I'm so glad. That does mean I can go back to Josh, doesn't it?"

Lavonda nodded slowly. "Eef that eez your wish, I can give eet to you. But you should understand that things are no longer as they were. You have changed circumstances for Josh."

"I don't care what his circumstances are. I love him with all my heart, and I want to marry him and have his children, whether he's a construction worker, a garbage collector, or the president of the United States."

"*Bien*. I must tell you also that eef you go forward again, eet will be your last journey. You will not be able to return to thees time."

"I assumed that was how it would be, and I've made the decision that if I have to say goodbye to everyone here in order to be with Josh, then that is what I must do."

"*Bien*. But your goodbyes would seem foolish to zee people here, as your shadow will continue with zee life you would have had without a change."

Beverly frowned. "I don't understand. I thought you said my shadow and I could not continue on two separate paths for any length of time, nor could we ever be in the same time and place."

"That eez correct. I know that you are aware of zee swelling een your breast, and that you have been to zee doctor here in thees time."

Lavonda's psychic abilities never ceased to amaze Beverly, regardless of how much she had witnessed. "Yes, and he told me it was nothing to worry about."

"He eez wrong. Though you must not blame him. He deed not know any better. At thees moment, eet eez not so bad, but een zee next three years, zee swelling will grow and change into a deadly cancer that will spread throughout your body. Your shadow will fade away, naturally in 1961."

Beverly could hardly believe her ears. "Fade away? You mean *die*?"

"*Oui.*"

"Dear God in heaven. Then that means my life was on the line here also." Suddenly, she felt angry. "Why didn't you tell me that?"

"I could not. For zee magic to work, you could not be concerned with yourself, and I could not tell you of your fate until you chose to live een zee future and not look back."

Beverly had to let that shocking discovery sink in before going on. "I'm very confused. Do I have a chance to live happily in the future, or not?"

"Een zee future, *oui*. Eef you go to see a doctor there and attend to zee swelling before eet changes."

Beverly exhaled with relief. "I can do that. And I'll keep going to see doctors until I find one who knows what's wrong and can take care of it."

"You will need zee money."

"Yes, I realized that, but I think I've got that problem solved."

"*Bien.* And I have something for you that you will need to smooth your path to your new life." She rose and went to her special cabinet.

Beverly was expecting another bottle of potion, and she could see Lavonda was holding one in her left hand, but first she handed her an official-looking document. "A birth certificate?" she asked, scanning the printed words. When she saw the name and birth date, she understood.

It said that she, Beverly Newcastle, was born in Mercerville, New Jersey, March 30, 1966. With this document, she could acquire a new driver's license, a marriage license, and so on. It wasn't strictly honest, but she couldn't manage very well without it.

"Do not ask how I do thees thing," Lavonda said before she could ask. "Eet eez a bonus for your good deed. But be warned, zee birth certificate eez only a piece of paper. Eet does not change reality here. You must not call such attention to yourself that would cause someone to investigate your past, for they would discover zee lie. Here eez another thing you must have."

She handed Beverly a social security card with her name on it. "Thees number eez listed in zee government records, so you should not raise questions when you file zee taxes. You must depend on your imagination to make up zee rest of your new life. You will, how you say, *improvise*."

She then placed the bottle on the table in front of Beverly. This one was made entirely of glistening mother of pearl, and the stopper was shaped like a seashell. "Drink eet only when you are absolutely certain you are ready to leave for good."

Beverly stood up clutching the bottle in one hand and her new identification in the other. "I understand." She could not resist giving Lavonda another hug. "Thank you. I don't know why you chose me, but I will be eternally grateful that you did."

Lavonda smiled at her. "I chose you, *ma petite*, because you were going to be leaving thees time soon anyway. Yet that alone would not have been enough. You were successful because of zee goodness in your heart. So eet eez I that must thank you for what you have done. Someday you will understand. *Adieu et bonne chance*, Beverly Newcastle."

"Before I go, I was hoping you could tell me how

I could help my friend Dee-Dee. I don't want anything bad to happen to her or her children."

Lavonda closed her eyes and took a slow breath. When she looked at Beverly again, she said, "Zee answer will come to you very soon."

Beverly was on her way out the front door before she realized that Madame Lavonda had not said her usual farewell line: *Nous nous verrons encore.* But then, she supposed it was unrealistic to think that they might see each other again someday.

Her mind raced the whole way home. She had succeeded! She could return to Josh and get married and live happily ever after!

From elation, her thoughts plummeted to desolation as she considered what her life would have held for her had she not been willing to take the risk of changing it. She would be dead in three years. She hadn't asked the exact day. She didn't really want to know.

Her heart filled with sadness as she realized that, although she would be happy in her new life in the future, only Hope and Dee-Dee would know about that. Her parents, Allen, and the rest of her friends and acquaintances would see her deteriorate with disease. They would cry at her funeral. She wished there was a way she could tell everyone that she was going to be fine, but that was completely illogical. No matter what she told them today, the minute her shadow returned, she would deny such a ridiculous story.

Who would believe it anyway, besides Hope and Dee-Dee? Peggy might, but she had more than she could handle in her head already.

Like a balloon popping in her own head, an idea

occurred to Beverly. There might not be anything she could do to spare her family and friends from heartache, but her death could be beneficial to someone.

As soon as she got home she located the insurance policy Billy had taken out for her just before they got married. It was a simple term-life policy with a low premium, so she had kept it up. The death benefit was twenty-five thousand dollars, which had seemed like an awful lot of money at the time. After Billy's death, she had changed the beneficiary to her mother.

It would be dishonest to increase the amount, knowing how soon it would have to be paid, but there was no reason she couldn't change the beneficiary again. She could take care of that piece of business first thing tomorrow morning.

Since she had already warned Josh that it might take a while for her to return, she knew he wouldn't be expecting her back so soon anyway.

She was about to get out of her uniform and take a shower when there was a knock at the door. Her visitors were the last two people on earth she had expected to see.

"M-m-mister Colby!" she stuttered upon opening the door and seeing him and his wife. She was even lovelier than her pictures. He was holding a beautiful bouquet of dozens of pink roses and white baby's breath.

"I hope you don't mind our dropping in on you like this," he said, "but a phone call or note just wasn't enough. We stopped by the diner first to say hello and return the cook's uniform, but they said you had left sometime ago. Pete gave us your address." He smiled down at the petite, dark-haired woman at his side. "Lucille, this is Beverly Newcastle, the waitress who spilled the stew on me and washed my clothes."

Lucille stepped forward and gave Beverly a kiss on each cheek. "I am so very pleased to meet you."

"These are for you," Mason said, thrusting the bouquet at Beverly. "Lucille thought you sounded like someone who would like pink."

"Pink is my favorite color of roses," Beverly replied, taking the flowers from him. "But I hardly think I deserve these just for rinsing off a shirt and pants that I dirtied to begin with." Despite her unease, she felt she had no choice but to invite them in for a visit. "Please come in and let me get you something to drink."

"My heavens, no," Lucille said. "You've been serving people all day, and you haven't even had a chance to get out of your uniform. We'll just be going—"

"I insist," Bev interrupted and drew her inside the apartment. "You drove a very long way to get here. At least come in and catch your breath before going back."

"I think you misunderstood about the flowers," Mason said as he closed Beverly's door. "It was our way of saying thank you for keeping me out of jail."

She knew exactly what he was talking about, but she wasn't sure how much she would have known if it wasn't for Lavonda. "Jail? The police came into Pete's this morning asking about you, but they didn't tell us what it was all about."

"I'll tell you what," Lucille said. "Let me get the roses in water and serve *you* a cold drink, while Mason fills you in."

"That would be very nice. Thank you. There's a vase in the cabinet under the sink. Soda pop in the fridge, and glasses over the counter."

Lucille took the flowers from her and headed for the kitchen while Beverly and Mason sat down.

Mason leaned forward with his hands clasped and his elbows on his knees. Beverly had seen Josh take the same pose when he was explaining something to her. "The reason the police questioned all of you was that I was suspected of murdering my boss Friday night."

Beverly gasped, as she supposed would be appropriate. "How terrible."

"His murder wasn't as big of a surprise as you might think. He was a mean, thieving, son-of-a— Pardon me. He wasn't a good man. Half the men that worked for him had an argument with him at one time or another. He was forever shortchanging our pay, or *forgetting* to pay us overtime after we'd worked, or docking us for the dumbest reason. Unfortunately for me, that day I was the man who everyone heard arguing with him.

"It had been raining pretty hard. Everything was slippery, and there was still a flash or two of lightning in the sky. But he was demanding that I get back to work. By the way, I'm a high-steel worker. And I'm real good at it, but I don't have a death wish. Well, we had it out. He called me names, and I called him a few right back. Then he told me if I didn't get to work, I was fired. There was a little shoving, then I walked out. That was the last time I saw him, and he was still alive.

"I went to the corner and had a couple beers to cool down." He bowed his head sheepishly. "I guess

I didn't have quite enough. I was still steaming when I got home. I don't usually let my temper get the best of me, but I was so mad I *could* have killed him. I really needed that job." He paused for a moment and glanced toward the kitchen. "You see, Lucille and I have been wanting to start a family and she'd get so excited every time we talked about it. I didn't want to tell her I'd been fired."

Beverly had to keep reminding herself that this wasn't Josh. Mason even made the same kind of face when he was feeling guilty. "So you ended up picking a fight with her instead."

"Yes, he did," Lucille confirmed as she came in and set a tray of cold drinks on the table. As she handed them each a glass of soda pop, she said, "And it made so little sense, that I knew something was terribly wrong, but he just stormed out the door instead of talking to me. I'm sure you know how men can be sometimes.

"Of course, now it turned out that that was the best thing he could have done, because while someone was murdering his boss, you accidentally gave my husband an airtight alibi. It might have been difficult to prove that he'd stayed home with me all evening."

Beverly almost reminded them of their nosy neighbor who kept track of all their comings and goings, but she stopped herself in time.

Mason continued the story. "Saturday, a man called the police, anonymously, and told them they saw me going into the boss's office, carrying a pipe, after I thought everyone had gone, that there was a loud argument, then I came out and threw the pipe in the back of my truck. When the police checked the truck,

they found the pipe, with blood and hair on it. I
didn't even know there had been a murder until they
tried to arrest me."

Lucille jumped in at that point. "As soon as the police told him when and where the murder occurred,
all Mason had to do was tell them the truth about
where he'd been, and you, and the stew, and the
other people he'd met at the diner. The story was so
extraordinary and so easy to verify, they ended up
only telling him to stay home until they could check
it all out."

"Have they found the real murderer yet?" Beverly
asked.

Mason shook his head. "No, but when they do, I
hope I get him alone for a few minutes before they
lock him up."

"Mason," Lucille said in a warning tone. "You
promised."

He made a face, but he conceded. "Yeah, I promised. I'll let the law handle it." He laced his fingers
with hers and kissed the back of her hand.

He was rewarded with a loving smile, and he returned one that was exactly the way Josh smiled at
Beverly. Suddenly she remembered what else had
happened Friday night. When Mason returned home,
they not only made up, they made a baby. A teeny
tiny Josh was inside Lucille right this minute. That
thought brought happy tears to her eyes, and she
quickly got up so they wouldn't notice. "If you'll excuse me for just a minute, I'd love to get out of this
uniform. The special today was liver and onions, and
that's all I can smell."

When she returned to the living room, she was
completely composed again. She could tell by the

flush on Lucille's cheeks that Mason had taken the opportunity to steal a few kisses.

To his credit, he drew Bev's attention to himself. "I also meant to thank you for introducing me to Ray and Oscar. What a pair of wise guys. And I mean wise. I was feeling so low when I walked into Pete's. I didn't know how I was going to tell Lucille what happened, or how I'd get her to forgive me for being so stupid. You know what they said?"

Beverly laughed. "Knowing the two of them, I wouldn't even make a guess."

"They said, buy her flowers, get down on my knees and apologize, then tell her the truth, especially about how I feel inside. They said the best way to keep my marriage a happy one was to always let her know what I was thinking, and never try to hide anything, not even to protect her from bad news."

Lucille smiled. "Personally, I liked the advice about always apologizing, even when you believe she's wrong."

"Like I said, they were a real couple of wise guys."

They chatted a little longer, but then Lucille reminded him that they still had a long drive home.

After they left, Beverly headed for the shower, but her mind was busy sorting out the problem presented by Mason and Lucille's unexpected visit. Now that she had changed history, what if they are still alive in 1996? They might not recall precisely what she looked like, but they wouldn't forget her general appearance. And there was a strong possibility that they might remember her name. They definitely would remember where she was from. How could she explain such an enormous coincidence?

Looking back on the evening, one thing had struck

her as very interesting. Josh had told her he never got to know his father, and yet they had similar mannerisms and facial expressions, besides looking nearly identical.

That was it. If an explanation became necessary, she would say she was the daughter of the Beverly Newcastle they had met. She had been given the same name as her mother because ... because why? Although a lot of fathers and sons shared the same name, she had never heard of a mother and daughter doing so.

Considering the fact that the original Beverly will have died long before then, she decided that a logical reason for the same names could be because her mother had died in childbirth. They didn't need to know she died five years before the new Beverly's birth certificate claimed she was born.

Lavonda had told her to improvise, but whenever possible, she wanted to have answers already made up before she was asked. Before she went to sleep, she got a small notebook and a pen and began to create a life history for herself. As long as she had everything written down, she could memorize it and avoid getting her answers mixed up later.

First thing Monday morning, she went to the office of her insurance agent and did not leave until she was certain everything would be handled the way she wanted. She signed a form that officially added Dee-Dee Giammarco as a second beneficiary. When her shadow died, her mother would get $12,500, which would cover funeral expenses and still leave some to help with Allen's college. That same amount would go to Dee-Dee. As an extra precaution, she prepaid the policy premium for four years, counting one for good measure.

When she got back home, she wrote Dee-Dee a letter, ordering her to use the money to buy her freedom. She warned her that she would check up on her in the future to make sure she had done it. She sealed the letter and the policy in an envelope to give to Hope for safekeeping.

With Dee-Dee taken care of, it was finally time to make her final preparations. So as not to overly upset her shadow, she decided to take only the clothes and shoes she was wearing. She had left enough with Josh to get by for a while longer.

She had gone by the bank on her way back from the insurance office and cashed her paycheck. That, plus all her tips, and the cash she had left from her window dressing job, came to almost four hundred dollars. She had her pile of comic books, but she had no idea how long it would take to convert those items to cash. Even though she and Josh were going to be husband and wife soon, she didn't want to arrive on his doorstep without some money of her own.

Looking at the Elvis Presley album, she decided, regretfully, that she would have to leave it there. If her shadow had been upset over missing shoes, she would go crazy if the album disappeared. Then she realized all she had to do was go to a store and buy another one to take with her.

What else? Perhaps she could take a memento or two that wouldn't be readily missed. With that thought, she got her souvenir box down from her closet shelf and began going through the same items she had when she had been looking for the James Dean packet.

Minutes after she began her walk down memory lane, her heart nearly leapt out of her chest.

The James Dean packet was back in the box, exactly where it had been before.

Chapter 15

How could the packet have gotten back in the box? She had left it in Josh's apartment. The previous time that she had popped back unexpectedly, her purse and shoes had stayed in his apartment and were still there when she returned to him. Why would this be any different?

She tried to think of what else she had left with Josh. With a little effort, she remembered what she was wearing the day she popped onto the construction site. Quickly she checked her drawers, the closet, and then the hall closet where they kept their coats and jackets. With each step, her heart pounded a bit harder. It was all there. The jeans, the sweater, the shoes, and the jacket. Everything she thought she had left behind at Josh's was now back here.

She didn't know what this meant. Lavonda had said Josh's circumstances had been changed by her act, but what did that have to do with her things? She gathered that outfit and placed the clothing with the comic books and the James Dean packet. There was no reason to leave those pieces behind since her shadow had already lost track of them.

She had a strong feeling that the return of her things held a terribly important meaning, but she couldn't imagine what it was. All she could think to do was go back and ask Lavonda. Thus, before heading to her parents' house she made a detour by Lavonda's.

She was very surprised to see a car in the driveway when she arrived, and even more stunned to read the sign that had been erected in the front yard. It welcomed visitors to tour the model home. The house looked different also. There were curtains in the windows that had not been there before, and flowering bushes had been planted on each side of the front stoop.

With her stomach churning nervously, she walked up to the front door and knocked.

A middle-aged man in a suit and tie opened the door and greeted her enthusiastically.

"Welcome to the home of the future. Would you like a tour?"

Beverly blinked and looked past him, into the living room. Lavonda's gaudy furnishings had been replaced by modern decor. "I, uh, no, I'm sorry, I . . ." She couldn't explain herself, but she collected her wits enough to ask a question. "Tell me, how long has this been a model home?"

The man looked at her curiously. "This is the first day we're open for business. Although we've been working on it for about a month to get it ready."

"A month," Beverly repeated. "I see. Thank you." She returned to her car, more confused than when she had arrived. How could Lavonda have been living here if the builder had been getting it ready to show as a model for the last month? She had no doubt that this was the same place she had been before, and her friends could confirm that. If it wasn't for Hope, Dee-Dee, and Peggy, she might wonder if she had lost her mind, or had dreamed the whole thing.

The mystery of the returned items came back to her. It was almost as if none of it had ever happened, but she remembered it too clearly for that to be true. Since Hope had come up with the correct explanation about why Lavonda had been unavailable for several days, she hoped that she might have an answer for this question as well.

She put her confusion on the back burner as she drove to her parents' house. They weren't expecting her, but she wanted to see them one more time before she left. She needed to say goodbye, without actually saying goodbye.

This visit was very much like the previous one, except that she had to stop herself from thinking about how this was the last dinner she would share with them, and how they would have to watch her shadow suffer and die, and never know that she was really okay and happy in another time and place. She felt like crying the whole time, and finally had to cut the visit short, saying she wasn't feeling well.

As she was leaving, Allen gave her a warmer hug than he had in years and whispered, "Thanks for the talk the other day. It helped a lot."

"I'm so glad. Always remember that I love you."

Hope was already home when she got to their apartment. "Boy am I glad to see you," Beverly told her. "Remember how I took the James Dean fan club stuff with me? Well it's back. And so are the clothes I wore the first time. And then when I went by Lavonda's to ask her what it all meant, her house had been turned into a model home." She stopped when she realized Hope was staring at her as though she were unbalanced. "What's the matter?"

Hope shook her head. "I was hoping you'd tell me. I didn't understand any of what you just said. Who's Lavonda? And what was that you said about James Dean's fan club?"

Beverly's nervous stomach acted up again. Hope didn't appear to be pulling her leg. "I'm sorry. I'm having a little dizzy spell. Would you mind getting me a glass of water?"

As Hope hurried to the kitchen, Bev really did feel dizzy and sat down before she fell. Something was wrong, and she wasn't sure how to get to the bottom of it. She looked in her purse and saw the three empty potion bottles and the new mother-of-pearl one. And Allen had referred to their talk the other day, so that had happened. It wasn't a dream.

When Hope returned, Bev could see that her friend was truly worried about her. *Improvise,* Lavonda had said. She took a slow sip of water to give herself another moment to think of how to proceed.

"Are you feeling okay now?" Hope asked, searching her face for a clue. "Jacob should be here soon. Maybe you should have him take a look at you."

Okay, Bev thought, Jacob was real. "That won't be necessary. I had a glass of sherry after dinner at Mom's. I guess it was stronger than I thought."

Hope sat down, satisfied that Bev's color had returned. "But what was all that you said when you came in? James Dean and . . . what was that other name?"

"Lavonda. Doesn't that name mean anything to you?" She watched Hope's face and knew she was telling the truth.

"No. Should I?"

"I guess not." Beverly needed to know exactly what was as she remembered and what had changed. "I know this is going to sound crazy, but I had the oddest dream last night, and I guess it was still in my head. You, Dee-Dee, and Peggy took me to a Gypsy fortune-teller for my birthday."

Hope laughed. "No kidding. How'd I get you to do something like that? A gun and a blindfold?"

Beverly was trying to piece the facts together, but her brain was going in ten directions at once. "I don't remember, but the Gypsy told you that you were going to marry a doctor."

Hope wiggled her eyebrows. "I like this dream. Did she say how much longer I have to wait before Jacob asks me?"

Beverly smiled. "Sorry. Can't help you there. She also told Dee-Dee about . . . something bad that was going to happen. Wait, I'll be right back." She went to her room, got the sealed envelope containing the life insurance policy and letter to Dee-Dee, and showed it to Hope.

"I took that part of the dream as a sort of omen and I did something about it. I'm not going to tell you what, and I want your sworn promise that you'll put this away somewhere safe and never mention it to anyone, including me. If anything ever happens to me, I want you to open this envelope."

Hope took the envelope, but she was back to wondering about Beverly's sanity. "Are you sure you're feeling all right?"

"Yes, but I'd like to ask you a couple of questions . . . just to make sure I've got the dream separated from reality. When and how did you meet Jacob?"

Hope answered in spite of her doubts. "In the emergency room, March 31st. When Stanley had his false alarm."

"Did the Grangers' house catch fire, and is Nina pregnant?"

"Yes and yes."

The pink roses caught Bev's eye. "Were those roses from a man named Mason Colby, because I spilled stew on him Friday night?"

Hope grinned. "They were and you did. Unfortunately, it was the closest you've come to having an exciting evening in years."

"Have I ever talked to you about traveling in time to the future?"

Hope laughed. "You? Miss I'm-Perfectly-Content-With-My-Life-The-Way-It-Is? I can't even get you to travel to Trenton, let alone into the future."

Bev tried to shrug it off. "I told you it was a crazy dream. One more thing. Did we have a conversation about . . . your eating habits?"

Hope finished. "Yes. And you don't need to keep bringing it up. I gave you my promise, and I intend to keep it. By the way, I peeked in your room when I got home. What are all the comic books for?"

"Oh, they're, um, for Allen. I forgot to take them with me today." Before Beverly could think of another question, Jacob arrived and Hope's attention was lost.

Before the couple left, Bev gave Hope a hug goodbye and held back all the words she had intended to say. They would only give Hope more reason to worry about her state of mind. As she went into her bedroom, she went over what she had learned.

Almost everything was as it should be. Only circumstances directly connected with Lavonda had changed. The bottles in her purse were proof enough for her to believe it had happened, but all other evidence of Lavonda's existence was gone. Perhaps she was an angel come to earth to make things right, and now that they were, only Beverly retained a memory of her.

She would probably never know for sure.

Feeling much less certain about everything, she decided to pack a few more essentials for her trip, whether it upset her shadow or not. By nine o'clock, she was ready to leave. Her money and new identification were in her purse. The comic books, James Dean packet, and a few souvenirs and photos were packed in a small suitcase with her clothes, toothbrush, and the like.

After one last look around her bedroom, she removed the seashell stopper from the bottle and downed the sparkling liquid. She waited for the kaleidoscope to whisk her away, but it didn't come. Instead she was slowly enveloped by darkness. There was no sense of movement, no sights or sounds; she merely floated in a void for an unmeasured time.

"May I help you, miss?" a man's voice politely asked.

She raised her eyelids and rapidly scanned herself and her surroundings. She was dressed as she was before. She had her purse, her suitcase, and the pretty bottle in her hands. She was standing in front of the double glass doors of a tall building. A uniformed man was on the other side of the doors, speaking to her through an intercom. Behind him was a luxurious lobby.

"Miss? Are you all right?"

Since the potion had always taken her directly to Josh, she hadn't expected it to be any different this time. Not knowing what else to say, she said, "I'm looking for Josh Colby. I understood I could find him here."

The man smiled. "Yes, ma'am."

That didn't tell her if he lived or worked here. Either way, it was obvious that what Lavonda had said about Josh's circumstances having changed was true. She put the bottle into her purse then tried to open the door, but it was bolted shut. That got her a reproving look. "May I come in, please?"

"One moment." He picked a clipboard. "Your name, please."

"Beverly Newcastle. I'm a friend of Josh's. He didn't know exactly what time I'd be arriving—"

"I'm sorry, there's no preauthorization for that name."

She was trying to be patient. "Well, would you please tell him I'm here?"

"I would, but he's not available at the moment, and I can't let you in without his authorization."

Josh had taught her all about the need for security in New York, but this was ridiculous. Then again, she was only assuming that was where she was since she didn't dare ask such a dumb question. "When is he expected to be available?"

"I'm not at liberty to say."

Don't get mad, Beverly. Get smart. Improvise. "Okay. Fine. Is there a motel nearby?"

"There is a fine *hotel* a few blocks north and west of here, or I could call you a taxi to take you . . . elsewhere."

She understood what he was implying. This was not a motel kind of neighborhood. "I'd appreciate your calling me a taxi. And could you give me Josh's phone number so that I could call him after I'm settled somewhere?"

"I'm not at liberty to release his private number."

"Would you at least leave a message for him?" He nodded and picked up a pen to write on the clipboard. "Tell him . . ." She couldn't even say where he could reach her. This wasn't the way it was supposed to be. "Never mind. I'll just try to catch him again tomorrow."

Her despair must have touched a soft spot in the doorman's heart, and he gave away more than he was at liberty to do. "I'm sorry, miss, that would be a wasted trip. In fact, Mr. Colby is not expected back until the end of the week."

"Oh. I see. Well, thank you for telling me." Something was very wrong about this.

"I'll call for a taxi now."

The cab arrived minutes later, and she thanked the doorman for his help, as little as it was.

As soon as she got in the car, she asked the driver, "How far is it to New Rochelle?"

He looked at her in the rear-view mirror. "This *is* New Rochelle, lady. Have you got an address?"

She gave him Mr. Fisk's address and prayed that he was home and had stayed up late, as usual. After what had happened at the apartment building, she asked the driver to wait while she made sure Mr. Fisk was home.

A white-haired woman answered the door.

"Is Mr. Fisk home?" Beverly asked, trying not to look too surprised at seeing the woman.

"Mr. Fisk? I'm sorry, there's no one here by that name." She tapped a finger to her cheek and looked thoughtful. "There's a Fisher family at the end of the block, but I don't know any Fisks."

Beverly forced herself to ask the next question. "How ... how long have you lived here?"

The woman had to think about that as well. "It will be twenty-three years this August."

"Thank you. I'm sorry I bothered you."

"Why, it was no bother at all. Perhaps you have the wrong street."

"Yes, I'm sure that's it. Thank you." Beverly was getting more nauseated by the minute. What was she to do now? Recalling that there was a motel near the mall, she told the driver to take her there.

The night manager was somewhat reluctant to accept her as a guest without a credit card, but when she offered to pay for two nights in cash in advance plus a fifty-dollar security deposit, the woman gave her a room.

Only when she was alone in her room did Beverly give in to the tears she had been fighting for hours. It was bad enough that she had to leave her family and friends behind and that Hope had lost her memory of Lavonda and her time-traveling adventures. To have arrived here without a soul to welcome her was devastating.

How had Josh come to live in such a fancy building? Why hadn't she popped to wherever he was, or at least inside his apartment? Where was Mr. Fisk? How had what she had done for Mason Colby in 1958 affected where Mr. Fisk lived in 1996?

Pulling herself together, she found the telephone book and looked up his name. He wasn't listed, but the toy store was. She had to go to the collectibles store tomorrow anyway. She would simply go see Mr. Fisk at his store.

She was about to put the phone book away, when she decided to look up Josh, just in case he was listed. He wasn't, but Mason Colby was.

Could it be the same Mason Colby whose life she had saved? Living here in New Rochelle? Of course it could. And he would know where Josh was. Whatever had gone wrong in the overall scheme of things, she now felt confident that she could get it back on track.

She had already planned out a whole story in the event that Mason was still alive and recognized her when Josh introduced them. All she had to do was turn it around. Tomorrow, she would go to his home, just as he and Lucille had once dropped in on her. She would introduce herself as the daughter of the woman who had given him the alibi that had kept him out of jail. How much conversation could it possibly take to find out where Josh was?

Certain that tomorrow would be a much more satisfying day, she slept soundly and awoke refreshed, ready to begin her new life.

The motel's breakfast buffet was surprisingly good and the front desk was able to provide her with an area map and bus schedule. When the mall opened at ten, she was already standing at the doors with a list of her comic book collection in her purse.

The first thing she noticed was the unappealing display in the toy store window. It was as if she'd never been here to redo it. A young woman was behind the counter.

"Hi," Beverly said. "Is Mr. Fisk in?" The woman frowned. "The owner, Mr. Fisk," Bev repeated.

"I'm sorry," the woman replied, shaking her head. "The owner's name is Middleton. He'll be in at three today."

"You don't know Mr. Fisk?"

The woman shook her head again. "Sorry."

"Thanks. I must have gotten the names mixed up." As she walked out, she glanced around the store and at the front display again. Mr. Fisk might not be the owner, but Mr. Middleton seemed to have the same problem with design that he had had. She would have to stop back here sometime and offer her services.

She had been counting on seeing Mr. Fisk, but she had no idea where else to look for him. It was almost as if he had never existed. Just like Lavonda. Slowly her brain put other similarities together. He'd called her "little one." She had called her *ma petite.* He had been such an enormous help to her when she had been here before, that she had called him a guardian angel. Then, just yesterday, she had been thinking that Lavonda might have been an angel.

Without any better explanation, she accepted that one as fact. She only hoped they were still looking down on her from wherever they were, because she needed all the help she could get.

Her next stop was only slightly more productive. The salesman on the floor in the collectibles store was a nice young man who reminded her of Allen, but knew next to nothing about comic books.

"I'm sorry. You'd have to talk to the owner, but to tell you the truth, I don't think he does much buying.

Most of the stuff in here is on consignment from other places or private sellers. If I had some old comic books to sell, I'd probably go to a store that specializes in them."

"Do you know where one would be?"

"No, but I know someone who would." He called a friend and came back with an address written on a scrap of paper. "He said for you to go here and don't talk to anyone but Earl. He also said to compare anything he offers you with the price list in the current *Wizard Guide to Comics.* That's kind of like the Bible in the industry."

"Thank you so much," Beverly said, putting the paper into her purse. "Did your friend happen to tell you where I'd find a *Wizard Guide*?"

"They sell them right there at the comic book store."

She thanked him again and he wished her good luck. Checking her street map, she found that the store's address was not far away, so she took a cab.

Her first shock was the size of the store. It was at least three times the size of the collectibles store in the mall and most of it seemed to be devoted to comic books. A young man was sitting behind the counter reading one of those books.

"Hi. Are you Earl?"

He dragged his gaze up from the story, then smiled broadly when he saw her. "No. I'm Kurt. Earl had to run out, but he'll be back in about a half hour. Can I help you with something?"

"Yes. I'd like to buy a current *Wizard Guide*." After she paid for it, she asked, "Would you mind if I sit down and look at this until Earl gets back?"

"We don't encourage people to sit and read here,

so there aren't any chairs, but you're welcome to hang around."

Beverly's second shock came when she figured out how to read the price guide and looked up some of the comics on her list. A few of them had little or no value, or weren't even listed. Most of them had values between two hundred and two thousand dollars.

One made her drop the book on the floor.

She had unintentionally picked up the Action Comics book in which Superman made his first appearance. Most recent sales price: One hundred twenty-four thousand dollars.

And she had left all of them in the motel room as though they were nothing but comic books! She realized selling something so valuable could call unnecessary attention to herself, so she decided not to let Earl see her entire list. She chose two to offer him— "Superman's Girlfriend, Lois Lane No. 1," $1,900, and "Challengers of the Unknown No.1," $1,400.

Earl returned on schedule, and she made sure he could see that she had been looking at a copy of the price guide as they spoke. "I was told that you might be interested in buying some old comic books. I just inherited a collection from my father."

His face remained poker straight. "That depends on what you've got and what condition they're in."

"Mint condition. Never even been read. He, uh, kept them in a special box so they wouldn't get yellow." His expression finally changed when he heard which books she was offering.

"You bring them in. I'll make you an offer when I see them."

She called for a cab and had the driver wait while

she ran to her room and fetched the two books. Before she left, she locked the rest of them in her suitcase and put the case under the bed.

Earl put on a pair of thin rubber gloves to examine the two books. "Incredible. What kind of box did your father have these in?"

Beverly shrugged. "I really don't know."

"The only time I've ever seen old issues in this good a condition was when someone kept them in a safety deposit box at a bank. Did you say you have more like this?" Earl was barely keeping his excitement under control.

She tried to remember all the little tips Mr. Fisk had given her about salesmanship. "Yes, but these are the only ones I want to sell right now."

"I'll give you fifteen hundred dollars."

She smiled. "For which one?"

He frowned. "I can't pay you book price. I have to make a profit, too. Two thousand dollars, in cash, right now."

"Make that twenty-five hundred, and I'll promise to come back to you when I'm ready to sell some more."

He asked her to stay put while he raced to his bank and back. The deal was satisfactorily completed within the hour.

At least she didn't have to worry about money this time around. She still intended to reestablish her business, however. Not only had she really enjoyed it, she wanted to be a woman of the nineties in every way, balancing home and career. But first she had to reestablish her relationship with Josh.

She returned to her motel and put on the one dress

she had brought with her. It was a simple style that she knew was still worn. Since the two times Mason had seen her she had had her hair in a ponytail, she let it hang loose now. She added a touch of lipstick for color, powdered her nose, and hoped she looked a little different, yet familiar enough for Mason to remember her.

Feeling very rich after her business deal that day, she took a cab again to go to the address listed in the phone book. She could see they were headed back toward the section of town where Josh's apartment was. Apparently the Colbys were doing quite well.

When the driver pulled up in front of a very large brick house, she asked him to wait, just in case this wasn't *her* Mason Colby after all.

A woman in a maid's uniform answered the door. Shock number . . . She quit keeping count.

"Is Mr. Colby home?" Beverly asked nervously, glancing back at the cab to make sure it hadn't left her.

"I'm sorry, he's not home yet, but Mrs. Colby is here."

"Would that be Lucille Colby?"

"Yes, that's right."

Beverly's spirits rose again. "I'd like to speak to her if she has a moment. My name is Beverly Newcastle. I believe she met my mother a long time ago, and I was hoping I could say hello."

The maid invited her in, so she waved the cab away. A few minutes later, an elegant, silver-haired woman came to greet her. She had aged, but Beverly had no trouble recognizing her. She almost said so when she remembered the part she had chosen to play.

"It's amazing," Lucille said. "You look exactly the way I remember seeing your mother." She held out her hand. "How do you do. I'm Lucille Colby. I can't tell you how many times we have thought of her over the years. How is she?"

Beverly put on a wistful expression. "She passed away when I was born. But my father had told me the story about Mason Colby and the spilled stew so often—he always called it her moment of heroism—that when I accidentally came across that name in the phone book, I had to check it out. And when your maid said your name was Lucille, I was certain you had to be the same people."

"We certainly are. Oh, Mason is going to be tickled to death to see you. You do have time to stay for dinner, don't you?"

"I don't want to put you out."

"I would be put out if you refused. Rosella! Set another place at dinner for Miss Newcastle. In fact, move dinner to the dining room. This is a very special occasion. Beverly, would you like a glass of wine or an iced tea while we wait for Mason?"

Knowing she needed her wits about her to keep her story straight, she opted for the tea.

"Two iced teas in the library, Rosella." Lucille then guided Beverly to a warm, masculine room with more books than she had ever seen in a person's home.

Lucille quickly got Beverly talking about where she had been and what she had done for the last thirty years, how she had come to New Rochelle to follow up on a business lead she had been given, and how she had accidentally come across their names. Beverly was very glad she had decided to have her whole story planned out ahead of time. She stuck close to the truth whenever possible and kept her facts simple when she had to lie.

It was also a good thing that she had memorized the details, for when Mason came home an hour late, he asked almost all the same questions Lucille had. Mason was now in his early sixties, and just as handsome as he had been when she had first seen him. It was fun to know exactly what Josh was going to look like when they grew old. She only hoped she would age as well as Lucille had. Overall, they looked fabulous for two people who had been long dead a few days ago.

Dessert was being served before they were both satisfied that they knew as much about Beverly as they possibly could.

Mason couldn't get over how much she looked like her mother. "I can't tell you how many times we've looked around us and wondered what would have happened if it wasn't for her and that damned stew."

"I'm glad you never had to find out," Beverly said, then tried to steer the conversation to the subject she was interested in. "What happened after you visited my mother? Did you ever have that family you'd planned to start?"

Mason laughed. "You even heard about that? What a memory your father must have had." He winked at Lucille. "Yes, we started our family. As a matter of fact, we're fairly certain Lucille conceived our son Josh the same night I ran into your mother."

"My goodness," Beverly said. "What a wonderful coincidence. Does your son live here with you?"

Lucille huffed. "As big as this house is, he likes to have his own apartment. But he keeps his old room here for when he and his father stay up late working on a project. Which is all too often, I might add."

"You and your son work together?"

"Oh, yes," Mason said with obvious pride. "The Colby Construction Company is into its twenty-fifth year of business."

"And doing very well, I gather," Beverly said.

"Josh gets most of the credit for that. He has degrees in both architecture and engineering. I would have been happy just to own our own company, maybe build a few houses, but he wanted to build skyscrapers. We compromised. We build both. If you plan to go into Manhattan, you might see our current project."

As he described the high-rise office building and gave its location, Beverly realized it was the building that Josh had been working on when she had been here before. Now, he had designed it.

"He was always fascinated with building things," Lucille added. "Even in the sandbox, while the other kids were making mountains, he was constructing castles. And in high school, when the other teenage boys were getting into mischief and only interested in studying girls, Josh was studying architecture and drawing buildings. He started working at his father's construction sites as soon as he was strong enough to lift a hammer."

Mason laughed. "I can still see him marching around in that hard hat. It covered his whole head, but he wore it constantly. I'm making him sound like he was some kind of weird kid. He wasn't. Our Josh was also the type that everybody liked. We always had a houseful of his friends running in and out. I remember weekends where we couldn't hear ourselves think. Now we can't wait until Livvie's kids grow up to bring some noise back into this house."

"Livvie is our other pride and joy," Lucille explained. "We had a daughter five years after Josh was born. She's not only beautiful, but she has a law degree that she's put on hold for a few years. She's married with two little ones, but as soon as they reach school age, she intends to get back to her career."

"In the meantime," Mason added, "Josh and I keep her skills up with all the legal problems we come up against. It never hurts to have an attorney in the family, even one who claims to be on sabbatical."

Lucille's eyes lit up with an idea. "Beverly, you must come to dinner Friday night. Josh is away at a business conference, but he'll be back that afternoon and has promised to be here for dinner."

Beverly felt a rush of relief that their reunion would be so easily arranged. This was exactly the kind of thing she had hoped to accomplish by this visit. "I would love to come. Thank you. After hearing you talk about him, I can hardly wait to meet him."

"I think I'll call Livvie and get her to bring the family, too. And I'm sure Josh will bring Elise. You know, both women are about your age. Since you don't know anyone in town, perhaps you'll become friends with them."

"Elise?" Beverly asked with a terrible sense of foreboding.

"Oh, yes. Josh got engaged this past Valentine's Day. Elise is his fiancée."

Chapter 16

Fiancée? Beverly felt the blood rush from her head.

"Beverly?" Lucille asked with concern. "Are you all right? You look as though you've seen a ghost."

Improvise! You can think about Josh later. Beverly rubbed her temples and blinked several times. "I'm sorry. I, uh, I've been getting dizzy spells recently."

"Have you seen a doctor?"

Beverly regained her equilibrium and her wits. "I intend to, once I get settled. Perhaps you could recommend someone."

"Of course. I'll give you our doctor's number before you leave. For a moment there, I thought it was something I said."

"Actually, it might have been. Not that it's your fault," she added quickly. "I . . . my fiancé was killed . . . in a car accident . . . about a year ago. I thought I was over it."

"You poor dear. And now, here you are, in a new city, alone, and not feeling well. I'm so glad you thought to visit us. Your spirit guides must have brought you here, knowing we could help."

Beverly tried not to react to that statement, but Mason noticed and misunderstood.

"Lucille," he said in a warning tone.

"Oh, pooh. I'm sure Beverly understands. I felt it immediately. She's a kindred soul."

Beverly forced herself to smile and concentrate on the new subject. If Lucille believed in supernatural things, it could be just the advantage she needed. "I know something brought me here, and it wasn't just a taxi cab."

"You see that, Mason? I keep telling you the younger generation is much more open-minded than people in our age group. It's a sign of the coming of the Fifth World of Peace."

Beverly leaned forward with sincere interest. "The fifth world? What is that?"

"Don't get her started tonight," Mason interrupted with a smile. "Unless you're prepared to stay for the night, and frankly, you look tired enough to fall off that chair."

Lucille clucked her tongue at him, then explained to Beverly, "I give lectures on the traditions and teachings of Native Americans. More and more people have become interested in reconnecting with the past, and I've been given the gift to answer their questions."

"That sounds fascinating," Beverly said. "I hope to get a chance to hear you speak sometime. But I'm afraid Mason's right. I am tired. I need to be going."

"I'll drive you," Mason offered. "There's no telling how long it would take to get a cab."

Beverly accepted gladly, and Lucille got the doctor's number for her. After repeated assurance that she would return Friday for dinner, she and Mason were about to walk out the door when Lucille said another sentence that made Beverly sway.

"Nous nous verrons encore."

Bev gaped at her. "What did you say?"

She repeated it. "It means, we will see one another again. My godmother was French-Canadian. She always said that phrase when friends or loved ones were leaving. She believed it would bring them back together again."

Beverly ordered herself to stay calm. "What . . . what was your godmother's name?"

"Lavonda. We named our daughter for her, but Livvie always preferred the nickname."

"Is your godmother still alive?" Beverly asked as delicately as possible.

Lucille shook her head sadly. "No. She passed over this past March."

Beverly managed not to outwardly react to that startling piece of information as she also managed to hold her panic at bay for the rest of the time she was with Mason, but the moment she was alone in her motel room, it attacked with a vengeance.

For a long while, she couldn't get her brain to work at all. The shocks triggered by Lucille's innocently spoken words paralyzed her limbs as well. She simply lay there on the bed, staring at a water stain on the white ceiling.

Eventually the confusion in her mind separated into individual questions. The easiest to deal with was Lavonda. She had told Beverly that she was grateful to her and that someday she would understand. That day had come quickly. Beverly wasn't familiar with all the ins and outs of the spiritual world, but it was quite clear that Lavonda had had a personal interest in the Colby family. Somehow, when Lavonda died in March she was given the power to set things right, and she had chosen Beverly to help her.

The chat with Mason and Lucille had been very enlightening. Seeing them alive was satisfying in itself, but hearing how wonderfully their lives had turned out was absolutely amazing. The biggest miracle of all had to be Livvie. She had not even existed originally and now she had children herself.

To think that so much changed because of one small act on her part. She mentally tiptoed into the area that she least wanted to think about. Josh. He now had a supportive family. He was successful, well educated, popular ... *engaged*. Not fictitiously engaged like Amanda had claimed, nor engaged by verbal promise as they had been. Beverly knew without seeing proof that his engagement to Elise would have been a formal affair, involving a very large diamond ring and a celebration party.

How could this have happened? Valentine's Day was before she met him, wasn't it? Could she have popped in a year early, before they had met the first time, or years later so that he thought she was lost to him and turned to someone else?

She lurched from the bed and checked the date on the newspaper that had been delivered that morning: April 29, 1996. It had been April 25, 1996 when she had seen Josh last. Only four days had passed.

Slowly, she let in the most frightening thought of all. What if Josh didn't remember her? Just as Hope's memory changed after the last visit to Lavonda, Josh may have forgotten their time together. Hadn't he once said that might happen? But she still remembered everything. Why wouldn't he?

It took Beverly a minute or two to sort out a reasonable explanation, and when she did she didn't know whether to cry or scream in fury.

By preventing Mason's imprisonment, she had changed everyone's lives around him from that moment on, including his son's. Josh never had to go through the difficult childhood or his troubled teen years. He never worked part-time at The Bullpen or lived in a cheap one-room walkup. The new, improved Josh had all the advantages a young man could start with, and he had made the most of them. This Josh hadn't needed a Beverly to pop into his life to show him what happiness felt like.

In fact, this Josh had never met Beverly at all, because there had been nothing wrong in his life for her to fix.

Worst of all was the realization that she no longer fit in this Josh's world. She had no place here.

Her next thought was that she would have to cancel going to the Colbys Friday night. There was no way she could stand to see Josh with another woman. She couldn't imagine being in the same room with him for hours yet not being free to touch him or even look at him with all the love that was in her heart.

So, what *was* she to do? She couldn't go back. She had made her choice and now she had to live with it. In a way, Lavonda had tried to warn her. At least she knew her way around this time and had an understanding of modern technology. She had proper identification and money and knew she would have no trouble getting her business off the ground again. She could manage just fine on her own if she set her mind to it.

But her mind had been set on spending the rest of

her new life with Josh. Hadn't she told Lavonda she didn't care what his circumstances had been changed to? She wanted him regardless.

But you're not in his class anymore, the pessimist in her head whispered. *Elise is probably a young debutante from some wealthy family. You can't compete with that.*

The old Beverly would have accepted that as fact and given up her dream of happiness. But this Beverly had already risked all she had to come this far. She wasn't about to give anything up at this point, at least not without a fight.

She remembered an early conversation she had had with Josh when he hadn't thought he was good enough for her, and her arguments against that attitude. Well, the same words pertained to herself, dammit! She was good enough for any man, regardless of his circumstances.

One thought kept repeating itself in her head, despite her doubts. All of what Lavonda had set in motion was to make things better. Beverly could not believe that she would have pushed her and Josh together only to separate them and leave her with a heartbreaking memory. Lavonda had said she had done well. She deserved her reward, not a loss.

Okay, so what was she going to do about the fact that Josh was engaged?

First, she had to go to the Colbys for dinner, no matter how difficult it might be. She would look Josh in the eyes and see for herself whether or not he had any memory of her. Then she would watch him and Elise together. If she was convinced that Josh looked happier with Elise than he had with her—which she found impossible to imagine—then she would bow out gracefully and get on with her new life, without him.

But if he had one glimmer of recollection, or didn't look ecstatic with his bride-to-be, then ... She didn't know precisely what she would do then, but it wouldn't be sitting back and watching him marry Elise.

When Bev awoke the next morning, she had to remind herself when and where she was. Since her situation was quite different from what she had expected it to be, she needed to make a new plan.

Sometime soon she would have to look for an apartment, but she decided to put that off until after Friday night. She would know better once she saw Josh whether she wanted to live in New Rochelle, near him, or look for a place on the other side of Manhattan.

That left her with four days to fill, and the most important thing was to take care of her health. A call to Lucille's doctor got her an appointment for a complete physical on Thursday morning. When she heard what the approximate cost would be, she realized that the money she had received for the two comic books would not last very long. That led her to decide how she would fill the next few days.

Although the books in her suitcase had considerable value, she had no way of knowing how high her medical bills would go before she was completely well. She needed to create an income for herself. Thus, she focused her attention on that need, and remembering everything Mr. Fisk taught her about business, she headed for the mall.

This time, she acquired business cards first and introduced herself to the mall manager, Ed Garwood, before approaching the toy store. Just as Mr. Fisk had, Mr. Middleton accepted her offer to redo his window display and store layout as a free sample of her talent. Of course, this time around she knew what she was doing in advance and was much faster about it.

When Beverly returned the next day to complete her work for the toy store, she was hardly surprised to see Mr. Garwood discussing the improvements with Mr. Middleton. After all, she had seen it happen before. And, as before, the kitchen store hired her that afternoon, and Mr. Middleton recommended her to his friend in White Plains.

Businesswise, everything seemed to be right on track.

Her Thursday morning appointment with Lucille's doctor ended up taking most of the day. Dr. Willard was a pleasant man who made certain that every opening in Beverly's body was thoroughly examined, and blood and urine specimens were taken for testing. When he felt the lump in her breast, however, his demeanor instantly changed from friendly to deadly serious. He asked her questions about when she had discovered it and how quickly it had grown, and she answered honestly.

"Have you ever had a mammogram?" he asked.

She didn't even know what that was. "No."

"That's okay. Half the time, this sort of growth doesn't show up on the x-ray anyway. It's a very good thing you didn't fool around about having this checked. We're not going to fool around either. I want you back here at three this afternoon for an ultrasound. We do it right here in the office. In the meantime, I'll have the receptionist make you an ap-

pointment with a surgeon. Just let her know how
your schedule looks before you leave."

He said a few more sentence, but Beverly didn't
hear a thing after the word *surgeon*. She was afraid to
ask any questions, not knowing what a woman her
age in this time period should know. What was a
mammogram? An ultrasound? Why did she need to
see a surgeon?

As the nurse guided her to the receptionist, she
promised Beverly that everything would be fine and
repeatedly told her not to worry, but that wasn't very
reassuring.

To keep her mind off why she needed a surgeon
during the time before she had to return to Dr.
Willard's office, she took care of another item of personal business. She went to a bank and opened a
checking account and a safety deposit box. She felt
quite a bit more secure having her money and the
valuable comic books in a protected place.

To Beverly's surprise, the bank clerk asked her if
she wanted to apply for a credit card while she was
there. Remembering how many things it could be
used for and how difficult a time she had had checking into the motel without one, she gladly filled out
the short form. Due to her lack of previous credit, she
agreed to leave a minimum balance in her account to
guarantee payment, and the clerk advised her that
her card could be picked up on Monday.

More than anything else so far, the thought of pos-
sessing "plastic" made Beverly feel as though she
now truly belonged in this decade.

Upon her return to the doctor's office, she was relieved that they took her in and performed the ultrasound without making her wait. It was a simple,

painless test, and Beverly was amazed to see the inside of her body on the small television screen. The lump in her breast looked exactly as it felt—like a marble.

"This is good," Dr. Willard said. "It appears to be a fibroadenoma. A solid mass. And it seems to be alone at the moment. We got you squeezed in for an appointment tomorrow morning with the surgeon, Dr. Verona. We'll see what she has to say, but my prediction is she'll be able to remove it without any problem."

"Re-remove it?" Beverly stuttered with a fearful expression.

Dr. Willard patted her hand. "Better to remove a small lump now than the whole breast later. Don't be frightened. Women are having this procedure done every day now."

All Bev could remember was having her tonsils removed when she was seven. It didn't matter that a zillion other kids had had that same surgery, it had hurt like the dickens.

Suddenly his comment about removing the whole breast echoed in her mind. How horrible! Her breasts were small, but at least she had two of them. Images of being disfigured for life flashed in her mind until she was afraid she was going to be ill.

Stop! she commanded herself. Lavonda said she would be fine, that she just needed to see a doctor and take care of the lump, and she was doing that. She tried very hard to hold that thought, but the fear refused to stay out of it.

Beverly slept very little that night. If only she could talk to Hope she knew she could be talked out of her state of terror. But she was alone here, without a friend to console her. What if Lavonda was wrong? She had used the word cancer. What if it had already developed and was hiding somewhere that the doctor's modern equipment couldn't find it? Had she taken a risk to change her whole life only to end up dying all alone in a strange time and place?

The problem of whether or not she and Josh would get together was completely replaced by the question of whether or not she had a future at all. As things were, he had a good life and was engaged to be married. She could not be so selfish as to wish for him, only to saddle him with a dying woman.

The appointment with the surgeon gave her a little more information, but no new hope. The bad news was that the earliest date she could be scheduled for surgery was ten days away. The good news was that it could be performed on an outpatient basis, and the tissue would be tested immediately after it was removed. She would know that day whether or not it was cancerous. Now all she had to do was keep from having a nervous breakdown during the waiting period.

Before she left the surgeon's office, she was advised of the costs she could expect, a portion of which were due in advance, since she had no insurance. It was apparent that she was going to have to pay Earl another visit a lot sooner than she had expected.

Rather than go back to the motel, where she knew she would only sit and brood, she went to the mall, determined to buy a new outfit for that evening. She was successful, but the pleasure of shopping was diminished by her worries.

As soon as she got back to her room, she called

Earl and read him the list of comic books she wished to sell. She offered him everything she had except the one she considered her jackpot. Not only was she afraid that selling it might attract unwanted attention to her, she also harbored the hope that she could keep it with the James Dean packet as a sort of dowry.

"I'm afraid I can't buy any more myself," Earl told her regretfully. "At least not immediately. But I know quite a few collectors who might be interested. If you're willing to pay me ten percent to broker a deal, I'll see what I can do for you."

Beverly agreed, but gave him a few terms of her own. "I need the money within one week, and I don't want my name involved."

"No problem," Earl said. "Private sales are normal in this kind of situation. Just give me a number where I can reach you if I've got an offer."

"Actually, I'd rather not. I'll call you Monday afternoon and see what you've come up with."

She wasn't sure why she had said that, but her instincts were telling her to keep her identity a secret, so she did.

With considerable effort, she put her fears about her health on hold and concentrated on looking the prettiest that she ever did in her life.

The simple aqua sheath was shorter than she was used to, yet she knew it was longer than the latest style. Once she got over how much of her legs were exposed, she thought they looked quite nice in today's sheer, seamless panty hose, especially after she put on the high heels she had bought to wear with the dress.

She wanted to do something modern with her hair,

but her talents were very limited in that area, so she let it hang freely around her face, the way it had been the last time Josh had seen her. A touch of makeup and she was ready to go, or at least as ready as she ever could be.

On the way there, she had the cab driver stop at a florist so she could buy a bouquet for Lucille. A few minutes before seven o'clock, she arrived at the Colbys' and rang the bell despite the last-minute urge to run away and forget the whole thing.

Lucille greeted her warmly and gushed appreciatively over the flowers. While she went to put them in water, Mason introduced Beverly to Livvie; her husband Zach; their three-year old son Zachary Junior; and their one-year-old daughter Lucy. Livvie was beautiful, a feminine Josh, her husband was a bookish type, with fair coloring and wire-rimmed glasses, and the children were absolutely precious.

Beverly had to get through several minutes of "getting to know each other" chitchat, before anyone mentioned the missing member of the family.

"Shall we take bets on what time their majesties will waltz in the door tonight?" Livvie asked with a twinkle in her eye.

Lucille's return look and the tone of her voice reminded her to be nice in front of company. "I'm sure they'll be here any minute."

"Oh, sure they will. Let's see, last time they were forty-five minutes late, the time before that it was an hour. You said dinner was at seven tonight. I say let's sit down and they can snack on leftovers in the kitchen when they finally get here."

To Beverly she explained, "My brother gets involved in a project and forgets that the rest of the world exists. But even when he remembers, Elise makes sure they never arrive anywhere on time. She simply must make an entrance."

"Livvie, I'm sure—"

"You told me Beverly was a kindred soul and to treat her like family. Well, I don't need to pretend in front of family."

Lucille cleared her throat and straightened her spine. "What I was going to say was that I'm sure they'll be here any minute because I told Josh dinner was at six."

Everyone chuckled over that, including Beverly, who suddenly felt a bit more confident. Elise had a flaw, and Josh's sister didn't care for her. On the other hand, Livvie seemed to like her, and she was certain that Mason and Lucille were firmly on her side as well.

Mason decided it was time to change the subject. "Honey, why don't you give Beverly the present you made her?"

As Lucille handed her a foot-square box, Beverly was glad that she had thought to pick up flowers. Inside was a navy blue hoop with blue-and-white threads interlaced in a weblike fashion, and white feathers hanging from the sides and bottom of the hoop. "It's beautiful," she said sincerely. "I've never seen anything like this."

"It's a dream catcher," Lucille explained. "You hang it over your bed, and when you go to sleep, it catches all the dreams that are floating around. Good dreams know the way through the center of the web and will slip through to you, but bad dreams are trapped inside until daylight comes and burns them away. In Native American tradition, giving a dream catcher as a gift is a sign of love and friendship."

Beverly hugged Lucille. "I'll cherish it always, especially because you made it. Thank you."

The doorbell announced more visitors at that moment, which pleased the family and sent a spear of panic through Beverly. She reminded herself to hide her feelings no matter what happened in the next few hours.

Josh and Elise entered and Beverly temporarily forget her self-reminder. As Josh apologized to his family for being late, she quickly noted the difference in his appearance. His hair was combed away from his face, trimmed short on the sides and barely brushed his collar in back. He was wearing loafers, dress slacks, and a knit shirt. He was incredibly handsome; he just didn't look like her Josh.

His frown was familiar, however. It was the expression he had worn when they had first met, before he discovered happiness. A glance at the couple gave hint to the possibility that they had been having a *discussion* about their tardiness before they arrived.

Elise wasn't exactly beautiful, but she made Beverly think of a model. She was nearly as tall as Josh in her heels, and her figure seemed perfectly proportioned. Her long, light brown hair had streaks of blond and was pulled up and back so that it fell in a cascade of curls. Her lipstick matched her manicured nails, and there was a diamond the size of New Jersey on her left hand. And she was *very* young, twenty-three at most. Between her youth, and classy appearance, and an extremely self-assured attitude, Elise managed to destroy what little confidence Beverly had without saying as much as a word.

"Josh, Elise," Lucille said, "I'd like to introduce our guest, Beverly Newcastle."

Beverly forced herself to smile as Elise briefly touched fingertips with her, then she had to force herself to breathe as well when Josh closed both his hands over hers and met her gaze.

"It's a real pleasure," he said. "Your mother's name was toasted to on so many occasions in this house, I feel as though you're part of the family."

Though his words sounded sincere, Beverly got the impression that he spoke them automatically, that his mind was occupied elsewhere. She looked deeply into his eyes, hoping to find a glimmer of recognition, but there was none. He truly had no memory of her.

As they all went into the dining room, Beverly's heart felt as though it weighed a ton. She had prepared herself for this, yet it was so much harder than she had imagined it would be. Perhaps it was best, considering the state of her health.

Suddenly she had the strangest sensation, as if someone had physically grasped her shoulders, shook her, and demanded that she stop such pessimistic thoughts. But no one in the room had done or said anything like that.

Mason held a chair for her while Livvie and Zach settled their children in a high chair and toddler seat. Then Lucille said a brief prayer of thanksgiving that gave Beverly a lightning flash of insight.

The sensation could have been caused by Lavonda. Maybe she really was hovering around, keeping an eye on her loved ones and watching to see how Beverly was handling her new life. She decided that what she had felt must have been a reminder that

Lavonda had told her she would be well and have a happy life if that was her wish.

And, by God, that was still her wish.

Throughout dinner, she discreetly observed Josh and Elise and came to an important conclusion. Although he didn't remember being in love with her, and wasn't showing any signs of instant infatuation, neither did he appear to be a man who was madly in love with his bride-to-be.

Instead of behaving as an engaged couple in the bloom of romance, they acted more like her parents—a long-married pair who got along fine and tolerated each other's annoying habits, yet had lost any feelings of passion they had ever shared. Knowing Josh as intimately as she did, she couldn't imagine his ever being so lukewarm with her.

There was also something very distant about Josh. His body was in the dining room with his family, but Beverly got the impression he barely heard a word of the conversation. Elise had to nudge him several times to get him to respond to a comment or agree with something she had said.

It was enough to convince her that Elise was *not* necessarily the best woman for Josh, no matter how young or striking she was. Unfortunately, she had no experience in the area she was thinking of venturing into. She just knew she had to find a way to show Josh that he could do better . . . with her.

She had once again built up her confidence that Josh was not yet lost to her when Lucille asked a question that triggered a new reason for anxiety.

"How are the invitations coming?"

Elise gave a dramatic sigh. "They're *finally* ready to go out. I cannot believe what incompetents those people were! But they seem to have gotten them right this time and absolutely guaranteed they would all be addressed and mailed by Monday morning. I only hope everyone who matters can rearrange their calendars to attend."

Livvie clucked her tongue at her. "The wedding is still six weeks away. Zach and I sent out our invitations four weeks in advance and that was plenty of time. Besides," she added, tinging her next words with sarcasm, "*anyone* who's *anyone* read your announcement in the *Times*."

Livvie's sarcasm was lost on Elise. "I hope you're right. It is just so embarrassing to be so late."

Mason coughed and Lucille pretended to be concerned that he had choked on something besides Elise's comment.

Beverly might have been amused if she hadn't been so stunned by the news of how close the wedding was. *Six weeks!* Of course, what else would they have but a June wedding? It went perfectly with the Valentine's Day engagement. How was she going to redirect Josh's attention in such a short time?

After dinner, as everyone moved into the living room, Lucille asked Beverly to stay behind with her for a moment.

"I didn't want to ask in front of the others," she said quietly, "but I couldn't help but notice that you seemed rather nervous this evening compared to how comfortable you were with us the other day. Is everything all right? Did you call my doctor?"

Beverly's instincts told her to confide in Lucille, so she did. To her surprise, Lucille had had a similar fright a few years ago, when her pap smear had come back showing an abnormality, and ended up having a hysterectomy. She quickly found herself sharing her feelings with the older woman. They both agreed that the waiting period was possibly worse than the surgery itself.

"I came out of my scare just fine," Lucille assured her. "And so will you. Although I obviously had some advantages. It would have been much more difficult if I'd been alone through it all. You said you had no family left back in New Jersey. Perhaps you could call a friend to come stay with you for a while."

Beverly shook her head. "I'm afraid not, but I'll be okay."

Lucille wasn't satisfied with that answer. "Have you found an apartment yet?"

"No. I'm still at the motel. I figured I'd start looking this weekend." Beverly could almost see Lucille's mind working.

"Mason would be able to help you find something nice, but I have a better idea. I'd like you to stay here with us for a while. At least until after your surgery. We have several empty bedrooms and I'd love to have the company."

Beverly knew this was exactly the kind of advantage she needed, but she felt obliged to protest a little. "That is so very kind, but I'm practically a stranger, and—"

"Nonsense. You weren't even a stranger the first day you walked through our door. In fact, I'm quite certain I owe you something from a previous lifetime when we were together, so unless you have a really good excuse, I won't take no for an answer."

Beverly wished she could discuss that "previous lifetime" with her, but as much as Lucille spoke as if she believed in the supernatural, she didn't dare take the chance of sounding unbalanced. She hesitated for a few more seconds, then gave in. "All right. But I insist on repaying you in some way. Does Rosella work for you full-time? Perhaps I could help take care of the house."

"If you're going to insult me, I'll withdraw my invitation. You will be our guest, and that's all there is to this discussion. Now, let's join the others."

Between cranky children and Elise's remembering that she still had numerous phone calls to make that night, the dinner party came to an end shortly thereafter.

Beverly was expecting Mason to offer to drive her home again, but Lucille had another surprise up her sleeve.

"Josh," she said as he was preparing to leave, "I wonder if you could do us a favor. You know how I worry about your father driving at night. Since Elise has so many phone calls to make, perhaps you could take her home, then drive Beverly to her motel, help her get her things together, and bring her back here. She's going to be staying with us for a while."

Chapter 17

Elise's mouth puckered as though she had just taken a bite of a lemon. Josh either didn't notice or he ignored the message she was trying to relay to him.

"No problem," he said, and ushered both women out to his black sedan.

Elise was clearly unhappy with the turn of events and didn't bother to try to keep up a conversation during the drive to her house.

They pulled up to a pair of gates that had to be opened by a control box before Josh could proceed to a house that made the Colbys' look like a cottage.

"You live here?" Beverly blurted out with a complete lack of sophistication.

Elise was amused. "Just until the wedding. Daddy insisted on keeping me with him until the very last minute, and considering the fact that our wedding present is a house of our own, I decided to humor him."

Josh walked around to the passenger side and opened the door for Elise. Before she left the car she said, "Lucille suggested that I introduce you to some people. I'll give you a call one day soon . . . now that I know where you'll be staying."

"That would be nice," Beverly lied. "Thank you." As soon as Elise got out, Beverly moved from the backseat to the front. Covertly, she watched the couple say good night to each other. Josh gave Elise a quick peck on the mouth, which seemed to be even more than she wanted, until she glanced at Beverly in the front seat of the car. Abruptly, she wrapped her arms around Josh's neck and pulled him to her for a passionate kiss before she allowed him to walk away. The expression on his face as he returned to the car was a mixture of bewilderment and embarrassment.

Beverly pretended not to have noticed Elise's little act of possessiveness and told Josh where she was staying. If she didn't care so much about making a good impression on him, she would have given him a hard shake and demanded to know why he was engaged to such a spoiled brat. Then again, from what she had gathered, Amanda had been a bit of a brat also.

Perhaps Josh just didn't have much sense when it came to choosing women companions in either of his lives. She didn't count since he hadn't had much choice about spending time with her. Obviously, she was going to have to find a way to arrange that again.

Josh was quiet for a while, then he said something that made no sense. "This is a good thing."

"What is?"

His gaze darted to her then back to the road. "Your visiting my mother. Not that she doesn't have plenty to keep her busy, but lately . . . I don't know. I think she just needs a new cause."

Beverly smiled. "And you think that's what I am to her?"

His cheek twitched. "I didn't mean it the way it sounded."

"That's okay. I understood, and I think you're right. She seemed really happy to be able to take me under wing."

"Like a mother bird?"

"Exactly."

They had exhausted that topic, and it was several more minutes before Beverly came up with a new one. "I'm anxious to see the new Colby building in Manhattan. Your father was telling me about it."

"Actually, you just saw one of our projects. We designed and built Elise's house a few years ago. That's how she and I met."

Beverly was torn between being impressed with his work and annoyed that it had brought him and Elise together, so she chose a response that would take the conversation away from Elise. "I think it's wonderful that you and your father work together. And I understand Livvie helps with her skills, too."

That was enough to keep him talking until they reached the motel. A half hour later, she had checked out, and her suitcase was in the trunk of the car.

As they headed back to his parents' house, he apologized. "I didn't mean to go on so long about my work. Sometimes I forget that other people aren't as interested in designing buildings as I am."

"But I am interested. In fact, on a much smaller scale, I do some designing myself." She started to tell him about her business and what she had done at the toy store, but she stopped when she noticed how he kept glancing at her with an odd look in his eye. "What's the matter?" she asked.

His brows narrowed and he cocked his head at her. "Were you talking about this at dinner? Sometimes I get lost in my own thoughts and don't hear everything people say."

"No. I meant to tell your parents my good news, but I didn't get to."

He shook his head. "That's strange. I would have sworn I heard all of that about the toy store before." A second later he cracked a smile. "My mother would call it déjà vu."

Her heartbeat increased a bit as she realized he might have actually had a recollection. "It sounds like you don't believe in such things," she said in a teasing tone.

"It's not that I don't believe at all. I mean, I was brought up to accept the theory that anything's possible. I just don't go out and give lectures on it like she does."

"Or discuss it with business associates," she added, and he laughed. It was a warm, wonderful sound, and she could barely control the urge to touch his face. "What about past lives?" she asked.

"What about them?"

"Your mother said she believes she owes me something from a past life when we were together. Do you think that's possible?"

He made a face. "Not really, but don't tell her I said that."

"How about time travel," she prodded. "Do you think that's possible?"

He seemed surprised that she was continuing this line of conversation, but he answered. "I can tell you that there is no scientific reason why time travel is not possible. From a purely physical standpoint, it could be accomplished. But there are several different schools of thought on why it wouldn't or shouldn't be possible." He went on to explain what he meant, using phrases like "breaks in the time-space continuum," "ripples in the pond of time," "the paradox threat," and "the creation of new time lines."

Beverly didn't understand all of what he said, but it didn't matter. While he was talking theory, she had already experienced it and knew exactly what happened when you went back and changed a tiny moment in time. It actually didn't matter what he was saying; she was simply enjoying his voice and the self-confidence he possessed in his knowledge and abilities.

Lavonda had told her she had done well, and she agreed wholeheartedly.

When they reached the house, Josh went inside to discuss something with his father. Rather than leave the men alone, Lucille served tea for the four of them in the library. While Josh updated his father about a new environmental issue that had been brought up at the conference he had attended that week, Lucille asked Beverly about her plans for the next few days.

She told her a little about her business and the appointments she had lined up during the next week.

"Didn't you say you had never been to New York?" Lucille asked.

Beverly didn't recall mentioning it, but she didn't want to take the chance of contradicting herself. "No, but I was thinking of doing some sightseeing this weekend."

"That's exactly what you must do. You really

should have a native escort you though. I could—Oh, dear, I just remembered, I have a meeting. Mason, what are your plans tomorrow?"

He looked at her curiously. "I told you I have a crew working overtime on the Dietrich house, and I need to be there. You said you didn't mind because you have a meeting."

"Oh, yes, that's right. Josh, what about you?"

Beverly wondered if either of the men were picking up the same feeling she was—that Lucille was only pretending not to know what everyone's plans were.

"I have to go to the city. We have an inspection Monday morning and I want to make sure everything's ready."

Lucille smiled and clapped her hands together. "Well, that's perfect then. I offered to show Beverly New York tomorrow, but now I can't. Since you're going in anyway, you can take her with you. You could take care of business and then show her some sights."

Now Beverly knew exactly what Lucille was up to and she could have kissed her for it, but again she knew a protest was called for. "Oh, no, really. I don't need a guide. I'm sure I could figure out the subway system on my own."

Mason laughed. "I remember the first time Josh took the subway on his own. He ended up calling us to come get him in Brooklyn."

Josh clearly remembered the incident, and it seemed to be enough to nudge him into agreeing to be her guide. "It's been a while since I've done the tourist routine. I wouldn't mind showing you around, if you wouldn't mind stopping at the site for a while first. You did say you wanted to see our building."

Just as Beverly knew when to protest, she knew when to stop. "I'd love that, thank you. What time should I be ready?"

"Would eight be too early?" he asked, making a slight face, as though he expected her to be horrified.

"Not at all. I'm an early riser."

"Good," said Lucille. "So are we. Rosella serves breakfast at seven. Which means it's well past time to say good night."

Having accomplished what she had set out to, Josh's mother smoothly brought an end to the evening.

When Lucille showed Beverly to the room where she would be staying, she didn't need to be told that it used to be Livvie's. It was bright blue and yellow, and feminine without being cluttered with frills and ruffles. She wished her "mother bird" a good night, without commenting on the reason behind her little orchestration of tomorrow's schedule. She had a feeling it would become clear with time.

Beverly was up with the sun the next morning. She kept thinking about Josh's déjà vu about the toy store, and decided that his memory might not be completely erased. It might just need some jogging. With that in mind, she dressed in the same outfit she had had on the day she had popped in on him at the construction site—the same site they would be going to that morning. She even carried the same jacket and pulled her hair back in a ponytail. She also knew exactly how they were going to spend the day.

She was very pleasantly surprised to see Josh sitting at the kitchen table with his father when she got there.

"Good morning," Mason said cheerfully. "My, but you look pretty. The image of your mother."

She thanked him for his compliment, but it was Josh's response that made her heart race. He had been about to take a sip of coffee when she had entered, but the cup never made it to his mouth. For several long seconds, he stared at her with his mouth open. His trance was broken when his cup tipped in his hand, spilling hot coffee over his fingers.

Mason cleared his throat and made a fatherly joke about Josh's coordination, but Beverly knew he had seen the same thing that she had—Josh's reaction to the sight of her. Of course, Mason would simply chalk it up to male awareness, but she knew it was deeper than that.

While she told Rosella what she would like for breakfast, Josh and his father got back to the conversation they had been having when she had arrived. Lucille joined them a few minutes later with a list of attractions she thought Beverly should see in Manhattan. It made Bev chuckle. She knew from experience that for them to cover all the places on Lucille's list would take a week, not a day.

For the remainder of breakfast, Josh's attention was focused on his father, but every so often he stole a quick glance at Beverly. She pretended not to notice.

At eight o'clock on the dot, she and Josh were walking out the door.

"Have you decided what you'd like to see today?" he asked as he opened the car door for her.

"Your building first, the Empire State Building second, then the Statue of Liberty and Ellis Island in the afternoon." She hoped the repetition of the pattern would jiggle his memory a bit more.

Although they had chatted comfortably last evening, Beverly had a difficult time drawing him into a conversation this morning. Even a question about the upcoming inspection failed to pull him out of his thoughts for more than a few seconds. Beverly could only hope she was part of what he was thinking so hard about.

When they arrived at his building, she was surprised to see how much further along the construction was from when she had been here before. Then she noticed the enormous sign that announced that it was a Colby Construction project. She felt so proud she almost hugged Josh, but she reined in the urge before she acted on it.

Looking up, she had a flash of herself standing on a beam, falling, and having Josh catch her just in time to prevent disaster. She watched Josh look up at the same spot, rub his eyes, and shake his head. She hoped it meant he was having similar flashes.

Josh offered her a seat in the construction trailer while he went about his business, but she asked if she could tag along and get a tour of the site. Along the way, she asked questions about how the finished building would look, and he was more than pleased to describe it to her. By the time they headed for the Empire State Building, he was back to being relaxed in her company.

The line to take the elevator to the top was relatively short, but it still required a wait. Beverly was in the middle of a sentence when Josh suddenly put his arm around her shoulders and pulled her close enough to whisper in her ear.

"Stay close to me."

That was no problem since that was what she wanted to do most, but she could tell there was more to his comment than affection. "What's the matter?"

"Don't turn around, but an old derelict followed us in here. I didn't think anything of it, but he keeps staring at you and inching closer. He might just want to get a closer look at a pretty lady, but keep a tight hold on your purse."

Instead of worrying about a possible purse snatcher, Beverly latched on to the fact that he had referred to her as a pretty lady.

A few minutes later, it was their turn to go up. There was a bit of commotion behind them, and when she turned to see the problem, she noticed the man Josh had spoken of. He pushed his way ahead of several others so that he could get into the elevator with them. As Josh had cautioned her previously, she avoided making eye contact with the man, kept a grip on her purse, and stayed pressed to Josh's side. It was a long, slow trip to the top, and by the time the doors opened, the derelict's body had everyone holding their breath.

The old bum was short, thin, very scruffy-looking, and definitely following them. As Beverly and Josh walked around the roof top trying to move away from him, he kept drawing closer. Josh's advice was to ignore him, but that became impossible.

"Beverly Newcastle!" the man exclaimed.

It was such a shock to hear her name, she turned and looked at him.

"It is you, you stinkin', lousy bitch!" He staggered forward, his dirty fingers reaching for her throat.

With little exertion, Josh shoved the man away before he touched her. "Beverly, do you know this man?"

She shook her head, but the man contradicted her. "You lyin' bitch. You know damn well who I am. You ruined my life and stole my family. Always puttin' ideas into Dee-Dee's head, then leavin' her all that money when you died—" He stopped abruptly as his clouded mind absorbed what he had just said. His anger turned to fearful confusion. "You . . . you were dead. I saw them put you in the ground."

Beverly could now see traces of the old Frankie Giammarco beneath the scraggly gray hair and beard, but she was too stunned to figure out what to say. Josh maintained his protective stance, but he was waiting to hear an explanation also.

She could hardly deny that she was Beverly Newcastle. "My mother," she said to Frankie. "You saw them bury my mother. I'm told I look like she did, and I have the same name."

He squinted at her. "She didn't have no children. I always figured that was why she did what she did to me. Jealous bitch."

Beverly hoped his brain was as pickled as it appeared to be and continued with an explanation to satisfy Josh. "If you remember my mother, then you should remember that she died in childbirth. You probably don't remember me because I was raised by my grandparents. Look at me. If my mother had lived, she would be sixty-eight today. Do I look that old to you?"

Her words confused him far too much to figure

out, so he jumped to a simpler train of thought. "Dee-Dee got that insurance money and took the kids and ran off." His watery eyes took on a distant look. "Followed them for years, but I lost them. Here in New York. But I'll find them. They can't hide forever."

As he staggered away, muttering to himself, Beverly was relieved that he had quit questioning who she was, but she felt a little sorry for him also. A heartbeat later she withdrew that compassion. He had probably continued to make Dee-Dee's life hell for many years even though she had the money to escape from him. At least she now knew that Dee-Dee had eventually gained her freedom. But was she happy? Did all the children survive unharmed? Hope would know—

"Crazy old bastard," Josh said. "Are you all right?"

She smiled up at him. "Yes, thank you for your protection. I don't know what he was talking about, but he apparently had a grudge against my mother."

"Thirty years is a hell of a long time to hold a grudge," Josh noted. "It obviously took a serious toll on his brain."

"Hmmph. A man like that was probably sick in the head to begin with. I don't want to think about him anymore. I want to see New York, starting with a peek through one of those machines."

The rest of the day went very much as it had the first time, right down to the establishing of an easy companionship between them.

At Ellis Island, all the pictures of immigrant families prompted Josh to ask Beverly a little more about her background. Fortunately, she had her answers ready.

"It must have been very difficult to grow up without your mother," Josh said compassionately. "What happened to your father?"

"Vietnam. He was killed a few months before I was born."

"Geez. I can't imagine what my life would have been like without either one of my parents."

That was one part of his old memory she hoped never came back to him. "It wasn't bad at all. My grandparents were very good to me. They were the main reason I stayed in Mercerville as long as I did. I waited until they had both passed away before I left."

By the time they returned to New Rochelle, dinner was nearly ready. Beverly had had such a lovely day, she thought nothing could spoil it until Lucille asked Josh if he would be joining them.

"Sorry," he said, and really appeared to be. "Elise is expecting me, and I've still got to go by my place and get cleaned up. She'll probably think I'm late just to pay her back for last night."

Lucille looked as though she had something to say about that, but she kept it to herself. "Remember, tomorrow is the powwow at the county fairgrounds. It would please your father if you could make it. Naturally, you know we'd love to have Elise come as well."

With tremendous effort, Beverly managed to keep her smile in place until she could excuse herself to go freshen up in her room. The day had been so perfect, so reminiscent of their first sightseeing excursion, she had been able to completely forget that he was engaged to another woman. How silly! How very self-centered of her to think he would be so bewitched by her charms that he would immediately drop Elise from his life. A man doesn't just fall out of love with his fiancée because he's had a pleasant day with a "pretty lady."

But was Josh truly in love with Elise? Surely he thought he was, or else why would he be marrying her? And yet, they had just spent an entire day together, and not once had he mentioned Elise's name to her.

If only he had simply dropped her off and left, she could have continued to remain oblivious to what he would be doing tonight. She could have made something up that wouldn't make her sick to her stomach. Instead, she couldn't help but think about him and Elise having dinner together, holding hands, talking about their future . . . making love all night long. It was almost more than she could bear.

But she had to. Lucille was expecting her to show up for dinner in a few minutes, and if she wasn't smiling Lucille might think she hadn't had an enjoyable day and feel guilty for sending her off with Josh. She gave herself a hard shake from head to toe, washed her face and hands, and forced herself to look content.

She found Lucille in the library sipping a glass of white wine.

"I had Rosella pour one for you, too, but don't feel you have to drink it if you don't care to."

Beverly accepted the offered glass, hoping it would help her forget what Josh was doing tonight.

"Have you ever been to a powwow?" Lucille asked as Beverly sat down in a big leather armchair.

The only powwows Beverly had ever heard of were in cowboy movies, but once again, she didn't know how ignorant she would seem if she admitted that. "No," she replied and hoped Lucille would explain without being asked. She needn't have worried; Lucille obviously loved teaching people about their traditions.

"Originally, a powwow was a gathering of the tribal peoples in the spring or summer to pray for a good harvest or a successful hunt, or give thanks afterward. Matters that were important to the nation were discussed, and goods were traded. It was also a social occasion, with a lot of singing, dancing, storytelling, and opportunities for unmarried members to look for mates.

"Times have changed, but we still have a need to gather together every so often, whether it's to give thanks, honor traditions, or just socialize. The powwow I mentioned to Josh will include a recognition ceremony for the son of friends of ours. He just graduated from college. I think you might find it interesting, if you'd like to come with us."

"I would love to," Beverly said without hesitation.

"I hope Josh decides to come. He missed the last one, and I've been a little concerned that he's losing touch."

Beverly noted how Lucille's expression changed and wanted to bring her smile back. "Josh doesn't seem like the type who would turn his back on his heritage."

"That's what I thought, but she— I really shouldn't say anything."

"Sometimes it helps to say something aloud, and I can promise you it won't go any further."

"Oh, I know it wouldn't. It's just that I try to live by the adage that if you don't have something good to say about someone, you shouldn't say anything at all." She paused as though she was going to heed that adage, but then she sighed and told Beverly what was bothering her.

"Elise is a lovely, well-educated young woman, from a good family. She also has enough money of her own that we know she isn't marrying Josh for financial security. She'll probably be a great help to him and his career from a social standpoint."

"But ..." Beverly prodded.

Lucille grimaced. "But there's something wrong. And Livvie agrees with me. It's more than the fact that Elise is somewhat spoiled and not always considerate of other people's time. She could outgrow those faults as she matures. It's something deeper, and I've never been able to put my finger on it. The first time I noticed it was when he brought her to a powwow. She didn't say or do anything negative, but I had the distinct impression that she ... I don't know ... that she *disapproved* of us. When the next gathering came up, she had something scheduled that required Josh to be with her at that time, but as I recall, it wasn't anything terribly important."

"Have you told Josh how you feel?"

"Heavens no. Josh isn't a child that I can tell him who to play with. I know love is blind, but I keep hoping he'll regain his sight before the wedding." She made a guilty face. "That was a terrible thing to say."

Beverly again assured her that it would go no further, while her heart was doing cartwheels inside her chest. She was tempted to push the confidential conversation a step further when Mason entered the library.

"Rosella said dinner's ready whenever you are," he announced, then stepped aside to allow the ladies to go first.

Beverly kept her eyes ahead, but she heard the couple greeting each other affectionately behind her. Mason and Lucille had been married about forty years, but they were still happy to see each other at the end of a day. *That* was what a loving marriage should be like. It was the way she had imagined it would be for her and Josh.

She could not, however, stretch her imagination far enough to see Josh and Elise that way. Why couldn't Josh see what everyone else in his family seemed to?

After dinner, they talked awhile then watched a little television. It was enough to prevent Beverly from dwelling on thoughts of Josh until she was alone in her bedroom. Then there was no help for it. Memories of the hours they had spent lying in bed together, kissing, touching, pleasing, loving kept coming forward, only in every scene she was being replaced by Elise.

She even tried fretting over the lump in her breast, but nothing worked. Finally, she got up, put on a robe, and went to the family room to watch a late-night show. No sooner had she gotten settled in a comfortable recliner than she heard what sounded like the front door opening and closing. The question of who might be coming or going at this hour was answered a moment later.

"Mom? What are you doing—" Josh stopped walking and talking when he realized it was Beverly and not his mother watching T.V. "I'm sorry. I didn't mean to intrude." He also didn't seem to know what he was supposed to do next.

Beverly's heart was racing, but she managed to keep her voice fairly level. "You're not intruding. I couldn't sleep. You're welcome to join me, but if you're looking for your mother, she went to bed hours ago."

"Yes, I know, I mean, I know she usually goes to bed early. I was just ..." He ran his hand through his hair. "I'm not sure what I was thinking."

Beverly took a hopeful stab at it. "If you were looking for someone to talk to, people say I'm a pretty good listener." Josh exhaled heavily, then sat down in the opposite recliner. If she was any judge of character, he was one confused man. She used the remote to mute the sound on the television and waited to see if he would fill the silence on his own.

As she had seen him do in the other time, he leaned forward with his elbows propped on his knees and his hands folded. "You're a woman," he began hesitantly.

"Yes, that's what I've heard."

He grinned despite the problem weighing on his mind. "Let me start over. You said you were engaged. Right?" She nodded. They had touched on the loss of her fiancé that afternoon. "So you were in love, right?"

"Definitely."

"What did that mean to you?"

Beverly was still off balance from having him walk in on her so unexpectedly, and the intimacy of his question would have knocked her on her bottom if she hadn't already been sitting. She had the feeling her answer could be vitally important to her future, so she didn't want to make a mistake.

"I'm sorry," he said. "I guess it's still hard for you to talk about him."

"No, that's okay," she said quickly. "I was just trying to think of how best to answer you. I guess I'd have to say that being in love is being the happiest you've ever been; that because this person has come into your life, everything is brighter and more colorful; that problems only weigh half as much."

That didn't seem to be clear enough for him, so she recalled how he had made her feel when they were together before. "Being in love is wanting to share the good *and* the bad, equally. It's cherishing the minutes when you're together and trusting that the love between you doesn't weaken in the hours or days when you're apart. It's also having a lot in common while accepting the differences between you."

For a long moment, he stared at his hands, then he asked, "Do you think love is supposed to be that way for men, too?"

"Most definitely. They just don't usually put it into words the way women do. Do you want to tell me why you're asking me these questions?"

He leaned back in the chair and crossed his arms over his stomach. "I'm not sure I agree with everything you said. It's too . . . *romantic*. But Elise and I had a big argument tonight about what love means, and I don't agree with everything she said either."

He paused, clearly trying to decide how much to reveal, then let out a frustrated sigh. "She had gone shopping with her friends today, and I had to go to the site, as you know, so we weren't going to see each other until I picked her up for dinner anyway. But when I told her I had taken you sightseeing, she went nuts. She wouldn't even listen to my explanation. She said if I really loved her, I would never have spent a day with another woman, no matter what her relationship to my family is.

"Then when I asked her if she wanted to go to the powwow tomorrow, it wasn't enough for her to say no, she insisted that I not go either. If I really loved her, I wouldn't want to do anything that she didn't want to do. Then she— Well, you get the gist of how it went. The thing that bothers me is that we've been arguing about a lot of things lately, and half the time I don't know what she expects of me, but it always seems to come down to my not loving her enough or not understanding her *needs*, whatever that means. It wasn't like this before we got engaged."

Beverly knew without a doubt that, not only was Josh not in love with Elise, he had never known love at all. She reminded herself that she was supposed to be a disinterested party in this discussion. "You know, Josh, sometimes engaged people get pre-wedding jitters and take their nervousness out on each other. Sometimes it helps to take an evening and remember how you fell in love to begin with and why you decided to get married."

He frowned. "Why does anyone get married?"

"Why don't you tell me why you asked Elise."

He ran his hand through his hair again and looked thoughtful. "It started on my thirty-fifth birthday."

"Is that when you met her?"

He shook his head. "No. That's when I realized I wasn't getting any younger. My parents already had two children by that time. You've seen my father and mother together. They have a great partnership. Can you blame me for wanting the same thing as I get older?"

"Not at all. So why did it take you until Valentine's Day to ask Elise to marry you?"

"Well, I didn't meet her until the next year, and none of the other women I'd dated fit the criteria."

Beverly's eyebrows raised. "The *criteria*?"

He returned to his explanatory pose. "You have to understand. I design buildings. To create a good sturdy building, you have to start with a plan. Everything has to be figured out in advance before the first stake is put in the ground. You have to consider what that building is going to be used for, how it has to appear to fit in with the other buildings in the area. It needs a strong foundation and an appealing exterior. And then there's the timing."

"Stop! I promised myself that I wouldn't stick my nose in your business, but that is the most awful, coldhearted thing I have ever heard. You can't choose a wife the same way you construct a building. Buildings don't have flesh and blood. They don't have hearts.

"If you want a relationship like your parents have, you can't make a list of *criteria* and order it up. You have to *feel* the attraction. You have to want to be with that person in spite of who her parents are, or how old she is, or how much money she has. The feeling comes from inside, far beneath the surface. You of all people should understand that."

He looked at her curiously. "Why would you say that?"

She realized too late what he was referring to. She mentally scrambled for an acceptable reason. "Because of how you were raised. I may not know your parents for very long, but I'm betting they never taught you to judge people by what's on the outside." That caused him to withdraw into his own thoughts. She may not have convinced him that she was right, but she had gotten him confused enough to question his relationship with Elise, and that was a start.

Beverly almost got up and went to her room to avoid making any more slips of the tongue, but she decided that she needed to reestablish their companionship before they parted again. So she turned the sound back on the television and asked him what he preferred to see. He said he never watched any of the late-night shows, yet he settled back in the recliner rather than going home.

Beverly didn't realize she had fallen asleep until Josh tried to rouse her sometime later. She had been dreaming and couldn't force herself to climb out of the comfy chair. "It's okay," she murmured. "I'll just sleep here for a while."

Josh's voice had a smile in it. "No, it's not okay. You'll wake up with a crick in your neck, and you'll feel miserable tomorrow."

She was drifting back to her dreamworld when she suddenly felt herself being lifted. "I can walk," she protested, or at least she thought she did, but he didn't put her down.

Even half asleep, she recognized the smell that was pure Josh, and she burrowed her nose closer to the opening in his shirt. Her palm pressed against his heart and felt the rapid beating. It didn't matter how she had gotten there; she was cradled securely in his arms, and she never wanted to be let go again.

As he lowered her onto her bed and pulled the covers over her, she knew it hadn't been real, but she sighed with contentment anyway.

Josh looked down at her, his physical senses blocking all logic. He reached out and brushed a lock of her hair off her cheek, his fingers lingering in the blond silk. It was completely insane, but more than anything he had ever wanted in his entire life, he wanted to lie down beside her. He was semiaroused just from holding her, but it wasn't that he needed to have sex with her. He simply wanted to embrace her, breathe her, *feel* her spirit touching his. If he didn't know better, he would have sworn he had been with her like that before.

He knelt beside the bed, physically unable to keep himself at a distance from her. What was it about this woman? He studied her face, looking for an answer. The word *innocence* whispered through his mind. But that made no sense either. She wasn't that young.

Was there something special about her, or was it just that his and Elise's relationship had gotten a little shaky lately? More than likely it was all the talk of love and feelings that had him acting like a boy with his first crush.

That didn't explain the weird déjà vu sensations he had been having around her, however. It was the myriad of those sensations he had had all day that had him returning to the house to seek out his mother. She was the only person he knew who wouldn't think such a thing was crazy. He had been hoping she could explain it for him. Instead he had ended up getting even more confused by Beverly.

She sighed in her sleep and her lips parted into a soft smile. God help him. He couldn't resist. He lowered his head and touched his lips to hers.

Instantly, he recoiled in shock. He couldn't believe what he had just done. The woman was sound asleep. She certainly hadn't invited his attention. He was engaged to another woman.

But the real shock was caused by the nearly electrical charge he had felt from the slight contact of their mouths. He quickly backed out of the room, determined to analyze whatever was going haywire inside his head and fix it before he did something embarrassing.

Chapter 18

As Mason drove to the fairgrounds the next morning, Lucille told Beverly a little about pow-wow etiquette. "The announcer lets everyone know when to stand, when pictures can be taken or not, and explains each dance or ceremony, but there are a few rules you need to keep in mind. Never point your finger; it's considered very rude. Touching anyone's outfit is also impolite. If an eagle feather falls from someone's regalia, don't touch it. It's considered sacred since it represents the soul of a fallen warrior."

"Actually," Mason injected, "I almost hope it happens so that you can see the ceremony that follows. It requires four war veterans to retrieve a fallen feather and return it to its owner."

Lucille added, "Many things in Native American teachings are in fours: the seasons, the directions, the peoples." Beverly's curious expression prompted her to explain further. "We're the two-legged people, then there's the four-legged, the winged, and the swimmers."

Beverly listened attentively since she didn't want to do anything irreverent, but part of her mind was wondering whether Josh would show up or stay away, as Elise had insisted.

For some reason, probably because of those cowboy movies she had seen, Beverly had assumed the powwow was a small affair, but this one didn't fall under that description. The fairgrounds were alive with activity. There were countless booths selling a variety of foods and beverages, all nonalcoholic, beautiful handmade crafts like the dream catcher Lucille had given her, and supplies such as feathers, beads, hoops, and leather to make the items.

It was a feast for the eyes. Lucille insisted she taste a Native American specialty called fried bread, and Beverly was delighted with that, too.

Mason and Lucille seemed to know at least half the people there, and she was introduced to each one as a special family friend. Around eleven-thirty, everyone began moving toward a large circle where Lucille told her the dancing and ceremonies would take place.

"The circle represents the Sacred Hoop of Creation," she said. "We believe life is never-ending, like a circle. Only those people invited may enter the ring."

Precisely at noon, everyone was asked to stand, the grand entry song began, and the veterans entered the arena carrying the flags. The music was unlike anything Beverly had ever heard before, a rhythmic sound created by a group of men beating on a large drum and singing in a Native tongue.

Lucille leaned close and whispered, "The drum is the heartbeat of the People. Don't listen, *feel* it."

Beverly remembered saying something like that to Josh last night and wondered if he had made the connection. As if thinking of him held some magic, Josh appeared at his mother's side.

"Sorry I'm late. I overslept."

Beverly glanced at him, but he looked away. She couldn't help but wonder if he was annoyed with her for sticking her nose in his business last night. However, the ceremonies and songs kept her mind occupied sufficiently not to worry about it for now. To her pleasant surprise, Mason participated in the first dance.

"You look like you're having a good time," Lucille said.

"Oh, I am. Mason is wonderful. But there are only men out there. Don't the women get to dance also?"

Lucille laughed. "Yes, and I'll be right in there with them, but it's all done according to long-standing tradition."

When that dance ended, a man walked up to Josh and said, "It's good to see you Crooked Runner. Come join us."

Josh hesitated, but went off after his mother's encouragement.

"What did that man call Josh?" Beverly asked.

She smiled. "Crooked Runner. That's his Mohawk name. He was given it as a boy because every time he competed in a race he zigzagged all over the field instead of staying in a straight line. You wouldn't know it by how straight and narrow he is today, but he used to say he zigzagged because it was too boring to only run from one point to another."

Straight and narrow certainly described this Josh, Beverly thought, but she knew he hadn't always been like that. Once upon a time he had worn black leather and an earring, and had hair as long as hers, and rode around on a big, flashy motorcycle. . . .

The next song began and Beverly stopped listening

to Lucille. All her attention was focused on Josh. She vividly recalled how gracefully he had balanced on the high steel beams, but that had been nothing compared to the grace he was now displaying in the dance. She was mesmerized by the movement of his body and the intense expression on his face. She knew he had to be feeling and not listening to the beat of the drum. To her it meant that he still had the ability to follow his heart, if he could just ignore his overlogical brain long enough to feel his pulse.

Josh and Mason returned and graciously accepted the lavish praise she and Lucille bestowed on them, but other than a quick glance, Josh continued to keep his gaze averted from hers. Two songs later, Lucille left them to join the women in a dance and Beverly was left standing next to Josh. The tension between them was too uncomfortable for her to ignore.

"I'm sorry if I overstepped myself last night," she said in a hushed voice.

He looked down at her and arched one eyebrow. "I beg your pardon?"

"I said more than I should have, I know, but you did ask. If I'd known you were going to get annoyed with me—"

"I'm not annoyed about anything you said."

"You're annoyed about something," Bev said. "And it sure seems to be at me." He cut her off by nodding his head toward the dancers. His mother was entering the ring.

Beverly's eyes followed Lucille through the dance, but her mind was searching for an answer to what was annoying Josh. If it wasn't her lecture about love and marriage, what was it? After their talk, they had watched the late show, and she had fallen asleep. Could he be annoyed that she fell asleep on him?

Suddenly she saw herself nodding off in the chair, but waking up in her bed. In between she had had some very intense dreams about Josh, but she had assumed the dream catcher had something to do with it. Only now did she realize they weren't all dreams. Josh had picked her up and carried her to bed. What else was real? She felt her cheeks grow hot. Surely she couldn't actually *do* any of those things and not remember them.

As soon as the song ended and before Lucille returned, she got Josh's attention again. "Did you . . ." She swallowed nervously. "Did you put me to bed last night?"

The muscle in his cheek twitched, and she knew his annoyance stemmed from something she had done while she thought she was dreaming. "Whatever I did, I'm sorry. I was half asleep and—"

"You didn't do anything," he interrupted, speaking as quietly and quickly as she was. "It was my fault. I should have apologized—"

Lucille's arrival cut off what he was about to say and Beverly had to wait for the next dance to begin before questioning him further. She tapped his arm and motioned for him to lean down so she could whisper in his ear. "Why did you say you should apologize? What happened?"

He gave her a curious look, then murmured in her ear. "Nothing happened. I just felt uncomfortable about putting you to bed without you realizing it."

She saw his cheek twitch again. He was lying. Something had happened, and he was feeling so guilty about it he could barely meet her eyes. It must have been very, very naughty, and she was very, *very* disappointed that she had missed it.

Her thoughts were interrupted when Lucille grasped her hand and gave her a tug.

"Come along," she said, including Mason and Josh in that directive. "The next one's a round dance. Everyone can participate."

"But I don't know—"

"It's easy," Josh said and lightly nudged her shoulder to get her to follow his mother.

The next thing she knew she was part of a circle of dancers and having a terrific time.

Shortly after that dance ended, Josh claimed he had to leave, but at least he no longer seemed annoyed; he was back to looking confused.

Beverly became a victim of bewilderment as well when they returned to the house and there was a message on the answering machine for her to call Elise as soon as possible. She was the last person on earth Beverly wanted to talk to, yet she could hardly ignore the message after both Lucille and Mason had heard it.

"The phone in your room is a separate line, if you'd like to use that one," Lucille said helpfully.

After a few minutes of arguing with herself, Beverly returned Elise's call.

"Oh, I'm so glad you got home in time," Elise gushed. "My girlfriend and I are going out tonight and I was hoping you'd join us."

Beverly cringed. What could she say? "That's so kind of you to ask, but, um, actually, I'm afraid I'll have to pass for tonight. I only brought a few outfits with me. My clothes were, uh, shipped and haven't arrived yet."

"No problem. Wherever we go, cazh is the code. Jeans always work. So we'll swing by there and pick you up about nine. Okay?"

"Nine. Of course. That would be fine," Beverly heard herself replying when no other excuse came to mind. After she hung up, she convinced herself that as uncomfortable as the thought of spending an evening with Josh's fiancée was, there might be a silver lining in the cloud.

She had gotten impressions of Elise from Livvie, Lucille, and Josh, and was fairly certain that Elise was not the best mate for Josh. However, in order to make a definite decision as to whether or not the forthcoming wedding should be derailed, she really should get to know her opposition firsthand.

Elise was only a half hour late for a change and showed up at the door wearing a shiny yellow raincoat and black patent leather boots that reached her knees. After a quick greeting and kiss on the cheek for both her future in-laws, she told them she was taking Beverly to the movies and to get a bite afterward, so it might be late when they got back. As soon as Lucille located a house key for Beverly, Elise hustled her out the door.

"Is it expected to rain?" Beverly asked as they approached a car that looked very similar to Josh's.

Elise laughed and unzipped the front of the raincoat. "Gawd, you really are the small-town girl, aren't you?" She removed the coat, revealing a black patent leather skirt that barely covered her hips, a flesh-colored, open-weave jersey, and short patent leather vest that showed off her cleavage. "I just didn't want Mummy and Daddy to have a shit fit over my outfit."

She opened the back door, tossed the coat inside, and waited for Beverly to get in. "Beverly, meet my best friend, Tamara."

Beverly greeted the plump, plain-faced young woman in the front seat and tried to get a peek at what she was wearing. She hoped it was closer to her jeans and sweater than Elise's outrageous outfit. Why would Elise have told her to wear jeans, then show up in something so flashy? She came up with an answer that seemed reasonable based on what she had learned about Elise thus far. It was the same reason that her best friend would be someone homely in appearance. Elise liked to be the main attraction.

"What movie are we going to see?" Beverly asked as they pulled out of the driveway.

Elise and Tamara both laughed. "*That* was also for the benefit of our elders. Josh pissed me off last night, so we're going out to howl tonight. Have you ever been to a male strip club?"

Beverly's mouth dropped open, but she quickly recovered. "Just once. It was . . . interesting."

"Well, wait until you see the lineup at The Bullpen. The woman that owns the place has the absolute greatest taste in men, and I have it on good authority that she personally makes sure that every one of them is actively hetero. And I do mean *actively*."

The Bullpen? Beverly cleared her throat. "Just out of curiosity, do you know the owner's name?"

"Of course. It's Amanda James. She and I share the same hairdresser, so you know what that means." She glanced in the rear-view mirror. "You might want to make an appointment with her while you're in the area. I'd be glad to give you a reference."

"Thank you," Beverly replied with a smile, as if

she didn't catch the insult. "I could use a trim." She had almost panicked when she heard Amanda's name, but then she realized that Josh wouldn't have been associated with that woman in his new life.

Elise was quiet for a moment, then asked, "So, how did you enjoy the *powwow*?"

Her slightly sarcastic tone of voice reminded Beverly of what Lucille had said about Elise possibly disapproving of them. She decided to see if that was true. Imitating Elise's tone, she simply said, "*Gawd.*"

Elise laughed. "No kidding. I thought I was going to die the first time Josh dragged me to one of his little Indian fests. Did he happen to show up today?"

Her question was asked lightly, but Beverly was beginning to get the picture. This "evening out with the girls" was Elise's way of checking up on her fiancé. "For about an hour."

Elise glanced at Tamara, then at Beverly in the mirror. "Don't tell me. He *danced.*"

Beverly imitated Elise's grimace.

"Dear God, what am I going to do with that man? I am trying so hard to civilize him, but every so often he slips back into all that savage crap his mother goes on about."

"Maybe he just needed to have one last fling before the wedding," Beverly offered sympathetically. "Surely you'll be able to control his primitive urges once you're living together." The words nearly made her ill, but they produced the desired effects.

"Hmmmph. I'll either control them or castrate them," Elise snarled. "Maybe you're right about a last fling. And if he can have one, so can I. Right, Tamara?"

Tamara giggled, but said nothing during the entire trip to The Bullpen.

The parking lot was so crowded, Elise pulled the car up to the lounge entrance. The doorman came forward with a stern look on his face until he recognized Elise getting out of the car.

"There's no place to park, Rick. Be a love and take care of it for me." She handed him her keys and some money, and like a queen waved for Tamara and Beverly to follow her.

Beverly had managed to forget about where they were going while she was studying Elise, but once inside the nightclub there was too much bare male flesh to ignore it. She *really* didn't want to be there. "It's terribly crowded," she said to Elise. "Maybe we should go somewhere else."

"Not a chance," she replied and motioned to one of the muscle-bound waiters.

"Hi, hon," he said and gave her a kiss on the cheek. "It's been a while, hasn't it?"

She laughed. "Yeah, but I'm back, and horny as hell. Amanda said she'd hold a table for us."

Minutes later, the three of them were seated right in front of center stage. Shortly after their drinks were served, a brassy woman with dark red hair came up to them.

"Amanda!" Elise squealed and allowed her cheek to be pressed by the owner's.

Beverly was stunned by the woman's appearance. She looked like an aging streetwalker. Her outfit was as revealing as Elise's, only cheaper-looking, and she was considerably older and had a much fuller figure. How could Josh have been attracted to her?

"Where have you been the last month?" Amanda asked. "The boys missed you."

Elise showed off her diamond ring. "I have a keeper now."

Amanda whistled over the size of the gem. "Is the rest of him as attractive as his bank account?"

Elise laughed. "If you saw him, you'd try to hire him on the spot."

"So what are you doing here instead of home getting laid?"

Elise rolled her eyes. "He does have this one *little* shortcoming."

"You're kidding! *You* and a miniman?"

"Well, he's not *that* small, but after you've had Elvis the Pelvis and his foot-long sausage . . . But the real problem isn't size as much as technique. Talk about bor-r-ring."

"Yeah. I know what you mean. Which reminds me, we have some new prime beef. I named him the Lone Ranger. And let me tell you, when they were handing out dicks in heaven, this boy got second helpings."

"Yes, but does he know what to do with it?"

Amanda winked. "You'd have to judge that for yourself."

Beverly was mortified. It was bad enough that she knew that any minute men would be taking their clothes off right in front of her, but the conversation she had just listened to was positively disgusting. She couldn't decide what upset her more—Elise making fun of Josh's private parts and inferior lovemaking, which she knew for a fact were bald-faced lies, or the possibility that Elise was as familiar with some of the male dancers as Amanda was.

Elise and Tamara were on their second cocktails before Beverly was half finished with her first. A third was brought to the table just before the floor show began.

Elise leaned toward Beverly as the first dancer, dressed as Charlie Chaplin, duck-waddled out on stage. "If you see anything you'd like to try on for size, Amanda can probably arrange it for you."

Beverly's cheeks flamed instantly, and Elise found that very funny.

Elvis was number three, but other than a glance, Beverly had stopped looking up by that time. As with the first two, he seemed to spend all too much time gyrating his hips toward the front center table.

It was finally the Lone Ranger's turn to strut his stuff, and if Beverly hadn't seen what Elise did with her own eyes, she wouldn't have believed it. The woman who was engaged to be married to the man Beverly loved wrote something on a cocktail napkin then wrapped it around a one-hundred-dollar bill. With a crook of her finger, she brought the cowboy to his knees in front of her, made sure he saw the amount of her "donation," then tucked it deep down inside his g-string. He shook his finger at her as her thumb "accidentally" brushed his incredibly swollen member, but his grin countered the reprimand.

Beverly had had enough. As soon as she could get Elise's attention, she told her she felt a migraine coming on and needed to go home before she became really ill. Elise looked annoyed until Beverly told her she would call a cab. Before the next dancer came out, she said goodbye and slipped away.

Fortunately, a taxi was waiting nearby and she was able to get back to the quiet of the Colby house in a very short time. Seeing Josh's car in the driveway erased all the bad feelings Elise had caused, but it raised a new dilemma. Should she say something about what she had witnessed this evening, or keep it to herself?

Since it was nearly midnight, she assumed Lucille was in bed, so she let herself in rather than ring the bell. The sound of the television drew her to the family room. There were no lights on inside the room and at first she thought no one was there. Then a soft snore made her take a closer look.

Josh was sound asleep in the recliner she had fallen asleep in last night. Why was he here? His parents had obviously gone to bed, and he had a choice of sleeping in his own apartment or here in his old room. It occurred to Beverly that he might have been waiting up, hoping to catch Elise when she dropped Beverly off. From what Elise had said, they hadn't made up from their tiff last night.

She supposed she should try to wake him up, but he looked so peaceful. She turned off the television, and he moved slightly in response to the elimination of the sound. The light in the hallway kept the room from being thrown into total darkness, and her eyes quickly adjusted.

For some time she stood there, just watching Josh sleep. It seemed like an eternity since she had touched him and felt his hands on her. She wanted to kiss him so badly she almost cried from the need.

She was happy that she had improved everyone's lives; she really was. But she missed his love so terribly. And now that she knew for certain what a mistake it would be for him to marry Elise, it was even harder to hold back what she was feeling.

Perhaps, she thought, while he was sound asleep, she could at least touch his face. Quietly, she moved closer and sat on the arm of the chair. If he woke up, she could always say she was trying to wake him.

Her fingers trembled slightly as they neared his face. She was about to withdraw her hand when he moved his head and her palm was suddenly cradling his cheek. He exhaled and his breath wafted over her arm. It was such a little thing, yet she still felt as though she were taking something she had no right to.

Josh's eyes opened slightly, and he smiled at her. She started to tell him she was trying to wake him up, but he eased her onto his lap and pressed his lips to hers before she could utter more than his name.

She had a fleeting thought that he must think she was Elise, but she really didn't care at the moment. His hands were caressing *her* and his mouth was making love to *her*. He pulled her body further into the chair, and she automatically fitted herself to him. She couldn't help but respond to his hungry kisses, for she was so starved for the taste of him.

Though he had been in a deep sleep a minute before, his body was now fully awake, reminding her that there was absolutely nothing small about him, despite what Elise claimed.

They were as close to having sex as two people could be with all their clothes on when wakefulness finally reached Josh's brain.

"Beverly?" he asked, blinking at her.

She tried to get out of the chair, but he stopped her easily.

"Wait, please. I don't understand how this happened."

She was extremely aware of his leg over hers and his arousal pressed to the heart of her womanhood. She took a shaky breath. "I . . . I was going to wake you up . . . so you could go to bed. I . . . I think you thought I was Elise." She expected him to let her up, but he didn't move.

"No. I didn't," he said, frowning in bewilderment. "I thought it was you. Why didn't you stop me?"

She lowered her eyes, but whispered the truth since he had been honest with her. "Because I was enjoying it too much."

He sighed and ran his fingers through her hair. "Do you have any idea how you're complicating my life?"

He didn't sound at all pleased about it, but Beverly was. "I'm sorry. But maybe your life needs a little complicating." He made a face. "Maybe it's time to remember how Crooked Runner got his name." His expression altered slightly, and forcing herself to ignore the positions of their bodies, she continued with what she had in mind.

"Once upon a time you thought doing what everyone else was doing was boring. Now you're running in such a straight line, you don't even need to look where you're going. Don't you ever get the urge to break away from the pack? Let your hair grow, put on a leather jacket, and take a ride on a Harley?"

He chuckled softly. "You just described me during the first two years at college. My mother called it my James Dean phase. But I was a lot younger then."

"And what are you now? An old man? Anyway, where does it say that there's an age limit for taking a risk and letting life get a little complicated? Is it the same book that says at thirty-five you should choose a wife based on a list of criteria?"

Instead of answering, he asked, "Why didn't Elise come in with you? She would have seen my car in the driveway."

"Um, she didn't drive me home. I took a cab."

"Why?"

"I was getting a headache, and didn't want to ruin her evening."

"Where did Elise take you tonight?"

If she said the movies, he might ask what was playing. If she told the truth, he might think she was only saying it to make Elise look bad because she was interested in him herself.

"Time's up," he said with a frown. "I smell cigarette smoke in your hair. There are very few places nowadays where the smoke gets that thick, and the movies are not one of them. Okay, let me get you off the hook here. Did she take you to The Bullpen?"

Her eyes widened with surprise.

"Yes, I know she used to go there quite often before we got engaged. I figured she'd outgrow her fascination with the place once we were committed to each other. I'm sure her taking you there tonight was just her way of punishing me for going to the pow-wow today." He waited for her to confirm his assumption, but when she remained silent, he asked, "Why do I get the impression that you're holding something in? What happened tonight?"

Did he really want to marry Elise enough to forgive her for the kind of behavior she had exhibited tonight? She would be lying if she told him nothing happened, and yet she knew she would sound like a jealous woman if she tattled. Even then, he would probably come up with an acceptable reason why Elise had touched that man's body and given him a hundred dollars.

She tried to rise again, but he tightened his hold on her. "Josh, please don't ask me to give you an excuse to make this okay between us. I don't want to be the woman you turned to because you were angry or hurt by your fiancée. I have never been, and never intend to be *the other woman* in a relationship. And I don't want to be considered a complication either. Now, please let me up."

He was back to looking confused again as she rose and walked away. At the door, she stopped and turned around. "You asked me last night what love was. I want to add two things to what I said. Being in love does *not* require you to overlook serious faults, and it definitely does not involve punishing the other person for disobeying your orders."

Chapter 19

Although she would have loved to remain under the covers all day Monday, Beverly had an appointment that morning in White Plains. On the way there she had time to think about everything that had happened last night, whether she wanted to or not. Unfortunately, at the end of her trip her mind was no clearer than it had been at the beginning.

Josh was clearly attracted to her and was having an occasional memory flash of their time together. *A plus.*

Josh was fixed on the idea that Elise fit his "criteria" and was the ideal woman for him. *A minus.*

Elise was an awful person and would be a terrible wife for Josh. *A plus.*

But he didn't realize it. *A minus.*

Josh's family didn't care for Elise. *A plus.*

The wedding was less than six weeks away. *A double minus.*

The minuses outnumbered the pluses, and Beverly had no idea how to change that.

Her business appointment resulted in a new client, which picked her spirits up considerably. From there, she checked in with Earl and learned that he had a buyer lined up and merely needed her to bring in the comic books to close the deal.

Deciding that she was on an uphill trend, she did something she had intended to put off until after her surgery. Running into Frankie Giammarco had been a real shock, but since that moment she had been dying to learn what had happened to everyone. She knew she couldn't just call home, announce that she was alive after all, and ask how her family and friends were doing and what they had been up to for the last thirty-eight years. Not only would it be impossible to explain, she knew it wouldn't be fair to deliver such a shock to people who had mourned her death. Yet her curiosity needed to be appeased.

She began with a call to the California Medical Association. Through them, she located Dr. Jacob Mauser in San Diego, and within a half hour she was talking to Hope. It was so easy that she glanced upward and thanked Lavonda for her help.

Beverly had her part rehearsed, and to be absolutely certain Hope wouldn't recognize her voice, she raised her voice a pitch and faked a southern accent. "Hello Mrs. Mauser. Y'all don't know me, but mah name is Nan Olsen. Ah graduated from Mercerville High with Allen Winetke, the brother of an old friend of yours, Beverly Winetke Newcastle."

"Oh my. Hello, Nan. What can I do for you?"

"Ah'm workin' on a reunion committee that would bring together twenty years of alumni, and Ah was given your name as someone who might be able to help me track down a number of people on our list."

"I'll be glad to help if I can."

"Great. First, Ah wasn't able to find any of the Winetkes."

"I'm afraid Beverly passed away a long time ago. And the parents are both gone as well. The last I heard, Allen was working for General Motors in Detroit, a design engineer, I think."

"Ah assume he's married and has children."

"I believe so, but I only kept in touch with him for a few years after Beverly died."

"How about Dee-Dee Giammarco and Peggy Roach?"

"Now those two I can tell you about. We all still exchange Christmas letters. Peggy was widowed some years ago and is happily married to her third husband. They live in Naples, Florida. And Dee-Dee just retired from her job with the State Attorney's office in Ohio. Of course, we're all grandparents now. Let me get those addresses for you."

Beverly wrote down the addresses and phone numbers, though she knew she would never use them. Before she hung up, she had to ask the one question weighing on her mind since she had seen Frankie. "Ah seem to remember Allen tellin' me somethin' about Dee-Dee runnin' 'way from her husband and children. How did that all turn out?"

Hope groaned. "What a nightmare that was. But everything ended up just fine for her and the kids. She even remarried after a while."

It was all Beverly could do to keep from telling her who she really was, but after a few more tidbits, she made herself say goodbye. She had to remember that if she hadn't left when she did, she would never have seen them again anyway.

Her list of things to be taken care of in her new life was practically finished. Unfortunately, the remaining obstacles were the most difficult to overcome.

She still had a week before her surgery, and though she had set aside any worry about it, the waiting period was tremendously aggravating. If it wasn't for Lavonda's having assured her she would be fine, she would probably be having a nervous breakdown over it.

However, because of that assurance, her mind had plenty of room to fret over Josh. She had no doubt she had made some progress with him, and that in time he would realize that he couldn't marry Elise because he was in love with Beverly. But unlimited time was not something they had. Repeatedly she went over the exact words Lavonda had said to her during their last meeting, and she always came up with the same recollection.

Although the Gypsy had assured her about her health and told her she could live happily in Josh's time, she had never actually guaranteed that Beverly could live happily *with* Josh. Instead, she had given her a warning about his circumstances having changed. That had to mean Lavonda couldn't arrange for her to have Josh; Beverly had to accomplish that through her own efforts.

If only she could hear what he was thinking . . .

"I think that was the best veal marsala I've ever tasted," Lucille told Josh as he picked up her plate and set it on his kitchen pass-through counter. "I had no idea you had become such a gourmet cook."

Josh laughed. "Survival instincts. You and your housekeepers spoiled me, and I got tired of eating out every night." He refused to allow her to help clear the table. "Would you like coffee or tea?"

"Tea would be fine." She had been pleased by his

invitation to come to his apartment that night for dinner, but she had been his mother too long not to know that he wanted to talk to her about something. However, none of the subjects they had touched on in the last hour needed her counsel. "You know, Josh, I'm delighted that you asked me to have dinner with you, just the two of us, but since you never thought of doing this before, I'd like to hear what was behind it."

"That obvious, huh?"

Lucille smirked at him. "Just bring me my tea and start talking."

Josh had no idea where to begin, partly because he wasn't all that sure what he wanted to talk to her about. Somehow he had been hoping that her maternal instincts would take over and she would simply read his mind, carve out the problem, and tell him what he should do about it.

"Since you invited me and not your father, I will assume we can eliminate business and financial questions," Lucille offered when he failed to get started. "That leaves matters of the spirit and the heart. Which is it?"

Josh sighed. "Both, I think. What do you know about déjà vu?"

"Probably no more than you do. What's the real question?"

He fidgeted in his chair. "I keep getting flashes of . . . things, and they feel like memories, but that can't be."

"Why not?"

"Because they didn't happen, so it isn't possible for me to remember them."

"There's a number of explanations for déjà vu. If

you accept the idea of reincarnation, the things you're seeing might have happened in a previous life. If you accept the concept of mental telepathy, you might be picking up someone else's thoughts or experiences. If that's too far out for you, you could simply have a very active imagination that's gotten kicked off by something that happened to you recently. It could be your subconscious mind's way of telling you to take a second look at something."

"Uh-huh," he sounded, but he looked more confused than before.

"Does Beverly have anything to do with this?" Lucille asked straight out. Her question deepened the color on his cheekbones. "Don't be so shocked. Anyone with eyes could see how you look at her. You are attracted to her, right?"

He made a face. "It makes no sense. I've tried to be logical about it, but I can't figure out exactly why the attraction is so strong."

"She's very pretty."

He shook his head. "I thought of that, but it doesn't explain these weird feelings I get when I'm around her."

"Weird how?"

He searched for an example suitable to tell his mother. "Like at the powwow, when she was dancing with us. Because she was having such a good time, I felt like ... like it was the first time I'd ever danced. And at the same time, I felt like she belonged there, as part of our family."

Lucille nodded slowly. "Unlike Elise, who wouldn't be caught dead dancing with us. Josh, you're engaged, which means you made a conscious decision that you're prepared to forgo romantic relationships with other women. But you can still have other women as friends."

"I don't want Beverly as a friend," he stated without hesitation.

"I see. I hope you're not asking me to condone your taking her as a mistress."

"I don't want that either."

"Postpone the wedding then."

He was shocked that she would suggest something so radical. "You know I can't do that. The invitations have already been sent out. Everything's been arranged. Elise would fry my—She'd never forgive me if I embarrassed her like that."

"So what is it you *do* want?"

"I was hoping you could tell me."

His mother sighed and shook her head. "I'm sorry, Josh, this is not something that I can decide for you. You're supposed to be getting married in less than six weeks. The fact that you've waited so long to take that step is important. My advice is to weigh all the facts with your feelings ... for both women. And when you do, imagine that there is no such thing as divorce or infidelity, that from the day you say 'I do,' you *do* until death do you part."

Lucille could have easily told him what he should do, for the answer was quite clear to her, but Josh needed to work it out on his own. The hardest part of keeping her opinion to herself was knowing that he had become so straight-line in his thinking and his behavior that there was a strong possibility that he would make the wrong choice. What she needed was to find a way to reawaken his heart before it was too late.

For the next six days she spent most of her time

making sure that Beverly was too occupied to worry about her surgery. When Beverly didn't have a business appointment, Lucille took her shopping for new clothes and urged her to come to classes with her. By the end of the week, they were the best of friends, and Lucille knew with absolute certainty that Beverly would be the ideal daughter-in-law.

Beverly never brought up Josh's name, but whenever Lucille did she could see that Beverly was very much in love with her son. She could also see that Beverly believed that the situation was hopeless.

Josh had not called or stopped by once since they had had dinner together the previous Monday. Lucille figured it was his way of crawling into his cave and following the advice she had given him to weigh all the facts with his feelings, but Beverly took his absence as a sign that he had lost what little interest he had had in her.

The morning of Beverly's surgery, an idea came to Lucille and she almost kicked herself for not thinking of using it sooner.

Beverly did her best to keep from showing her fear as the surgeon was talking to her. She reminded herself that Lavonda had assured her that the lump was not deadly at this time and that she would be fine as long as she had it taken care of immediately. It helped that they had given her a shot of something that made her feel like she was floating on a cloud. It also helped that Lucille was beside her, holding her hand.

She heard the doctor telling her about the general anesthesia and a two-inch incision, and how it would all be over in a few hours. She could go home by that afternoon.

"Hi."

She turned toward the voice that sounded like Josh and blinked her eyes to get him in focus. When she couldn't do it, she figured he was just a figment of her imagination, but she tried to answer him anyway. "Hi. What are you doing here?" Her voice sounded as blurred as her eyesight. She felt his fingers stroke her cheek and sighed. What a lovely hallucination this was.

"I would have been here sooner," he said softly, "but I didn't know about this until Mom called a half hour ago. You should have told me."

She smiled and tried to tell him it was okay, but her mouth wouldn't cooperate.

"I wanted to see you before . . . before the operation, and tell you that I finally understand what you were trying to tell me . . . about being in love, and—"

"I'm sorry," a nurse interrupted. "Beverly's number just came up in the OR. Time to go. If you want to wait in the family room, the doctor will come out and update you in about an hour."

Beverly waved at Lucille and Josh, then gave in to the lovely, lovely medicine.

"The mass was benign," Dr. Verona told Lucille and Josh with a smile. "There's nothing to worry about. We're going to keep her in recovery for a while though. She'll have some discomfort for about a week. Make her rest tonight, but she can get up and around tomorrow. Here's a prescription for some pain medicine if she needs it."

After the doctor left, Josh and Lucille both took deep breaths of relief.

Josh kissed his mother's cheek. "I have something to take care of that I've put off too long already. Tell Beverly . . . no, don't tell her anything. Not yet. I'll come by and see her tomorrow, after the drugs wear off."

Lucille smiled happily. Her idea had paid off.

As Josh stepped outside, he took a moment to notice how very bright the sun was that day, how beautiful the trees looked with their new spring leaves, and how the sky was the color of Beverly's eyes. It was exactly the way she had told him being in love was supposed to be. Everything was brighter and more colorful now that she had come into his life.

He supposed his subconscious knew it the first moment he saw her, but it took a panic attack to make him consciously aware of his feelings. When his mother called that morning, his heart took over his thought processes. She had sounded so worried about Beverly, fretting over the kinds of terrible accidents and unexpected tragedies that can happen during the simplest surgical procedures.

By the time they had hung up, he was picturing Beverly in a casket, taken away from him before he could logically figure out what he wanted to do about her and Elise. And he knew he couldn't let that happen.

All the things Beverly had told him about being in love were how he felt about her. What he felt for Elise didn't begin to compare. He had rushed to the hospital without analyzing what he was going to do about that. He only knew that he had needed to tell Beverly that he loved her.

And that he was certain he had loved her before.

Somewhere between his mother's explanation of déjà vu and seeing Beverly in the hospital, he had come to that conclusion. He didn't know where or when, and it wasn't of any importance now. What was important was that he needed to rearrange his life to be with her and to show her that Crooked Runner was still alive and well inside him.

From the hospital he drove directly to Elise's house. He always believed in getting the hardest tasks out of the way first, and breaking his engagement to her was probably one of the hardest things he had ever had to do.

He had kept giving her excuses for not seeing her all week, and she had fluctuated between being irritated with him and worried that she had done something to upset him. In spite of the fact that they had been arguing a lot lately and that she had returned to her old hunting grounds to punish him, she hadn't actually done anything to warrant his ending the relationship. The change was within him.

He felt horribly guilty about the hurt this was going to cause Elise. If there was any way he could spare her the embarrassment of being jilted, he would. He figured he would let it appear that she had changed *her* mind and broke off with him for whatever reason she wanted to give. After all, he did care for her, he just didn't *love* her.

He was somewhat surprised when he reached her house and she wasn't home. Normally she didn't even leave her bedroom before noon. He had no choice but to take care of the second item on his agenda first—bringing Crooked Runner back from oblivion.

When he returned to his apartment later that afternoon, he called Elise, but all he got was her machine. Now that he had made his decision to break the engagement, he found it very aggravating that he couldn't get it over with.

You must go by zee house again. Elise eez there.

Josh's gaze darted around his living room. He would have sworn he heard a voice. He had already hung up the phone, neither the television nor radio was on, and he had never before heard voices coming from another apartment. The oddest thing about it was that the French-accented voice sounded just like his "Aunt" Lavonda, his mother's godmother who had passed away a few months ago.

Go now. Do not wait.

Josh's heart thumped in his chest. It wasn't his imagination. Lavonda was giving him a message. He had respected that woman all his life. He wasn't about to start disobeying her orders now.

Elise's car was parked in the driveway when he arrived at her house, and as soon as he touched the cool hood he knew she hadn't just gotten home. No one answered the door, which only meant that the housekeeper wasn't around. It was highly possible that Elise was inside and simply didn't want to be bothered.

He was about to ring the bell again when a feminine squeal reached his ears. It seemed to have come from the backyard, so he headed that way to investigate.

It took his brain several seconds to register what his eyes took in.

The squeal had come from Elise, but she was not in any danger, as he had feared. She and a long-haired young man were frolicking in the pool . . . minus their bathing suits. The boy saw him first, and it was his expression that alerted Elise that they had company.

"Don't bother to get out on account of me," Josh said. "I just stopped by to let you know that the wedding is off." He turned on his heel and left before Elise could close her mouth. Instead of feeling angry or betrayed, Josh laughed out loud.

So much for feeling guilty.

"You were right again, Lavonda," Beverly said aloud when she awoke Tuesday morning. Her left breast was tender, but bearable, her mind was clear, and she was hungry. Feeling like a hundred-pound weight had just been lifted from her shoulders, she got dressed and headed to the kitchen.

"Good morning," Lucille said cheerfully. "How do you feel?"

"Very well, considering how bad I felt yesterday." She fixed herself some orange juice and toast and felt even better a few minutes later.

Josh had told Lucille not to say anything to Beverly, but she couldn't resist giving away a little something. "Do you remember Josh coming in to see you yesterday morning?"

Beverly narrowed her brows in thought. "He did?" She could almost see him in her mind, but not quite. "Boy, that was some medicine. I thought I had imagined him."

"No. He was there, but he couldn't stay. Had some business to take care of."

"Oh," Beverly said, trying not to show any disappointment over his not sticking around to see how she fared.

"He called to check on you last night, but you were asleep."

"Oh," she repeated, feeling somewhat mollified that at least he was concerned for her. A sound drifted into the kitchen from outdoors. A ferocious, roaring sound that made her think of Josh in black leather.

"He had some interesting news," Lucille said casually.

The sound grew louder until she felt it as much as heard it.

"He broke his engagement to Elise."

Beverly lurched up from the table and rushed out the front door toward the sound. For several heartbeats she stood there, gaping at the manly figure dressed from neck to toe in black leather. A black helmet shielded his identity, and between his legs was a powerful creature, rumbling its discontent at being forced to sit still.

Josh revved the engine twice, then held out his hand to her.

Her heart sang out in joy, yet she needed him to speak the words.

When she remained on the front porch rather than accept his invitation, Josh removed his helmet so that she could see his eyes. "I broke up with Elise."

She took a step forward. "Why?"

"Because I'm in love with you."

She moved a little closer. "How can you be sure?" He smiled and his eyes told her all she needed to know.

"Because you make me happier than I've ever felt in my life. Because you make my world more colorful. And because a voice in my head warned me that if I let you go, I'd be miserable for the rest of my life."

She cocked her head to one side. "By any chance, did the voice have a French accent?"

Josh's surprise was obvious. "How do you know that?"

Beverly closed the distance between them and stroked his cheek with her fingertip. "Ask me that question again on our tenth anniversary." She kissed his mouth, then fearlessly joined him on the wild beast, for she knew she had tamed its master's heart . . . just in time.

📲 TOPAZ

Journeys of Passion and Desire

☐ **TOMORROW'S DREAMS by Heather Graham.** Beautiful singer Penelope Parrish—the darling of the New York stage—never forgot the night her golden life ended. The handsome businessman Seth Tyler, whom she loved beyond all reason, hurled wild accusations at her and walked out of her life. Years later, when Penelope and Seth meet again amid the boisterous uproar of a Denver dance hall, all their repressed passion struggles to break free once more. (406842—$5.50)

☐ **YESTERDAY'S ROSES by Heather Cullman.** Dr. Hallie Gardiner knows something is terribly wrong with the handsome, haunted-looking man in the great San Francisco mansion. The Civil War had wounded Jake "Young Midas" Parrish, just as it had left Serena, his once-beautiful bride, hopelessly lost in her private universe. But when Serena is found mysteriously dead, Hallie finds herself falling in love with Jake who is now a murder suspect. (405749—$4.99)

☐ **LOVE ME TONIGHT by Nan Ryan.** The war had robbed Helen Burke Courtney of her money and her husband. All she had left was her coastal Alabama farm. Captain Kurt Northway of the Union Army might be the answer to her prayers, or a way to get to hell a little faster. She needed a man's help to plant her crops; she didn't know if she could stand to have a damned handsome Yankee do it. (404831—$4.99)

☐ **FIRES OF HEAVEN by Chelley Kitzmiller.** Independence Taylor had not been raised to survive the rigors of the West, but she was determined to mend her relationship with her father—even if it meant journeying across dangerous frontier to the Arizona Territory. But nothing prepared her for the terrifying moment when her wagon train was attacked, and she was carried away from certain death by the mysterious Apache known only as Shatto. (404548—$4.99)

☐ **RAWHIDE AND LACE by Margaret Brownley.** Libby Summerhill couldn't wait to get out of Deadman's Gulch—a lawless mining town filled with gunfights, brawls, and uncivilized mountain men—men like Logan St. John. He knew his town was no place for a woman and the sooner Libby and her precious baby left for Boston, the better. But how could he bare to lose this spirited woman who melted his heart of stone forever? (404610—$4.99)

*Prices slightly higher in Canada

Buy them at your local bookstore or use this convenient coupon for ordering.

PENGUIN USA
P.O. Box 999 — Dept. #17109
Bergenfield, New Jersey 07621

Please send me the books I have checked above.
I am enclosing $_____ (please add $2.00 to cover postage and handling). Send check or money order (no cash or C.O.D.'s) or charge by Mastercard or VISA (with a $15.00 minimum). Prices and numbers are subject to change without notice.

Card #_____ Exp. Date _____
Signature_____
Name_____
Address_____
City _____ State _____ Zip Code _____

For faster service when ordering by credit card call **1-800-253-6476**

Allow a minimum of 4-6 weeks for delivery. This offer is subject to change without notice.

BREATHTAKING ROMANCES YOU WON'T WANT TO MISS

☐ *Wild Bliss* by Cassie Edwards   (405854—$5.99)
☐ *The Duke* by Catherine Coulter   (406176—$6.99)
☐ *Whisper My Name* by Raine Cantrell   (406052—$4.99)
☐ *A Taste Of Heaven* by Alexis Harrington   (406532—$5.50)
☐ *Falcon's Fire* by Patricia Ryan   (406354—$5.50)
☐ *Touch Of Lightning* by Carin Rafferty   (406133—$5.50)
☐ *Petticoats And Pistols* by Margaret Brownley

     (406184—$4.99)

☐ *The Thistle And The Rose* by May McGoldrick

     (406265—$4.99)

☐ *Bed Of Roses* by Suzanne Simmons   (405196—$4.99)
☐ *Stormswept* by Deborah Martin   (405293—$4.99)
☐ *Moonspun Dreams* by Elizabeth Gregg   (405730—$4.99)
☐ *Stolen Hearts* by Melinda McRae   (406117—$5.50)

from **TOPAZ**

Buy them at your local bookstore or use this convenient coupon for ordering.

PENGUIN USA
P.O. Box 999 — Dept. #17109
Bergenfield, New Jersey 07621

Please send me the books I have checked above.
I am enclosing $_____ (please add $2.00 to cover postage and handling). Send check or money order (no cash or C.O.D.'s) or charge by Mastercard or VISA (with a $15.00 minimum). Prices and numbers are subject to change without notice.

Card #_____ Exp. Date _____
Signature_____
Name_____
Address_____
City _____ State _____ Zip Code _____

For faster service when ordering by credit card call **1-800-253-6476**

Allow a minimum of 4-6 weeks for delivery. This offer is subject to change without notice.

WE NEED YOUR HELP
To continue to bring you quality romance
that meets your personal expectations,
we at TOPAZ books want to hear from you.
Help us by filling out this questionnaire, and in exchange
we will give you a **free gift** as a token of our gratitude.

- Is this the first TOPAZ book you've purchased? (circle one)

    YES   NO

    The title and author of this book is: _____

- If this was not the first TOPAZ book you've purchased, how many have you bought in the past year?

    a: 0 - 5   b 6 - 10   c: more than 10   d: more than 20

- How many romances in total did you buy in the past year?

    a: 0 - 5   b: 6 - 10   c: more than 10   d: more than 20 ____

- How would you rate your overall satisfaction with this book?

    a: Excellent   b: Good   c: Fair   d: Poor

- What was the main reason you bought this book?

    a: It is a TOPAZ novel, and I know that TOPAZ stands
       for quality romance fiction
    b: I liked the cover
    c: The story-line intrigued me
    d: I love this author
    e: I really liked the setting
    f: I love the cover models
    g: Other: _____

- Where did you buy this TOPAZ novel?

    a: Bookstore   b: Airport   c: Warehouse Club
    d: Department Store   e: Supermarket   f: Drugstore
    g: Other: _____

- Did you pay the full cover price for this TOPAZ novel? (circle one)

    YES   NO
    If you did not, what price did you pay? _____

- Who are your favorite TOPAZ authors? (Please list)

- How did you first hear about TOPAZ books?

    a: I saw the books in a bookstore
    b: I saw the TOPAZ Man on TV or at a signing
    c: A friend told me about TOPAZ
    d: I saw an advertisement in_____magazine
    e: Other: _____

- What type of romance do you generally prefer?

    a: Historical   b: Contemporary
    c: Romantic Suspense   d: Paranormal (time travel,
       futuristic, vampires, ghosts, warlocks, etc.)
    d: Regency   e: Other: _____

- What historical settings do you prefer?

    a: England   b: Regency England   c: Scotland
    e: Ireland   f: America   g: Western Americana
    h: American Indian   i: Other: _____

- What type of story do you prefer?

    a: Very sexy   b: Sweet, less explicit
    c: Light and humorous   d: More emotionally intense
    e: Dealing with darker issues f: Other

- What kind of covers do you prefer?

    a: Illustrating both hero and heroine   b: Hero alone
    c: No people (art only)   d: Other_____

- What other genres do you like to read (circle all that apply)

    Mystery   Medical Thrillers   Science Fiction
    Suspense   Fantasy   Self-help
    Classics   General Fiction   Legal Thrillers
    Historical Fiction

- Who is your favorite author, and why?_____
_____

- What magazines do you like to read? (circle all that apply)

    a: *People*   b: *Time/Newsweek*
    c: *Entertainment Weekly*   d: *Romantic Times*
    e: *Star*   f: *National Enquirer*
    g: *Cosmopolitan*   h: *Woman's Day*
    i: *Ladies' Home Journal*   j: *Redbook*
    k: Other:_____

- In which region of the United States do you reside?

    a: Northeast   b: Midatlantic   c: South
    d: Midwest   e: Mountain   f: Southwest
    g: Pacific Coast

- What is your age group/sex?   a: Female   b: Male

    a: under 18   b: 19-25   c: 26-30   d: 31-35   e: 36-40
    f: 41-45   g: 46-50   h: 51-55   i: 56-60   j: Over 60

- What is your marital status?

    a: Married   b: Single   c: No longer married

- What is your current level of education?

    a: High school   b: College Degree
    c: Graduate Degree   d: Other: _____

- Do you receive the TOPAZ *Romantic Liaisons* newsletter, a quarterly newsletter with the latest information on Topaz books and authors?

    YES   NO

    If not, would you like to?   YES   NO

    Fill in the address where you would like your free gift to be sent:

    Name: _____

    Address: _____

    City:_____   Zip Code: _____

    You should receive your free gift in 6 to 8 weeks.
    Please send the completed survey to:

Penguin USA•Mass Market
Dept. TS
375 Hudson St.
New York, NY 10014